to Dream, PERCHANCE to Live

NESSA L. WARIN

Dreamspinner Press

Published by
Dreamspinner Press
5032 Capital Circle SW
Ste 2, PMB# 279
Tallahassee, FL 32305-7886
USA
http://www.dreamspinnerpress.com/

Cover Art by L.C. Chase
http://www.lcchase.com

ISBN: 978-1-61372-761-4

Printed in the United States of America
First Edition
October 2012

eBook edition available
eBook ISBN: 978-1-61372-762-1

To Lisa for her help polishing not just this story but others as well. To Krista for providing the gentle (and sometimes not-so-gentle) pushes I needed to get this finished.

Part One

Chapter One

THE room shifted, its warm walls and soft carpet melting into a bleak landscape. Skeletal trees cast long shadows over the few tufts of brown vegetation poking out of the flat, dusty ground. The sun was close to the horizon, just enough below the thick clouds that the shadows took on a sharp, menacing edge as they crept along the ground. An asphalt path stretched off into the distance, heat rising from it in waves untouched by the shade of the closest trees.

Wyatt rubbed a hand over the back of his neck as he took in the scene. Behind him, it was much the same, though only a moment earlier he'd been crossing a comfortable living room, heading toward a well-stocked kitchen and the beer that beckoned him. It hadn't been any more real than the landscape in front of him, but it had been a nice dream, one of his own, and he'd been pulled from it and stuck into someone else's head in the time it took to blink his eyes.

Muttering under his breath about the unfairness of his lot in life—though not too loudly, as he was never sure how much the people who owned him could see or hear from him when he was in the Dreamscape—Wyatt started forward, slowly and deliberately putting one foot in front of the other as he trudged toward the horizon. He moved cautiously, constantly alert for the one out-of-place thing that would let him know why he was here and what he needed to accomplish before his owners would let him retreat to the safety and comfort of his own dreams. There, he could pretend he was awake and living a real life instead of lying flat on a table or floating in a vat of life-sustaining fluids with more drugs flowing through his veins than most junkies, and more machines monitoring him than most ICU patients.

He walked for what felt like hours, though the sun never moved in the sky. His gaze roamed over the unchanging landscape. The trees had begun to repeat themselves not too long into his journey, and Wyatt felt as though he were stuck in some sort of unimaginative video loop. "The guy could at least have a soundtrack in his head," he muttered, his voice sounding unnaturally loud in the silence broken up only by the snick of his sneakers against the blacktop. It could have been worse—he'd once been put into a dream where "Pop Goes the Weasel" played incessantly in the background—but when coupled with the monotony of the landscape, the silence was disturbing. There was nothing here for him to grab on to, no way for him to twist the dream, just bleak emptiness and the steady thud of his footfalls.

Sighing, Wyatt stopped, rested his hands on the small of his back and bent backward, letting his spine crack as he moved. Reaching for the sky, he stretched up on his toes and groaned as sore muscles stretched and tight joints popped. He needed water, would need food soon, but without control of the dream, he couldn't manifest anything. Stretches would have to suffice to give him some energy until he could figure out why he was here.

Feeling a little rejuvenated, he started moving again, plodding on with one foot in front of the other, his eyes and ears alert for any changes in his surroundings. He would find the secret eventually. Ultimately, the Dreamscape always yielded to him.

As WYATT trudged, Marcus Kittel frowned at the monitors in front of him, giving an especially evil look to the one showing a short, balding man sprawled across a queen-size bed, drooling into the silk-covered pillow. The man had been easy to deceive; he'd fallen completely for the flirtatious looks and teasing smiles their fetcher, Deanna Brill, had sent his way and succumbed to the drugs in the wine before Deanna had to do more than coyly fend off his clumsy attempts at kissing her. Now that he was asleep, however, he was proving quite recalcitrant. He'd been out for nearly eight hours, and the monitors still indicated Wyatt had found nothing in his dreams.

"You think the kid's just being stubborn?"

Marcus tore his attention away from the monitors, sparing a quick glance at his partner, Soren Embry, before letting his gaze settle on the still figure floating in the fluid-filled tank. Only Wyatt's face was above the liquid, his head cushioned on the same foam that supported his limbs and torso at strategic points and kept him motionless so the various IVs wouldn't pull free of his skin. "Why?" he asked, returning his gaze to Soren. "He knows if he wants to dream for himself, he has to give us what we need. Besides, it's not as if he has any choice in the matter. He's stuck in the dream same as our friend over there."

"I guess." Soren wandered over, his hands tucked in the pockets of his lab coat as he stared at the numbers and lines that recorded Wyatt's vitals. "It's just—" He paused, shaking his head. "Do you ever think he'd want to wake up?"

"No."

"But—"

"We let him, a little over a year ago, just before you started. It was his twenty-sixth birthday, the ten-year anniversary of us getting him, and Deanna managed to talk the boss into it. She said he deserved a little break." Marcus snorted indelicately as he looked at the hazy image of dead trees that had occupied the largest monitor for the better part of eight hours. "We let him dream whatever he wanted for a few days. Got him out of the tub, settled him in the room over there, and let him really wake up, not just the brief vitality checks he gets every month or two. Deanna had even gotten cake, not that we expected him to be able to eat it after ten years of IV nutrition."

"What happened?"

"Kid didn't even know it wasn't a dream. He kept trying to change things, like he will once he figures this out." He nodded at the large monitor. "When nothing changed and Deanna just kept talking to him and telling him how grateful we were and how much he was helping us, he panicked. We had to sedate him so deep he couldn't dream and leave him there for near a week. It was another two before we could send him into anyone else's head. The kid is better off asleep."

"Yeah, I guess. Why hasn't he done anything with that, then?" Soren tilted his head toward the center monitor and its unchanging image.

"I guess he hasn't figured out what he needs to do to change it." Marcus looked at his watch and sighed as he eyed the video feed of the sleeping man. "I'd best give him another dose. We can't let him wake up before Wyatt finds what we need."

"God forbid," Soren replied, punching some buttons to adjust the drugs flowing into Wyatt's body. "That should give the kid a boost, but you'd better give our friend over there another dose anyway. And warn Deanna she's going to need a better story than he passed out from the wine. At this rate, the guy is going to be missing a whole day before he wakes up."

"I'm on it." Marcus pulled a vial out of the small refrigerator and slipped it and a syringe into his pocket as he headed toward the door. "Keep an eye on wonder boy here. Don't let him get up to anything too wild."

Soren rolled his eyes and responded dryly. "I'll be ready for it."

The first sign anything was wrong went unnoticed by Marcus and Soren. They were busy running the machine that kept Wyatt's muscles from atrophying and didn't notice the way the man in the other room stilled. The snort-snuffle of his breathing quieted to shallow gasps missed due to the lack of sound on the video feed. By the time they turned back to the screen, he simply looked as though he'd fallen into a deeper sleep.

"Looks like our friend has settled a bit," Marcus said.

Soren punched a few buttons, sending another stream of medication into Wyatt. They'd never kept him in a dream this long, but the plan to pull him out was strictly theoretical and highly dangerous. They'd never needed it before. "Maybe his dream will change and the kid will finally find something."

"God, I hope so." Marcus rubbed at bleary eyes. "Come on, kid," he muttered, fixing his eyes on the center screen with its unchanging image. "You've never taken this long before. What's going on?"

The sleeping figure in the tank behind him didn't answer.

An hour later, shrill, high-pitched alarms jerked Marcus awake. He flailed in the chair, tumbling to the ground with a crash that would have been deafening if not for the ear-piercing shriek of every alarm in the room. "What the hell?" he asked, clambering to his feet as he stared at the flat lines and terrifyingly low numbers on the monitors. "What happened?"

"I don't know!" Soren was already at the tub, his hands immersed in the fluid as he tried to reattach leads pulled loose by Wyatt's thrashing. Blood seeped from Wyatt's arms where the IVs had come free, sending rivulets of red across the clear, goopy substance that surrounded him. "He just started seizing!"

Marcus glanced at the now-blank dream screen and then looked at the video feed of the other room. "We have to pull the kid out of the dream. I'll go see if I can wake our friend up."

Soren nodded, still trying to attach the leads to Wyatt's wet, seizing body. "Hurry, or we'll have to institute Plan B."

"I'm on it." Marcus ran into the other room and grabbed the other man's shoulder to shake him awake. His fingers found the pulse point on the man's neck and lingered there for only a moment before Marcus barreled back into the other room, cursing loudly. "Time for Plan B."

"What?" Soren shot another glance at the monitor showing the other room. It looked the same, with their subject sprawled across the bed, but....

"He's dead." Marcus cursed again as he yanked open the cabinet at the back of the room and began spinning the knob of the safe inside. "Still warm enough it must have just happened, but definitely no pulse and no breath."

"Shit."

"Yeah."

They both knew there was a chance they could resuscitate the subject, but if they took the time to try, they'd lose Wyatt for sure, and the kid was definitely more valuable in the long run. Someone else would have the knowledge they were trying to glean from their subject. They would have a lot of trouble obtaining anyone else with Wyatt's abilities.

The seizure stopped just as Marcus got the safe open. "Thank God," he breathed, pulling out the syringe preloaded with the drug they believed would jerk Wyatt from deep sleep to full wakefulness. He crossed the room in three quick steps, lifted Wyatt's arm from the fluid, and plunged the needle straight into the vein.

Nothing happened.

Soren grabbed the kid's shoulder and started shaking him with a force that rivaled the seizure. "Wyatt! Come on, kid! Wake up!"

MARCUS and Soren laid Wyatt on his back behind the dumpster, artfully disheveling the too-big, ragged clothes they'd dressed him in before dragging him out to the car. The clothes wouldn't provide much shelter against the elements, but neither Marcus nor Soren expected Wyatt to live long enough for it to matter. Dreamers didn't usually survive when the person they were dreaming with died, and both Marcus and Soren knew what it meant that Wyatt hadn't woken up, even with the drugs.

"What now?" Soren asked, his hands shoved in his pockets as they walked back to the car with brisk steps.

"We take Mr. What's-his-name home and make it look like he died of a heart attack, then tell Deanna she's going to have to get her information some other way."

"No." Soren shook his head. "With the program. We just left our only Dreamer in an alley."

"We start looking again. There are other Dreamers out there. They can't all be protected. We'll find one that's not Bonded and desperate, get another kid, maybe. Buy off another set of clueless parents who desperately need the money and don't understand what a real Bond is." Marcus smirked as he climbed into the driver's seat. "It'll take time, but we'll find someone else. Someone no one at work has any affection for."

Soren climbed into the passenger seat and slammed the door shut. "That'll make it easier."

"Yeah, it will." Marcus pulled the car out into traffic, glancing briefly at the alley in the rearview mirror. He didn't see the hand that was sticking out from behind the dumpster with twitching fingers and a slowly blinking green light on the bracelet around its wrist.

Chapter Two

AIDAN DONECOFF stumbled along the sidewalk, leaning heavily against the brick and stone of the buildings as he drunkenly struggled to put one foot in front of the other. He hadn't meant to get drunk, but then his ex-boyfriend had shown up, and even though Aidan was really over him—it had been months and he was not pining, no matter what Ratri and Olin said—the sight of Kevin with his tongue down his new girlfriend's throat had been too much. The six Red-Headed Sluts he'd downed had seemed appropriate at the time. Kevin was kissing one, so Aidan would drink as many as he could to get back at him.

He was never again allowed to make any sort of decision after more than one beer.

Rough bricks scraped his shoulder as he staggered forward, his hands clenched around his suddenly rebelling stomach. He pressed his lips tightly together, willing the bile to stay down his throat until he could at least get off the road. A public restroom was too much to hope for, but there was an alley ahead, and the unlit pavement between the looming buildings would provide him privacy while he spewed the contents of his stomach.

Aidan's gut lurched as he broke into a shambling run, desperate now, unable to hold off any longer. He lurched around the corner, reeling forward to lean against the dumpster, his head resting on his arm as he vomited the evening's food and drink at his feet. He didn't move for several minutes after he had finished, trying to ignore the pounding in his head as he waited to see if his stomach was going to rebel again.

Gradually, the scent of the bile at his feet overwhelmed the scents of rotting food and old piss that permeated the ally, and Aidan stood, then pushed himself back to lean against the wall as he focused on breathing through his mouth and gathering his addled wits together. He was blocks from home. He had to keep himself together, had to keep moving or he risked being found and tagged as a vagrant. He had an apartment, a job, and friends, so it wouldn't stick, but it would take days for his lawyer to sort it out, and Aidan had heard stories of the holding cells. If Carina couldn't get him out quickly enough…. Aidan shuddered at the thought as he took a deep breath and pushed himself from the wall.

As he moved, a light on the ground caught his eye, and he turned, frowning as he noticed flashing on a thick metal bracelet tight around a pale wrist. His gaze followed the arm and he dropped to his knees, ignoring the muck on the ground. "Oh God." His fingers fumbled as he dug in his jacket pocket for the phone he desperately hoped he hadn't left at the bar.

"WELL, fuck."

"I said that already."

"Not while we were here."

Aidan looked up at his friends and shrugged. "Yeah, well, it wasn't exactly something I could wait to say."

"No shit." Ratri Chavez squatted down next to Aidan, heedless of the puddles left by the melting snow, and gently touched the cool metal bracelet. "That's—"

"A slave bracelet, I know. The kind that requires surgery to remove, too." Aidan shuffled forward a few more steps, one arm extended toward the wall for balance. The worst of his drunkenness had faded the moment he laid eyes on the limp body behind the dumpster, but he didn't want to risk falling in the muck around the unconscious young man, or worse, harming him further.

"So what is he doing back here?" Olin Chavez, Ratri's Bondmate, crouched down as well, lifted the unconscious man's limp wrist and turned it over to examine the bracelet from all sides.

"It's like he was thrown away," Aidan murmured as he brushed a damp brown lock back from the man's forehead. "Like they thought he was done, useless."

"Maybe he is." Ratri gestured to the bracelet before shoving his hands back into the pockets of his leather coat. "These special bracelets check a lot. There'd be more than one blinking light if he was okay."

"Obviously he's not okay!"

Ratri stepped back in surprise, exchanging a worried glance with Olin that Aidan didn't miss.

Aidan sucked in a deep breath and blew it out slowly, trying to get his taut nerves to relax and to let go of some of his anger. The urge to find whoever had done this and deck them boiled deep in his gut, bubbling up every time he looked down at the unconscious man lying on the asphalt.

As he exhaled, Aidan brushed his fingers over the man's cheek, his boiling rage calming to a simmer at the contact. "That doesn't mean he deserves this," he said, looking up to glare defiantly at Ratri. "You don't just throw people away."

"Someone did." Olin's motions were gentle as he laid the man's hand back on the wet pavement, but his harsh tone conveyed his true feelings on the matter. "They left him for dead."

Aidan glanced once more at the limp figure before turning a hard gaze to his friends. "Well, we can't."

"We weren't going to. God." Ratri pulled his phone out of his pocket. "I'll call the hospital."

"No!" Aidan snatched the phone away from Ratri. "No hospital."

"Give it back," Ratri said with a growl, holding out his hand and narrowing his eyes. He was shorter than Aidan, with long, dark hair pulled into a ponytail at the nape of his neck and a stocky frame that gave his glare true menace. Aidan could easily hold the phone out of Ratri's reach, but they both knew Ratri could take Aidan down one-handed and drunk, and neither of them was in the mood to try it.

"Don't call the hospital," Aidan said as he handed over the phone, attempting a glare of his own. It wasn't nearly as effective as Ratri's, but it got his point across.

"Fine." Ratri rolled his eyes as he shoved the phone in his pocket, already convinced this was going to turn into another of Aidan's crazy ideas. "What do you want to do with him, then? We can't leave him here."

"I know." Aidan glanced down at the man, unsure why this was so important to him, but knowing this was what he needed to do. "I'll take him back to my place and call Kyler."

"Why?" Olin came up to stand next to Ratri, the two men a contrast in everything from color to attitude. He flung his arm over Ratri's shoulder with a casual intimacy only he could get away with, soothing away some of Ratri's surliness, and gave Aidan a level look. "What can you do that a hospital can't?"

"Keep him safe." Aidan glanced back at the man on the ground, somehow unable to have him out of sight for more than a few minutes. "The first thing a hospital is going to do is find who owns him. That's probably the same person who left him here."

Olin nodded, also looking at the man on the ground. "And if it's not?" he asked, not missing the way Aidan's gaze was constantly drawn down.

Aidan sighed, pushing his hair back from his forehead as he looked up at his friends. "Look, I'll call Carina," he said, referring to his lawyer. "She'll look into it discreetly."

Ratri snorted, amused by the idea of Carina doing anything discreetly. "Right. I hope Kyler can pull off a miracle, or it won't matter what Carina finds. This guy won't last."

Aidan crouched down again, curling his hand around the man's shoulder as he tried to suppress the fear that raced through him at the thought. "I know."

He still had to try.

"TOOK you long enough." Kyler Jedry pushed off the wall next to Aidan's apartment door as Aidan, Ratri, and Olin maneuvered out of the elevator, carrying the unconscious man. "I've been here for ten minutes."

Aidan glared as he shifted his grip, trying to keep the man's arm around his neck while he fumbled with his apartment keys. "Yeah, well, it was a little harder to get everyone here than usual."

"I can see that." Kyler picked up his black physician's bag and took the keys from Aidan just as he was about to drop them. It would have been comical to try to watch him open the door while maintaining his grip on the unconscious man, so it was safer for Kyler to do it. Given the precarious way Aidan, Ratri, and Olin were holding the guy, Kyler wasn't sure Aidan would have succeeded.

He slid the key into the lock, stepped inside, and held the door open for his friends and their passenger. Aidan and Olin each had one of the man's arms looped around their neck and one of their arms behind his back. Their other hand held the man's arm to keep it from sliding off, something it had threatened to do while Aidan was fumbling with his keys. Ratri had the guy's feet, one in each hand, and steered as Aidan and Olin shuffled along sideways. It worked, but it looked like Ratri was pushing a wheelbarrow with Aidan and Olin as the wheels.

The thought made Kyler smile as he watched them squeeze through the door, but his smile faded as they moved past him and he got a good look at the man Aidan had called him here to treat. "Shit," he said, taking in the man's labored breathing and blue-tinged lips. He was thin, though not emaciated, and the slave bracelet stood out starkly on his wrist, the dark metal contrasting sharply with his pale skin.

"That's one word for it," Aidan agreed, leading the way to his guest bedroom. He felt better now that they were safely in his apartment, free from the risk of being seen on the street or by one of his neighbors, but his skin itched with the urge to get the man into a bed and have Kyler look him over thoroughly. "That's why I brought him here. Whoever did this to him doesn't deserve him back."

Kyler exchanged a look with Olin as they set the man down on Aidan's guest bed. Ultimately, it wasn't going to be up to Aidan, and they both knew it. "It's not your decision," he said softly, not backing down when Aidan glared.

"I know."

"Do you?" Ratri had watched the way Aidan hovered over the guy on the way here, never once breaking contact after they'd picked him up in the alley. "Because you seem attached."

"I'm not." Aidan had to force himself not to look down. He couldn't deny that he was drawn to the man, faced with an overwhelming urge to protect him though he didn't know why. Yet, he had no desire to own a slave, particularly not one he'd be saddled with for the rest of their lives. "I just want to make sure he's okay. The courts can find him an owner once he's healthy."

Kyler shrugged. "All right. Let me take a look." He pulled his stethoscope from his bag, followed by a thermometer and a tablet, and started checking the man's vitals.

Olin and Ratri watched for a moment, both feeling more awkward by the second. Discomfort echoed along their Bond, each of them feeding off the other until they itched with the need to be elsewhere. "We'll wait outside," Olin said, already halfway out the door. "Let Kyler work in peace."

"Wait." Aidan looked at him imploringly. "Stay. Please. Just in case."

Ratri narrowed his gaze as he looked between Aidan, Kyler, and the unconscious man on the bed. "You want witnesses."

Aidan nodded. "Yeah." He hadn't heard back from Carina yet, his phone screen remaining worryingly blank despite the text messages he'd sent and voice mail he'd left. "I don't know what Carina's going to tell me to do, and I'm not calling the cops until I talk to her, but I don't want anyone to accuse me or Kyler of doing something to hurt him."

Ratri nodded in understanding. "Sure," he said, pulling Olin back into the room. Permanent slavery could only be assigned by the courts, and most people who merited it were owned by the government and fastidiously tracked. The mere fact they'd found this man in an alley indicated that he was privately owned, and they would need all the aid they could get if they had to go up against someone that rich and connected.

"Thanks." Aidan pulled his phone out of his pocket and stared at it, as though watching would make the screen light up with Carina's call. It didn't, and he sighed and slid it back into his pocket as Kyler plugged his tablet into a small port on the side of the man's bracelet. The pad immediately beeped, sounding unnaturally loud in the quiet room, and Aidan stepped forward, leaning in to look though he knew he wouldn't understand most of the information. "What is it?"

"I don't know." Kyler frowned down at the pad, tapping the screen a few times. "None of the data I'd expect is on here. Most of it doesn't make any sense, but the bits I do understand…." He looked up at Aidan with wide and startlingly blue eyes. "Aidan, he's a Dreamer, and he's been dreaming for a *really* long time."

"How long?" Aidan's stomach twisted tighter with every passing second of silence from his friend. "Kyler. How long?"

"I don't know. Too long, though." Kyler stared sadly at his patient for a moment and sucked his bottom lip between his teeth as he contemplated how to best phrase what he next wanted to say. "He's been dreaming for long enough he may never regain consciousness. Or he might wake up tomorrow. I don't know."

Ratri stepped away from the wall, his elbow bumping against a picture on the dresser. "Is he dreaming now?"

"He's sleeping." Kyler shrugged. "If anyone nearby is asleep, he is."

The apartment below Aidan's was laid out the same as his, so chances were good that someone was asleep in the room below this. Aidan shifted uncomfortably at the thought, strangely disturbed by the idea of the man dreaming with someone else and suddenly anxious to go to sleep.

"It's late," Aidan said, glancing at the clock on the nightstand. "Almost everyone is asleep." He would be sleeping as well if he hadn't stumbled across the man. It was almost three in the morning now, nearly two hours after he'd left the bar, and he was grateful he didn't have anywhere to be in the morning.

"We'll tell your neighbors tomorrow, if Carina thinks we should keep him here," Olin said, leaning forward in his chair and rubbing his hands over his face. "We can't do anything about it tonight."

"Aidan can sleep somewhere else." Ratri glanced at Kyler. "You sure he's not going to wake up tonight?"

"Fairly." Kyler unplugged the tablet from the bracelet and poked at the screen a few times, e-mailing himself the information he'd downloaded. "I can't tell when—or if—he'll wake up, but I doubt it would be tonight."

"Good enough." Ratri turned to Aidan. "You can crash at our place tonight."

Aidan didn't even consider the idea. "No. I'll be fine."

Ratri clenched his hands, his concern warring with his frustration. "You don't know that."

"Yes, I do." Aidan smiled softly. "He's not the first Dreamer I've known. Hunter used to dream with me all the time before he Bonded."

"Dreaming with someone you know isn't the same as dreaming with a stranger, Aidan." Olin pushed his hair back from his forehead as he looked up. "We don't know what might have gone wrong. You don't know what this guy can do."

"I'll figure it out." To Aidan, it was that simple, and he wasn't going to argue further. "Just leave it, okay? Please," he asked, rubbing the back of his neck as the weight of the evening came crashing down. "I'm going to bed. You are welcome to crash here if you want. Otherwise let yourselves out."

"I'll be back tomorrow," Kyler said as he slipped the tablet back into his bag. "Call me if you hear from Carina?"

"Of course. Thanks." Aidan clasped him on the shoulder, squeezing briefly before shuffling off to his bedroom, more anxious than he would admit to fall asleep and find out more about his unwitting houseguest.

AIDAN dreamed he was back in the bar, only this time the bar top was cracked, the stools uncomfortable, and the tables covered in a sticky film that made his skin crawl. Half the lights were out, which cast deep shadows across parts of the bar, and the group around the pool table yelled loudly every time someone took a shot, but it wasn't enough to hide either the sight or sound of the couple in the corner. At the moment, they were exactly as they'd been when Aidan had first seen them in the bar, the man pressing the woman against the wall as they passionately kissed. It wouldn't stay that way for long, Aidan knew, and he turned away so he wouldn't have to see what he remembered coming next.

The group around the pool table only had time to take one shot before the couple was in front of Aidan again, kissing as though they were being paid to put on a show. The girl climbed up the guy and wrapped her legs around his waist as she pushed her tongue into his mouth. His hands came around, slipped under her skirt, then cupped her ass, and she giggled, then slowly slipped down his body until their crotches pressed together. His moan when she started bouncing was loud enough to be heard clearly over the din of the bar, and he swung her around so her back was pressed against the counter as he deepened the kiss.

"Dammit!" He grabbed his drink and downed it as he swiveled around, once more putting his back to the couple. They were in front of him again in an instant, making out against the wall where he'd first seen them. Aidan turned again, then again, trying partial turns and full circles, but it didn't matter how fast or far he moved. Whenever he stopped, Aidan's ex and his new girlfriend were right there, flaunting their relationship with a display that would have gotten them arrested if this weren't a dream.

Desperate, Aidan spun the stool around as quickly as he could. The room blurred around him, turning into streaks of colored light and shadow as he moved faster, but the couple remained there, looking like a cartoon head on a spinning background, following him wherever he looked. He pushed faster and harder, spinning the stool as quickly as it would go, but it didn't matter. The couple stayed clear, and after a few more moments, Aidan let the stool slow.

When it stopped, the room kept wobbling, almost sending Aidan tumbling to the floor when he tried to stand. He cursed as he staggered to his feet, thinking maybe he just needed to leave, and stumbled toward the door, pushing his way through the thick crowd. He bumped into someone with practically every other step and apologized at every turn, but somehow the couple managed to stay in front of him, the guy carrying the girl as they continued to kiss.

It was almost enough to drive him mad. All he wanted was a good night's rest and maybe to meet the man he'd rescued. Instead, he was trapped by the memory of what had driven him to drink too much in the first place, unable to get away from it no matter how hard he tried. When he bumped into another person and found the couple in front of him again, he stopped, completely overwhelmed, and tangled his hands in his hair as he looked down at the scuffed wooden floor.

Aidan half expected to see the couple down there as well, miniaturized versions making out on his feet just for the added torment, but all he saw were the brown tips of his boots as well as the black scuff marks and pale stripped areas that covered the old floor. As ugly as it was, it was a relief, and Aidan found himself relaxing as he took a deep breath and blinked.

Then he blinked again.

The floor, or whatever he was standing on now, was gray instead of the brown it had been when he'd closed his eyes. The din of the bar was gone, too, replaced by complete silence that was more disturbing than the lewd comments coming from the pool table or the moans of the couple as they shoved their tongues down each other's throats. That, at least, had been explainable. This wasn't, and fear curled in Aidan's gut as he looked up to find the bar was gone and he was standing on a featureless gray plane, alone except for a solitary figure in the distance.

"Hello?" Aidan took a cautious step forward, not transferring his weight until his foot hit what felt like solid ground. He glanced down when it did, confirming there was just gray nothingness there and steeling himself to take another step. When he looked up again, the man stood right in front of him.

Aidan blinked at the unexpectedly familiar sight. The man's skin had better color and his muscles were more toned, but he was clearly the same man who lay unconscious in Aidan's apartment. Here, the ends of his brown hair fell into his eyes and the limbs that looked gangly on the bed fit his body perfectly as he moved. He was about six inches taller than Aidan now that they were both standing. Aidan tipped his head back to look up at him. "You're here. I thought you weren't going to show up."

"You were expecting me?"

"Yeah. Kyler said you were a Dreamer, and I thought I'd be the closest person, but then you didn't come and I started to wonder if there was someone in another apartment who was closer." Aidan looked down, flushing slightly at his eager rambling. "But now you're here, in my dream. Or what used to be my dream, anyway," he added, looking around at the featureless gray plane again.

"It's still your dream. I just hijacked it. It looked like you wanted out." As Aidan nodded vehemently, Wyatt dipped his head once, glad he had gotten that right. "I'm Wyatt Mettler, by the way." He pushed ear-length dark brown hair out of his eyes and held out a hand, grinning at Aidan's babbling. It had been a while since he'd gotten to talk to someone else. "Figured I should introduce myself since I'm dreaming with you."

"Aidan Donecoff." He took Wyatt's hand, marveling at how well it fit with his own. "It's nice to actually meet you."

Wyatt narrowed his eyes as Aidan again referenced being near him physically. That wasn't possible. "*Actually* meet me?"

"Yeah." Aidan shifted nervously as he realized he'd forgotten that bit of information. "You're in my guest bedroom. Someone dumped you in an alley. I found you and brought you here." He shoved his hands in his pockets as he tried to downplay the awkwardness of the situation. He always felt weird talking to slaves about being owned, and tonight it felt more awkward than usual. "I didn't take you to the hospital 'cause I thought maybe it was your owner who left you there. Was it?"

"I. Um." Wyatt shook his head. It was easy to imagine Elliott abandoning him in an alley if he ever lost his usefulness, but he hadn't, and he knew Elliott wasn't going to give him up that easily. It was wishful thinking, his hopes bleeding into a rare dream not orchestrated by his captors. "I can't be."

"You are." Aidan rocked back on his heels, his gaze drifting around the empty space as he tried to pick his words carefully. "You're safe. I've called my lawyer, too, and if your owner has hurt you, we'll make sure you don't go back to him. You can tell me."

"There's nothing to tell."

That wasn't good enough for Aidan. He needed to know who he'd rescued, who he was going to be up against if it came down to a legal battle, and he wasn't going to leave until he had answers. "There is. I wouldn't have found you in that alley otherwise."

"There's nothing to tell," Wyatt repeated in a slightly firmer tone, hoping but not believing it would be effective. "Please stop asking."

"I will!" Aidan promised, truly intending to do so as soon as he got a name. "I just need to—"

"No." Wyatt shook his head and smiled sadly. He'd hoped to have a real conversation, but it couldn't go like this. "You have to wake up now."

Aidan opened his mouth to protest, but before he could say anything, Wyatt was gone and Aidan was lying on his back, blankets pooled around his waist and the familiar fixtures of his bedroom lightly illuminated by the pale strips of sunshine that seeped through the partially drawn curtains. He sat up, looked around carefully, and flopped back down onto his back. He'd definitely messed that one up.

Chapter Three

MARCUS slipped quickly into the building and headed straight up the stairs, not bothering to turn on the lights. The glow from the emergency exit sign illuminated the stairwell enough for him to see the shadowy rise of the stairs, and he didn't need anything more to scurry to the top without stumbling. He pushed on the door at the top, hoping the emergency lighting in the hallway would be sufficient for him to unlock the lab door without having to find the hallway lights, and froze as the door opened.

The hallway wasn't dark.

Swallowing hard, Marcus stepped into the hall, letting the stairwell door close behind him. He slowly walked down the hall, moving out of the shadows toward the open door at the far end. Light from the lab spilled into the hall, a bright beacon warning him of the danger ahead.

Marcus's heart pounded heavily in his chest, thumping so loudly he could barely hear himself breathe. His feet moved forward almost of their own accord, falling rhythmically against the tile floor despite the extra weights that seemed to have slipped into his shoes, propelling him forward faster than he wanted to move. Long before he was ready, Marcus reached the open door and found himself sucking in a deep breath before stepping in to face his fate.

The scene wasn't one Marcus had witnessed in the entire eleven years he'd worked here, nor one he'd ever expected to see. Boxes covered every available surface, all of the equipment they'd used to monitor Wyatt stuffed into them or loaded onto carts. The tank that had long been the central feature of the room was empty, looking strange without Wyatt's sleeping body suspended in it.

Soren sat in a chair near the door, his hands folded in his lap and his eyes fixed on the floor. He'd had the same idea Marcus had, get here early and take care of things, but both of them had been too late.

"Nice of you to join us, Marcus. I was starting to wonder if you were going to show up at all."

Marcus flinched as he turned to face the man sitting at what had been his work station. "I'm early, sir." He wasn't scheduled to be in for another two hours.

Elliott Sloan made a show of looking at his watch before looking straight at Marcus. "You're about thirty hours too late." He pressed the tips of his fingers together and looked at Marcus and Soren over them. "I shouldn't have found out from your colleagues that my asset is missing."

Soren looked down, unable to meet Elliott's gaze any longer. He'd heard stories about what had happened to people who held his position before him, and now that he was seeing his boss's anger, he believed them. "Sorry, sir. We were just trying to clean up the mess."

"This isn't a mess for you to clean up." Elliott smiled coldly, the slight thrill from seeing Soren cower in front of him doing little to mitigate his anger. "You should have called me right away."

"Of course." Marcus looked down as well. He'd had more experience handling Elliott Sloan, but he doubted he was going to survive this encounter as unscathed as he had in the past. If he survived at all. "There wasn't anything you could do. We didn't think it was worth bothering you over."

"This program is *always* worth bothering me over, Marcus. You should have learned that by now." Elliott sat back in the chair and stretched out his legs, crossing them at the ankles. "Now where is the boy?"

"Dead, sir." It would be true by now, Marcus hoped. He managed to look up for a brief moment before fear forced him to look down again. The white tile of the floor wasn't pretty to look at, but it was preferable to actually seeing Elliott's cold gaze or the way his casual pose belied his anger. "We dumped him in an alley after we disposed of the subject."

"And didn't tell anyone?"

Soren tried to subtly shift his chair away from Marcus so Elliott could only glare at one of them, but stopped when the feet screeched over the tiles. "We were going to write up reports this morning," he said, doing his best not to cringe as the full force of Elliott's attention fell upon him. "It wasn't—" He swallowed. "We couldn't—"

"Obviously." Elliott stood, giving both his employees a long, hard look and biting back a sadistic smile when Soren jumped to his feet. "You will find me someone to replace the boy. Quickly."

"Of course, sir." Marcus straightened, weight lifting off his shoulders as Elliott headed toward the door. He'd expected that to be so much worse than it had been, and he bit back a sigh of relief as Elliott stopped in front of him.

"Pack up your things and take these down to the storeroom in the basement." Elliott swept his hand around the room to indicate the packaged equipment. "Until you find me someone, your office is down there. HR will provide details of your new job. It is a pay cut."

Marcus and Soren nodded, more than happy to accept a demotion over sharing the fate of Wyatt and their latest subject. "Thank you, sir," Marcus said, finally daring to look Elliott straight in the eyes. "We won't let you down."

Elliott smiled, the sinister curve of his lips sending a chill down Marcus's spine. "I know you won't."

AIDAN resolutely turned his back as the show in the corner started for yet another night, his ex sliding his hands around the lithe redhead and pulling her in for the first of many passionate kisses. "I really wish they'd stop doing that."

"It's your dream." Wyatt twisted the Dreamscape just enough to create a shot of whiskey and slid it toward Aidan. He clearly needed it. Aidan's skin looked paler than the last time Wyatt had seen him and the light smattering of freckles across his nose and cheeks was more obvious. His short brown hair was a mess, but most telling were the dark circles under his green eyes. Sleep had clearly not been restful for Aidan, and Wyatt was determined to do something about that. "You keep seeing it because you keep thinking about it."

"I know." Aidan tossed back the shot, grimacing as it burned its way down his throat, and slammed the glass on the counter. "I just wish I knew why."

"It bothers you." Wyatt created another glass of whiskey and handed it to Aidan. Other than his presence and the whiskey, he hadn't changed anything while dreaming with Aidan tonight, despite the temptation to rescue him from the endless repeat of a scene that clearly disturbed Aidan more than he cared to admit.

Wyatt could whisk him away from it with a thought, as he had last night, and banish the uncomfortable scene from Aidan's dreams as long as Wyatt dreamed with him, but Wyatt was reluctant. Aidan was the first person besides Elliott who had directly talked to him in years. Though Wyatt could change Aidan's dream without his knowing, it felt wrong somehow. Wyatt didn't want to take advantage of him, even if it would temporarily relieve his pain.

"Of course it bothers me." Aidan downed the second glass of whiskey and let his head fall forward into his hands. "We were together for years. Part of me knew it wouldn't last—we never Bonded—but I still hoped. And to see him with *her*...." He fumbled for a glass, not noticing Wyatt fill it with a thought as he lifted it to his lips, and downed the whiskey in a single gulp. It didn't have any effect here in his dream, but it felt good going down. "He told me he couldn't imagine being with a girl, that guys were it for him, and convinced me to admit I was gay. Guess he was wrong."

"I'm sorry." Wyatt filled Aidan's glass again, created one for himself, and knocked them together before downing his. "That sucks." Wyatt had never had any sort of romantic relationship, but he'd known long before he was sold that he was attracted to men and remembered the fear he'd felt when he told his parents. He could imagine how Aidan would feel betrayed.

"It's stupid." Aidan glanced over his shoulder, ignoring the flash of pain he felt as he saw Kevin's lips pressed against the girl's, and turned his back on them for what he was determined would be the last time. "It's been over between us for months. I should focus on something else." That was what Ratri and Olin had been trying to tell him when they'd dragged him out, but he hadn't seen it until now. He probably wouldn't have seen it at all, if not for the way his heart quickened more when Wyatt dreamed with him than it ever had when he'd been with Kevin.

The couple in the corner started to fade away from the dream as Aidan refocused, and the disturbing events of the previous night dulled in importance. The bar changed too: the light brightened, the crowd thinned, and the seats widened slightly. They were subtle shifts, hardly noticeable individually, but together they transformed the bar into a welcoming place instead of the dingy dump tainted by bad memories that had dominated Aidan's dream.

Wyatt relaxed into the more comfortable chair, marveling at the way Aidan seemed to lighten with the room, his shoulders straightening and his eyes brightening. He was a gorgeous man—Wyatt had noticed it the moment he first stepped into Aidan's dream—but without the weight of his past hanging over him, he was positively radiant. Wyatt couldn't look away.

"Like what?" Wyatt tipped his head to the side as he wondered what else he could find out about Aidan. He wanted to know everything.

Aidan didn't miss Wyatt's curiosity, and he would have been happy to satisfy it to keep Wyatt happy, but he needed more information to find out who Wyatt belonged to. "Well, I don't know anything about you except your name and that you're a Dreamer."

The room darkened again, as the Dreamscape shifted to accommodate Wyatt's mood. The night had been going so well. Why couldn't Aidan just leave it alone? "There's nothing else to know."

"Of course there is." Aidan did his best to ignore the rapidly cooling room as he hoped that he'd get some answers before Wyatt woke him up. "Where are you from? What's your family like? Who owns you?" The last question almost stuck in his throat, but he needed to know, if only to protect Wyatt from further harm.

"I don't have a family." Wyatt twisted away, his desire to talk to Aidan as long as possible warring with his need to not think about this. When he could pretend it was his choice or it was real, it wasn't so bad living in the Dreamscape, but talk of where his body really was and how he ended up there always reminded him of what he could never have.

"Okay." Aidan wanted to scoot closer and tell Wyatt everything was going to be all right—even though it was probably a lie—but he could feel the hurt radiating off Wyatt and decided to let it be. It wouldn't matter once Carina helped him ensure Wyatt wouldn't be handed back to the people who'd hurt him when they turned him over to the proper authorities. As much as Aidan wanted to know about Wyatt's past, it wasn't worth hurting him, not when there were other things he needed to know more. "What about your owner?"

Wyatt squeezed his eyes shut, wondering if this had all been some sort of cruel trick on Elliott's part to see if Wyatt would squeal on him if presented with the opportunity. It felt real. *Aidan* felt real, unlike anyone he'd encountered in the Dreamscape before. Wyatt was drawn to him, but the idea had occurred to him while Aidan was awake, and he wouldn't put it past Elliott to have engineered the whole thing to torment him.

A warm hand gripped his shoulder, turning him back around on the seat, and all Wyatt could think was that it shouldn't be warm because it wasn't real. It was a dream, nothing more. He shouldn't have let himself hope.

"It's okay. You can tell me. I'm going to make sure he can't hurt you again." Aidan tried to smile reassuringly, but it was difficult without knowing he would be able to keep this promise.

He couldn't stop Elliott, and Wyatt didn't want him to try. "I don't—"

The room shook around them, bits of it spiraling off into nothing despite Wyatt's attempts to hold it together. Aidan turned to him, flickering in the dream as he started to wake up, and put his hands on Wyatt's shoulders. "I just want to help you."

"I can't—" Wyatt started, and then Aidan vanished, leaving Wyatt alone in the fading dream and waking to his phone ringing next to his ear.

CARINA arrived an hour after Kyler woke Aidan. She blew into Aidan's apartment like a whirlwind and dropped her bag on the couch next to him before he'd fully registered she was there. He jumped to his feet with a startled yelp, spilled coffee on his T-shirt, and scurried off toward the kitchen before she could say anything. He regretted giving her a key. Carina on a good day was a handful. When she had *that* expression on her face, Aidan wasn't going to deal with her while anything less than properly dressed and caffeinated.

By the time he returned to the kitchen after changing his lounge pants and T-shirt for crisp jeans, a sweater, and shoes, the fresh pot of coffee was just done brewing. Aidan poured two mugs, turned, and almost spilled them on himself again when he saw Carina in the middle of the kitchen, brandishing her phone like a sword.

"Thirteen messages, Aidan? Thirteen! And not one of them telling me what's so important! Not even one!" Carina stepped forward, waving the phone in Aidan's face, not caring that it was coming dangerously close to his nose. "And then—*then*—you get up and walk away without saying so much as hello when I got here!"

"Good morning?" Aidan hazarded, pushing a mug into Carina's free hand. It had been waving as wildly as the one holding her phone, but it stilled as her fingers curled around the mug.

Carina lifted it to her lips, taking a sip and nodding in satisfaction as the rich, warm liquid rolled over her tongue. Aidan always bought the expensive coffee, and the price showed in the flavor. "All right. You're forgiven. If—!" She brandished her phone again, waving it under Aidan's nose and smirking when he stopped short. "If you tell me right now why I came back from what was supposed to be a relaxing weekend and had *thirteen* messages from you, all predicting doom and gloom."

"Yeah, sorry about that." Aidan rubbed the back of his neck. "I didn't want to be specific in case someone else got the messages."

"Specific about what?" Carina tucked her phone into the pocket of her blazer. "Aidan, what did you do this weekend?"

"Nothing!" Aidan held up his free hand like he was taking an oath. "I swear. I went out drinking with Ratri and Olin, that's all."

Carina narrowed her gaze, glaring at Aidan as if a mere look could pull the information out of him. It didn't, and she spoke after a moment of complete silence from Aidan. "Then why did you leave me so many messages, Aidan?"

"I found someone. A slave." Aidan rubbed at the back of his neck again, well aware of how strange the situation seemed. "He was unconscious in an alley, and we brought him here. I need you to tell me what I should do."

"You *found* a slave?" Carina focused on that first, because at least it sort of made sense, though she could hardly believe it. She didn't want to think about the second part of what Aidan had said. "How do you *find* a slave?"

Aidan shrugged, wishing he knew. "He was dumped. I'll show you. Come on." He headed into the hall without waiting to see if Carina followed. When he got to the guest bedroom where Wyatt was sleeping, he leaned in, blocking the view from the hall with his body. "How's he doing?"

Kyler looked up from his tablet and blinked at Aidan as he mentally switched gears. "The same, I think." He held up the tablet, showing Aidan its screen full of incomprehensible jargon. "I can't understand this any more than I could when you brought him here, but his vitals are stable."

Aidan nodded as he stepped into the room, leaving the door open so Carina could follow him. "Good."

"It's not bad, anyway." Kyler shrugged. "I wish I could tell when—or if—he'll wake up." He unhooked the tablet from Wyatt's bracelet and started packing it up. "I took another blood sample to see if any of the drugs in his system have worn off, but given how long he's been out, he might not be able to wake up even if they have."

"How long has that been?" Carina asked as she stepped around Aidan. She glanced at Kyler and nodded a greeting, but her gaze was drawn to the bed where Wyatt lay motionless and pale, connected to tubes and wires. The room looked like it belonged in a hospital rather than Aidan's apartment, but the soft sounds of the equipment revealed Wyatt was alive.

"Months, at least." Kyler blew out a frustrated breath as he tucked his tablet into his bag. He wished he could give a better answer, but unless he figured out how to decipher the data on the bracelet, he wasn't going to be able to give one. "Probably longer."

"God." Carina stepped closer, trying to wrap her mind around the idea as she looked Wyatt over again. Up close, it was clear that he'd been unconscious for a long time, and her stomach churned as she thought about it. She'd heard stories about the things done to slaves, particularly ones sentenced to permanent slavery, and had even done legal work on their behalf, but this was the first time she'd seen the results for herself. It made it hard to focus on the reason she was here. "Do we know anything?"

"His name is Wyatt Mettler," Aidan said as he sat down in the chair in the corner. "And he's a Dreamer. I've asked him about his owner, but he won't tell me anything."

"His name is a start." Carina leaned in and picked up Wyatt's wrist, turning it back and forth as she looked at the bracelet. The serial number was worn away from years of use. "Between that and this serial number, I should be able to find out something." She set Wyatt's arm back on the bed and turned to look at Aidan. "Why'd you bring him here?"

"I didn't want to return him to his owner if they did this to him."

Carina nodded. It was what she'd expected, but she had to ask. "You can't keep him."

Aidan barked out a short unamused laugh. He hadn't suddenly started desiring a slave in the past two days, though it made him wonder what his friends were seeing that they kept pointing that out. "I know. That's why I called you. I don't want him to go back to whoever did this to him, but I need to tell someone."

"Right." Carina mentally reviewed her contacts at the police station, settling on who to talk to first. "Let me record the serial number, and I'll see what I can find. Don't do anything else until I get back to you."

"I wouldn't dream of it," Aidan said, a weight lifting off him as Carina pulled out her phone and typed the serial number from Wyatt's bracelet in the memo section.

"It might be a few days," Carina warned. "Can you take care of him that long?"

"Of course," Kyler said, and Aidan nodded along with him. He didn't mind the delay at all, though he wouldn't admit that to his friends yet. A few more days taking care of Wyatt meant a few more days dreaming with him, and Aidan was definitely looking forward to that.

Chapter Four

AIDAN dreamed he was in the bar again, as he had every night for the past week, though thankfully Kevin and his new girlfriend hadn't made an appearance since that second night. It was comfortable and easy, and though intellectually Aidan knew Wyatt would find him no matter what he dreamed, he thought about it every night before going to sleep, just to be sure. Tonight, however, he had other plans.

He sipped his whiskey as he waited for Wyatt to arrive and smiled when he noticed the subtle changes that indicated Wyatt had entered his dream. It wasn't much, just a slight switch in the way things felt, but since the first night he'd dreamed with Wyatt, he'd learned to pick up on it. "Hi," he said, not bothering to glance to his right as someone slid onto the barstool next to him.

Wyatt grinned, impressed with how quickly Aidan had learned to recognize him, and bumped shoulders with him. "Hi. What are we talking about tonight?" They'd discussed a lot in the past week: mostly Aidan's life, since every time his came up, Wyatt changed the subject or ended the dream, but he was running out of questions to ask.

"Nothing." Aidan finished his drink and set the glass down on the counter. "Let's get out of here."

Wyatt raised his eyebrows. "Out of here? Where to?" They'd spent every night for the past week in the bar, until it was time for Aidan to wake up. It hadn't occurred to him that Aidan would want to go anywhere else.

"I dunno." Aidan shrugged, affecting nonchalance though this was part of his plan. If Wyatt wouldn't talk about himself, maybe he would show Aidan something. "Where would you like to go?"

"Um." Wyatt's eyes widened in shock. "I don't—"

"Sure you do. What's your favorite place to visit?" Aidan held up a hand as Wyatt opened his mouth. "And *don't* tell me you don't have one. You have to."

Wyatt thought for a moment. There was one place he liked, but taking Aidan there was—well, it wasn't actually any more dangerous than sitting in the bar chatting with him. Either way, his handlers would find out soon enough, and he might as well enjoy this time with Aidan before it was ripped away from him. "You sure?"

Aidan slid off his stool and held his hands wide, presenting himself at the ready. "Take me wherever you want to go."

The world swirled and faded around them, the dim light and stifling air of the bar replaced by sunlight and a fresh breeze. When Aidan's vision cleared, he found they were standing on the grassy shore of a lake that sparkled in the sun. Wildflowers grew along the shoreline, peeking out from behind rocks and through tufts of grass in a riot of color, and the sky overhead was a pale blue dotted with fluffy, white clouds.

It was gorgeous. Aidan could feel the tension draining from his shoulders as he gazed out over the placid water, and when he turned and saw Wyatt sprawled on the grass, his heart swelled. "This is your favorite place? You can take us *here*, and we've been hanging out in a *bar*?"

"I wanted you to be comfortable."

Aidan's jaw fell. "You thought I'd be more comfortable sitting in a dark bar than *here*? Are you nuts?"

"Maybe." Wyatt shrugged and sat up, pulling his legs up to his chest. "It's a place you've been before. Most people dream about things they know."

"I've had some pretty weird dreams before."

"But underneath all the weirdness, they're things you're familiar with. Even if your mind distorts them in your dreams, they're still familiar if you look closely. I didn't want to upset you by pulling you away from that into, well, this."

"*This* is supposed to be upsetting?"

"It could be." Wyatt shrugged again. "You don't know me, Aidan. I know it feels like you do, but that's because I'm in your head. I could make you feel whatever I wanted."

A surge of annoyance flashed through Aidan, but then he reviewed how Wyatt had phrased it and sat down on the soft grass next to him, looking him straight in the eyes. "*Are* you making me feel anything?"

"No, but that doesn't mean that you can just believe everything you see and feel. Dreams aren't like reality, Aidan."

"Obviously." He looked around with one eyebrow arched, glancing pointedly at the impossible colors of the wildflowers and the perfection of the distant snowcapped mountains. "I don't think I could find a place like this in the real world."

"You couldn't," Wyatt replied, momentarily sidetracked. "It's a conglomeration of memories and dreams, mostly other people's. I come here sometimes when I want a little peace. You're the first person I've brought."

They both knew Wyatt hadn't had an opportunity to bring anyone else, but Aidan felt honored anyway. "It's amazing," he said. The description felt woefully inadequate, but he couldn't think of another word that would work better.

"Yeah." Wyatt flopped back, tucking his arms behind his head when he hit the grass, and let out a contented sigh. "It is." He patted the grass next to him. "Come on. Lie back. You can't get the full experience without watching the clouds."

It wasn't how Aidan had planned to spend the night, but as he stretched out an arm's length away from Wyatt, he had to admit that, as dreams went, this was a pretty good one.

THE next night, Aidan jumped when he felt a hand on his shoulder. He was in an art museum, contemplating the latest exhibit of fantasy art, oohing and ahhing over pictures and paintings and wishing the ones he created were even half as incredible as these. Ratri and Olin told him all the time that his art was fabulous, and he had enough work as a graphic designer and occasional illustrator to keep him living in comfort and then some, but that was different. Ratri and Olin were his friends, so they *had* to tell him it was fantastic, and the ability to get clients did not mean his work was museum quality.

His art was good. This stuff was stunning.

He hadn't expected anyone to be here with him, but when he turned and saw Wyatt grinning at him, he couldn't help but smile. "Hey!"

"Hi." Wyatt stepped closer to the painting Aidan was contemplating. "You do this stuff, right?"

"I wish." Aidan turned back to face the painting. "My stuff isn't anywhere close to this good."

"Uh-huh."

"It isn't! Nothing I've done comes even close to being good enough to get into a museum."

Wyatt doubted that, but he could admit he was biased, so he didn't say anything about it, just slung his arm over Aidan's shoulder and tilted his head to the side so he could better consider the wooded scene before them. "So, a museum, huh? I'm surprised we're not in the bar again."

"I do dream about things other than getting completely trashed, you know."

"Well, I do *now*, but I didn't until tonight. Every time I'd go looking for you in the Dreamscape, you'd be in that bar!"

"I think it was because I knew you could find me there," Aidan muttered, ducking his head so Wyatt couldn't see the blush creeping its way up his cheeks. "I don't even really like that bar."

"I can find you anywhere in the Dreamscape. I'm drawn to you, really. It's weird."

"That's because I'm the closest person to you." Aidan slid his arm around Wyatt's shoulders as he started to walk to the next exhibit. "In the real world, I mean. You never Bonded with anyone, so you'll dream with whoever is closest to you unless you go looking for someone else."

Wyatt tensed at the implication. They'd had this conversation before, and he didn't want to have it again. "Uh-huh."

"Look." Aidan turned toward Wyatt as they stopped at the next painting. "I know it's hard to believe, but if you would just try to wake up—"

"I *can't.*"

"Wyatt...."

"Don't." Wyatt pulled back from Aidan, then crossed his arms as he leaned away. He hated this conversation. "We've been over this. I can't wake up. I would love to, but I can't. I'm never going to get to, so stop trying to convince me. *Please.*"

Aidan wanted to say more, but he knew from the experiences he'd had over the past several nights that if he pushed it, Wyatt would wake him up. He'd have trouble falling back to sleep, and even if he managed it, Wyatt wouldn't show himself again until the following night. It wasn't something Aidan was willing to risk. He woke up feeling so much more refreshed when he spent the whole night talking to Wyatt in the Dreamscape.

"Sorry," Aidan said and turned his attention to the painting. This one was a lake scene, strikingly similar to the lake Wyatt had taken him to, and Aidan couldn't help but smile as he looked at the sprites dancing above the water. It was easy to imagine them at Wyatt's lake as well, and he wondered as he saw the look on Wyatt's face if they'd be there the next time they visited.

"It's okay." Wyatt stepped back toward Aidan but tucked his hands in his pockets so he could resist the urge to pull Aidan close again. That was too complicated. "So, uh, what kind of art do you do?"

"I'd love to do this." Aidan gestured at the painting in front of him, "Though I mostly use digital media instead of pencil and paint. Usually, though, I'm designing advertisements. Nothing too exciting."

"But you do get to do this sort of thing occasionally, right?" Wyatt followed as Aidan moved on to the next painting. "I mean, you don't just create boring advertisements, do you?"

"No. I do some of this in my free time, and I illustrate children's books occasionally."

"Sounds nice."

"It is. I'll show you some of it when you wake up." The words came out before his brain caught up with his mouth.

"Aidan…." Wyatt stepped back again, his heart sinking. He hated doing this, but he hated listening to Aidan talk about things that could never be even more. It hurt too much to hear night after night. "You promised."

"I know! It's just, I know you want to see them, and I can't show you here, but if you wake up, then—"

"Good-bye, Aidan. I'll see you tomorrow."

Aidan was awake before he could say another word.

THE next time Wyatt didn't go to Aidan. As soon as he felt Aidan in the Dreamscape, Wyatt crafted another one of his favorite places and pulled Aidan to it. The look on Aidan's face when he saw the bright flowers and low wooden buildings that made up the park entrance made it worth the effort.

"I went on a field trip here once, when I was a kid," Wyatt said, taking Aidan by the wrist and drawing him farther into the zoo. "I'd never been to a zoo before, and had never seen half the animals outside of pictures in our textbooks, and it was just the most amazing thing ever." He flashed a grin at Aidan as they walked up the gentle slope of the entrance to the main thoroughfare. "The big cats were the best, I think, but the wolves were pretty cool, too, and they're right by the entrance, so we'll start with them."

There were so many things Aidan wanted to say—how he was sorry he'd ruined their visit to the art museum, how upset he'd been all day, and how much he wished Wyatt would try to wake up, just once—but instead he nodded and let himself be pulled along and caught up in Wyatt's enthusiasm.

They stopped just short of the tram tracks, and Wyatt turned to Aidan with a worried look on his face. "You *are* okay with seeing the wolves first, right?"

Aidan laughed. Wyatt was so earnest, so eager to please, and Aidan just wanted to give him a giant hug and tell him they would do whatever Wyatt wanted all night long. The next night, too, and the night after that, if that's what it took to keep Wyatt's eyes sparkling with joy. "Absolutely."

Wyatt's grin widened as he dragged Aidan across the tram tracks into the viewing area for the wolf enclosure. It was large and open, with trees along the sides, and it took them a minute to find the animals, but once they did, the wolves were marvelous. They were sleek and gorgeous and so realistic that it was hard to remember this was only a dream. It felt so real.

After the wolves, they made a circle around the zoo, stopping in to see birds, reptiles, and monkeys before they finally made it to the cat house. As they waited for a woman to convince her two small children they really did want to walk through the door, Wyatt bounced on his toes. "When I came here on my field trip, I wanted to take every single one of the cats home. And I'm a dog person!"

"It's the way they look at you," Aidan replied sagely. "Or rather, the way they don't look at you. It just makes you want to break down that aloof barrier and ruffle their fur."

"That and they're absolutely adorable," Wyatt agreed. They stepped into the air conditioning with twin sighs of relief and started following the directed path around the building. It started with the smallest cats first, little things that could live as house cats if they weren't wild, and slowly progressed to the larger animals. The largest—lions, cheetahs, and tigers—were outside in Big Cat Canyon, but the ones inside reached a size bigger than Aidan wanted to meet away from the safety of the zoo.

Wyatt took Aidan's hand as they wandered and grinned when Aidan didn't pull away.

At the end of the day, they walked out of the zoo, still hand in hand. Wyatt's steps were a little slower than they had been when the dream started, but he was smiling widely. "I haven't visited here in ages."

"I can see why you liked it." Given how excited adult Wyatt was about visiting the dream version of this zoo, Aidan could only imagine how thrilling it had been for him to visit the real thing as a child. "We'll have to come back some time." He bit back the urge to suggest they visit it in the waking world. That never ended well, and Aidan had learned his lesson.

He would just keep hoping that Wyatt would wake up on his own soon and keep enjoying their nightly visits until he did.

He wasn't going to let himself think about what might happen after Wyatt woke up. He didn't want to consider the possibility that the night before Wyatt woke up would be the last night they dreamed together. Instead, he let Wyatt nod enthusiastically and start rambling about other favorite places he could take Aidan.

Wyatt was thrilled by how well the night had gone. He didn't want to wake Aidan up, but he knew that if he didn't end the dream soon, it would be ended for them when Aidan's alarm went off, and as hard as it was to send Aidan away, it would be harder if the dream ended without any warning.

"I'll see you tomorrow night," he said as they paused in the parking lot. He pulled Aidan in for a tight hug, resisting the urge to kiss Aidan's forehead, and twisted the Dreamscape to send Aidan back into the waking world.

The whole dream dimmed as soon as Aidan was gone, and Wyatt left it swiftly, returning to his own dreams until he could visit with Aidan again.

Chapter Five

"WYATT'S waking up."

Aidan blinked blearily at Kyler as he tried to wrap his tired brain around the words. "He is?" He sat up straighter and peered critically at the sleeping figure.

Wyatt was definitely stronger. After the time in Aidan's and Kyler's care, all the lights on his bracelet were steadily lit, and he'd begun to move in his sleep instead of lying eerily motionless. Aidan hadn't let himself hope, however. He couldn't, not with Wyatt telling him every night that he would never awaken.

"Yeah." Kyler moved around the bed, checking Wyatt's stats and IVs. "He was practically unconscious before, but now it's normal sleep. And he's getting restless."

"Restless is good?"

"Restless is very good." Kyler brightened. "It means he's almost ready to wake up. Physically, anyway. Mentally...." He shrugged and looked pointedly at Aidan. "Have you tried to convince him to wake up when he dreams with you?"

"I've asked. He doesn't think he can." Aidan leaned forward, resting his head in his hands as he sighed. "He doesn't believe me when I tell him he's safe now."

Kyler squeezed Aidan's shoulder gently as he tried to impart reassurance he didn't really feel. "He will."

Aidan looked up, smiling uncertainly. "I hope so."

WYATT'S room was dark when Aidan awoke. He winced and groaned in pain, his back and neck muscles tight from sleeping in the chair. The clock told him what his body already knew, that it was the middle of the night and he should go back to sleep—this time in his own bed, where he had a chance of resting even if Wyatt didn't manage his nightly visit.

It was sad that the worst part of falling asleep in the chair wasn't the kinks in his muscles or that he awoke feeling as if he'd been awake for days instead of sleeping for hours. The worst part was he couldn't remember if he'd dreamed and so knew he hadn't been visited by Wyatt while he slept. He shouldn't have become used to the nightly visits so quickly, shouldn't feel an ache in the pit of his stomach at the thought of even one night without Wyatt.

He was well and truly fucked, and he couldn't tell anyone.

Sighing, Aidan clicked on the light by the bed so he could check on Wyatt one last time before shuffling off to his own room. It was just a small lamp, but after sleep and pitch darkness, it was bright, and he blinked and moaned, rubbing at his eyes.

It was only after he opened his eyes again that he realized he wasn't the only one groaning.

Bright hazel eyes blinked up at Aidan from the bed, tears pooling in the corners as Wyatt tried ineffectually to lift a hand to shield them. The arm twitched and flopped but didn't make it nearly as far as Wyatt's face.

"Sorry," Aidan whispered, pulling the lamp away from the bed and angling it so it shone into the corner of the room.

Wyatt kept blinking, trying to figure out this strange dream, but his eyes stopped watering as he peered up at Aidan. "Thanks."

The hoarse sound only superficially resembled the warm baritone Aidan heard in his dreams, but even superficial resemblance was more than Aidan had come to hope for in the waking world, and his brilliant smile matched the warmth spreading through his chest. "You're welcome." He sat on the edge of the bed and brushed at the floppy hair that had settled into Wyatt's eyes. "How are you feeling?"

Wyatt opened and closed his mouth a few times, huffing in frustration as he failed to produce any noise. "Hurts," he finally managed, the word sounding more like a croak than speech.

Aidan leaned closer, already cursing the fact that his phone was in the other room and he didn't dare leave Wyatt even long enough to grab it. He needed to call Kyler, needed to let him know Wyatt had awakened, that Wyatt was in pain, that Wyatt needed care Aidan didn't know how to provide. "What hurts? Where? How badly?"

"Throat." Wyatt swallowed hard, wincing at the burning pain. He tried to focus on making it go away, and when that didn't work, on changing the whole dream to something more pleasant, but the room never dissolved around him and the pain in his throat stayed. "Thirsty."

"Oh!" Aidan jumped to his feet, took two steps, and whirled back around, afraid Wyatt would think he was abandoning him. "I'm just going to get you a glass of water, okay? I'll be right back, I promise."

Wyatt nodded, confused, and Aidan dashed from the room. He grabbed the first glass he found in the kitchen cabinet and filled it with water before grabbing his phone and punching in Kyler's number. "He's awake," he barked. "Come over. Hurry!" Kyler started to answer, but Aidan hung up before he could. He was back in Wyatt's room in under a minute.

"Here." Aidan stopped just short of knocking his knees into the bed and thrust his hand forward to hold the glass above Wyatt's chest. "Water."

Wyatt rolled his eyes as he lifted a shaking arm to take the glass.

Aidan cursed silently. He was clearly an idiot. "Sorry," he muttered, setting the glass down on the nightstand. He slipped an arm behind Wyatt's shoulders, carefully avoiding the tubes and wires still attached to him, and helped him sit up. Wyatt was gaining a little control over his muscles as he woke, but the weeks lying in Aidan's spare room had taken their toll.

Wyatt gulped greedily at the water as Aidan held it to his lips. "Thanks," he whispered, his voice sounding a little more like it did in the Dreamscape, though quiet and rough around the edges. He let his head flop back to rest on Aidan's shoulder. "This sucks."

"Yeah." Aidan didn't think it did, not with Wyatt heavy and warm against his chest, finally talking to him in the real world. "It'll get better."

"I guess." Wyatt guided the glass to his mouth, though Aidan kept a firm grip on it, and downed the rest of the water. "This is a weird dream."

"It's not a dream. You're awake."

"I don't get to wake up, Aidan. I've told you that. I never will." Wyatt tried to sit up, settled for scooting over a little so he could turn his head and look at Aidan's face. "I'm surprised they let me keep seeing you, though maybe these are my dreams now, and I'm just wishing you were around," he added softly. "I used to dream about the dog that I had as a kid, before. Maybe this is like that."

"What happened to it?"

"The real one? I don't know. It was still with my family when they, when I—" He waved his hand limply in the air. "You know." He couldn't say the words, even after all these years. "The dream one just vanished one day. I stopped thinking about it when I was dreaming, I guess, and when I was in the Dreamscape, I stopped being able to manifest it. It hurt too much."

"I'm sorry."

"Don't be." Wyatt managed a small smile despite the aching in his chest. "It'll happen to you eventually, and I don't want to waste the time we have."

Aidan shifted, propping Wyatt up on pillows and turning around so he could look the other man in the eyes. "What do you mean it'll happen to me?"

"If this is my dream, I'll eventually stop thinking about you, and I won't see you anymore. If it's your dream, they'll find a way to keep me from finding you. Either way, you won't be around anymore."

"Wyatt." Aidan took the other man's hands and leaned forward a little. "This isn't a dream. Whoever *they* are, they left you for dead in an alley. I found you, and my friends and I brought you here. You've been sleeping in my guest room for two weeks."

"No, I haven't." Wyatt pulled his hands free and wrapped his arms around his chest. "They wouldn't let me go any more than they'd let me wake up. It's a nice thought, though. I'd like it if it were true."

"It *is* true."

"Please stop saying that."

"But Wyatt—"

"Can I have more water?" He met Aidan's eyes with a silent plea. "Please?"

"Yeah. Sure." Aidan took the glass from where he'd left it on the nightstand and walked to the kitchen, trying very hard not to think about the lost, broken tone in Wyatt's voice.

"HE DOESN'T believe he's awake."

Kyler blinked as he pushed his way past Aidan into the apartment. "What do you mean?"

"I mean," Aidan said as he shut the door and locked it, "that he still thinks he's dreaming. He's convinced that this is just some fucked-up dream and that I'm just some dream version of me that he's remembering, because— I don't know—but he did it for a dog once, but then he realized that the dog wasn't real and he stopped dreaming about it, and he's convinced that the same thing is going to happen with me, and I don't know how to convince him otherwise!"

Kyler watched with concern as Aidan paced and ranted. "Breathe."

"I can't. Fuck!" Aidan sank onto a chair. "I don't even know why it's so fucking important to me that he realizes that he's awake. I don't even know the guy, not really, even though he has been dreaming with me for two weeks."

Kyler tried to give Aidan an excuse. "You rescued him, Aidan. It's natural to have some interest in his well-being after that."

"It's more than that, though, Kyler." Aidan let his head fall forward into his hands. "I care that he's okay, yeah, but want him to know that he's awake, with me. That this is real. That *I'm* real."

"You have feelings for him."

"I shouldn't. He's been lying helpless in my guest bedroom since I met him and visiting my dreams because I'm the closest person, and that's all he knows."

"Aidan...."

"And worse," Aidan went on, ignoring Kyler, "if he ever does realize that he's awake, he'll feel obligated to me or something." He looked up, meeting Kyler's eyes with a desperate gaze. "I can't be feeling this."

"Sure you can." Kyler crouched in front of Aidan so he could look straight into his eyes. "He's attractive. And you've seen what he's like when he's awake, even if you were both asleep," he added mischievously. "He has to be even more attractive moving around than lying in a coma."

"It's not even that. I mean,"—he hurried on as Kyler's eyebrows shot upward again—"he's attractive, yeah. And you're right; he's even more attractive when he's awake." Aidan started to smile but suppressed it. He was *not* going there. "But it's more than that. I fell asleep in the chair tonight, and when I woke up, I could barely move I was so sore, but the thing that hurt was that I *didn't dream*."

"Shit."

"Yeah."

"Aidan, you know what this means, right?"

"No." He didn't. He shook his head, his stomach churning at the expression on Kyler's face.

"You're Bonding with him."

"No." Aidan jumped to his feet, pushing past Kyler to pace the room. He tore at his hair, his hands clenching into fists to tug at the short brown locks. "I can't be."

"Why not?" Kyler settled in the chair Aidan had vacated, looking curiously amused. "You never Bonded, right? And he obviously hasn't."

"I haven't, but, Kyler, if I were going to Bond, I would have done so by now. I'm thirty-one years old. You know as well as I do that most Bonds are formed before either partner turns thirty. Most Dreamers Bond before they're twenty. I'll be lucky to find a long-term companion. I'll never have that connection."

"Most isn't all, Aidan," Kyler said with a fond smile as he watched his friend pace around the room in agitation. "And it's not like you could have met earlier. He's been locked up for years. *Since before he was old enough to form a Bond.*"

"It doesn't matter." Aidan stopped pacing and sank onto the couch, his eyes wide and pleading as he looked at Kyler. "You don't have to rationalize it. I haven't Bonded because I suck at relationships. No one could possibly want to put up with me for the next seventy years."

"Or maybe the person who could has been asleep somewhere the whole time you've been looking. Bonds don't happen when you try for them; they happen when you least expect them to."

"Kyler. Please." Aidan couldn't talk about it, couldn't think about the possibility of a relationship, of a *Bond*, not when the spectacular failure of his last attempt was what had led him to find Wyatt.

"Yeah, sure. Sorry." Kyler looked down at his hands, twined his fingers together as he tried to think of a way to change the subject gracefully. "I, uh, should probably go check on Wyatt. Has he told you anything other than that he thinks he's dreaming?"

"Not really. We didn't talk long. I got him to drink some water, 'cause his throat hurt. I called you while I was getting it." Aidan shrugged, wished he had more to share. "He mentioned that this was a weird dream after he drank, and I tried to tell him it wasn't a dream at all, but he wouldn't hear it. He asked me to stop telling him that it was real and when I wouldn't he—" He jumped to his feet and dashed into the kitchen. "Shit! He asked for more water, and I was on my way to get it when you got here," he called back over his shoulder.

Kyler leaned against the doorframe between the kitchen and living room, watching, but held up his hand when Aidan tried to hand him the glass. "You should take it to him. Tell him who I am. He's already spooked enough, I'm sure."

"Yeah, and me freaking out and taking twenty minutes to get a glass of water isn't going to help."

"Hey. He doesn't need to know you freaked out. You can tell him you were updating me. Which you *were*," Kyler added quickly when Aidan opened his mouth to protest. "We should probably go, though, so he doesn't get too worried."

"Yeah. Or fall back asleep. How could I be such an idiot? I should have brought the water back before I opened the door. He's going to think I abandoned him, that he dreamed me away, and then he's going to freak out when I come back because it's just another thing he can't control, and I don't know what I should do or say or... Fuck!"

"You done?"

"Yeah, I think so." Aidan took a deep breath and forced a smile onto his face. It felt unnatural, but it was better than letting Wyatt see how worried and unnerved he was. He couldn't let Wyatt see that.

"Good. Go introduce me to the guy I've been taking care of for the past two weeks, then."

"Yeah, okay." Aidan started toward the bedroom, doing his best to ignore the twisting feeling in his gut as he wondered how Wyatt would react to his absence. "Try not to scare him, yeah?"

"As if." Kyler stopped just outside Wyatt's door and laid a hand on Aidan's arm. "I know you don't want to hear this, but that reaction in there? That's exactly how I felt when I first met Nell. Like the worst thing that I could possibly do was upset her or make her worry."

"Kyler," Aidan growled, stepping forward to loom over the slightly shorter man.

"All I'm saying is that Wyatt might not be the only one in denial about the reality of this situation. Just keep that in mind, okay?" He grinned and opened the door, stepping inside the bedroom before Aidan could reply.

Chapter Six

AIDAN leaned against the door to Wyatt's room. "You have to sleep sometime."

"I am asleep, remember?" Wyatt didn't lift his eyes from the book he was reading. "I don't need to sleep in my dreams."

"Wyatt...." Aidan crossed the room and sank down into the chair next to Wyatt's bed. The young man had been awake for thirty-six straight hours and had been content to spend most of them propped up against the headboard, reading or talking to Aidan and Kyler.

"Aidan...." Wyatt echoed. He stopped reading and smiled, but his eyes stayed focused on the page.

"When will you believe that this isn't a dream? It's been a day and a half."

"Time flows differently in dreams." Wyatt turned to look Aidan in the eye. "It's probably only been five minutes in the real world."

Aidan's gut twisted painfully at Wyatt's denial, but he pushed the feeling aside. He couldn't think what it might mean, couldn't consider the possibility that Kyler was right, until Wyatt accepted he was awake. "What can I do to convince you?"

"Nothing!" Wyatt turned his most pitiful expression on Aidan, trying to convey the way his own gut was twisting every time Aidan said something he *knew* couldn't be true. "There is nothing you can say or do or show me or anything. I know that I'm never going to actually wake up, okay? Please stop rubbing it in."

"Wyatt. Please."

Wyatt didn't answer, didn't give in to the want pooling in his stomach or the tingling feeling on his arm where Aidan's hand had been a moment earlier. He forced his eyes to move over the page, understanding little and remembering less, but anything was better than continuing the conversation. He wouldn't look back, no matter how long Aidan held out.

"I'M GOING to sedate him."

"What?" Aidan said, his panic evident in his voice.

Kyler sank into the leather armchair and gratefully accepted the beer Ratri pushed toward him. He took a long swallow before answering Aidan. "Wyatt needs to sleep. He's hurting himself by fighting it. He'll crash eventually from sheer exhaustion, but I'd rather not wait that long. If he won't sleep on his own, I'll make him."

"And you think he's just going to let you sedate him?" Wyatt had removed the IVs and leads within a half hour of waking, and though he'd grudgingly cooperated with everything else Kyler had requested, he'd adamantly refused electronic monitoring and needles.

"No." Kyler smiled despite his serious concerns. "I was going to slip it into his dinner. If we're lucky, he won't ever know."

"And if he finds out?" Aidan asked in a rough voice, his eyes narrowed as he glared at Kyler. "What then?" His chest clenched at even the idea of doing anything to Wyatt against his will.

"I'll explain it." Kyler set his beer on the coffee table and leaned forward so he could look Aidan in the eyes. "I'm hoping that when he wakes up again, he'll realize that he's really awake and that he'll understand why I had to make him sleep. He needs to dream and then wake up so he can realize how it's different."

"And who is he going to dream with? Brent from across the hall isn't going to be dreaming about anything that will help convince Wyatt."

"You." Kyler held up a hand to forestall Aidan's protest. "I know you just slept. I'd like to sedate you too so we'll know who he's dreaming with, and you can try to dream about something that will help. Maybe you'll be able to convince him that he really has woken up."

"Well, that ought to be easy, convincing him that he's awake when he's really asleep," Aidan muttered wryly, frowning at his empty beer bottle as he spun it between his fingers.

"You know what I mean," Kyler said, his tone a mix of gentle prodding and fond exasperation.

"Yeah. All right."

"Oh hell no!" Ratri grabbed Aidan's hand, stilling the bottle. "You are *not* agreeing to this."

"Ratri."

"No. Sleeping while he's here is dangerous enough!" Ratri shuddered at the thought. "If you're sedated, you won't be able to wake up until the drug wears off. He'll be able to do anything to you."

"Ratri."

"No." Ratri twisted to face Kyler, his hand firmly gripping Aidan's arm. "Why does the guy have to dream, anyway? Aidan has tried to convince him that he's awake, and he doesn't want to hear it. Why would he listen when he's asleep?"

"He might not," Kyler answered in a calm voice, his soft tones a stark contrast to Ratri's angry growls. "We need to try, though. I can't take that bracelet off until Wyatt realizes the reality of the situation, and the longer we leave it on, the greater the chance that he'll be found."

Aidan's gut twisted at the thought. They hadn't gotten any answers from Carina, though she had confirmed Wyatt wasn't a legally registered slave in Clardon. That left the other provinces, though, and it took time to get answers from them. "They left him for dead. Why would they be looking for him?"

"The bracelet is still transmitting," Kyler explained, his eyes darting toward Wyatt's bedroom as though he expected Wyatt to come running at the words. "They aren't watching it—they'd have been here weeks ago if they were—but there is always the chance someone will notice. Or the court who sentenced him could request an update. When they trace the bracelet and find it's not where it's supposed to be, they'll want it—and him—back."

"Fuck." Aidan closed his eyes, took a deep breath, and then looked straight at Kyler, ignoring Ratri anxiously hovering on his left. "You can sedate me after we eat." He stood, shrugging off both Ratri's hand and his protests, and carried his empty beer bottle into the kitchen. He definitely needed another one.

AIDAN slowly rubbed the washrag over the counter, pausing occasionally to scrub at imaginary spots. He was stalling, but he was inexplicably terrified and wanted to wait until the last possible second before letting Kyler stick him with a needle and send him off to sleep. His kitchen would be spotless before he was done.

"I think it's clean." Ratri pulled out a beer and set it on the counter before leaning against the refrigerator with his hands in his pockets and his eyebrows raised as he eyed the smooth gray of the granite countertop dubiously.

"Yeah." Aidan gave the counter one last wipe and tossed the wet rag into the sink. A moment later he snatched it back out and folded it in half before draping it neatly over the faucet.

"You don't have to do this, you know."

"Yes, I do. It's the only way I can help Wyatt right now."

"Why do you feel like you have to help him?" Ratri asked uncertainly.

Aidan leaned forward, resting his elbows on the counter and staring down at the slick, damp surface. "When you and Olin Bonded," he started softly, deliberately not looking at his friend, "what did it feel like?"

"What does—?"

"Can you just tell me? Please?" He risked a glance but quickly returned to focusing on the tiny droplets left behind by the washrag. "When it first started, before it was an actual Bond, what did it feel like?"

"That was years ago, Aidan."

"I know." Aidan pulled his bottom lip into his mouth, worrying it as he contemplated his next sentence. "Kyler thinks I'm Bonding with Wyatt."

"What?" Ratri crossed the room, spun Aidan around, and looked closely into his eyes. "Why does he think that? It's crazy!"

"That's what I said. I'm too old. *Wyatt* is too old. Kyler said that doesn't matter." He sighed and closed his eyes, hating that he had to explain this and dreading Ratri's answer. "I haven't slept well in two days because he's awake, because he's not dreaming with me." Aidan slumped back, leaning heavily against the cabinets. "It's only been two weeks, and I don't sleep well without having him in my dreams."

Ratri stepped back, his arms dropping to his sides. "Shit."

"Yeah. Pretty much." Aidan shrugged sheepishly. "I'm stalling right now because once Kyler sedates me, I'll dream, and I'll have to tell Wyatt that *we* are the ones who made him sleep. He's either going to think I'm nuts or that I betrayed him or I don't know, but it won't be good. That's what I'm worried about."

"Shit," Ratri repeated, sitting down hard in one of the wooden chairs at the table. "I think Kyler is right. As soon as Wyatt realizes he is really awake, that Bond is going to snap into place."

"We're too old," Aidan protested, ready to rehash all the arguments Kyler had already discarded. "And we barely know each other, even if you count two weeks of dreaming."

"*Most* people Bond by a certain age, not all. And Bonds form quickly, Aidan, especially for Dreamers, and especially in stressful situations. Wyatt is a Dreamer in a stressful situation. He's going to Bond quickly given the opportunity."

"And what about me? I'm just a good opportunity? The poor un-Bonded bastard who just happened to find him? Never mind that I couldn't manage a relationship if my life depended on it and that I'm just going to do everything wrong and fuck him up even more than he already is. I was *convenient*. Is that it?"

"No. Well, you are the poor bastard who found him," Ratri corrected with a smirk, "but maybe you were meant to. Maybe you would have met him years ago if things had been different. Maybe he doesn't need someone who can manage relationships and do all the right things, but someone who just wants to help as best he can."

"Because my best is so fantastic." Aidan laughed as the hysteria building inside him bubbled to the surface. "Even if that's true, he's still a slave. I can't change that."

"If you Bond, you can petition the courts for ownership. They'll probably grant it," Ratri said softly. It wasn't a good answer, he knew, but there was nothing else he could offer Aidan. Wyatt was a permanent slave, and whatever he'd done to merit that, Bonding wouldn't change it.

"I don't want to own him." Aidan rubbed his hand over his face, trying to maintain his composure. "If I Bond with someone, I don't want that between us."

Ratri sighed and leaned back in the chair as he tried to figure out what to say. "I don't know what to tell you, man."

"That's not the worst." Aidan leaned back, letting his head thunk against the cabinets. "I don't know what he did, either." For the past two weeks, he'd managed to avoid more than idle curiosity about what Wyatt had done to merit permanent slavery, but with the prospect of a Bond hanging over his head, it suddenly mattered a lot more. "It had to be something bad."

"Not necessarily." Ratri shifted uncomfortably. Most people sentenced to permanent slavery had committed serious crimes. Locking up only the violent offenders kept the jail populations down and forced the criminals to support society. "Maybe it was a car accident."

"You're being awfully optimistic."

"Government wouldn't dump him," Ratri pointed out wryly. "So he obviously owes somebody something."

Aidan nodded. It was a valid point. "Whatever happened, whoever had him probably deserved it," he muttered, thinking about how they had treated Wyatt.

"Probably." Ratri shrugged. He wasn't too worried. "Carina will figure out who they are. They'll get what they deserve."

"Yeah. I guess." Aidan sighed, not feeling nearly as happy about that as he thought he should. "That doesn't solve my problem, though. He's still a slave."

"Does it matter? Really?" This wasn't the first time Ratri had talked Aidan down from overthinking things, but he suspected it might be the most important. "You like him, right?"

"That's the problem. I hate thinking that he's done something to merit this." The idea that it was accidental was a little easier to swallow, but it didn't eliminate any of the issues they'd be facing if Kyler and Ratri were right.

"So don't think about it." Ratri stood and flipped the chair around to sit backward. "Talk to him. Maybe he'll tell you when he knows he's awake."

"Maybe." It was a logical approach, though it wasn't going to stop Aidan from worrying. "Why are you being so logical about this?"

"You're Bonding with him." Ratri shrugged and leaned to rest his chin on the back of the chair. "He can't be all bad."

Aidan stared at his friend for a long moment and then shook his head. Ratri wasn't supposed to be the logical one in their friendship. "My life is officially weird." He pushed off from the counter. "I'm going to let Kyler knock me out. Maybe things will make sense while I'm asleep."

THE apartment was quiet. When Aidan had lain down, his arm tingling where Kyler had administered the shot, he'd been able to hear the soft sounds of the television playing in the living room and the subdued shuffling of Kyler and Ratri as they settled in to wait for Wyatt and Aidan to awaken. Now there was a deep silence, like in the dead of night after a deep snowfall, heavy and almost sacred in its absoluteness. Even the radiator was silent, the hum more noticeable in its absence than it ever was when present.

Aidan climbed from the bed, taking care that the bedsprings didn't creak, and plodded down the hall, his steps slow and deliberate. The living room was empty and spotlessly clean: blankets folded over the back of the couch and chairs; remotes lined up neatly on the end table; video games, DVDs, and books all in their proper places on the shelves. There wasn't a glass, beer bottle, or even a stray magazine to be seen. "What the hell?" Aidan sank onto the couch as he looked around with wide eyes. He wasn't a slob, but his apartment usually looked lived in. This was showroom clean—definitely *not* how he'd left it.

He was wondering what would happen if he put a movie into the DVD player when he heard a noise down the hall and the guest room door opened to reveal Wyatt, borrowed pajama bottoms hanging low on slender hips and chocolate-brown hair curling behind his ears and falling into his eyes. Aidan's heart fluttered and his stomach flipped as his gaze roamed over Wyatt's chest, and he had to force himself to look up and focus on Wyatt's face—not that his face was hard to look at either.

Wyatt was well-built in the dream, his muscles well-defined and his stomach flat. Muscle tone was the one area in which dream-Wyatt beat real-Wyatt, and Aidan was happy to look, his eyes drifting lower again as Wyatt walked down the hallway, rubbing at his eyes and running a hand through his hair.

"Hey."

Wyatt stopped and met Aidan's wide grin with an uncertain one of his own. "Hi." He blinked, frowning, and swallowed experimentally a few times. "This is weird."

Aidan agreed. He never thought of his apartment as this clean or empty, and it was odd that he would dream it that way. He doubted that was what Wyatt meant, though, so he assumed a curious expression, his head tilted slightly to the right, and asked, "What do you mean?"

"This." Wyatt finished crossing the room and sat on the couch next to Aidan, waving his hands vaguely as he moved. "I was sore and exhausted and my throat hurt horribly, and then all of a sudden I have plenty of energy and I don't hurt at all. I could hardly talk, and now it's easy. You're going to have to interrupt me or I'll ramble."

Aidan laughed. "You can ramble. I'm okay with that."

Wyatt shook his head in mock sadness, the effect completely ruined by the smile he found himself unable to suppress. "You really shouldn't be. I'll go on and on forever and bore you to death."

"No, you wouldn't." There was no way Wyatt could ever bore Aidan to death. If his words were boring, Aidan would just concentrate on the sound of Wyatt's voice or the way he couldn't seem to stop moving even when he was sitting still or—

"Yeah, I would," Wyatt protested, his eyes sparkling in a way they had yet to do when he was awake.

Aidan's chest tightened as he shook his head and forced his face into a more serious expression. He couldn't let his mind wander down that path. Sedatives or no, they'd only stay asleep for so long, and he'd have to deal with the real world again. "You're not tired right now because this is a dream."

Wyatt immediately sobered, his whole body deflating as he sank back into the couch cushions, frowning. "It's *always* a dream, Aidan," he said in clipped tones. He stared back at the doorway to the bedroom with such intensity that Aidan was afraid Wyatt was going to flee before he had a chance to push the issue.

"Wyatt, please." Aidan placed a hand on Wyatt's arm, drawing the other man's gaze. "Just listen, yeah? I promise, if I can't convince you tonight, I'll stop trying to."

"Fine." Wyatt shifted into a slightly more comfortable position but kept the scowl on his face and his arms crossed. "Why should I believe that I'm awake?"

Aidan couldn't stop the small twitch of his lips. "Well, you're not right now. Kyler gave us both a sedative so we could dream and talk."

"So you put me to sleep so I would believe that I was awake?" Wyatt asked skeptically.

"It sounds stupid, I know, but we couldn't think of anything else to try. Kyler really wants to get your bracelet off, and he's afraid to do it until you accept that you really have woken up. It's dangerous to leave it on, but it's dangerous to take it off, too, I guess." He shrugged, unsure how he would answer if Wyatt wanted a deeper explanation.

"Bracelet?" Wyatt held out both arms, frowning. "I don't have a bracelet."

Shit. Aidan didn't know if he should laugh or cry. It was a stupidly easy solution to his problem, but he didn't want to break the news to Wyatt. "In the real world, you have a slave bracelet on your right wrist, the kind that requires surgery to remove. Whoever had you before, they really wanted to keep you."

"But when my father—" Wyatt bit his lip, shook his head. "When they took me, they didn't put anything on me. They just drugged me."

"Took you?" That put an entirely new spin on things, one Aidan hadn't considered. Slavery was legal, an institution designed to help people pay off debt or repay damages caused by their crimes, but it was a legal process, handled by the courts. No one was supposed to be taken against his or her will.

If Wyatt wasn't legally a slave, that changed everything.

"I didn't agree to spend the rest of my life asleep, Aidan." Wyatt pulled his legs up to his chest, resting his chin on his knees as he tried to make himself as small as possible. He hated talking about this. "I was drugged, and—"

"And you've been asleep ever since?"

"Basically." Wyatt took a deep breath, trying to center himself again. "Apparently they sometimes kind of wake me up, to make sure everything still works, but I haven't really been awake in a long time."

"You were yesterday. And you will be in the morning."

Wyatt squeezed his eyes shut. Thinking about that was even worse than thinking about how he'd ended up trapped in the first place. "Aidan...."

"Just listen, okay?" Aidan waited for Wyatt to nod before continuing. "You don't have the bracelet here because you don't remember it. I don't know what all is involved in putting a slave bracelet on, especially the permanent kind, but I know it's complicated and painful and it has to be easier to do when the person getting it is unconscious. It's not like anyone *wants* one, right?"

"Doubtful."

"You look about the same in dreams as you do awake," Aidan pushed on, afraid that if he stopped he'd lose his momentum and never start again. "I don't know how; maybe you're pulling images of yourself out of the dreams of people who have seen you. Maybe it's something to do with whatever the people who had you did to you. Maybe it's just an innate sense of who you are. I don't know. Point is, though, that even if the person you're dreaming with has seen the bracelet, it doesn't matter, because to you it's just like clothes—something you can change at will. When you're awake, though, it's grafted to your arm and monitoring all sorts of stuff in your body, and you can't just take it off."

"Aidan, I can't change anything there. Why would the bracelet be any different?"

"The fact that you can't change anything should be your biggest clue!" Aidan closed his eyes and silently counted to ten. "Look, if you don't believe me about the bracelet, pick up the book you finished yesterday. It'll still be the same tomorrow, and you *know* that doesn't happen in dreams!"

"It can if you know it really well." Wyatt twisted his hands together as his protests grew weaker. "It's possible."

"I don't know it that well, and neither do you." Aidan grabbed Wyatt's hands, trapping them between his own. "Please, Wyatt. I'm trying to help you, but we're all in danger if we can't get that bracelet off. I know it's hard and terrifying and confusing, but what other explanation is there?"

"I don't know." Wyatt stared at their joined hands for a minute and then nodded, the small, jerky movement barely noticeable. "I'll try," he whispered, looking up to meet Aidan's eyes with a gaze full of fear and hope.

Aidan's heart felt as though it was going to burst from his chest as he leaned forward and pressed his lips to Wyatt's in a chaste kiss. "Thank you," he replied, his mouth still against Wyatt's, their hands still joined together.

Wyatt tangled one hand in Aidan's hair as he deepened the kiss.

Chapter Seven

WYATT opened his eyes and blinked into the darkness, trying to discern the shapes of furniture from the shadows cast by the ambient light of the street and hallway. It was the first time he could remember opening his eyes since *before*, and the weird sensation almost convinced him to believe Aidan without performing any of the other tests he'd agreed to. The sensation of moving between deep unconsciousness and his own dreams or his own dreams and the Dreamscape wasn't quite the same. There was the similar sensation of settling into a new reality—though this one felt more familiar than any except the ones he knew were in his own head—but this time there was the sensation of physical weight, of movement, and of actually opening his eyes rather than simply letting the world change around him.

It was an oddly familiar sensation, and thinking back on it, he remembered feeling similarly the last time he ended up here. He hadn't noticed then because he hadn't been looking for it, but it was definitely a clue that Aidan might be right.

Slowly, wincing at the pain of underused muscles (another clue, if he was being perfectly honest with himself), Wyatt sat up and pulled his right arm into his lap. Even without turning on the light (and that was yet another clue, that his eyes hadn't adjusted immediately to the dim light), Wyatt could see the bracelet, the ten evenly spaced LED lights glowing softly in the darkness. He poked hesitantly at it with his left index finger, wincing when he pushed too hard and the skin on his arm moved with the bracelet. It was definitely attached or grafted or whatever Aidan had said, then.

Shit.

There was only one more thing to check.

Conscious of his weak, aching muscles, Wyatt scooted to the edge of the bed and flicked on the light. The book he'd read yesterday—some sort of courtroom drama that was barely memorable enough for this test to be effective—lay next to a glass of water and a stick of lip balm. His hand shook as he picked it up, flipped it open to the first page, and began reading. The beginning was the same, as was the ending, and the middle bit that he flipped to was familiar enough that Wyatt knew it was the exact same book he'd just finished.

The books in his dreams rarely even had *words* inside, and the text on the covers changed every time he looked away. For this to be the same book—same title, same words, same characters, same story, same *everything*—it could only mean one thing.

Aidan was right.

The book fell from Wyatt's suddenly limp fingers, hitting the hardwood floor with a rustle of pages and a dull thump. Wyatt sat, frozen, his eyes fixed on the new crease in the cover, unable to move, to think, to breathe. There was a loud *thud, thud, thud* inside his head, and the bed felt like it was going to tip over and dump him to the floor at any second, but nothing was moving, or changing, or dissolving away, and now there were gray spots in front of his eyes, making it impossible to focus on anything. His hands clenched the fabric of his unfamiliar pajama pants as the spots grew larger and larger and darker and darker until all he could see was the cover of the book inside a long, gray tunnel that kept growing narrower and narrower.

Then everything went dark.

"WYATT!" Aidan rushed through the door and skidded to a stop in front of the bed just as Wyatt toppled forward, falling limply against Aidan's shoulder. His heart pounding and his hands shaking, Aidan pushed the unconscious man up, settling him back on the bed. "Come on, Wyatt," he encouraged, sitting on the bed next to the lax figure and gently shaking Wyatt's shoulders and stroking his cheek. "Wake up."

Wyatt made a small sound of protest, his nose scrunching as he turned his cheek into Aidan's hand, but he didn't otherwise move, didn't open his eyes.

"Kyler!" Aidan yelled out, glancing over his shoulder only long enough to direct his voice toward the door and not into Wyatt's ears. "Help!" He didn't wait for Kyler to respond but turned immediately back to Wyatt, his hands fluttering between shaking Wyatt's shoulders and patting his cheek, mumbling encouragement all the while.

Kyler slid through the doorway, his socks slipping on the polished wood as he turned the corner and skated to the bed. He shoved himself between Wyatt and Aidan, pushing Aidan's hands out of the way as he began his own examination of Wyatt, lifting his eyelids and checking his pulse before turning to Aidan. "What happened?"

"I don't know." His eyes wide and full of terror, Aidan blinked at Kyler. "I had convinced him to, uh, test things, I guess, when he woke up, and I was coming to see if—if he was going to believe me this time and actually accept that he was awake." His eyes flicked back to Wyatt, and Aidan picked up the slack hand near his hip, holding it between his own as if it were the most precious thing in the world. "Only when I got here," he continued, his eyes back on Kyler, "he was sitting up, and he looked, I don't know, shocked or something, and then he just toppled forward. I ran in and caught him, but I don't think he even saw me." Aidan squeezed Wyatt's hand tighter, pressing it to his chest as he silently begged Kyler to fix the situation.

Kyler nodded, running his hands over Wyatt's limbs and again checking his pupil dilation and pulse. "I think you might have succeeded," he murmured, pulling the blankets up over Wyatt again, tucking them up to his chin but leaving the hand Aidan clenched free.

"What do you mean?"

"He passed out, probably from shock. Give him a few minutes, and he should wake up again. Just go gentle on him, okay? And bring him out if he's feeling up to it. He should meet Ratri and Olin."

"Um, yeah, okay." Aidan didn't move until he realized Kyler was walking out of the room. "Wait!" he shouted, turning after his friend. "Why are you leaving?"

"He's fine, Aidan." Kyler turned and looked Aidan straight in the eyes. "He's likely already starting to wake up. I don't think I need to be here, but I'll be right in the other room if you need me, okay?"

"Okay," Aidan parroted, his attention already back on Wyatt's face, searching desperately for any sign of consciousness. He didn't notice when Kyler left, closing the door behind him.

KYLER sighed, taking a minute to run his hand over his face and center himself. He'd put on a confident front for Aidan, and Wyatt would be all right, but Aidan's scream and the initial sight of Wyatt limp on the bed had shaken him more than he would ever let Aidan know. Kyler sucked in another deep breath and released it slowly, feeling the residual tension drain from his muscles before he headed back out to the living room.

"He's fine," he said, nodding at Ratri and Olin as he stepped into the room. "Wyatt passed out—from shock, I think—but he'll be all right."

"So he realized he's awake, then?" Olin sat back on the couch, relaxing a little now that he knew there wasn't going to be another problem to deal with.

"I think." Kyler shrugged and veered toward the door when a knock sounded. "He's not awake at the moment, so I can't be sure, but from what Aidan said, I think he fainted."

"So it could be something else." Ratri crossed his arms and scowled at Kyler. "There could be something wrong with him."

"Maybe." Kyler leaned up and peered through the peephole, immediately opening the door when he saw Carina shifting impatiently from foot to foot in the hall. "His vital signs were good, though, and that's all I can check until he wakes up again. Hello, Carina."

"Problems?" Carina slipped through the doorway, heading toward the couch with barely a glance at Kyler.

"Wyatt's awake, or he was." Kyler locked the door behind Carina and followed her, dropping into the arm chair with a sigh. "We were trying to convince him that he was awake. I think Aidan succeeded, but he passed out."

"Or worse," Ratri muttered, sinking further into the couch and ignoring the looks Olin and Kyler both shot him.

"He seemed fine," Kyler repeated, clenching his teeth. "I wouldn't have left the room if he didn't."

"Right."

Carina, long used to Ratri's sullenness, ignored him and turned to Kyler. "When do you think he'll wake up?"

"Soon." Kyler shrugged. If he were honest, he would admit he didn't really know, but he'd focus on that later, if Wyatt didn't wake up again. For the moment, he distracted himself by casting a curious glance at Carina. "What brings you by?"

"News, actually." She paused a moment, deciding if she should wait to tell Aidan—and Wyatt, she supposed, though it was going to take seeing him awake for her brain to accept that—then decided it might be better to tell Kyler. Just in case. "We've gotten the records searches back from all the provinces. Wyatt isn't legally a slave."

"He said he wasn't," Olin murmured as he leaned forward, his gaze and attention both locked on Carina.

She pulled some papers from her briefcase and set them on the coffee table. She knew Aidan wanted to believe, but what she'd found directly contradicted the information Wyatt had given him. "There were papers filed in Ambridia where he agreed to ten years of slavery in exchange for money being sent to his parents. Allegedly," she added when all three men gave her an incredulous look. "That was eleven years ago, however, and there is no record anywhere of Wyatt Mettler being sentenced to permanent slavery."

"So he's free, then, regardless of whether the papers you found are right." Olin waited for Carina's nod before sitting back, his worry lifting. If Wyatt was free, he didn't have to worry about Aidan as much.

"I had court papers drawn up to that effect." Carina tapped her finger on one of the envelopes she'd put on the table. "There was never an official contract termination filed, but since there wasn't an extension filed either, the courts will give him an official decree."

"What about the bracelet?" Kyler had slowly begun to interpret the data the silver band surgically attached to Wyatt's wrist gave him, but he always felt strange plugging his tablet into it, like he was cheating or relying too heavily on a crutch. "If he's not a permanent slave, how did he get one?"

"It's from a batch that was reported stolen." Carina pointed to another file on the table. "They went missing off a transport twelve years ago, just after it left the manufacturing facility. The serial numbers were reported stolen, but the rest of them turned up a week later in a box left outside a police station. Three were still missing after they checked them all in. Two more turned up later, but the last one was never found."

"No one looks at serial numbers of attached slave bracelets." Ratri's scowl deepened. "Why would they? Everyone assumes they deserve it and tries to have as little to do with them as possible."

"And usually they're right." Kyler sighed. He didn't like the situation any more than Ratri did, but he understood it. Permanent slavery was reserved for the most serious crimes, and most people didn't want to have anything to do with criminals. "The police couldn't exactly check every bracelet attached to every slave, either."

"It wouldn't have done any good," Olin pointed out. "They took Wyatt across the country and kept him asleep. No one had the opportunity to see him."

Ratri leaned forward and picked up one of the envelopes, carefully unfastening it and pulling out the papers inside. "So why give him a bracelet at all, then?"

Kyler shrugged. "I don't know. Insurance, maybe. If someone stumbled into wherever they were keeping him, they'd assume he was there legally."

"Possibly." Carina nodded at Kyler, admittedly a little impressed. That was the most likely reason. "Or maybe it was so they could track him, just in case."

"Speaking of, since it's not legal, I can remove it, right?" Kyler hadn't taken it off for fear of repercussions, but if all he had to worry about was Wyatt's health, he wanted to get rid of the bracelet—and the tracker—as quickly as possible.

"Yes." Carina pulled one last sheet of paper from her briefcase, which she then snapped shut. "There's your official authorization. The judge signed it an hour ago."

"Thanks."

"You're welcome." Carina stood and smoothed her skirt. "You'll pass this information on to Aidan?"

"Well, yeah, but where are you going?" Olin didn't mind passing on good news, but he'd honestly expected Carina to stay around and tell Aidan herself. "Shouldn't *you* tell him?"

Carina smiled. "I'll be in touch later. I don't want to distract him right now." Then, leaving Kyler, Ratri, and Olin gaping behind her, she left, slipping out the door.

WYATT'S eyelids fluttered, and he made a soft noise somewhere between a whimper and a groan. The fingers of the hand Aidan held twitched, curling briefly around Aidan's before relaxing again, and Wyatt's nose wrinkled, scrunching up adorably in a way that made Aidan's heart quiver.

"Wyatt?" Aidan asked, leaning close and brushing the back of his left hand against Wyatt's cheek. His right hand still held Wyatt's, pressing it against his chest as though feeling Aidan's heartbeat would help Wyatt wake up.

"Mmmm," Wyatt moaned again, his eyelids fluttering more rapidly as he turned his face into Aidan's hand.

Aidan broke into a wide grin as he gazed down at Wyatt's long, dark eyelashes and pale cheeks. "Come on, Wyatt," he whispered. "Open your eyes."

With agonizing slowness, Wyatt blinked his eyes open. "What happened?" he asked in a rough voice, pulling his free hand from under the covers to rub at bleary eyes.

"You passed out."

Wyatt bit his bottom lip and thought about that for a moment. "Oh."

"How are you feeling?"

"Um." Wyatt kept chewing on his bottom lip. "Am I awake?"

"Yeah." Aidan leaned over, not letting go of Wyatt's hand, and snagged the book from the floor. "You are. See?" He shifted his grip a little so Wyatt could see the bracelet on his wrist and handed him the book.

Wyatt glanced at the cover, then thumbed it open and looked at the first paragraph. It was still the same. "Oh." He closed his eyes and let the hand holding the book fall to the bed. "That's, um, oh."

Aidan chewed on his bottom lip and idly thought that at the rate they were going, they would both have horribly chapped, split lips before the conversation was over. "Are you...?" He trailed off, not sure what he was asking.

"Am I what, Aidan?" Wyatt looked up. "Am I okay? Am I hurt? Am I going to freak out? What are you asking me? 'Cause honestly, I don't know the answer to any of that. Do you have any idea how long I've been asleep? What they did to me? And now you keep telling me that I'm here and I'm awake and everything is going to be okay and—and I don't even know where here is or what okay means anymore or—or anything, really!" His breath came in short, heavy gasps as the words tumbled from his mouth.

"Breathe," Aidan soothed, rubbing his free hand up and down Wyatt's arm. "We'll figure things out."

"How?" Wyatt was close to panicking, his heart thudding in his chest as he struggled to keep his voice from quivering. "I don't even know where I am or how long they had me!"

"Do you know when they took you? Where you were?"

"It was my sixteenth birthday, the nineteenth of Glio, 798. I, um, we, uh, lived in New Altz, in, uh, Ambridia."

"Okay." Aidan struggled to keep his voice calm. Kyler had said a long time, but Aidan had been thinking months, not years. "Today is the seventh of Cembre, 809, and we're in Clardon. In the capital actually. Haverdsford."

"That's...." Wyatt did the math in his head and blanched. "I think I'm going to be sick."

Aidan didn't say anything as he helped Wyatt sit up and pulled the trash bin over to his feet. Wyatt heaved, spitting up what was left of the water and soup he'd had for dinner, then gagged on stomach acid as he tried to wrap his mind around eleven years of forced dreams. He'd known it had been a while, known he had grown and changed physically as he'd come into his abilities, but he had never dreamed it had been that long since his parents had betrayed him.

He almost wanted to go back to sleep and never wake again.

Chapter Eight

AIDAN slumped in his chair and scowled at the computer monitors. Everything on them was crap, worthless for the advertisement they were intended to be used in, and certainly not acceptable for a portfolio. A twelve-year-old with a simple graphics program and a working knowledge of computers could do better. Someone with Aidan's experience and credentials could do better blindfolded and drunk.

Graphic design was easier blindfolded and drunk than worried out of his mind.

His scowl deepening, Aidan hit the save button in case there was something that could be salvaged from the mess on his screens and closed the program. When the screen showed only the desktop background—a soaring dragon he had drawn the previous fall—he slumped further and sighed deeply. There was no way he was going to accomplish anything, no matter how much he needed to, not while Wyatt was undergoing surgery in the next room. The advertisement would have to wait, as would the next illustration for Marissa's book and the samples he'd promised to send to a prospective customer.

He paced and fretted, walking into the hallway several times, but Kyler had made it clear that he was *not* to come into Wyatt's bedroom until the surgery was complete, so he stopped himself just short of barging in. His palm itched each time he looked at the doorknob, and eventually he returned to his office and his computer so he wouldn't stare at the door to Wyatt's room and wonder what was happening on the other side.

He was halfway to losing his tenth consecutive game of Free Cell when Kyler poked his head in. "Hey."

Aidan immediately jumped to his feet, sending his chair rolling across the room. "How is he? Is he okay? Can I see him?"

"He's sleeping."

Aidan tried to barrel past, unsure if he should head to Wyatt's room or his own bedroom, but Kyler grabbed his arm.

"He's too drugged to dream right now."

Aidan's gut clenched. "But you can't! He needs—"

Kyler cut him off with a squeeze on his shoulder. "He needs to let his body heal. He needed to be deep enough that he wouldn't feel or dream about what I was doing. The drugs will wear off in a few hours, and he'll be able to dream then."

"Yeah, okay." Aidan pulled free of Kyler's grip and crossed the remaining steps to the door. "Can I see him now?"

"Of course."

It was all Aidan could do to keep from running to Wyatt's room, but once he got inside, he stopped short. Wyatt again looked weak and pale—not as bad as he had when Aidan had first rescued him, but close. His eyes were closed, lashes long and dark against too-pale cheeks, and the dark circles that had almost faded from under them were back. His lips were parted slightly, and his arms rested on top of the covers, the left by his side, the right resting on his stomach. White gauze surrounded his right wrist where the slave bracelet had been removed, the soft fabric blending surprisingly well with Wyatt's light skin.

Looking at him, it was painfully obvious why Kyler had waited as long as he did to remove Wyatt's slave bracelet.

"It went well," Kyler said from behind Aidan before moving into the room to stand and stare down at his patient. "It came off more easily than I'd hoped, and if he's able to leave it alone to heal, scarring should be minimal. In a few months, only someone looking for a scar will see it."

"Good." Aidan finally convinced his feet to carry him to Wyatt's side. He let his fingers hover over Wyatt's bandaged wrist for a moment before gently taking Wyatt's hand in his own and sinking down to sit on the bed next to his unconscious friend. "Is he going to be in pain when he wakes up?"

"Some, but I'll leave things to help with that. When he wakes up, I'll show you both, in case you need to take care of something when I'm not here."

Aidan's stomach churned at the thought of Kyler not being here to help him take care of Wyatt as he healed, but he knew Kyler couldn't stay. Other patients were counting on Kyler, too, and his Bondmate probably missed him, with all the time he had been spending over here. "Okay," Aidan said, flashing a strained smile without moving his gaze from Wyatt's face.

Kyler squeezed Aidan's shoulder. "He's going to be fine, Aidan."

"I know. I just... I don't like seeing him this still. I don't like knowing he can't dream right now. I want to talk to him, make sure he feels okay."

"Yeah." They waited in silence for several minutes, both looking down at Wyatt as he slept, unaware of his visitors. "He knew I was going to drug him, Aidan," Kyler said when the silence began to stretch thin and Aidan fidgeted with the need to do something. "I told him that I wanted to put him under so he couldn't dream, and he was okay with that. I wouldn't have done it otherwise."

That got Aidan to look up, and he met Kyler's eyes for the first time since entering Wyatt's room. He smiled slightly and squeezed Wyatt's hand a little tighter, taking comfort from its warmth and doing his best to ignore the way it wasn't moving. "Thanks."

IN A small, windowless room on the other side of the city, a tiny box buried in a pile of discarded equipment lit up and started emitting a shrill beeping sound. There was no one there to hear it, the room dark and its daytime occupants already gone for the weekend, but the box's battery was strong. The alarm would still be blaring when the work week started again.

"LEAVE it alone," Aidan said two days later as he took Wyatt's left hand in his right, lacing their fingers together and squeezing gently. He told himself it was only to keep Wyatt from picking at the gauze wrapped around his right wrist, but when Wyatt squeezed back, he thought of all the things they'd done in dreams but had thus far avoided in reality.

Wyatt sighed dramatically and held his right arm up, examining the gauze with critical eyes. "It itches. And hurts. And I think it's almost time to change the gauze anyway."

"Kyler will be here in an hour or so."

"We could go to him."

"I don't think—"

"Never mind." Wyatt huffed and pulled his hand free of Aidan's. "Don't worry," he said in response to Aidan's surprised look, "I won't pick at anything. I wouldn't want to damage myself any more."

"What?" Aidan sat up straighter and looked at Wyatt with wide, surprised eyes. That was *not* the response he'd been expecting. "What the hell do you mean by that?"

Wyatt held up his bandaged wrist again, this time looking at it in disgust. "I don't know why you bothered to take this off me."

"Because you don't belong to them," Aidan said in a dubious tone. He was beginning to feel as though he and Wyatt were having two completely different conversations. "You don't belong to anybody."

"I don't? Are you sure?"

"Yes?" Aidan had no idea what Wyatt was getting at, but he didn't like how agitated he was getting.

"Really?" Wyatt sprang to his feet and paced to the other side of the room. His steps were surer now, but he leaned against the wall for support when he got there, his arms crossed and his eyes narrowed as he glared back at Aidan. "It doesn't seem that way."

Now Aidan was completely lost. "It doesn't?"

"I'm as much a prisoner here as I was—" He paused, waved his hand around. "*There*. At least they didn't pretend."

"Prisoner? What—?"

"I haven't left this apartment since you brought me here, Aidan!" Wyatt waved his arms wildly, nearly hitting the television with one particularly wild swing. "I've spent more time than I care to think about in that damn bed, and now I can't even go see the doctor you have treating me. I have to wait for him to come here! What else am I supposed to think but that I'm *not allowed* to go out?"

Aidan sprang to his feet, his teeth clenched and his hands balled into fists at his sides. "I'm trying to help you get healthy so you *can* go out, Wyatt!" he spat. "You were practically *dead* when I found you. You still can't stand or walk for long. You wouldn't make it to the end of the block without collapsing, and then what?"

"We could drive somewhere." Wyatt crossed his arms again and leaned more heavily against the wall while trying to look like he was just affecting a casual pose. Aidan was right about his strength, but that didn't mean Wyatt was going to admit it.

"Not today we can't." Aidan smiled ruefully and held up a hand when Wyatt opened his mouth to protest. "Kyler has my car. I let him borrow it 'cause his is in the shop and he needed to spend some time at the clinic before he came back here to check on you. I didn't realize you'd want to go out yet."

"Can we go somewhere when he gets here?"

"I don't know." When Wyatt's mouth gaped open again, Aidan crossed the distance between them and rested his hands on Wyatt's crossed arms.

"We'll talk to Kyler, okay? I don't want to do something that will set back your recovery. And I don't know how safe it is."

Wyatt blinked, trying to wrap his brain around this new twist. Every time Aidan cleared up one thing, he said something else that made no sense, and Wyatt's head was swimming. "What do you mean?"

"The people who had you could probably tell when Kyler removed your bracelet," Aidan said softly. "They're not designed to be removed, and the ones that the government issues have alarms built in to keep people from getting them cut off. There's no reason to think that yours didn't. If there is an alarm and it went off, they'll know you're alive." He slid his hand along Wyatt's arm until his fingers brushed the edge of the gauze. "There aren't many things that leave a wound like this, and I can't imagine that there are many people who recently had permanent slave bracelets removed walking around the city. They're rare, and the courts don't just release someone who was sentenced to wear one. If someone powerful is looking for one…."

He didn't have to finish the sentence. Wyatt shivered and nodded. "Okay. Sorry."

"Don't be." Aidan pressed his lips to Wyatt's ear. "Once you're healed enough, I promise, we'll go out. I'll show you around the city, we'll get your favorite food, get your hair cut, buy you some clothes that fit… whatever you want."

Wyatt grinned at Aidan. "Pants that actually come down to my ankles?"

"Yep." Aidan returned the smile. "Long-sleeve shirts that come down to your wrists too. And real shoes and a jacket for the winter."

"Sounds great." Wyatt's smile faded and he let his head fall forward again. "How am I supposed to pay for that, though?" Aidan's shirt muffled his voice, but the worry in it came through just fine.

"I'll pay for it."

"And then what?" When Wyatt looked up, his eyes were brimming with tears. "I come back here and live in your apartment and eat your food and wear clothes you paid for and do what—keep the place for you while you work? I don't have any money, and I don't have any way to get any, either."

"Yes, you do."

Wyatt snorted and closed his eyes. "Aidan, I've been asleep since I was sixteen years old. I don't have any marketable skills. The only thing I know how to do is dream."

"So dream. I'm serious." Aidan waited until Wyatt opened his eyes, curiosity sparking within them. "Look, my best friend from when I was a kid and her Bondmate, they're both Dreamers, and they use their ability to support themselves. If they can, so can you. I can ask them to help you, if you want."

"Maybe."

"They're out of town right now, but if you're feeling up to it when they get back, I'll introduce you. I'm sure they'll have ideas to help you find a job. And until then"—Aidan stretched up onto his toes and leaned forward until his lips were only inches from Wyatt's—"I am happy to help you out."

Wyatt uncrossed his arms and slipped them around Aidan's waist, pulling Aidan closer, which forced Aidan's hands up to his shoulders. "Oh? And what's in it for you?"

"I get to keep you around."

"Really?" Wyatt lifted his eyebrows teasingly. "Why would you want that?"

"I'm hoping that this is as good while we're awake as it is while we're asleep," Aidan whispered before sliding a hand up to tangle in Wyatt's hair and moving the last few inches to push their lips together in a gentle kiss.

It was. Wyatt's lips were soft and pliant under Aidan's, parting easily when Aidan slid his tongue across them. When they were dreaming, Aidan never noticed how Wyatt tasted, but here, now, Wyatt tasted of chocolate and the hazelnut coffee he had drunk with breakfast.

Wyatt slipped his tongue into Aidan's mouth, sliding over the roof and sending a shiver down Aidan's spine. His arm tightened around Aidan's waist and shifted his hips in a way that sent all of Aidan's blood rushing straight to his groin. Aidan moaned, his breath puffing into Wyatt's mouth as he shifted further, rubbing their hard lengths together through layers of cotton and denim. Aidan's world narrowed to Wyatt's mouth on his, Wyatt's body pressed against him, Wyatt's hands digging into his hips. He couldn't move, couldn't think, couldn't breathe, couldn't do anything but lose himself in the soft warmth of Wyatt's embrace.

Too soon, Wyatt pulled back and looked at Aidan through hooded eyes. "Damn, Aidan. I was having trouble standing *before* you did that."

"Does that mean you want me to stop?"

Wyatt's eyes darkened and he leaned forward, catching Aidan's bottom lip between his teeth. "Hell no."

Their first kiss had been mind-blowing, but this one was all-consuming. Aidan moaned deeply and desperately delved into the depths of Wyatt's mouth.

Wyatt brushed his hands over Aidan's back, one hand coming up to cup the back of his head, the other slipping under his waistband, one teasing finger sliding under his underwear into the cleft of his ass. Aidan gasped into Wyatt's mouth and rocked his hips, urging additional contact. He stroked down Wyatt's arms, then up under his shirt, his fingernails scraping down Wyatt's sides, his thumbs gliding over Wyatt's chest and brushing over sensitive nipples.

"How did you learn to kiss like that?" Aidan asked in a breathy voice as he pulled back to gasp for air, his lips brushing against Wyatt's. There was no way someone who had been asleep since he was sixteen should be able to make Aidan feel like *that*.

Wyatt sucked Aidan's bottom lip into his mouth. "Dreams can be very explicit." He kissed his way down Aidan's neck, across his collar, and back up to his mouth. "I learned all sorts of things dreaming with people."

Aidan growled, rode the surge of jealousy that flooded him at the thought of anyone else dreaming about kissing Wyatt, and shoved his mouth against Wyatt's. Their teeth clashed as Aidan thrust his tongue deep into Wyatt's mouth, determined to touch every spot, to claim him.

Wyatt reciprocated, rolling his hips forward as they battled for control. His hand slid further under Aidan's waistband, warm and soft against Aidan's ass.

"God, Wyatt." Aidan was going to come in his pants if they didn't stop, and it didn't look like Wyatt was much farther behind. He pushed his hips forward, rubbing hard and fast against Wyatt's groin as Wyatt squeezed his ass and rocked his hips, increasing the friction between them. Aidan came hard, gasping and yelling into Wyatt's mouth, and Wyatt followed, his whole body shaking as Aidan pressed him tight against the wall.

Wyatt sagged when he was done, his head once again resting on Aidan's shoulder, his arms tight around Aidan's waist. "Fuck."

"Yeah." Aidan carefully slid his hands between Wyatt and the wall. "You think you can make it back to your bedroom? We should, uh, change before Kyler gets here."

"I don't think I can move," Wyatt groaned, but he managed to stand a little straighter.

"Come on," Aidan said, slipping easily under Wyatt's arm and looping his fingers into the belt loops of Wyatt's borrowed pants. They wove down the hall, both a little weak in the knees, their steps unsteady as they maneuvered around the television and bookcases before stumbling down the hall and collapsing onto the unmade bed in Wyatt's room, arms and legs tangled together.

"We should move," Wyatt said after a minute, and Aidan nodded, though if they were going to be found tangled together with come inside their pants, the bed was a much better place than on the floor of the living room, where it would have looked like they were horny teenagers who had come hard from making out.

They weren't teenagers, and thirty-one was far too old to lose control from rubbing and kissing against a wall.

Too bad Aidan desperately wanted to do it again.

ON THE other side of the city, Marcus Kittel took a deep breath, steeling himself to knock on the wooden door in front of him. "Let's get this over with," he muttered, rapping his knuckles hard against the door and wincing as the staccato taps echoed down the empty hallway. Behind him, Soren Embry shifted from foot to foot, his shuffling the only noise after the echoes faded, and both men held their breath as they waited for the door to open.

A minute passed, then two, and just as Marcus was about to knock again, the door opened, revealing a tall man with white hair and a round face. He looked Marcus and Soren up and down, disdain clear on his face, and raised one eyebrow as he met Marcus's eyes. "What?"

The venom in his tone was enough to make Marcus flinch. It was expected—Elliott had never addressed him in any other tone—but it still bothered him. "This, sir. It was going off when we arrived this morning." He held out the small box he and Soren had found beeping when they arrived that morning. "It means Wyatt is alive and someone removed his bracelet."

"WE NEED to talk."

Wyatt looked up from his folded hands and flashed a strained smile at Aidan. He'd been expecting this ever since he'd fallen asleep and changed the pleasant beach Aidan had been dreaming about to the apartment so Aidan would know he was there. The sand and waves had been soothing, but they weren't the setting Wyatt wanted for the conversation he knew they were going to have. "Yeah, I know."

Aidan sat down on the bed and pressed his shoulder against Wyatt's, soothing him a little. His presence usually had a way of keeping Wyatt calm. It had been that way at the store a few days ago when Wyatt had finally ventured outside for the first time in years, and earlier, when Carina had stopped by to let them know the paperwork she'd filed had finally gone through.

Wyatt appreciated the gesture, but it wasn't helping as much as he'd hoped. The idea of telling Aidan about his past was too overwhelming for anything to truly comfort him. The urge to flee from the dream and avoid the conversation for just a little longer was almost overwhelming. Wyatt ignored it—or tried to, anyway—focusing instead on Aidan's thumb as it rubbed back and forth over the inside of his wrist. "Sorry."

Aidan's heart broke as he took in the shattered expression on Wyatt's face, but he swallowed and put his free hand under Wyatt's chin and lifted it so their eyes met. "It might help," he offered, though he regretted saying it the moment the words left his mouth.

"Maybe," Wyatt agreed, almost as surprised as Aidan by the answer. His chest tightened and his heart started to pound just thinking about it, but Aidan's hand on his gave him strength he didn't know he had and courage he didn't know he needed.

"You don't have to tell me." Aidan was offering an out, but Wyatt couldn't take it. It would only be a delay, and they both knew it.

"Yes, I do." It wasn't worth the delay it would cause. Now that his past had come up, Wyatt needed to let Aidan know what he'd been through, needed to share his past with the man who seemed destined to be part of his future.

The moment Wyatt made up his mind, the air in front of them shimmered, the dream changing to share his story.

Chapter Nine

"Happy birthday, baby."

Wyatt scowled at his mother, his fingers clenching tightly around the fork in his hand. "I'm not a baby, Mama," he protested, puffing out his chest. "I'm sixteen."

"So you are," she agreed, patting Wyatt on the head. He ducked, his scowl turning to an O of surprise as he tumbled into his little sister.

"Watch it, Wyatt!" Tabatha shoved Wyatt back, though there was no malice in it, just general sibling annoyance that didn't go away just because it was Wyatt's birthday or because they were eating at an actual restaurant for the first time in years. "I'm trying to eat."

Wyatt stuck his tongue out at his sister, doing his best to ignore the dizziness that made him fall in the first place. "Make me," he taunted, deliberately leaning against her and using his superior weight and height to his advantage.

It would have worked, too, but his older brother was sitting on Tabatha's other side, and he reached across her to shove Wyatt off. "What are you, sixteen or six?"

Wyatt moved sluggishly, and glared at Damon as he tried to stop swaying back and forth. "Sixteen."

"Could've fooled me."

"Damon," their mother chided. "Leave him alone."

"He has a point," Wyatt's father groused. "Sixteen is an important birthday. It comes with a lot of responsibilities. Wyatt should act like he's ready to accept them."

"There's no harm in letting him have a little fun while he still can, Lorne."

"He needs to grow up, Ursula." The look on Wyatt's father's face was thunderous, and Wyatt cowered even though it wasn't directed at him.

"Sorry," he said, shifting so he was in the center of his seat with no part of him even close to touching his sister and then slumping so he didn't topple unexpectedly as he tried to sit up. "I'll behave."

"See to it that you do."

Their server set dessert in front of them then, the cheesecake distracting Wyatt from his father's harsh response. He dug in with gusto, shoveling forkfuls into his mouth as quickly as he could manage and swallowing so fast he barely tasted it. A few bites in, he slowed. He told himself it was so he could relish the flavor, though in reality it was because he lacked the energy to move any faster. The fork seemed heavier with each bite, and after he'd taken a few more, it was too much effort to even lift it.

"I'm tired, Mama," Wyatt said, setting his fork down and leaning against the table. His eyes didn't want to stay open, and it was only through supreme effort that he managed to avoid falling face first into the remains of his cheesecake.

Someone whisked it away as his mother patted him on the head one last time. "It's okay, Wyatt," she told him in a soft voice. "Rest. You've had a long day."

There were reasons he shouldn't sleep here, Wyatt knew, but it was too much effort to think of any, so he gave in, letting his mother gently guide his head down to the table and closing his eyes as he rested his cheek against the soft tablecloth. It was amazingly comfortable, and he sighed as his muscles relaxed, sleep claiming him quickly.

WYATT came to slowly, stirring grudgingly in a warm cocoon made of thick covers on a soft, lavish mattress. He was more comfortable than he'd ever been upon waking, wrapped in more luxury than he'd ever experienced in his life, and it was with great reluctance that he pushed the covers down to reveal cream walls and dark mahogany furniture that looked like it cost more than everything in his house.

Moving slowly so he wouldn't break anything he could never afford to replace, Wyatt pushed the covers down farther and lifted his head to take in the rest of the room. The bed he was lying on had a curved headboard and footboard made of the same mahogany wood as the rest of the furniture, and it was covered with a hunter-green quilt that felt like velvet as he rubbed his hands back and forth across it. The quilt was nice, not what he would have picked, but it didn't clash with the cream-colored walls or the large landscape scenes adorning them, and it had done its job well enough that Wyatt wasn't going to complain about the uninspired design.

Nor would he complain about the rest of the room, given that it couldn't possibly be his, though it seemed crowded despite the large size. A dresser with an attached mirror stood against the far wall, a chest sat at the foot of the bed, and three plush armchairs were clustered around a low table in front of a curtain-covered picture window. A tall, unfamiliar man with thick shoulders sat in the chair closest to the window, gazing out through the tiny gap in the navy curtains. He turned as Wyatt sat up, and the smile he wore sent a shiver down Wyatt's spine.

"Hello, Wyatt," he said in a voice as oily as his slicked-back white hair.

Wyatt pulled his knees to his chest and scooted as far back as possible, pressing his back against the headboard and focusing his gaze on his hands as he twisted his fingers. "How did you know my name?"

"I know everything about you, Wyatt." The man leaned forward, resting his elbows on his knees, his suit jacket bunching under his arms. "My name is Elliott, and we're going to become great friends."

"Right. Whatever." Wyatt forced himself to look up and meet the man's eyes. "Can I go home now?"

"Oh, Wyatt, this is your home now. Well, not *this* precisely—this is my dream, after all—but you'll create your own soon enough, and you're free to base it off this if you'd like. It's much nicer than what you're used to, I know."

"A dream? It can't be." The bed was too solid, the sheets too soft. They were real, they had to be.

"Wyatt, Wyatt, Wyatt." Elliott shook his head and pursed his lips into a disapproving frown. "You know you're a Dreamer; you have for some time. I know you're a Dreamer. So let's not beat around the bush or go into hysterics. Just accept the fact that you're dreaming with me, all right?"

Wyatt swallowed hard. Being a Dreamer was just an abstract concept that had simply meant he occasionally shared his sister's or brother's dreams and that his mother looked at anyone he showed interest in as a potential Bondmate. He was only beginning to come into his full powers, and he hadn't given the slightest bit of thought to what he would someday do with them. He knew it wasn't this, though. "But I don't know… I don't understand."

"It's quite simple, really. Your parents want things—a nicer house, well-educated children… a good night's sleep." Elliott smiled cruelly. "We want an un-Bonded Dreamer. Your parents were quite pleased with the offer, though your mother did get a bit teary at the end there."

Wyatt's heart dropped into his stomach. "What are you saying?"

"You're *my* Dreamer now, Wyatt. Well, more accurately, my company's Dreamer, but that's just semantics. I'm the only one you'll be talking to for awhile."

"But you can't—"

"You're bought and paid for, Wyatt. Your parents signed the paperwork for you, just like we wanted them to, and there's nothing you can do about it. You're not going to be awake to." Elliott leaned forward, his smile widening. "You have no idea how hard it was to wait for you. We were so afraid that you were going to Bond with your friend Lilly." He stood. "But you didn't, and now I'm free to make you dream with whomever I want." He leaned over and patted Wyatt's knee. "You're mine, Wyatt. For the rest of your life. I'll leave you to get used to the idea."

He vanished, the room along with him, and Wyatt was left with his own dreams.

WYATT floated in a gray void, left alone, free to dream of his sister's laughter and his brother's teasing jokes. His friends made regular appearances, Lilly kissing him lightly on the cheek and the guys taunting him about his lack of skill with the video game systems he only got to play at their houses. Occasionally, he would dream of his mother's soft smile and the way she had patted his head that last day before he fell into never-ending sleep.

He never dreamed of his father.

He never wanted to.

DAYS, weeks, or maybe months later, when Wyatt was playing a racing game and winning for the first time ever, the living room faded around him and he found himself back in the opulent bedroom, sitting on one of the plush armchairs instead of sprawled on a ratty couch. He looked around with wide eyes, his spine tingling and his heart thudding before he laid eyes on Elliott. "What the...?"

"Hello, Wyatt." Elliott gestured to a steaming mug on the low table between them but didn't otherwise move from his relaxed position in the other chair. "Would you like some hot chocolate?"

Wyatt barely glanced at the glass. "I want to leave."

"Then wake me up."

"What?"

"If you want to leave this room," Elliott said slowly, as though speaking to a small, dim-witted child, "all you have to do is wake me up. This is my dream, and it will end when I awaken."

It was only the terror and confusion roiling in his stomach that let Wyatt avoid rolling his eyes and making a snarky comment. The guy seriously had said *awaken*. In his *dream*. Not that there was anything wrong with the word, it just wasn't anything that people of Wyatt's acquaintance used regularly. Then again, Elliott was the only person Wyatt was really acquainted with anymore. All the other people in his dreams were made from memories, no more real than the invisible friend he'd had when he was five. "And how do I do that?" he asked, his head held high as he met Elliott's gaze.

"Telling you would take all the fun out of it." Elliott's eyes lit up in a way that scared Wyatt more than anything else had since he'd first seen this false room. "It's a basic skill, instinctive for Dreamers, or so I've been told. Of course, the fact that you'll never wake yourself up might be a hindrance, but I have the utmost confidence in your abilities."

Wyatt snorted as he stood and paced back and forth, running his hand over the smooth, cool surface of the dresser and the beveled edges of the picture frames. His first thought was to simply walk out of the room, but the opulent setting lacked a door, so that option was out. Busting through the window was an idea, but Elliott was perched in front of it and the curtains were closed. Even if he got past Elliott, he had no idea how close he was to the ground. With his luck, he would tumble down just far enough that he'd break every bone in his body. Either that or the window was really a curtain-covered frame on the wall and there wasn't anything on the other side.

That idea discarded, Wyatt explored further, pulling open drawers to find them filled with empty boxes. The books on the shelves were filled with blank pages, not a single word written in any Wyatt pulled from the shelf, though the titles were some he recognized as favorites from before he was.... From *before*.

The room had seemed large enough when Wyatt first became aware of it, but now, as he paced back and forth along the wall farthest from the window, it seemed painfully small, jerking his stride short and forcing him to turn every ten steps. He eyed the fixtures, the furniture, the wall, and Elliott, but nothing in the room or Elliott's satisfied smirk gave him any clues to how he could possibly wake the other man. Wyatt could try touching him, but he wasn't that desperate, and something told him that was the wrong path anyway. Dreams didn't always allow for touch, and Dreamers could *always* wake anyone up, including themselves.

Except for Wyatt, apparently.

Fixated on that fact rather than the mechanics of waking Elliott, Wyatt crossed the room to slump back in the armchair. His hands trembled as he leaned forward and rested his elbows on his knees, his eyes meeting Elliott's once again. "Why can't I wake myself up?"

"Because we're keeping you drugged. See?" The room changed to a sterile-looking lab, all gleaming metal and white tile. A bank of monitors took up one wall. A dark-haired, balding man slouched at the desk in front of them, his eyes glazed as he watched. "That's Marcus," Elliott said. "Over here, we have Paul and Victor, otherwise known as the Dynamic Duo." He gestured to two men in the corner who were adjusting dials on a large machine with a purpose Wyatt couldn't discern. It was all buttons and lights and wires that led to—

Oh God.

"And there you are." Elliott's smile was the scariest Wyatt had ever seen it, all perverse pleasure and unholy glee as Wyatt's gaze flickered between it and the tub in the center of the room.

Wires and tubes snaked down from machines and bags and attached to a scrawny figure floating in a vat of liquid. He was nearly naked, only a small pair of shorts preserving any modesty, and his ear-length light brown hair spread around his head like a halo. Various liquids dripped through the tubes to the needles in his arms and chest, providing nutrients and—Wyatt guessed—controlling his slumber even as all the wires sent information to the machines mounted around the room.

"Is this… is this where I am?" he asked, his lips barely moved as he fought to keep bile from rising in his throat.

"More or less. It's my memory of the last time I was in here, at any rate, which was about five or six hours ago now. I'd guess that at this very moment only the Dynamic Duo is monitoring you. Marcus and the Rookie of the Week have probably gone home for the night."

"R-rookie of the Week?" Wyatt stammered as his brain desperately struggled to latch on to anything other than the sight of himself in that tub.

"We've had… a bit of trouble filling the fourth position on the team. This latest is the fourth attempt, and you've only been here for three months." Elliott shook his head in mock-sadness. "Such a shame too. They had such promising careers, such promising lives. To have to cut them short… it's a tragedy."

Wyatt's stomach churned, and he leaned forward, his hands on his knees as he gasped for breath and tried really, really, *really* hard not to look at himself in the tub or think about people's *lives* being cut short because they didn't want to help do this to him. He needed to leave, needed to go, needed to be anywhere that wasn't here with Elliott's memory of his sleeping body and the men who were keeping him that way and Elliott and—

The room twisted around him, becoming his old bedroom with its too-small bed and shabby, dented furniture. It was exactly how Wyatt remembered it, with the exception of Elliott standing in the middle of the room, looking around, his expression wavering between shock and disdain. Wyatt sank onto the bed, smiling a little at the creak of the bedsprings, his eyes closed so he could pretend Elliott wasn't there.

"You could go anywhere you want," Elliott commented, his sneering voice grating down Wyatt's spine, "and you brought us *here?*"

The small bit of peace Wyatt had collected vanished, leaving his blood boiling as he clenched his fists hard enough to leave marks in his palms and opened his eyes to glare at Elliott. "I didn't mean to bring *us* anywhere. I just wanted to get out, to get away, to not be there, not be with them, not be with *you.*"

"You can't ditch me. This is *my* dream. You can change it, but the only way to get rid of me is to wake me up." He gave Wyatt a satisfied look. "Good job on changing things, by the way. I didn't think you'd grasp something like that for months. It's a bit backward to get that before being able to wake me up, but it just goes to show how strong you really are. I'm going to *enjoy* working with you."

Wyatt clenched his fists tighter and stood, stretching to his full height as he stalked forward until he was toe to toe with Elliott. "*Go away,*" he said and pushed with his mind, harnessing the desperation he'd felt in that other place. Elliott's mouth dropped open as the room swirled into nothing, taking him with it. Wyatt watched until both room and man were gone and then embraced the gray nothing surrounding him, the only thing that granted him oblivion.

Chapter Ten

"THEN what happened?" Aidan hated to ask, hated the way Wyatt's body stiffened in his arms, but he knew that if he let Wyatt stop now, he'd never hear the rest of the story.

"He, um, he kept coming back, goading me into learning how to do things. Then one day he told me he needed me to find something, to get information from this guy. I thought I was good at controlling the Dreamscape then, but suddenly I was in someone else's head, and he wasn't even aware I was there. It took forever to figure out how to take control of his dream so I could get what Elliott wanted. He wasn't very happy about my timing when I was pulled back into his dream, but what was he going to do? I'd gotten what he wanted, and it wasn't like he could punish me any more."

"Shit, Wyatt." Aidan put effort into keeping his voice calm and steady. The last thing Wyatt needed right now was Aidan getting angry and righteous, even if it was on his behalf and even if the assholes who had done that to him deserved Aidan's ire.

He took a moment to calm himself, focusing on breathing steadily as he rubbed Wyatt's back and waited for his indignation to recede. "Is that all that you had to do, or was there more?"

"No. Yes. Shit." Wyatt huffed and sat up, pulling himself free of Aidan's arms and running a hand through his hair. "No, that wasn't all I had to do. Yes, there was more. I guess. Um." He jumped to his feet and began pacing the room, his hands waving in front of him aimlessly as he tried to come up with the words. This wasn't something he *wanted* to show Aidan, but Aidan had asked, so Wyatt had to tell him somehow. And he would, just not while wrapped in Aidan's arms as though he was a love-struck teenager who needed comforting.

"What else was there?" Aidan kept his voice soft, though he sat up and leaned forward, his eyes fixed on Wyatt walking around the room. He stayed on the bed but scooted closer to the edge, ready to jump up and grab Wyatt again if he looked like he was going to flee.

Wyatt stopped, looked at Aidan for a moment, and then sank into the chair in the corner. "More of the same, mostly. Elliott would pull me into his dream room, tell me what he wanted, and then they'd somehow send me into someone else's dream. I don't know how," he added, shaking his head and forestalling Aidan's question. "I don't know how they did anything, really. That one glimpse I got of Elliott's memory was the only time I ever saw anything even remotely real. I just kept going from dream to dream, and eventually I learned to figure out when they were my dreams and when they were someone else's. Elliott stopped pulling me in as often, too. I'd just go from my dream to some poor person's—I don't know how Elliott and his coworkers got them to agree to it, if they even did—and I'd just explore until I found what they wanted. It was always the same kind of thing: business secrets, and whatnot, mostly things I didn't even understand at first, though I kind of got the hang of them, I think. Maybe."

"Got the hang of them?"

"Of understanding the secrets, the things I was supposed to find out. They started to make sense, at least, though I guess I really have nothing in the real world to compare them to, so maybe I was completely wrong. I could have been. I don't know." Wyatt took a deep breath. He was rambling, he knew, but if he stopped, if he thought about what he was saying, he'd panic and push Aidan out of the dream, and then—then he'd have to have this conversation while they were *awake*, and he couldn't do that. It was much better when they were asleep, even if they would remember it when they woke up.

"We can check, if you want," Aidan offered softly. He stayed where he was on the bed, his legs crossed in front of him and his hands clasped loosely in his lap, the casual pose belying the tension running through his frame. "Or not," he added with a smile as Wyatt tensed at his words.

Wyatt flashed a grateful smile but pushed on, focusing on the fact that *this* dream was one of his choosing and that he would never again be forced into doing the things it was churning his stomach to even describe. "I thought for a while that I'd never see Elliott again—though I have no idea how they were getting the information I was finding once he stopped pulling me back into his little dream room. But then one day he pulled me in again and told me that he wanted me to make the person do something. He told me—" Wyatt stopped and shook his head, correcting himself. "They made me go in and change this woman's dream so she started dreaming that this project or something was going to go really well. I don't think it worked that time, but he made me do it again and again—to different people—and eventually, he seemed happy. I mean, as happy as he ever seemed."

Aidan's eyes grew progressively wider as Wyatt talked, and when he stopped, slumping forward and resting his forehead in his hands, Aidan could barely make his own mouth work to form the words. "Wyatt, that's... they were, God, using you to influence decisions about business. Or investing. Or, well, anything. Was it all business?"

"I don't remember, really." Wyatt didn't look up, couldn't make himself meet Aidan's eyes and face the horror he was certain he would see in them.

"God, Wyatt, that's… horribly illegal."

Wyatt looked up then, his eyes wide. "And the part where they kept me prisoner wasn't?"

Aidan let out a sharp, unamused laugh. "Of course it was. They gave it a veneer of legality by having your parents sign, but that wouldn't have held up to any real scrutiny. No one can sell someone else, not even parents selling their children. If you'd wanted to indenture yourself to help them, you could have set that up, but even then, there are rules about what they could do, about how they had to treat you, and they broke every one of them. What they did, what they made you do…." Aidan shook his head, trying not to think about it too much. "They shouldn't have been able to do any of it."

"They did, though." Wyatt let his head fall back into his hands. He was too tired, too worn out, and too emotionally wrought to keep it up. "It doesn't matter. I shouldn't have told you. It's not your issue."

"Yes, it is," Aidan responded firmly. He stood, gently grabbed Wyatt's wrist, and pulled him back to the bed. "Not in the same way, no, but the things that happened to you, they affect me too."

Wyatt laughed, the sound hollow as it echoed around a room that was suddenly far too big. "How? You didn't even know me. You should just—just make me leave and never think about me again."

"Do you really think that?"

Wyatt opened his mouth, ready with an emphatic "yes," but the pain he saw in Aidan's eyes as he uttered the soft words went straight to Wyatt's gut, leaving him feeling as though someone had cut off all the oxygen in the room. "No," he whispered, shaking his head only slightly so his eyes never had to leave Aidan's.

"Good." Aidan leaned up and pressed his lips lightly against Wyatt's. "Because I could never do that. I couldn't make you leave. Not ever. I don't think I could even *let* you."

Wyatt didn't think he could leave, either—the mere idea of trying to survive without Aidan by his side set his heart thumping wildly with panic—but it made no sense. Sure, Aidan had rescued him, saved him from dying, but he'd only known the man for a few weeks, and he already felt like Aidan was the most important thing in his life. "I know." And he did, which was even more confusing. "It just...." He shook his head. "You hardly know me. I hardly know you, and yet—"

"It feels like we've known each other forever," Aidan finished, beaming. He had hardly let himself believe, despite what he felt and what his friends said they saw. It had been too much to hope for.

"Yeah." Wyatt nodded and twined his hands around Aidan's. "I just... I don't understand why. Or how."

"We're Bonding." Aidan had said the words aloud before, but this time he was sure of them. "This feeling between us, like we've known each other forever, it started before you even woke up, and it just keeps growing. I can feel when you're upset, and it makes me happier to have you around, and I can't imagine not having you here, loitering outside my door when I'm working and watching all sorts of crazy shows on the television and being amazed by the silliest things that have changed or come out in the last decade."

Wyatt blushed. "They're not silly when you haven't seen any of them before. I bet you were amazed when they came out."

"Some of them," Aidan admitted with a laugh. "But everyone was amazed then. Now it's just you."

"It's not my fault." The words came out sounding petulant, and Wyatt wished he could take them back the moment they left his mouth.

"I know. I'm just stating a fact," Aidan said in an amused tone. "Besides, I think it's kind of cute."

Wyatt hadn't thought his cheeks could get any hotter, but they did. "*Cute?*" he protested, his eyes wide and his face flaming. "It's not *cute*." He stood, stepping around Aidan as he moved to pace the room, which conveniently lengthened to accommodate his long stride and need to get a little distance from Aidan. "It's not cute, or adorable," he continued when he turned back, "or sweet, or any of that."

"Then what is it?" Aidan asked, still sitting on the bed and watching Wyatt with an amused expression. "Because it looks rather cute to me."

"It's embarrassing, is what it is." Wyatt flung himself on the bed, landing flat on his back with his feet hanging off the edge.

"It shouldn't be." Aidan moved to sit on the edge of the bed, looking down at Wyatt with a fond expression on his face. "I like it."

Wyatt couldn't stop the warm feeling that welled up inside him any more than he could stop the protest tumbling from his lips. "Yeah, but—"

"No." Aidan stopped him with a hand over his lips. "No buts. That adorable awe is part of who you are, and *I* like it. So there," he finished with a nod, sticking out his tongue.

"Yeah, but—" Wyatt stopped short when Aidan raised an eyebrow. "I just—" He cut himself off, shaking his head. "I don't like *why* I'm that way, you know? That's hard to get past."

The goofy grin dropped from Aidan's visage as they were once again faced with the heart of the issue. "Neither do I. But it's something we have to deal with. And yes, it is something *we* have to deal with," he continued, pushing over Wyatt's spluttering protests. "Even if there wasn't a Bond forming between us, I'm the one who rescued you. If we ever find out who the people who had you are, or if they ever find you, there will be legal ramifications. They'll fight it, I'm sure, even without any legal ground to stand on. I'm tied up in this, Wyatt. I was from the moment I stumbled into that alley."

"Sorry." Wyatt sat up but didn't meet Aidan's eyes, instead focusing on his hands as he twisted them together in his lap. "You should have just left me there. Then you wouldn't have to deal with this."

"No. I shouldn't have." Aidan ducked his head to catch Wyatt's gaze. "You're a person, Wyatt, not a means to an end that can be discarded when it's not useful anymore."

"I know, but now you had to nurse me back to health, and now you might have to deal with whoever it was that had me, and there's this whole Bonding thing, and you didn't ask for any of it. You were trying to be nice, and now you're in this huge mess," Wyatt said quickly, frantic to get his point across.

Aidan shook his head and smiled fondly. "Okay, first of all, I didn't do much nursing. Kyler did. I hovered and drove Kyler crazy."

"Okay, but—"

Aidan held up his hand, not letting Wyatt lodge any more protests. "Second, the people who had you might not ever find you. We might not ever find out who they are," he added firmly, pushing past his own doubts and only giving voice to his hopes. "If either of those things happens, we'll deal with it when it does. I'm not going to worry about it until then. And as for this whole Bonding thing," he pushed on, not letting Wyatt get a word in, "it's not something we 'have to deal with', it's something we're lucky to have found."

"Are you sure?"

"Yes. More than." Aidan leaned forward, never breaking eye contact, and put all the conviction he felt into his words. "This thing between us, it's something magical. One day soon everything will just snap into place, and it will be the most amazing thing ever, this indescribable connection that will make us both better and stronger. It'll mean," he continued in a softer voice, "that no matter who those people who had you are, that no matter what legal bullshit they try to pull, they won't be able to touch you. They won't be able to make you do anything for them, because no matter where you are or who is nearby, you will always find me when you dream."

"Always?"

"Unless you choose to look for someone else, yeah. Some people think that's why most Dreamers Bond so young. Protection against the random dreams of whoever is sleeping closest, I guess."

Wyatt had to laugh at that. There had been times, back before, when he'd found himself sharing dreams with his siblings or his parents, and he'd learned things that no fifteen-year-old needed to know about the people he was related to. "That would be nice. Though how do I know your dreams are going to be any less traumatic than my sister's were?"

Aidan laughed as he pressed a swift kiss to Wyatt's forehead. "Somehow, I doubt you'll mind my dreams. But if you're worried, when we wake up, you can, ah, give me some things to dream about."

The dream bedroom was suddenly far too small and unreal. Wyatt was searching for that spot he could nudge and wake Aidan up before he opened his mouth. "Yeah," Wyatt agreed in a breathy voice. "I'll just wake you up, and then you can—"

"No." Aidan kissed Wyatt again, this time on his lips. "Wake us both up."

Dread filled Wyatt at the thought of disappointing Aidan. "I don't know if I can. I've never woken myself up before."

"So try." Aidan smiled as he looked into Wyatt's eyes, putting all of his faith into his gaze. "It's something all Dreamers can do. I'm sure you know how. You just don't know that you do."

He said it with so much conviction that Wyatt agreed without thinking, nodding as he found himself believing too. "Okay." He took a deep breath, steeling himself to try something he'd never dared try before. "Okay."

Aidan kissed him again. As nice as it was, Wyatt didn't want it, not here in the Dreamscape. He closed his eyes and leaned into the kiss, focused on that place he used to push Aidan out of the dream, then found it for himself as well. He took one last moment to enjoy the kiss, drawing strength from Aidan's belief in him, and pushed.

Chapter Eleven

WYATT blinked up at the ceiling, letting his eyes adjust to the darkness. He was awake: he'd forced himself out of the dream, and as the realization settled over him, a giddy feeling rose in his chest. He'd done it, the one thing he'd never learned how to do in his dreams, and he'd managed it with Aidan's encouragement.

Practically bouncing with excitement, Wyatt scrambled out of bed and dashed into the hallway, his feet sliding on the wood floor as he took the corner without slowing. He made it three steps out of his room before he saw Aidan and grabbed him on the fourth, pulling him into a passionate hug and resting their foreheads together. "I did it."

"Yeah." Aidan returned the hug, but before he could do more than agree, Wyatt's mouth was on his.

It was some time before Aidan was able to form a coherent thought and even longer before he could make his mouth do anything other than respond to Wyatt's passionate kisses with licks and nips of his own. When he finally managed to pull back long enough to speak, he growled, "Bedroom."

Wyatt didn't say anything. They stayed tangled together as they stumbled down the hallway, crashing into the first bedroom—Wyatt's—and tumbling onto the bed. Aidan landed on the bottom with Wyatt's weight heavy and solid on top of him, and Wyatt dug his fingers into Aidan's back. They gasped for breath as they paused, staring at each other with dilated eyes and matching grins.

"I love you," Aidan whispered, feeling giddy as he gave voice to the words for the first time.

Wyatt's answering smile was blinding. "I love you too," he whispered as he brought his lips down to Aidan's in a tender kiss that was completely unlike the ones they'd been sharing just moments before.

Sparks flew between them as they moved together, with Aidan's hand cupping Wyatt's cheek and Wyatt's tongue slipping leisurely into Aidan's mouth. All the urgency from before was forgotten as warmth spread through their limbs. It wasn't anything either of them had felt before, but they both knew what it was, and as they both realized this was their Bond starting to form, the connection between them clicked more firmly into place.

Aidan moaned as Wyatt pulled back, his teeth tugging lightly on Aidan's lips and his eyes sparkling. Aidan pressed their lips together without ever breaking eye contact.

Everything slowed. The world narrowed to just the two of them and the crackling air that surrounded their bodies. Aidan's heart rate surged, skyrocketing before settling into a faster-than-normal pattern, the beats thumping in his ears with a strange echo. He was hyperaware of Wyatt on top of him, his skin tingling everywhere they touched, leaving him especially conscious of the layers of denim and cotton that separated them in so many places.

"Fuck," Wyatt whispered, his lips never leaving Aidan's. The idea of pulling back, of relinquishing even the tiniest bit of contact with Aidan was unfathomable.

"Yeah." Aidan slid his hands down Wyatt's back and up under Wyatt's shirt, seeking additional contact. When he was satisfied that as much of his skin was touching Wyatt's as possible without drastic movement, he briefly deepened the kiss, then pulled back, catching Wyatt's eyes and shaking his head when Wyatt tried to follow. "We need to—"

"Right." Wyatt rolled after looping his legs around Aidan's so the other man came with him. When they lay on their sides, torsos pressed together and legs intertwined, he pushed Aidan's shirt up toward his shoulder.

When both their shirts had been moved as far as was possible without them pulling their bodies apart, Aidan sucked in a deep breath. "Ready?"

They moved together, separating only as far as was necessary to pull the shirts off their arms and over their heads. Wyatt flung his shirt away and wrapped his arms back around Aidan as Aidan's shirt hit the wall. "Much better," he whispered as he nuzzled his nose against Aidan's.

"For now," Aidan agreed. "We're going to have to—"

"I know." Wyatt pulled Aidan closer, letting his hands roam over the firm muscles of Aidan's back. It was strange, the way he could hear the end of Aidan's sentence in his head before Aidan said it aloud, but nice too. It certainly made the way Ratri and Olin talked to each other more understandable, and a small part of Wyatt was looking forward to returning the favor the next time he and Aidan saw their friends. "Let's just enjoy this for the moment, though, okay?" Despite the heat of their passion on the couch earlier and the niggling pressure of their newly formed Bond, Wyatt was completely content to stay right where he was, relaxed in Aidan's arms.

"Okay." Aidan lightly kissed Wyatt's cheek and snuggled in closer, tucking his head beneath Wyatt's chin and tightening his arms around Wyatt's waist. He had heard everything Wyatt hadn't said, and he pushed his awareness of the tingling of his skin and the pressure in his groin to the back of his mind, concentrating instead on the warmth of Wyatt's chest against his and how right it felt to lie half-naked, tangled together on the guestroom bed. He was contemplating how lucky he was when his eyes closed and he drifted off into sleep.

AIDAN'S eyes snapped open as he jumped from deep slumber to full wakefulness in less time than it took to draw a breath. He was lying on his side, wrapped in and around Wyatt, and he instinctively burrowed closer, seeking more contact, trying to move Wyatt's still-lax arms so they would touch a different part of his back and ease the burning pain that prickled his skin in every spot not in direct contact with Wyatt's.

Before Aidan's brain made it past *hot* and *pain* to wake Wyatt up, Wyatt's eyes snapped open and he hissed. He flexed his fingers against Aidan's back as he squirmed and squeezed tighter, crushing their bodies together in a desperate attempt to find relief. "Aidan."

"We shouldn't have slept."

"I didn't."

"We're going to have to—"

"I know."

Aidan braced himself, squeezing his eyes shut as he tried to remember if he kept any supplies in this room or if they'd have to brave a dash down the hallway to the master bedroom. He couldn't remember, so he just lunged, biting back a whimper as his fumbling in the nightstand drawer pulled him away from Wyatt and the soothing touch of skin-on-skin contact.

Wyatt rolled over and wrapped his arms around Aidan again, pressing his chest to Aidan's back and providing a little relief to them both, but they were past the point when close contact would do much good. Their Bond demanded acknowledgement, and nothing short of giving in would make them feel any better.

The nightstand drawer was almost empty, but Aidan ran his hand methodically through it, his eyes squeezed shut against the pain. The rough wood of the drawer's bottom scraped horribly against his suddenly ultrasensitive fingertips. The cool, smooth plastic of the lube bottle brought some relief, and he sighed as he pulled his hand back. "Got it."

"Good." Wyatt squirmed, hissing as the burning on his skin increased, and struggled out of his pants before turning his attention to Aidan's. The button fly on Aidan's jeans took longer to undo than Wyatt's zippered one, and their fingers bumped awkwardly as they fumbled, desperate to get it open. The flashes of coolness they felt as their fingers brushed together weren't nearly enough to relieve the burning pain that was driving them desperately forward.

The moment Aidan's jeans and boxers were free of his legs, Wyatt pounced, pinning Aidan to the bed and capturing his mouth in a brutal kiss. Their tongues darted in and out and around each other's as their noses bumped and their teeth scraped hard over too-sensitive skin, leaving them both panting as Wyatt drew back just enough to be able to talk. "How are we doing this?"

Aidan didn't stop to think. "You. In me." It had been close to a year since the last time he'd bottomed, but Wyatt was a virgin, at least outside of the Dreamscape, and the desperation driving them wouldn't give them the luxury of being gentle.

"You sure?"

Aidan shifted under Wyatt until their cocks brushed, and they both gasped. "Yes. Hurry." He frantically opened the lube and pressed the bottle into Wyatt's hands.

It hurt to pull back even for this, but Wyatt wasn't going to just push into Aidan with no preparation, so he poured the slick gel over his fingers and slid his hand down between Aidan's legs, moving as quickly as he dared but pausing when his finger pressed against the tight hole of Aidan's ass. "Aidan?"

"Please." Aidan pressed against Wyatt's finger, forcing the digit to breach the tight circle. "Need you." He moaned as Wyatt pushed farther in and twisted his finger in such a way that if Aidan had been in a position to think about anything other than Wyatt's finger up his ass—and how desperately he needed *more now*—he would have wondered what, exactly, Wyatt had learned in the Dreamscape.

Wyatt slid his finger out and pushed it back in with a second one beside it and scissored them quickly, stretching as fast as he dared. His skin burned, and the strange pressure inside his body urged him faster, faster now, *now*. He couldn't take the time to be gentle, couldn't take the time to explore and figure out what Aidan liked or kiss his way down Aidan's firm chest and abs, couldn't make sure every moment of this was as pleasurable for both of them as possible. There wasn't time for tenderness and care. There was only raw burning need that had to be assuaged.

Aidan moaned again as Wyatt inserted a third finger, stretching him uncomfortably and not providing the relief they both needed. "Hurry," he gasped, fingers clenching in the sheets as he silently willed Wyatt to stop prepping and stretching and get on with fucking him already. His hips jerked as Wyatt's fingers brushed his prostate, sending a jolt of pleasure and pain through his already hypersensitive body. "Now!"

"Yes." Wyatt jerked his fingers free of Aidan and wrapped his already lube-slicked hand around his own hard cock, stroking once, twice, wiping as much of the lube on it as he could before he lifted Aidan's legs and positioned himself to push in.

"Now," Aidan growled, tightening his legs around Wyatt's waist and pushing downward, moaning in pleasure as the slick head of Wyatt's cock breached his body.

Wyatt bore down without warning, pushing himself fully inside Aidan in one swift movement. He didn't stop, didn't pause to give Aidan time to adjust, just pulled out and pushed back in, again bottoming out and pulling back immediately. As he rocked, his movements swift and desperate, he leaned forward, trapped Aidan's hard cock between their bellies, pinned Aidan's hands to the bed above his head, and captured Aidan's mouth in a bruising kiss, his tongue gliding in and out at the same rhythm as his dick.

Aidan squirmed and struggled, his tongue battling with Wyatt's and his legs tightening around Wyatt's waist. Wyatt's movement over him provided just enough friction on his sensitive cock, and it felt like they'd barely begun when his breath hitched and he came with a yell down Wyatt's throat, spilling sticky white fluid over their bellies and clenching his ass tightly around Wyatt.

"Gonna—" was all Wyatt managed before he, too, came, his whole body shaking as he squirted his seed directly into Aidan's ass, and then collapsed on top of Aidan without pulling out.

Just like that, it was done: the painful burning and intense pressure gone, replaced with a feeling of warmth, contentment, and connection unlike anything Aidan had ever experienced. He let his legs relax and his feet fall to the bed on either side of Wyatt and debated how long he could manage to not move. It was uncomfortable with Wyatt on top of him and the sticky come pooling on his belly and beneath his ass, but it also felt fantastic, and he was reluctant to lose the contact, even though it was no longer demanded by their Bond.

He could wait a few minutes, he decided, as he turned his head and pressed a quick kiss to the tip of Wyatt's nose. Wyatt's sleepy contented smile broadened, but he didn't open his eyes and made no other attempt to move. Aidan smiled back and let his own eyes fall closed for just a few seconds before he opened them again, wriggled a hand free, and started pushing at Wyatt's shoulder.

As reluctant as he was to move, he definitely couldn't let them fall asleep like this.

"IS THAT going to happen again?" Wyatt wrapped himself around Aidan after they climbed back into bed, resting his head on Aidan's chest and slinging a leg over Aidan's hips. They had stripped the guest bed so the sheets could be washed in the morning, showered together in the large corner shower-tub combination in the master bathroom, and were now contentedly entwined in Aidan's bed, eyes drooping.

"No." Aidan didn't have to ask what Wyatt was talking about. He just knew, the same as he knew that Wyatt was too exhausted for them to dream that night and that he was worried Aidan would be disappointed in him because of it. He wouldn't be.

Wyatt lifted his head and looked sleepily at Aidan. "Are you sure?"

"Of course." Aidan met Wyatt's lips, kissing him softly but thoroughly before pulling back. "A Bond is mostly mental. It just needs the physical aspect to fully form. After that, we could never touch again, as far as our Bond is concerned." Not as far as Aidan was concerned, but that wasn't the point of the conversation. "We can *definitely* have sex again, but it won't be like that. Our Bond won't force us into it or hurt us if we don't anymore."

"Oh." Wyatt regarded Aidan seriously for a few moments and then smiled. "So no more frantic, must-have-you-right-now, desperate, mind-blowing sex?"

Aidan laughed loud and hard, surprised by the teasing lilt in Wyatt's voice. "Well, not with pain like that involved." He let his grin turn predatory as he rolled, pushing Wyatt down to the bed with one swift motion, then leaning down to growl in his ear. "We can definitely have more frantic, must-have-you-right-now, desperate, mind-blowing sex, though."

Wyatt swallowed hard, his mouth suddenly dry and his palms sweaty. Aidan's gravelly, come-fuck-me-now voice had his cock springing to attention, and his eyes rolled back in their sockets as Aidan licked his ear, swirling his tongue over the shell before sucking the lobe between his lips and tugging on it with his teeth. Wyatt bucked. "Aidan. You're killing me."

"Not yet." Aidan slowly slid along Wyatt's body, licking and sucking at his pulse point and collarbone, then taking the time to lavish attention on both nipples, leaving them red and aching for more. As he kissed his way down Wyatt's stomach, swirling his tongue in Wyatt's belly button, Aidan grabbed Wyatt's wrists before sliding his tongue downward, tasting the sensitive skin just above Wyatt's cock. When he reached it, he stopped, his face hovering just above the moist tip of the erect organ.

"Aidan." Wyatt squirmed, groaning with displeasure as Aidan lifted his head further, a mischievous smile playing on his lips. The look set Wyatt's heart racing. "*Please.*"

"Too messy." Aidan climbed to his knees, brushing his erection against Wyatt's. "I don't want to have to change this bed tonight too."

"It's a big bed," Wyatt ground out through clenched teeth. "We can take care of it in the morning." He rolled his hips up, deliberately brushing his cock against Aidan's, silently begging him to do something, *anything*, about the erection he had caused. "I'll sleep in the wet spot. Just. *Please.*"

Aidan's grin widened as he climbed over Wyatt, situating himself facing Wyatt's feet with his knees at Wyatt's shoulders and his penis bobbing over Wyatt's face. "Less mess this way." And then, before Wyatt had a chance to process what was happening, Aidan leaned over and licked the length of Wyatt's cock just once before slipping his mouth over the end and sucking.

Wyatt moaned, his eyelids fluttering and his brain trying to catch up, so lost in the warm heat of Aidan's mouth and the sudden onslaught of delightful sensation that it took him several moments to untangle his fingers from the sheets and guide Aidan's cock to his lips. He mirrored Aidan, licking and sucking, scraping with his teeth, moving purely on instinct, lost in the pleasure and pure electricity between them. He pulled back as far as he could, swirling his tongue over the tip of Aidan's dick and then swallowed it whole, humming around the engorged flesh.

Aidan had to pull back, gasping and mumbling incoherently as his elbows buckled at the surge of pleasure. "Oh God." His vision grew hazy, and he returned his attention to Wyatt, taking special care to lick every inch of Wyatt's cock before opening his throat and taking it all the way in.

The combined sensations of Aidan in his mouth and Aidan's mouth on him were too much for Wyatt. He didn't try to hold back and willingly tumbled over the edge, his hips bucking and his fingers clenching in the sheets as he screamed Aidan's name around his cock and spurted his come down Aidan's throat.

The vibrations of Wyatt's scream and the warm, salty liquid pouring into his mouth were enough to send Aidan over as well. He barely managed to swallow before he was yelling Wyatt's name, his hips jerking as he came down Wyatt's throat. His limbs shook as he fell to the side, pulling free of Wyatt's mouth and gasping for breath as he lay bonelessly next to his lover, their sweat-slicked bodies pressed close together on the large bed.

Wyatt licked his lips, caught a dribble of come that had escaped, and swallowed it. "That's less messy?"

"Nothing. On the sheets."

"Except sweat." Wyatt sat up and pulled at Aidan, manhandling him until they faced the same direction.

Aidan sagged limply, letting Wyatt maneuver his lax limbs. "Doesn't count," he mumbled, burying his face in Wyatt's shoulder. "I sweat at night anyway."

"That's attractive." Wyatt laughed, his chest shaking under Aidan as he moved them to the untouched side of the bed. "Way to ruin the mood."

"The mood was over." Aidan wrapped his arms around Wyatt and snuggled down, his head pillowed on Wyatt's chest and his eyes closed. He didn't move as Wyatt reached across him, grabbed tissues from the nightstand, and wiped them both as clean as possible while pinned by Aidan. "Besides, you love it."

Wyatt chuckled and kissed the top of Aidan's head. "That I do. Now sleep. You're exhausted." He let his eyes drift closed as he wrapped his arms around his lover in a loose embrace, content for the moment to just sleep and let his dreams take him where they willed.

Chapter Twelve

A SHRILL ring broke the silence and echoed loudly in the mostly empty space of the large office. If the occupant had been a nervous person, he might have startled, but Elliott Sloan hadn't gotten where he was by being nervous. He picked up the phone on the second ring, making a cursory note of the number displayed before sliding his finger across the screen and holding it up to his ear. "Yes?"

"I have news. About that name you asked me to watch for." The voice on the other end was rushed and low, almost overwhelmed by the background noise.

"What?" None of Elliott's curiosity leaked into his tone, but he did pick up a pen and pull a pad of paper close.

"You're going to pay me, right? Like you said you would?" the informant, a man almost as desperate as Wyatt Mettler's parents had been eleven years earlier, pressed. "I could get in trouble for sharing this."

Elliott's eye twitched slightly as he considered whether threatening or cajoling would work better with this particular contact. "Of course," he said, settling on cajoling for the moment. "What did you find?"

"Residency paperwork filed for Wyatt Mettler."

Elliott's fingers clenched tightly around the phone. "Does it list an address?"

Papers rustled on the other end of the line. "No. Just the city."

"I see." Elliott forced himself to stay calm. An address would have made things easy, but the lack of one wasn't insurmountable. "Thank you."

"If he stays in Haverdsford—"

"That will be all." Elliott didn't need the clerk to put anything together once he managed to locate Wyatt. "You'll be compensated."

"Thank you, sir. If there's anything else—"

Elliott disconnected the call with a swift jab to the screen and set the phone down, then pressed the tips of his fingers together and stared at the blank wall as he pondered what to do next. Any sign of Wyatt had been all he'd hoped for. The knowledge that Wyatt was alive and presumably well was beyond Elliott's wildest dreams.

And to think, Wyatt probably thought he was safe. The possibilities, as far as Elliott was concerned, were endless.

AIDAN leaned against the door to the laundry room, his arms folded loosely over his chest, and watched with amusement as Wyatt poked at the buttons of the washer. Wyatt's nose wrinkled more with each unsuccessful jab, scrunching up until his brows furrowed and his forehead creased, and Aidan had to say something before Wyatt gave himself a migraine glaring at the offending machine. "I can do that you know." He'd been planning on it, but while Aidan was in the shower, Wyatt stripped the master bed and shoved both sets of sheets into the washer before Aidan was able to stop him.

It was a good thing Aidan had sprung for the more high-tech, high-capacity washer. Wyatt clearly didn't know what the words "washer capacity" meant.

"I know." Wyatt flashed a strained smile before returning his attention to the buttons, his tongue poking out as he continued to try futile combinations. "I wanted to."

"Do you want help?" Aidan asked slowly, shifting his weight so he was ready to step into the room the moment Wyatt gave him the go-ahead.

"No!" It came out harsher than Wyatt intended, but the worry and concern echoing over their new Bond was putting Wyatt on edge. Last night it had been fabulous, but when he'd awakened, the sense of Aidan *right there* had been almost oppressive, and he'd been trying to distract himself. "I got it!"

Aidan stumbled back into the hallway, his hands held up in surrender as he tried to ignore the sharp smack of *leave me alone* that had shot down their Bond. "Okay. It just looked like you could use some help. Sorry."

"I'll figure it out." Wyatt's cheeks flamed as he returned his attention to the complex array of buttons, frowning at them so he wouldn't look at Aidan. The sense of worry increased, but at least it wasn't the shock and hurt he'd felt as Aidan retreated. That had hurt Wyatt, a surprising stab of pain in his chest that left him desperate to make sure Aidan never felt that again. "I'm not stupid." Only he was, really. Too stupid to figure out the washer, too stupid to avoid hurting the best person he'd ever met.

The look on Wyatt's face was enough to drag Aidan back into the laundry room. He felt Wyatt's anguish and self-loathing through their Bond, and it ensured that he moved faster than he ever had before, crossing the linoleum in three swift steps and resting his hand on his lover's shoulder. "I never said you were." And he never wanted to hear those words again. "Laundry-challenged, maybe," he added, his tone light and his thoughts focused on cheering Wyatt up so Wyatt would *know* he was joking, "but not stupid." He let the smile fall from his face and gently turned Wyatt's chin so they looked straight at each other. "I'm not going to think any less of you if you let me help. Really."

Wyatt looked at Aidan for a moment before slumping forward, pulling free of Aidan and resting his elbows on the washer and cradling his forehead in his hands. It was all too much. Yesterday had been overwhelming, and now with the complicated washer and the realization that the Bond entailed more than just awesome sex and peaceful dreams, Wyatt's brain was about to shut down. "I want to do it. I just—" He lifted his head a little and looked at Aidan with brimming eyes, willing him to understand. "I feel like you do everything sometimes, like you *have* to do everything sometimes, and I hate it. I'm twenty-seven years old. I should be able to do a load of laundry."

Aidan opened and closed his mouth several times, gaping like a fish as he struggled to find the right words to say. His hand hovered just inches over Wyatt's shoulder, but he was afraid to touch, afraid that whatever he did or said would just make matters worse. He could feel the maelstrom of Wyatt's frustration, shame, and anger through their Bond, but the knowledge of what Wyatt felt did not come with the knowledge of what to do about it. Every thought that crossed Aidan's mind was a ridiculous combination of empty platitudes and meaningless gestures, and he wouldn't demean what Wyatt was feeling like that. Still, he had to do something, so he settled for a tight squeeze of Wyatt's shoulder and a weak offer to teach him. It sounded pathetic, even to his own ears.

Wyatt let his head fall back into his hands. "You shouldn't have to. That's the point. I should have already learned, only…. Before, my mother always did the laundry so she could combine it into as few loads as possible. And then, well. Obviously, I didn't need laundry. I didn't until now. Here. And you've been doing it, but I thought about it this morning, and I thought I could figure it out, but…. Well." He gestured at the machine and managed a weak smile. "Your washer is really complicated."

"Yeah, well, it's a gadget." Aidan grinned broadly as the tension drained from his body. It was only a small change in Wyatt's tone and demeanor, but the feelings echoing along their Bond were less stressed and more rueful. It was a change Aidan could definitely live with. "I know that the books are the most prominent thing in this apartment, but I can't believe you haven't noticed how many gadgets I have. Come on." He bumped his hip against Wyatt's, moving him just enough that they could both stand in front of the washer, and began slowly pushing the washer buttons, making sure Wyatt could follow what he was doing.

"I noticed." Wyatt bumped Aidan's shoulder, his smile growing more genuine as he focused on learning and pushed his failures to the back of his mind. "I just didn't think it would apply to laundry. Clearly, I hadn't fully thought it through."

"Clearly," Aidan echoed, struggling to keep a straight face through his euphoria. It seemed ridiculous that a simple genuine smile from Wyatt— visual confirmation of the feelings echoing through their Bond—could leave him feeling so giddy, but he wasn't going to question it. It had been ages since he'd felt this wonderful.

"You can stop feeling so smug now."

Wyatt's playful accusation left Aidan feeling even better, and he grinned blindingly. "I wasn't."

"Whatever." Wyatt shook his head, his own smile widening as he jabbed the start button, his finger reaching it just ahead of Aidan's. "I figured that part out almost immediately, you know. It was the other settings that were giving me trouble. Thanks, though," he added dryly. "Glad to know you didn't think I could figure that part out."

"You are very welcome." Aidan struck a cheesy pose: his hands on his hips, his nose in the air, and a smug expression on his face. "You can begin showing your gratitude at any time. Worshiping is strongly encouraged."

Wyatt managed to hold back for all of ten seconds before he doubled over, peals of laughter spilling from his lips and echoing off the walls of the small room. "In your dreams, Aidan. In your dreams."

It was too good of an opportunity to resist. Aidan waited until Wyatt calmed a little and straightened enough that they were looking each other in the eye. He let his lips twist up into a pleased smirk as he stepped backward toward the door, never breaking eye contact with Wyatt. "Promise?"

The surge of *want* along their Bond gave him all the answer he needed.

WYATT kept his promise that night, worshiping Aidan in a variety of exotic locales first pulled from Aidan's dreams and then from Wyatt's memory of other dreams he'd had. Each time he switched their location, Wyatt started again, paying homage to every inch of Aidan's body, worshiping him with hands, tongue, and cock until the night was half over and Aidan had been reduced to a quivering, boneless mass of satisfaction. When he was finally done, Wyatt climbed back up Aidan's torso and kissed him thoroughly before rolling over to lie next to him, fully taking in their surroundings for the first time.

They were on a beach, or at least what Wyatt hoped was a reasonable facsimile of one, cobbled together from memories of dreams Wyatt had walked in. They were alone, the sand smooth and cool beneath them, the full moon shining down and reflecting on the gently lapping waves a few feet away. The sand was white and pristine and—since this was a dream—well behaved, shifting gently beneath their fingers and toes without getting caught in any inconvenient places. Not realistic, perhaps, but Wyatt could make the Dreamscape do whatever he wanted, and after years of being forced to use the ability to serve other people, he was enjoying using it to his own advantage.

"You're thinking," Aidan murmured, propping himself up on one elbow and gazing down at Wyatt. His heart fluttered with so much love and adoration that it seemed likely to pop from his chest and float free on the euphoria.

"Just enjoying this." Wyatt languidly waved his hand around, indicating the sand, ocean, and sky, before using it to pull Aidan down so he could capture his lips in a tender kiss. "It's nice, being able to do what I want with it, not worrying about whose head I'm going to end up in when I close my eyes, not having anything I *have* to do when I'm asleep."

Aidan winked. "Except worship me."

"Yeah. Except that." Wyatt kissed Aidan again, deeper this time, and marveled at how much *more* everything between them was now that they were Bonded, even in dreams.

"Would you mind, though? If you had other things you had to do in dreams?" Aidan asked when he pulled back, staring down at Wyatt with intense worry. "Not like before," he continued in a hurry as Wyatt's spike of fear stabbed at his senses. "Just. Like a job, I mean. Helping people. Or companies or the government, I guess, but if people knew ahead of time what you were going to try to do, would you mind, really?"

"I guess not." Wyatt hadn't really thought about it. It had never occurred to him that purposefully dreaming with people who knew what he was going to do was an option. Aidan knew, of course, and Wyatt was pretty sure that had he and Aidan waited much longer to Bond, they would have been required to warn the neighbors, just so they would know there was a possibility he would visit their dreams. But he had thought most people wouldn't want a complete stranger entering their mind, particularly when it was vulnerable in sleep. "Why?"

"I was thinking about it." Aidan shrugged. "Hunter and Brianna should be back after the new year. I thought maybe when they came over, you could talk to them about what you could do."

Wyatt blinked, trying to wrap his mind around the whole idea. "Who are Hunter and Brianna?"

"My friends who are Dreamers." Aidan tapped his finger on the sand. "I told you about them the, uh, the day you panicked waiting for Kyler."

"Right." Wyatt vaguely recalled the conversation, though what he remembered most was the kiss afterward. "Sure, I guess." He shrugged, figuring it couldn't hurt. Even if he decided he never wanted to dream with anyone but Aidan again, he still wanted to know how other Dreamers used their abilities. "Just, uh, when's the new year?"

"Sunday. Today's Cembre 29. Or, it was the twenty-ninth when we went to sleep," Aidan corrected. "I guess it could be the thirtieth by now."

"Right." Wyatt didn't really care what the date was—it had been too long since it actually mattered—though he supposed he should start paying attention. Mostly he just wanted to know how long he had to fret about meeting more new people. He'd have to get over it someday, he knew, but at the moment, it made dread coil deep in his gut. "So I'll meet Hunter and Brianna in a week or so, then?"

"Something like that." Aidan took Wyatt's hand, trying to reassure him. He almost wished he hadn't brought it up, but he didn't want to spring his friends on Wyatt without giving him time to prepare. "I'll let you know when as soon as I talk to them. Don't worry about it."

Wyatt looked down at the sand so he wouldn't have to meet Aidan's eyes. "That's easier said than done."

"Then let me distract you." Aidan brushed stray strands of hair back from Wyatt's forehead before kissing him softly, their moist lips pressing together with gentle tenderness. Not for the first time, Aidan marveled at how realistic everything was when Wyatt dreamed with him. It wasn't perfect—if he looked carefully, he could see where the beach and ocean simply stopped existing instead of vanishing at the horizon—but up close, where it mattered, where their bodies were lying close together in the sand, every detail was perfect. He took advantage of that as he slid down Wyatt's body, pampering Wyatt as Wyatt had pampered him, paying attention to every bit of skin under his hands and lips.

Wyatt squirmed with pleasure as Aidan kissed his way down his torso, his soft touches driving all thought of their conversation from Wyatt's mind. "Aidan, *please*," he moaned, digging his fingers deeper into the sand and arching his back, pushing his torso closer to Aidan's talented tongue and soft, sweet lips. He was hard and close, and after a night of seeing to Aidan's pleasure, he was about to come without Aidan's hands or mouth roaming below his waist.

Aidan increased his pace, focusing his attention on Wyatt's nipples and chest. He could feel Wyatt trembling beneath him, could feel *want* and *need* echoing along their Bond, and Aidan wanted nothing more than to see his lover fall apart beneath him in the sand.

It didn't take long. Aidan swirled his tongue in Wyatt's navel, and without warning, Wyatt shuddered beneath him, breathing his name as sticky, pearlescent fluid spilled between their bodies. Aidan followed, shaking and collapsing on top of his lover, gasping for breath.

Wyatt lay pliant, sated and happy as Aidan crawled up and sprawled on his chest, their legs tangled together in the sand and his come sticky between their bodies. With a thought, he cleaned them up, amused at Aidan's startled look when sweat- and fluid-covered skin was suddenly clean and dry.

"I keep forgetting you can do that," Aidan murmured, laying his head back on Wyatt's chest and letting his eyes slip closed.

"Even after I kept taking us to new spots without you ever getting off your back?" Wyatt laughed, kissed Aidan's forehead, and carded fingers through his hair. "Dreaming does have a few advantages over reality. It'd be silly not to use them."

"Hmm. True." Aidan's limbs were heavy with exhaustion, and he drifted until morning, lost in the warm body below him and the light touches of Wyatt's hands as they ghosted over his back.

Chapter Thirteen

A WEEK later, Wyatt scrubbed at an invisible stain on the kitchen counter. He'd spilled coffee earlier to justify—even to himself—the pressing need he'd felt to scrub already pristine counters and floors, but it had been that or starting on the bathrooms for a third time. At least cleaning the kitchen kept him away from the back office where Aidan was finishing an important project, and out of the living room, where he might be caught unprepared when their guests arrived.

Eventually even the invisible spots were gone, and Wyatt was again left with nothing to do. He was contemplating the merits of pulling out the refrigerator to mop behind it when Aidan came in, wrapped his arms around him from behind, tugged the damp rag from his hand, and tossed it on the table. "It's clean."

"I know. I just...." Wyatt trailed off, waving his arms aimlessly as he struggled to express his overwhelming need to *do* something.

Aidan slid his hands over Wyatt's arms, stilling the wild movement, and rested his chin on Wyatt's shoulder, his lips right against Wyatt's ear. "Calm down. There's nothing to worry about." He focused on calming his own rapidly beating heart, revved up by Wyatt's anxiety even when in the other room, and hoped his calm would transmit to his Bondmate.

"Easy enough for you to say," Wyatt muttered, though he welcomed the calm Aidan was sending along their Bond and tried to capture some of it. He wasn't very successful—a week's worth of practice at using their Bond didn't make him an expert, despite the fact that it was at least half instinct—but he did manage to calm a little bit. He twisted in Aidan's arms so they faced each other. "They like you."

"And they'll like you too." Aidan lightly kissed Wyatt's lips before stepping backward and snagging the cloth so he could toss it in the laundry pile. "All my friends do. Hunter and Brianna won't be any different."

They were, though. They were Dreamers, the first Wyatt would meet since being freed, and that made all the difference in the world, from Wyatt's point of view. If Hunter and Brianna didn't like him, all of his tentative plans would be for naught. "If you say so." He managed a small smile for form's sake, though he didn't mean it and Aidan would know that.

"I do." Aidan started forward, ready to try to reassure his Bondmate further, but there was a knock on the door. He stopped short, holding out the damp cloth. "You want to take care of this so I can go get that? It's probably them."

Wyatt nodded, taking the rag with shaking fingers. "Yeah. Okay." With a strained smile, he forced his feet to move, pulling each one from the floor with a good deal of effort. It was like trying to walk through molasses.

Aidan caught Wyatt's hand as he walked by and squeezed it, his gaze sympathetic as he wished he could do more to reassure his lover. "Take your time, okay? We'll wait for you." He waited for Wyatt's small, reluctant nod before letting go. He kissed Wyatt on the corner of the mouth and then headed to the door to greet friends he hadn't seen in far too long.

BY THE time Wyatt gathered the courage to come out to the living room, Hunter and Brianna were settled quite comfortably on the loveseat, pressed close together as they talked excitedly with Aidan about their trip. Wyatt hovered in the hallway, just out of sight, and learned that Brianna hated flying, Hunter lacked the patience to drive long distances, and they'd been gone for close to three months, a combination of work and play keeping them away from home for longer than ever before and testing their tolerance for both methods of transportation. It wasn't until the conversation moved to what Aidan had been up to that Wyatt managed to take that final step and enter the room.

As soon as Wyatt crossed the threshold, Aidan turned and held one hand over the back of the couch toward him. "Hey." He'd felt Wyatt hovering but hadn't wanted to draw attention to him until he was ready. "Come here."

Wyatt beamed at the affection in Aidan's tone, and he clung to that feeling as he crossed the room and settled on the couch next to Aidan. "Hey."

The notion to take things slowly and ease Wyatt into the conversation was discarded when Hunter unwrapped his arm from Brianna's shoulders and leaned across the coffee table, his hand extended. "You must be Wyatt. I'm Hunter."

Wyatt blinked and slowly took Hunter's hand, pleased at how steady he was. "Y-Yeah. Hi." He expected a hearty shake, so when Hunter pulled him forward, practically dragging him across the coffee table to wrap him in a loose hug, he squeaked, his free arm flailing as he struggled to regain his balance.

"Hunter!" It was impossible to say who sounded more outraged, Aidan or Brianna, though the resounding smack Brianna planted on Hunter's side weighed the argument slightly in her favor.

"He has to get used to me eventually." Hunter threw out insolently. "No sense sugarcoating it, right?" He pulled back, leaving one hand on Wyatt's shoulder, balancing him. "You all right, man?"

Wyatt was a little shocked, a bit overwhelmed, and he *really* wished that Aidan had warned him about Hunter, but he found himself nodding anyway. "Yeah. I'm good."

"Awesome." With a grin that Wyatt would soon come to relish and dread in equal proportions, Hunter pushed, sending Wyatt tumbling back into Aidan before resuming his seat next to Brianna and putting his arm back around her shoulder.

Brianna slapped his chest with the back of her hand and wriggled out of his grip. "Don't mind him, Wyatt," she said, standing to lean over the coffee table and kiss his cheek. "He's obnoxious, but he kind of grows on you."

Hunter yanked her back to the loveseat with a playful growl, his fingers dancing over her sides and stomach as she squirmed and squealed in his lap. Wyatt watched them for a bit, before he turned and directed his wide-eyed gaze at Aidan. "Why didn't you warn me about them?"

"You were nervous enough." Aidan tugged him closer and kissed him softly. "Would you have come out at all if you'd known ahead of time what they were like?"

"Maybe?" Wyatt glanced at Hunter and Brianna, wondering how Aidan could possibly have explained them. Their playful tickling had turned into a mock-fight and it was nothing short of a miracle that they hadn't fallen to the floor. "I might have been more curious than afraid if you'd tried."

"And you might have locked yourself in the guest room and refused to come out for anything. I couldn't risk it."

It was a fair point, and Wyatt conceded gracefully. He rested his head on Aidan's shoulder as he twisted to watch Hunter and Brianna again. "True." He found Aidan's hand without looking and laced their fingers together. "You would have coaxed me out eventually, though."

"Too much work," Aidan protested, trying hard not to think about the things he could have promised Wyatt to coax him out. He pushed them to the back of his mind, saving them for later. "Besides, how would I have described them?"

Wyatt laughed, his whole body shaking in Aidan's arms as nervous amusement bubbled up and out. "I don't know that you could have. They do seem to be, uh, *unique*." It was the politest word he could think of, though the way the two were completely wrapped up in each other, Wyatt wasn't sure civility mattered. They didn't seem likely to notice if Wyatt called them all sorts of horrible names.

Their complete lack of regard was oddly comforting. In Wyatt's mind, he'd pictured Hunter and Brianna as imposing figures who would make him work hard to impress them, despite his relationship with Aidan. The laughing couple rolling on the love seat was so far from what Wyatt had imagined that it was impossible not to be comfortable with them even though their over-the-top affection was a little disconcerting.

Or, rather, very disconcerting, Wyatt mentally amended as Hunter's hands started roaming places Wyatt definitely didn't need to see them go. He turned and buried his face in Aidan's shoulder, his eyes squeezed tightly shut as he tried not to think about what he'd just witnessed. "Are they going to stop any time soon?"

"Only if we make them." Aidan grabbed a pillow, tossed it at the other couch, and raised a fist in victory when it hit Hunter square in the back of the head. "Yes!"

The pillow sailed back and hit Aidan straight in the face. After that, all bets were off. Pillows, blankets, and couch cushions flew around the room in a crazy fight reminiscent of a childhood slumber party, only without the sleeping bags or pre-teen girls.

Cotton and feathers soared with wild abandon until two pillows and a couch cushion hit Wyatt all at the same time and he curled in on himself, a throw pillow clutched tightly to his chest. He didn't make a sound.

The laughter immediately stopped.

Brianna was the first to move, her tiny hand outstretched and her bottom lip caught between her teeth as she leaned over the arm of the loveseat toward the corner of the couch where Wyatt huddled. "Wyatt? Are you okay? We didn't mean to get you all at once."

"Yeah, man, come on. They're just pillows, right?" Hunter's heart thumped loudly as his eyes flicked between Wyatt and Brianna, his serious expression and worried tone belying the lightness of his words. "You're not hurt, right?"

Wyatt slowly lifted his head and blinked at the pair on the loveseat. "I, um." He looked down, smiling slightly, and lunged. The pillows and blankets piled on top of him all flew toward Hunter and Brianna, and Wyatt landed on Aidan, pinned him to the couch, and kissed him soundly. "Gotcha."

"You jerk!" A pillow flew back, but Aidan knocked it away before it came close to hitting Wyatt. "I thought we'd upset you! I was terrified!" Brianna continued to fling pillows, her rage and Hunter's halfheartedly restraining arm making most of them go wide. "You upset us all," she continued, settling back against Hunter with a huff when the supply of pillows around her was exhausted. "Right, guys?"

Hunter nodded agreement, but Aidan shook his head. "No."

"What? How?"

Aidan had to laugh at the outraged expression on Hunter's face. It wasn't often that Hunter was on the receiving end of such tricks. He played them often enough that he saw through most attempts at deceiving him. That Wyatt had managed to do so within twenty minutes of meeting Hunter was astounding, and it made Aidan's chest swell with affection. "The same way you'd know if Brianna was really upset or not, Hunter. I wasn't sure what I was getting from Wyatt, but I knew he wasn't really hurt or angry."

"Whatever. I'll get you back. Just wait," Hunter grumbled.

"Of course you will, dear." Brianna patted Hunter's knee and smirked when he stuck his tongue out. "Of course you will."

"I will."

"Mm hmm." Brianna ignored him as she turned to Wyatt. "Aidan said you wanted to talk to us about something?"

"Yeah." Wyatt rubbed his hand on the back of his neck as he tried to settle the sudden roiling in his stomach. He'd been over this several times in the past week, rehearsed an entire speech in his head, and yet he still froze at the idea of actually saying something. He knew, deep down, that Hunter and Brianna were Aidan's friends and that they'd try to help him for no other reason than that, but it didn't make it any easier to get his mouth to move.

"What did you want to talk about?" Brianna asked after a moment, leaning forward curiously and resting her elbows on her crossed legs.

Her casual pose loosened Wyatt's tongue. "I need your help."

It was as easy as that. Hunter and Brianna listened intently as he told his story, both asking pertinent questions in soft voices as Wyatt narrated what he remembered, what they'd pieced together, and what had happened since Aidan had found him. When he stopped, his hands folded in his lap and his head down, Brianna leaned forward again and waited until he looked up enough to catch her eye. "What do you need us to do?" she asked, her voice quiet. "As much as I'm sure Hunter would love to help prosecute them, if we don't know who had you, there isn't much we can do."

"I don't need help with that. I mean, I might. Eventually. But not now."

"Then what do you need help with?"

"I, um." Wyatt closed his eyes, swallowed hard, and gathered his courage. He focused on Aidan's calming presence next to him, opened his eyes, and continued with renewed determination. "I just—what am I supposed to do now? I don't know how to do anything other than dream, not anything marketable anyway, and I don't know what to do with dreaming. Aidan said—" He paused, his gaze moving briefly to his lover before he pressed on, his voice soft and uncertain. "Aidan said you might be able to help with that. Have some ideas, or something."

As it turned out, Hunter and Brianna had quite a few ideas. Hunter worked for the courts, entering witness's dreams to help better reconstruct what they'd actually seen and providing expert testimony in cases involving other Dreamers. He also helped calm distraught victims and witnesses after they testified; giving them at least one night of pleasant dreams, should they want it.

At the hospital, Brianna spent a lot of her time giving restless patients a few hours of peaceful sleep, helping them heal. She also helped keep patients asleep when they needed to be sedated and drugs weren't advisable, and she urged coma patients toward wakefulness once their bodies had sufficiently recovered. The two of them also had a side business they ran from their house, helping quell nightmares or getting to the root of troublesome, repetitive dreams.

The advice didn't stop with that. According to Brianna, the list of places that hired Dreamers was endless—businesses that wanted help with employee morale, health spas, cruise lines, doctor's offices, and research centers, just to name a few. Wyatt shuddered, unable to contemplate getting a job at a place that did any sort of experimental testing, even if it was completely legal, voluntary, and aboveboard.

Brianna nodded her understanding when he voiced the thought. "I won't put any feelers out at those places, then. Anywhere in particular you'd like to work?"

Wyatt shrugged, his face flushing with embarrassment as he shifted uncertainly. "I don't... I mean, I haven't really thought about it." Not beyond avoiding whoever had held him before, and staying close to Aidan, anyway. "I want to be able to come home every night, so not a cruise line. Other than that...." He shrugged again. "I think I'd like to do something where I feel like I'm helping people, but I don't think I can afford to be picky. I don't exactly have an employment history, or references, or anything." Or really any idea what was required to get a job, when it came down to it. His knowledge was entirely gleaned from the Dreamscape. People did dream about applying and interviewing for jobs, fortunately, but Wyatt was certain his idea of the process was skewed.

"I'm sure we can find something."

Wyatt had never been more grateful to someone for avoiding the issue of his life. He really didn't want to rehash their earlier conversation, and Brianna's simple acceptance of his employment barriers meant more than he could express. "Thanks."

"No problem, man. We're glad to help." Hunter flashed a quick smile as he climbed to his feet, tugging Brianna with him. "We need to be going, though. We still have *way* too much to do before work tomorrow."

"Nothing like a vacation to make you need one." Aidan swiftly hugged Briana and Hunter, patting them on the back as he pulled away. "Thanks."

"Don't mention it." Hunter planted a sloppy kiss on Aidan's cheek before hoisting Brianna over his shoulder, ignoring her squawk of indignation, and waving at Wyatt. "Nice to meet you, Wyatt. I'll see you both around, yeah?"

He was out the door before Wyatt could stop gaping long enough to formulate a response.

Fix this.

The two-word e-mail sent a shiver down Elliott's spine that intensified as he clicked on the attached spreadsheet to reveal the fourth-quarter numbers. Not all the results were in—they were only a week into the new year—but the trend was obvious, and the final numbers wouldn't change it. Profits had dropped drastically in the last month of the year.

Steeling himself, Elliott sat straighter in his chair and typed up a quick e-mail. *Working on it.* He considered saying more, something about loss of personnel contributing to the decline in profits, but he decided against it. His boss didn't know about the Dreamer program, and Elliott wanted to keep it that way. It was his project, his alone, and with that thought firmly in mind, he hit send.

The answer came back almost immediately. *Work faster.*

Elliott sucked in a deep breath and blew it out slowly, trying to calm himself. In the past when he'd gotten e-mails like that from his superior, he'd taken it out on Wyatt, throwing the boy into someone's nightmare and watching him suffer, but that wasn't an option anymore. He could take it out on Marcus and Soren, but there wasn't much else he could do to them without making people suspicious, and he needed them to continue their search for someone to replace Wyatt.

Or did he?

Elliott's anger morphed into twisted pleasure as he fired off an e-mail to Marcus and Soren, instructing them to start the paperwork to stop the payments still being sent to Wyatt's parents. As soon as the e-mail was sent, he pulled up his Internet browser and started typing in the search bar. He needed someone to help him get Wyatt back and keep him, and he knew just where to start looking.

He'd have the results he wanted before the quarter was out.

AIDAN flopped back on the couch after closing the door behind Hunter and Brianna, scooted over until his shoulder pressed against Wyatt's, and propped his feet up on the coffee table. "You okay?"

"Yeah." Wyatt propped his feet up next to Aidan's. "Just overwhelmed, I guess."

"It's a lot to think about." Aidan honestly hadn't imagined there were so many different things Dreamers could do with their skills. His head was spinning with all the information, and he'd already known half of it. He could only imagine how bad it had to be for Wyatt. "But you have time."

"I know." Wyatt could try to get a job right away if he wanted—Carina had taken care of all the paperwork, and he'd gotten his ID the day they'd gone down to the courthouse to register their Bond—but he wasn't ready yet. He wanted answers first, and Carina hadn't heard back from her investigators yet. "You'll take care of me until then, right?" he asked in a teasing tone, though he knew the answer.

"Of course." Aidan grinned. As far as money was concerned, Wyatt didn't need to get a job. Aidan made enough to support both of them, and he was happy to do so as long as Wyatt needed it. "Though I might require some compensation."

Wyatt raised an eyebrow and rolled his head to the side so he could look at Aidan. "Such as?"

"Go out to dinner with me?"

Wyatt's whole body warmed from the inside out. He sat up and moved to straddle Aidan's hips with one swift movement. "Are you asking me out on a date?" he joked, kissing along Aidan's collar bone and up his neck.

Aidan squirmed, trying to maintain his composure in the face of Wyatt's amorous advances. "Maybe? I just thought that we hadn't yet, even though we've, well, done just about everything else." He sucked his bottom lip through his teeth and chewed on it as he peered at Wyatt through half-lidded eyes. "Are, uh, are you saying yes?"

It was tempting to rib Aidan further, but he was so adorably earnest and unsure that Wyatt didn't have the heart to do it. "Of course I am," he whispered before pressing his lips against Aidan's in an all too brief, all too chaste kiss. "You can wine and dine me all you want."

It was a promise Aidan intended to hold him to.

Chapter Fourteen

WYATT growled low in his throat as he pushed the end button on the phone harder than was necessary, jamming his thumb into it with all the force he could muster. That was the eighth dismissal he'd gotten in the last half an hour, and he was starting to think he was never going to get the answer he wanted. Everything had been going so well—Brianna had come up with several job leads for Wyatt, and he was finally becoming comfortable and confident around people other than Aidan—but it felt like it was falling apart now.

He was starting to wonder if he'd ever be able to accomplish the things he wanted.

Scowling, Wyatt jabbed at the phone again, clearing the just-called number from the screen, and yelled angrily as he threw it into the end of the couch, where it bounced and fell between the cushions. He glared at the couch for a moment and then dug the phone out, not satisfied with the effects of sending it bouncing harmlessly into the soft surface. He wanted it to hurt, to shatter, to break, to make some horrible noise that would bring Aidan running and leave the neighbors wondering what actually went on in their apartment. A dull thud against padded couch cushions was not enough to express his frustration.

He squeezed the phone tight as he looked around the room with wild eyes, anger and frustration building up inside until the phone casing started to crack under the pressure of his grip. He was about to hurl it into the television or the glass doors that led out to the balcony, just for the satisfaction of breaking something.

Aidan grabbed his hand before he could, pried his fingers open, and pulled the phone free with surprising strength. "What did the phone do to you?"

"Nothing." Wyatt crossed his arms, a petulant glare on his face, and began pacing. The anxious, furious energy he'd been focusing on the phone needed a new outlet. "It's the people on the other end."

Aidan's voice remained calm and his gaze serene as he struggled to fathom what was bothering his lover so badly. "And what did *they* do?"

His untroubled tone only served to rile Wyatt further, and he kicked at a couch cushion that had fallen to the floor, sending it flying over Aidan's head. "They won't talk to me." He was aware that he sounded like an ill-tempered child, but at the moment, he didn't care.

Everyone he'd called had treated him as though he was the uncertain, uneducated barely sixteen-year-old boy his parents had sold to some unknown company. It didn't matter what had happened to him or what he'd been doing for the past eleven years, all they saw was that he didn't have a degree, hadn't graduated from secondary school, and had nothing to back up his abilities as a Dreamer. They never even got as far as a lack of references or work history. He wasn't hirable, plain and simple.

"Who won't talk to you?" Aidan laid a hand gently on Wyatt's crossed arms, sending tranquil thoughts and feelings along their Bond to counteract the aggravation that had drawn him out of his office.

"Anyone." Wyatt let Aidan lead him back to the couch, where he sank down into the soft cushions and stared morosely at his feet. "I've been calling the new list of places Brianna gave me, but no one wants to talk to me. Same as the first list. They hear that I never graduated or that I don't have anything to verify my skills as a Dreamer or whatever the magic phrase is for that particular place, and I get told that no, they're not really interested and best of luck. I can't even get an interview."

"It'll happen."

"Yeah? When?" It wasn't going to happen soon enough. He'd hoped to have something by Aidan's birthday, but that had already passed, and he'd spent it tagging along to the party Ratri and Olin had thrown. He'd felt completely stupid and out of place because he hadn't contributed anything, hadn't even been able to get Aidan a present, and Aidan was *his* Bondmate. Everyone had told him that it was okay, that they understood, that they hadn't expected him to do anything given the circumstances, and that he would make it up next year, but that hadn't made Wyatt feel better.

"I don't know, Wyatt. It'll happen." It had to, or Aidan was going to go as crazy as Wyatt. He couldn't let himself believe otherwise, couldn't let himself send anything but confidence and determination along their Bond. "Someone will be willing to hire you, I promise."

"Yeah, well, it doesn't look like it. I don't have anything they need: no references, no employment history, not even a secondary school degree or equivalency test. And half of them want to know what kind of Dreaming credentials I have, and I don't have any! I don't know where to get them! Or how!" He ran his hands through his hair. "I'm stuck. I can't get a job without these things, and I don't know where or how to get them or even if I can!"

Aidan pulled Wyatt's hands from his head, holding them tightly in his own. "Hey. We'll figure it out. I know where you go to take equivalency tests. We can set it up in a few minutes. That's easy enough to do. And we'll ask Hunter or Brianna about Dreamer credentials. I think there are tests or something for those too." He wasn't sure of the details, but he'd heard Hunter mention them once or twice, usually in relation to an unaccredited Dreamer who had caused problems for the courts. "We'll figure it out. I promise."

Wyatt stared at his lover for a long moment, trying to read the truth in his words through their Bond. "Yeah, okay." He collapsed against the back of the couch, exhaustion overtaking him as his anger draining away. "Can we wait until tomorrow, though? I'm not sure I can handle any more frustration today."

"Sure." Aidan leaned in and gently kissed Wyatt, slipping his tongue slowly between Wyatt's lips and moving his hand to cup the back of Wyatt's head. "Whatever you want."

"Whatever I want?" Wyatt teased as he rubbed his hands over Aidan's back, slipping them under his shirt and splaying them wide across his warm skin. "That's a pretty dangerous promise, Aidan."

Aidan chuckled. "Oh, I'm sure I can handle it."

THE testing center was in the middle of downtown, in an area Wyatt had never visited before, and he looked around at the towering buildings, zooming cars, and racing trains that deposited riders every few blocks. Aidan had driven and parked his car in a lot not far from the building they were visiting, but the walk along the sidewalk was both nerve-wracking and illuminating at the same time. Wyatt had never seen so many people in one small area, and he watched with awe as people moved around each other as if they didn't see anyone else, their gazes focused on their toes or on the addresses of the buildings they passed.

Wyatt almost caused a traffic jam when he paused at a storefront, gaping at the display of clothing in the window. He had thought that clothing was one thing that hadn't changed much in the eleven years he'd spent asleep, had clung to that when everything else seemed so painfully new, but this display showed him differently, and he began to wonder just how out of fashion Aidan and his friends actually were.

"No one actually dresses like that." Aidan tugged at Wyatt's arm, pulling him farther down the sidewalk. "No one real, anyway. You might see someone in those clothes if they're at a big hoopla for the who's who of town, but other than that, no one buys them. No one can afford to." He glanced back at the uncomfortable-looking, highly impractical dresses and suits, shuddering at the thought of wearing one. "No one would want to anyway. Can you imagine?"

Wyatt tried to picture himself wearing one of the outfits he'd seen in the window and failed miserably. "No, not really."

"Me either. So stop worrying about it. You saw what people were wearing and what they were selling when we went shopping. That's what everyone is wearing, same as you. No one is looking at you funny."

No one was looking at him at all, and in the mass of people, Wyatt found that odd and rather disturbing. "I know. I kinda wish someone was, though. How do they do that?"

"Do what?"

It was only then that Wyatt realized Aidan was doing the same thing: tugging Wyatt along the sidewalk and through crowds of people without actually looking at or really seeing any of them. "This!" he exclaimed, pulling his wrist free of Aidan's hand. "You aren't seeing any of these people, and they aren't seeing us! That's just weird."

"They're all on tight schedules. If they stopped to browse and people-watch, nothing would ever get done. No one would get anywhere on time."

"But—"

Aidan grabbed Wyatt's hand again and laced their fingers together. "We're on a tight schedule too. Our appointment is in ten minutes, and you don't want to be late. That wouldn't make a good impression."

Wyatt had thought that his test scores were what mattered, not what the staff thought of him, but he didn't argue, just let Aidan guide him along as he watched the scenery and people that flew by. It was good that Aidan was navigating, because Wyatt would have been run over ten times by the time they stopped in front of a large glass-faced building. "Is this it?" He peered around, trying to find a sign, but Aidan just nodded and dragged him through the automatic doors.

When they reached the desk, Aidan briefly asked for directions to the office they wanted and then pulled Wyatt to the largest group of elevators he had ever seen. Aidan pushed the Up button for the bank labeled Floors 70-100.

Wyatt blanched. "How high are we going?" Aidan's apartment was on the tenth and top floor of his building, and to Wyatt, that had seemed high. Back in Ambridia, he had never been downtown in a big city. New Altz was a small town, and Wyatt had spent the whole time he'd been living with Aidan on the outskirts of the city. He hadn't realized what a truly large downtown could be like.

"They said it's on the 88th floor." Aidan looked at Wyatt's pale face, took in the shaking hands and the quivering uncertainty he felt over their Bond. "Is that a problem?"

"Not so long as I don't have to look out any windows." Wyatt shuffled his feet as he tried to latch onto Aidan's calm instead of his own nervousness. "I, um, don't think I've ever been that high before."

"Ever? Really?"

"We didn't live in a big city when I was a kid, and we didn't travel much, either." Wyatt looked down, his cheeks reddening. "I thought your apartment was high up."

Aidan's laugh echoed off the metal-plated walls as he threw his head back, his whole body shaking with mirth. "My apartment? Really?" It was difficult to imagine, especially since he'd moved to his current building partially because the building *wasn't* very tall. Penthouse views could be nice, but they were horrible to reach if the elevator malfunctioned.

Wyatt's blush deepened, but Aidan's laughter released some of the pent-up anxiety in his chest. His giggles soon joined Aidan's guffaws, and he found himself clinging to Aidan and struggling to stay upright as he wondered how his near-terror had turned into something to laugh about. The situation wasn't at all funny, not from Wyatt's point of view, and he blamed his laughter on Aidan's amusement echoing through their Bond coupled with his own nerves.

All too soon, the elevator doors opened, and Aidan pulled him inside. Wyatt spared a moment to be thankful they were solid-walled elevators, and though the space was tight and claustrophobic, he was able to relax in Aidan's presence in a way he wouldn't have been able to had they been riding in a glass-walled elevator. It was one less thing to worry about. All he had to concentrate on was passing this test. And doing so on the 88th floor.

WHEN the testing was done, a slip of paper with the number to call the next day for his results tucked in Wyatt's back pocket, they headed farther into downtown. Aidan was determined to show Wyatt the sights of a big city now that he realized Wyatt was unaware of the pleasures to be found there. Aidan led him down tight alleys Wyatt was sure could only lead to trouble but in reality held hidden treasures: shops that delighted Wyatt and left Aidan charmed by his reaction. They went into tiny boutiques that housed knick-knacks of the kind Wyatt had longed to collect when he was a child—and how Aidan discovered *that* he would never know—and got lunch at an out-of-the-way diner that had the best barbecue Wyatt had ever eaten. Dessert was at a locally owned ice cream parlor, the only one of its kind in the city and definitely worth the half-hour wait in line.

As they waited to be served, Aidan turned to Wyatt, noted his fidgeting, and smirked. "It's this busy all the time. Get used to it. Everyone wants some."

Wyatt could believe it. The ice cream was thick and creamy and like nothing else he'd ever tasted. He took one bite and declared that he was never, ever eating any other kind of ice cream ever again.

Aidan bought four pints, packed with ice in a cooler so he didn't have to worry about it melting. Wyatt's smile about the ice cream had been the first genuine, noncoerced one Aidan had seen all day, and he wanted to be sure he could delight Wyatt like that again.

Their next stop was the park in the center of the city. Surrounded on all sides by buildings towering over one hundred stories, it was a strange oasis free from the bustle of the concrete streets. A few people sat on benches eating bagged lunches or food they'd taken out from nearby restaurants, but it was mostly deserted due to the cold weather and time of day. The pond in the middle, however, was full of life, and Wyatt reacted to the fish and fowl with childlike eagerness.

"Did you see?" he asked, pointing at the spot where something had just disappeared into the water and craning his neck as though he would magically be able to see beneath the placid surface if he tilted his head just the right way. "What was that? It jumped!"

Aidan resisted the urge to roll his eyes as he shook his head. "I don't know. I'm not an expert. I really don't want to know what's actually in this lake." He'd heard rumors, and though most of them were too wild to believe, he didn't want to be in a position to confirm or deny any of them.

Wyatt stuck out his tongue and dragged Aidan farther along the shore, shaking his head and muttering under his breath about worthless tour guides. Aidan followed a few feet behind, beaming with delight at Wyatt's reaction to each new sight.

By the time they returned to the car, they were just early enough to get out of the city before the rush of people leaving work crowded the roads and trains. Wyatt continued his babbling monologue for the first few miles, but by the time the tall buildings began to give way to their smaller, less stately counterparts, he was asleep, his head resting on Aidan's shoulder and his breath fogging the cool window glass.

AIDAN glanced over at Wyatt and then back at the light in front of him. When he saw it was still red, he returned his attention to the phone in his hand, thumbing out a quick reply and hitting Send before the light changed and he had to devote his attention to the road once more. At the next light, he turned and headed away from the apartment and toward the business district a few blocks away. He soon parked in front of a squat, homely looking building with lights and music spilling out the door every time it swung open, and gently shook Wyatt's shoulder. "Hey."

Wyatt blinked bleary eyes at Aidan and rubbed at them with one knuckle as he yawned. "We home?"

"Change of plans." Aidan peered closely at his companion, but his assessment from the road seemed correct. Though still half-asleep and a bit groggy, Wyatt had been refreshed by his nap and would be glad of their new destination once he finished waking up. "Ratri texted me, asked us to meet him at the bar."

"Oh." Wyatt peered out the windshield, blinking at the neon green sign proclaiming McGrudy's Pub and waited for his brain to catch up. "Okay," he said, shaking his head to clear the rest of the cobwebs. "They have food here?"

Aidan shook his head as he climbed out of the car. He could have guessed that would be the first thing on Wyatt's mind. "Of course."

Inside, the pub was decently lit, with a lamp fashioned to resemble a candleholder on each table and overhead lights hanging above the bar and the pool tables in the back corner. Ratri, Olin, Kyler, and Carina were sitting in a corner booth, and as he looked around, Aidan saw Hunter and Brianna throwing darts at the back wall with a man he didn't recognize. He immediately led Wyatt to the table and squeezed them into the warm seats that he assumed had until recently been occupied by Hunter and Brianna. "Hey."

Their friends greeted them exuberantly all around, and two beers were pushed across the table from the cluster in the middle while Kyler went to get more, stopping to say something to Brianna on his way to the bar. Wyatt gulped down his beer, feeling the need for some fortification, and Aidan laid a hand on the small of his back to calm him.

"So," Aidan said, looking around at all of the others as he handed a menu to Wyatt. "What's going on?"

Everyone became very interested in their drinks. "What makes you think something's going on?" Carina asked when she realized the cup she was showing such interest in was completely empty. "Maybe we just wanted to get the whole gang together for some fun."

Aidan gave each of his friends a piercing stare, directing an especially hard look at Carina. "You're all still sober, and Ratri doesn't send multiple text messages unless he's drunk or it's important. I got four in the five minutes it took me to stop at a light so I could read them. Now, you want to tell me why?"

"Soon." Ratri beckoned the lone waitress over to their table. "Get some food. We should wait until everyone gets back anyway."

The waitress arrived about the same time as Kyler. Wyatt ordered a burger and some fries, and Aidan added his own order—a club sandwich—and turned expectant eyes on his friends. "Well?"

Kyler and Carina exchanged looks and then waved at Hunter and Brianna, signaling for them to come over. The man they'd been playing darts with followed, piquing Aidan's curiosity. This didn't seem like a discussion that should include strangers.

"What's going on?" Wyatt's voice was barely a whisper in Aidan's ear, but it felt loud in the sudden quiet at the table, and both men flinched at the way it seemed to echo in the stillness. Wyatt pressed closer to his lover, suddenly feeling insecure, a ridiculous notion as it had been this very same group that gathered only a week earlier to celebrate Aidan's birthday and he'd spent plenty of time with all of them since he'd first awakened in Aidan's apartment.

Aidan shook his head, his eyes fixed on the man trailing after Hunter and Brianna. Wyatt wasn't the only one feeling suddenly insecure.

"Wyatt. Aidan. I'd like you to meet Zane Gaulk." Carina gestured to the man at the end of the table. Zane was tall and dark, his hair wavy and his expression serious. "He's the investigator I sent out to Ambridia to look into things out there. I thought you might want to hear what he found out."

Chapter Fifteen

IF AIDAN had been taking a drink, he would have spit the liquid across the table in shock. As it was, his jaw dropped so far that a train could have driven into his mouth. He said nothing, unable to speak as his brain tried to process the fact that Carina wanted to have this conversation *in a bar*.

"Here? Now?" Wyatt expressed what Aidan couldn't. "Why?"

Carina shrugged. She wasn't surprised by the protest and had warned Zane before he'd arrived at the bar to expect it. She had expected it to come from Aidan, but either way, it didn't matter. "I thought it would be easier than bringing strangers to your apartment."

"We don't have to do this here if you don't want to," Zane offered, stepping closer to the table and letting his arms fall to his sides. The last thing he wanted was a scene in the middle of the bar. He came here a lot—both on business and otherwise—and he didn't need a bad reputation. "We can go back to your place, if you'd prefer, or some other public place if that would make you more comfortable."

"He does a lot of business here," Carina added, "but if you'd rather not do this here, we'll go elsewhere."

"Don't think we won't all tag along, though," Hunter said, leaning across the table and staring hard at Aidan to convey how serious he was. "We want to hear this too."

"Here's fine." Wyatt was suddenly a lot less comfortable than he had been only moments earlier, but having everyone here would keep him from having to repeat the same story multiple times. He'd done that enough and appreciated the opportunity to avoid a similar situation with whatever Carina's investigator had uncovered. "We already ordered food. Might as well stay."

Carina pulled her briefcase from under the table, removed a folder, and slid it across to Aidan and Wyatt. "There's the written summary, along with contact information for your family and friends in Ambridia, Wyatt."

Wyatt's eyes widened, and he gulped down his beer. "I thought—" He cleared his throat, trying to force the words around the tightness there. "I thought they wouldn't know anything." Every muscle in his body was screaming *run*, *leave*, *danger*, and it was only Aidan's presence next to him that kept him anchored in the seat, his whole body trembling with the effort of staying still.

"They don't. I didn't contact them." Zane pulled a chair over from a nearby table and sat on it turned backward, resting his hands on the chair back as he dipped his head so he could meet Wyatt's eyes. "The only information that's there is public record. Your family moved not too long after you were taken, and your brother and sister don't live with them anymore. They've both graduated college and don't seem to have much contact with your parents. I had to guess on your friends, though," Zane added. "I had some clues from school records and the like, but I probably missed a few, and I might have included someone you never spent any time with at all. If there's someone I left off who you'd like to contact, just let me know, and I'll get you their information as well."

"I don't *want* to contact anyone." Wyatt's lips narrowed into a thin line as he flipped past the first page—the one with names, addresses, e-mails, and phone numbers—without looking at it. Maybe later, but not now. Probably not ever. The idea of facing anyone from his past, even his old friends who had probably missed him when he disappeared, was enough to make his stomach churn. He wasn't going to think about it. "What else did you find out? Everyone isn't gathered here to see a list of names and addresses."

"You have some very persistent friends, Mr. Mettler." Zane held up a hand to forestall Wyatt's protest. "We didn't speak to them. We didn't have to. Lilly Kaden and Quinton Spicer are still maintaining a webpage looking for you. They are both convinced that you were taken against your will and that your parents lied about where you had gone."

"Where *did* my parents say I had gone?" Wyatt wasn't going to touch the idea that he had been taken against his will. Everyone here already knew that. There had never been any question.

"Boarding school." Zane reached over and pulled a pamphlet out of the bottom of the folder. "They told your friends you'd won a scholarship to a prestigious school in Beridsdale and had to leave immediately."

"And they believed that I was there for eleven years?"

"No." Zane shook his head, biting back a chuckle. From what he'd seen, Wyatt's childhood friends didn't believe anything anyone in authority told them. "They didn't believe it at all, if the webpage is anything to go by. Your parents didn't think things through very well. Boarding school explained why you were gone, but not why you didn't write or call or ever visit. Prison would have been more believable."

Wyatt choked on his beer, coughing and sputtering as he tried to wrap his brain around the notion of prison being in any way believable. He'd been an extremely straight-laced kid, the one who said no to everything that was remotely wrong, even when he was presented with a perfect opportunity and very little chance of being caught. "I don't think that they would have believed that either. I never even skipped class or copied someone else's homework. Lilly and Quinton never would have believed that I'd committed a crime."

Zane cleared his throat as the laughter continued. "Anyway, they pestered your parents for a while, and when they didn't get any answers there, they started their own campaign. They set up a website, put flyers up around the school and neighborhood, even pestered the police, though they didn't get anywhere with that."

It was difficult for Wyatt to fathom. He'd been good friends with both Quinton and Lilly, had considered dating Lilly once or twice, but he'd been sure they had long since forgotten about him. There was little reason for them to keep looking for someone who had disappeared without so much as a good-bye. He lifted his head and peered at Zane. "They're *still* doing this?"

"Well, they only update every couple of months now, but they do keep it relatively up-to-date. The web address is in the folder, if you want to look at it later."

"Thanks." Wyatt pulled the folder a little closer but didn't look down. Maybe someday, but Lilly and Quinton would have to wonder for at least a little bit longer.

Aidan squeezed Wyatt's knee and bumped his shoulder into Wyatt's. "We can look it up when we get home, if you want," he offered quietly.

Wyatt ducked his head and shrugged, not sure how to explain his reluctance, or if he even should. "Maybe."

"Whenever you want," Aidan assured him with another squeeze. "*Whatever* you want."

He blushed, grateful that his Bondmate understood, and returned his attention to Zane. "What else did you find out?" There had to be more than just updates on a couple of his old friends to merit a gathering of everyone he knew in Haverdsford.

"There are a few things about your family in there as well. What they're doing, where they live, that sort of thing."

Wyatt rolled his eyes and gave Zane an exasperated look. "Anything else?" He could read about his family later, should he decide he wanted to. Right now, he wanted to know if they'd found out anything that was going to affect him here and now. "Nothing you've told us so far is very earth-shattering."

Zane leaned forward, his gaze once more focused on Wyatt. "We don't know who your parents sold you to, but we may have a way to track them down. Your parents are getting payments each month, deposited directly into one of their accounts at the bank. They come from an escrow company, which in turn gets the money from a dummy corporation. We're going to have to trace it back, but we should be able to figure out where the money is coming from."

"And that would be who had me?" Wyatt wasn't sure he wanted to know, not really. He would just as soon put the whole thing behind him.

"Not necessarily." Zane scooted his chair closer and pulled a notepad from his pocket and began scribbling on it, drawing boxes and connecting them with lines. "I suspect that we'll find the money ultimately comes from a holding company. Usually, the subsidiaries that the money goes through would be the ones involved in any given transaction." He drew an arrow straight down one chain of boxes. "Given the lengths that they went to with this, however, it could be any one of their subsidiaries." He poked at the paper again, this time drawing a curved arrow from one line of boxes, back through the top box, and down another line. "One subsidiary could be financing something for another subsidiary. They're shady business practices, but we already know they're not above those."

"So, what then? Even if you chase the company down, you won't know who held him. How does that do us any good?" Aidan asked.

Zane nodded. "True. We won't know for sure, not without some other form of proof. We can probably narrow it down based on location and business transactions, but it's going to take time."

"And then what?" Wyatt peered down at the drawing, a frown pulling at his face. This was far more complicated than he'd imagined. "We can't do anything with suspicions." He knew they couldn't do anything without iron-cast, unassailable proof, and even then it would be risky.

"Once we have suspicions, we work on narrowing it down further," Carina said. She leaned back and directed a serious look at Wyatt. "Anything you can remember about the things they had you dream would be helpful, Wyatt. We can use what you remember to further narrow down which company held you."

"I don't—"

"Just think about it, okay?" Carina let her gaze soften as she watched Wyatt fidget. She knew what she was asking wouldn't be easy, and she wished she didn't have to ask it, but if they wanted to have any sort of case at all, Wyatt needed to do this. "You don't have to tell us anything now. Just think about it, and write down whatever you remember. It's the only way you'll ever get justice."

Wyatt was suddenly very aware of the people crowded around the too-small table with him and even more so of the countless strangers mingling around the pub. It felt like every single eye was on him, even though he could see that most of the other patrons were fully occupied with other things. "I don't really want justice," he admitted in a soft tone. "I just want to know that they'll leave me alone and let me live my life."

Aidan pulled Wyatt close, pressed his lips to his temple, and stroked his fingers through his hair. "Just think about it, okay?" He rubbed his hand up and down Wyatt's arm and concentrated on sending comforting thoughts to his lover. "You don't have to do anything you don't want to do. We'll do everything we can to make them leave you alone."

Wyatt nodded as all his friends seconded Aidan's assertion. "Okay." He would agree to anything for Aidan. He could manage to think about something for at least a little while.

"If you don't do something, they'll be able to do that to someone else," Brianna pointed out quietly, her eyes sad as she looked at Wyatt. "They'll buy off some other clueless and desperate parents, trap some other kid who doesn't know anything about being a Dreamer and steal his life."

"Or hers," Hunter added, sounding more serious than Wyatt had ever heard him.

That tore a hole in Wyatt's gut. His own memories were horrible, and he felt bitter and completely lost inside every time he thought about the fact that he'd spent *eleven years* asleep because someone else decided he would best benefit them that way. The idea of some other kid going through the same thing, only maybe never waking up, maybe dying there like Wyatt almost had, was unthinkable. "I'll do what I can. I just… I can't promise anything, okay?"

"Of course." Carina nodded in thanks. "Whatever you can do will help."

The shrill chimes of Brianna's ring tone interrupted the conversation. She dug it out of her purse, scowled at the screen, and slipped under the table, crawling on the floor to avoid making anyone move to let her out. "I'll be back, guys," she said as she shimmied out from under the table. "I have to take this." She darted across the bar, lifting the phone to her ear as she went, and disappeared out the front door.

Everyone at the table followed her progress with stunned looks on their faces.

Zane was the first to recover, and he cleared his throat to bring attention back to him. "We didn't find out much else. It was clear early on that your brother and sister didn't know anything. We're doing what we can to track down anyone who might."

Wyatt nodded, though he really had only processed about half of what he'd been told. "Thanks."

The waitress came by then and dropped off their food, and by the time they'd settled in to eat, Brianna was back, smiling broadly at Wyatt as she bounced on her toes. "That was my friend Renee. She works with me down at the hospital. I had lunch with her the other day, and I told her about how you were looking for a job. It turns out that her department is looking to hire someone, 'cause the last *three* people they've hired have been let go within a month. She's already talked to her bosses about you, and they want to give you an interview! It's entry level, so it's not going to pay a ton, but it has benefits, and there's a chance for promotion, and if you hate it, you'll at least have some work history when you go out looking for something else. They're actually pretty desperate, because one of the other Dreamers is going on maternity leave soon, so they need to get the spot filled."

It sounded great. Too great. "What about…?" Wyatt trailed off, waving his free hand vaguely in front of him. Hunter and Brianna knew all the issues he faced with getting a job, but none of their other friends did, and he didn't want to talk about it.

Brianna's eyes widened almost comically. "Oh! They know. I told Renee, and she told her bosses, and anyway, she said that they want to interview you, and then if they like you and you need to get other stuff taken care of, they'll give you a chance to do that then." She snagged the pen and notepad from the table, flipped it to a clean page, and scribbled down a number. "Renee said to call her here tomorrow, and she'll get stuff set up."

Wyatt took the paper with trembling hands. "Thanks." The word stuck in his throat, and he had to clear it before he repeated himself, louder this time. "Thanks. Really." He even managed a smile, though it was mostly automatic reflex, as he was in far too much shock for the real thing.

"You're welcome." Brianna gave him a quick peck on the cheek and then crawled back under the table, giggling when Olin and Kyler both tried to kick her as she crawled by. "Behave, boys."

Aidan snorted. "They'll never behave, Brianna. It's a lost cause."

"A girl can hope."

"Good luck with that." He took the paper from Wyatt's hand and tucked it in his pocket. "You okay?"

"Just a lot to take in."

"Yeah." It was, and it had come on top of an already busy day. Aidan couldn't blame his lover for looking and feeling a bit frazzled. "Mostly good, though."

"I guess. It's all rolling around in my head, and I can't process all of it yet."

"Stop trying to process any of it."

The corners of Wyatt's lips twitched. "That's easier said than done."

Aidan looked around the table. Their friends had all broken off into private conversations, some serious, some not. Farther out, the other patrons of the pub were involved in their own amusements, the din of chatter and clanking silverware almost painfully loud when he listened to it. Across the room, the waitress who had taken their order was carrying a heavy tray with what looked like their food and refills for the dozen empty glasses scattered around the table. The moment was perfect.

He turned back to Wyatt and slipped his hand under his chin, turning it so they were looking into each other's eyes. "I love you," he whispered before leaning in to softly kiss Wyatt.

Wyatt relaxed into Aidan, the frustrations of the day melting away under Aidan's touch. "I love you too."

CRISPIN ALLER slid the crisply folded piece of paper off the mahogany desk, glanced at the number written inside, and nodded. It was enough to keep him comfortable for a few years, longer if he managed to invest it without alerting the authorities. "Do you want him picked up immediately?"

"No." Elliott's leather chair creaked as he leaned back, folded his hands in his lap, and regarded Crispin thoughtfully. His shaved head contrasted sharply with the snappy cut of his suit, but his expression was all business and he hadn't batted an eye at Elliott's request. "I need a way to keep him first. He Bonded a few weeks ago."

"Ah." Crispin nodded, understanding now why the offer had been so high. Bonds complicated things. "You'll need to break it, then." He didn't know what Elliott was planning—didn't want to know—but he knew that was true regardless of what Elliott was after.

"I plan to." Elliott leaned forward, ignoring the creaking of his chair, and rested his arms on the desk. "I need to you obtain a dose of Vinculex before you pick up Wyatt Mettler."

Now the high offer made even more sense. Vinculex was highly regulated and not available as a street drug. Obtaining it would be complicated and time-consuming. "How much are you willing to pay?" Crispin held Elliott's earlier offer up between his index and middle fingers. "I'll find it for this, but a vial isn't going to be cheap."

Elliott smiled as he wrote another number on a piece of paper, this one double what he'd offered Crispin to bring Wyatt back. "If you need more, call. This has to work."

Crispin put both sheets into his inside jacket pocket. "Anything else?"

"Find someone to watch Wyatt Mettler's family. I need to know if he's in contact with them." It seemed unlikely, but Elliott wasn't going to risk it. Getting Wyatt back was too important. "I need to know if his family is likely to cause trouble when their money stops as well."

"Of course." Crispin stood, straightened his jacket, and nodded at Elliott. "I'll send you weekly reports and stop in if I learn something."

"Very well." Elliott waited for the door to close behind Crispin, then sat back, his smile slowly widening as a feeling of satisfaction spread over him. The weeks of research he'd put in before hiring Crispin had clearly paid off. Wyatt Mettler would soon be his.

Part Two

Chapter Sixteen

WYATT parked his car in the lot at McGrudy's and was pleased to recognize familiar cars parked in the lot. From the looks of things, everyone was already inside, making Wyatt the last to arrive. Late to his own party. There were worse things, and it couldn't be helped. He'd been tied up at work, creating a fun-filled fantasy for a little girl while her doctors performed what otherwise would have been painful tests. The dream had gone a little bit long, but he'd been having fun too.

For the last two months, he'd been working at Sacred Heart—the same hospital Brianna worked at—in the pediatric department. Though there was a downtown hospital dedicated solely to pediatric care, the department at Sacred Heart always stayed full, and Wyatt and his coworkers were kept busy making sure the children had restful nights and naps, and occasionally keeping them asleep while the doctors performed tests or procedures.

Wyatt loved it. He loved working with the kids, knowing he was helping them, and especially loved all the fun scenarios he got to treat them to in the Dreamscape. All the things he'd wished he'd gotten to do as a child, from going to simple festivals to swimming with exotic animals, were incorporated into the children's dreams, and Wyatt cherished enjoying it with them.

He loved it so much that he hadn't hesitated when Gwendolyn, one of the other Dreamers in the department, had asked him to cover a shift that afternoon. It was his birthday, the first one he'd gotten to celebrate in more than a decade, but Aidan had work to do during the day and the shift would have ended well before the scheduled party. It was Wyatt's fault that he'd been late.

It was his party. He could be late if he wanted to.

Shaking his head at the ridiculous thought, Wyatt climbed from the car and, as he had every time for the past month, paused to admire its sleek black lines and to marvel that it was really his, bought with his own money on his own merits. He remembered the day he'd bought it with startling clarity. Aidan had been driving him around to car dealers for a week, ever since Wyatt had passed his driving test and added an official driver's license to the other identification cards he kept in his wallet, but he hadn't yet found something he both loved and could afford. His salary was decent and certainly enough for him to contribute to the everyday household expenses, but he hadn't wanted to risk stretching himself too thin. Nothing within his budget had felt right.

This car, however, had been perfect. Wyatt had noticed it as soon as they had set foot on the lot, the sleek lines and powerful curves calling his name as they gleamed in the sun. He'd approached it slowly, afraid of what the price tag was going to say, bracing himself for more disappointment, and almost hadn't been able to look at the tag stuck in the window. It had taken Aidan poking him in the side and muttering under his breath something about it taking long enough for Wyatt to look. When he had, he'd marched right inside and started the paperwork immediately. He hadn't needed to drive it to know that it was meant to be his.

With a last fond look at the car he was so proud to own, Wyatt tucked his hands into his pockets and headed across the lot to the pub entrance. It was a gorgeous day outside, sunny and not too hot or cold, and after spending most of it inside, asleep, Wyatt was almost reluctant to head back indoors. If he'd known what the weather was going to be like, he would have suggested they go to the park or the fair he and Aidan were planning on visiting over the weekend, instead of hanging out in the pub where they spent a lot of their free time. Still, McGrudy's meant something to their group, and the owner had apparently been willing to give his friends some sort of deal, so the party was here, whether Wyatt wanted it to be or not.

He would make the best of it, he thought as he pulled the door open. It could hardly end up worse than the last birthday he'd been awake to celebrate, and any sort of party at all would be better than the ones he remembered from his childhood. His parents had tried, at least when he was young, but they'd never had much money and that fact was always felt most keenly during times of celebration, particularly when Wyatt had been able to see his friends and classmates get things he could only dream of.

No, this party would be much better than those barely remembered days, even if it turned out to be just a normal night at the pub.

With one last glance at the bright sky, Wyatt pulled the door open, stepped inside, and stopped short, one hand holding the door open behind him.

McGrudy's had never looked like this, not once in the four months Wyatt had been coming here. It was usually semi-dark, packed with people, and full of the sounds of drunken conversation and music playing in the background. Now it was well-lit, brighter than Wyatt had ever seen it, the polished wood of the bar and tables sparkling under the overhead lights. The wood paneling had been covered with blue and green streamers and a set of tables had been pushed together in the center of the room, covered with a tablecloth, and decorated with what looked to be confetti. A large cake sat in the middle of the table, a whole pile of wrapped boxes and festive bags covered one of the pool tables, and the scents of Wyatt's favorite foods wafted through the room.

Most surprising was the lack of noise and people. The only sound was a low murmur coming from the group of people clustered near the back of the room, and there wasn't a single person visible who Wyatt didn't count as a friend.

His hand fell to his side as he took a few halting steps forward, his eyes full of wonder, and the door swung shut, the hinges creaking loudly and drawing all eyes to him.

"Wyatt!" The change in volume was staggering as his friends surged forward, laughing, hugging him, and clapping him on the back as they wished him a happy birthday. Brianna literally climbed up him to plant a kiss on his cheek, squeezing him tight before dropping back to the ground and grinning widely. "Happy birthday!"

Wyatt blushed, his entire body turning red as his friends made a big deal of him in a way that had never happened before in his life. It was ridiculous that he'd had to wait until he was turning twenty-eight to get a proper birthday party, but based on the sights and smells he'd taken in before the squeaking door had betrayed his presence, he was sure it would be worth the wait. Assuming he could stop blushing long enough to enjoy it.

He shuffled forward, his blush deepening with each birthday greeting. The ten people around him felt like a hundred as he waded his way through, trying to gracefully accept the attention yet, at the same time, wishing it would all end.

And then it did. Warm hands curled around the back of his head and soft dry lips pressed against his, replacing the myriad of voices and touches. Aidan. Wyatt's world narrowed to just the man in front of him. Aidan's brilliant green eyes were hidden behind dark lashes as their lips moved together, promising so much more before the night was over. Wyatt moaned into the kiss, his hands coming up to cup Aidan's face as his tongue entered a dance with Aidan's, twining together with sensual strokes that left both men weak in the knees.

Slowly, Aidan broke the kiss, keeping his body pressed against Wyatt's as he looked up, meeting his lover's eyes for the first time that evening. "Happy birthday."

Wyatt knew his grin was bright enough to light the whole room, but his voice was as soft as Aidan's had been. "Thanks."

"You're welcome."

"Did you bake?"

Aidan's gaze flicked to the table, and he flushed, his face turning almost as red as Wyatt's had been only moments earlier. "Yeah," he offered, his eyes finding Wyatt's once more.

"Yes!" Wyatt pumped his fist, shimmied his hips, and wrapped Aidan in a giant bear hug that lifted his feet from the ground. They kissed again, the cake and presents and friends gathered around them all forgotten. Aidan tasted of coffee and chocolate and something sugary sweet that Wyatt couldn't identify, though he certainly tried, his tongue exploring every cranny of Aidan's mouth as their lips moved together.

Then a damp rag landed on them, draping over Aidan's head and catching on Wyatt's ear. They ignored it, and it was followed by a shower of peanuts that Aidan deflected by sliding a hand up to shield Wyatt's face. "I think they might want our attention," he murmured into Wyatt's mouth as he tilted his head and made sure Wyatt's eye was protected from the flying legumes.

"Yeah?" Wyatt tugged at Aidan's bottom lip with his teeth. "Think we should give it to them?"

A firm hand gripped Aidan's shoulder tightly and a low voice growled in his ear, "Break it up or I'll tell Hunter to start throwing alcohol."

Aidan turned to glare at Olin. "You wouldn't."

"Try me."

Aidan turned back into the kiss, but it quickly became impossible to continue as Hunter jumped on Wyatt's back, ruffling his hair and shouting "Molest the birthday boy!" He smirked at Aidan's shocked look, putting on an innocent face as Aidan's eyes narrowed. "What? I thought that's what the game was. This *is* a party, right?"

Wyatt rolled his eyes, pecked Aidan on the lips, and leaned back until Hunter was forced to stand on the floor again. "Fine. Let's party. What's first on the agenda, oh impatient one?"

"Food! And then presents. We'd do it the other way around, but I'm afraid that you'd eat the presents if we made you wait any longer for dinner. You were about to eat Aidan, there."

Wyatt shook his head as he twined his fingers in with Aidan's. "Later, yeah?" he asked as he squeezed, putting promise into his voice and his touch.

Aidan squeezed back, his smile growing. "Definitely."

CRISPIN pulled the door shut as he ducked into Elliott's office, putting a solid barrier between them and anyone who might still be in the office despite the late hour. He hadn't seen a soul since passing the security guard at the front desk, but it wasn't worth the risk.

Elliott waited until Crispin sank into the chair across the desk before leaning forward. "You have something for me?" He managed to keep most of the anticipation out of his voice, but inside he was buzzing with the expected thrill.

"Information." Crispin sat back, resting his elbows on the armrests. "I found a source for Vinculex."

It wasn't what Elliott hoped for, but he took care not to let it show. Information on where to get Vinculex was more than he had at the moment. "Yes?"

"I found a worker at the plant licensed to make Vinculex locally." Crispin crossed his legs and met Elliott's gaze evenly. "They only do one batch a month because it's used so infrequently, but he said he could tag a good vial as damaged the next time they make it. He'll sneak it out if the price is right." Crispin didn't mention the money he'd already spent tracking down the man and convincing him to name a price. That was included in his fee. The vial wasn't.

"How much?" Elliott clasped his hands together as the almost giddy feeling returned. A man inside willing to sell was almost as good as having a vial in his hands. Whatever he wanted, Elliott would double it, just to be sure he stayed loyal.

Crispin pulled a slip of paper from his pocket and slid it across the desk. "Less than you offered."

Elliott glanced at the paper, his eyes widening slightly at the surprisingly low amount. He could triple it and not pay what he'd been prepared to offer, though he wouldn't needlessly be that generous. Doubling it would be enough to ensure the man inside remained his. "I can have it tomorrow." He tucked the paper away. "Cash, I presume?"

"Please." Crispin nodded. "He said it would be a few weeks, but I want the money on hand so there's no delay when he gets it. I'll call in some favors, and we'll move on Wyatt as soon as we have the vial."

"Send it to me first. I want to give it to him." Elliott smiled at the thought of severing the Bond Wyatt had dared form. "I'll tell you where to bring him when I give you the cash. I have to make sure the new facility is ready."

"Of course." Crispin nodded again as he stood. "I'll await your call."

He left as quickly as he'd come, stepping into the empty hallway and leaving Elliott with a pleased smile on his face. Everything was finally falling into place.

WYATT slung his arm over Aidan's shoulder as they stumbled down the sidewalk. "Tonight was fun, man. Thanks."

"Wasn't just me," Aidan said, pressing his lips to Wyatt's neck. "The others did most of the work." They'd done all of it, actually, except make the cake, but it didn't really matter. The point had been to give Wyatt a great party, and they'd succeeded.

Wyatt leaned in close, his eyes sparkling under the bright moon. "I'll thank them later," he whispered, his breath warm against Aidan's cheek. "I have ideas for you tonight."

Aidan's dick twitched with pleasure at the thought, and he hurried his steps, anxious to get home so Wyatt could show him what he was thinking. "Do you, now?" He guided their steps back toward the middle of the sidewalk, keeping them clear of the street, and waggled his eyebrows.

"Maybe." Wyatt sent mirth and lust echoing along their Bond. "Or maybe," he added, his fond gaze becoming a leer. "I think you have plans for me."

Aidan did, but that didn't mean he was going to reveal them now. They could wait, and would be all the more fun for it. "You'll see when we get home," he offered.

"Is that a promise?"

The low, gravely tone of Wyatt's voice went straight to Aidan's groin, and suddenly he was the one having trouble walking in a straight line. "Definitely."

"Good." Wyatt's grin was predatory as he tugged Aidan forward, picking up their pace just enough that they both started to stumble a little. "Because I have to say that while all those presents were awesome, none of them were what I *really* wanted."

"Oh?" Aidan teased. "And what would that be?"

As they turned the corner, Wyatt looked as though he couldn't decide if he should be amused or exasperated. "What do you think?"

Aidan knew exactly what Wyatt wanted; the sheer *desire* echoing along their Bond erased any doubt he may have had and ensured he wanted the exact same thing. "I don't know," he joked as he slipped the key into the door of their building. "It looked to me like you got everything you could possibly want."

The pile of presents had been impressive. Every one of their friends had gone out of their way to get Wyatt something he would enjoy but wouldn't think of buying for himself, and they'd all come up with some very thoughtful and surprising ideas. The results of their efforts had filled the back of Carina's car and left Aidan privately wondering where they were going to put all of it when Carina dropped it off in the morning.

"Not everything," Wyatt growled, his voice seductive in Aidan's ear. "There wasn't a present from you in that pile."

Aidan's gift for Wyatt was hidden safely away in his office, but the wrapped box tucked deep in the file drawer wasn't what Aidan had in mind as he dragged Wyatt across the lobby to the waiting elevator. Every nerve in his body vibrated with desire as he pushed Wyatt into the car and slammed him into the back wall, only belatedly remembering to hit the button for the top floor.

The ride up was both too long and too short. Wyatt pulled Aidan tight against him, their groins rubbing as their lips met in a heated kiss.

He would never tire of kissing Aidan, never tire of his taste or the way his hands and tongue constantly begged for more, even as he left Wyatt trembling at his mercy. He would never tire of the way their feelings ricocheted back and forth along their Bond: love, need, and want building and building until reaching an explosive crescendo that felt as though it could never be reached again and yet always was.

This time was no different. By the time the elevator opened on the top floor, they were both desperate.

Aidan stopped first, noticing the man waiting outside their door only because he had turned away from Wyatt in an effort to get into their apartment as quickly as possible. Wyatt took two more steps before he realized Aidan wasn't moving and turned to ask why.

The pleasant expression dropped from Wyatt's face as his eyes landed on the tall man. Every good thing about the day was suddenly meaningless and inconsequential, as a fabulous birthday turned into something terrible.

His brother had found him.

Chapter Seventeen

AIDAN stepped in front of Wyatt, pushing his Bondmate away from the man by their door. It was a ridiculous response—the man was taller than both of them, and Wyatt was certainly capable of defending himself—but there was something in Wyatt's tone and body language that triggered all of Aidan's protective instincts.

"Wyatt," Damon Mettler said, propelling himself off the wall and taking a step toward them in one fluid motion. "You, uh, you look good."

Wyatt just stared, his eyes wide and breathing heavy as he clutched tightly at Aidan's hand. He couldn't speak, couldn't move, couldn't process anything beyond his older brother standing in the hallway in front of them looking older, more mature, but basically much the same as he had twelve years earlier when Wyatt had last laid eyes on him.

"Can I help you?" Aidan asked. He wanted to fight, to defend Wyatt's honor and make this man hurt for the way he made Wyatt look, or barring that, to flee, taking Wyatt far away to someplace safe where this man wouldn't be able to find them. But his mother had taught him manners, and though Wyatt was shocked and terrified and a few other things Aidan couldn't identify, the man hadn't yet done anything to threaten either of them. He kept his voice and mannerisms polite, though barely.

"I'm, uh." Damon looked down and rubbed his hand over the back of his neck. "I'm Damon. Wyatt's brother." He looked up, met Aidan's eyes and then Wyatt's, letting them see the worry and concern he felt. "I just found out where he was, and I wanted to see him, make sure he was okay."

Muttering obscenities under his breath, Aidan tugged Wyatt forward, taking care to keep himself between the two siblings. "This isn't a conversation we should be having in the hallway," he said tersely as he opened the door, letting Wyatt scurry inside before he gestured for Damon to follow. "Have a seat."

Damon crossed the room and sat uneasily in the armchair closest to the patio door, but Wyatt kept moving, heading to the back of the apartment with swift steps. Aidan followed after flipping the deadbolt on the front door, not giving thought to the fact that he was leaving a complete stranger unattended in his front room.

The bedroom door was closed when Aidan reached it, but not locked, and he slipped through with little noise, easing the door shut behind him. The room was empty, but the sliding door leading to the balcony was open, and through the glass, Aidan could see Wyatt pacing back and forth in the enclosed area.

Wyatt stopped when Aidan stepped outside to join him. "I won't leave."

"Why would you?" Aidan asked in a puzzled voice as he stopped behind Wyatt and slowly rubbed his back, calming him in a way he hadn't needed to in months.

"Damon. He'll tell our parents. Or bring them here. Or take me to them. And then—" Wyatt swallowed hard as he turned and looked over his shoulder at Aidan. "And then I'll have to go back there."

"No. You won't." Aidan slipped under Wyatt's arm, squeezing himself between his lover and the rail. "They can't make you. Damon can't make you go anywhere you don't want to go. And if your parents come here, we won't let them in."

"You let Damon in."

"I did. I want to talk to him."

Wyatt's heart thudded in his chest, and he shut his eyes tightly. He didn't want this answer, but he needed to know it. "Why?"

The word was filled with so much fear and pain that Aidan wanted to throw Damon out and barricade the apartment so no one else could ever enter. "I need to know how he found you. And why he started looking. Carina said nothing was filed in Ambridian courts. I don't know how your brother knew to look."

"And then you'll make him leave?"

"That depends on why he came."

"But—"

Aidan cut Wyatt off with a soft kiss. "Look at me." He took Wyatt's chin in his hand and rubbed his thumb over Wyatt's cheekbone until the hazel eyes fluttered open to regard him with a fearful, almost betrayed expression. "He might not want what you think he wants. He didn't try to grab you out in the hallway, and he hasn't come back here. Maybe he really did just want to make sure you were okay."

It was almost impossible to believe. If the idea had come from anyone other than Aidan, Wyatt would have discarded it without a thought, but Aidan looked at him with an earnest expression, and Wyatt couldn't find it in himself to deny him. "You'll just talk? I can't. I mean… you have to talk to him."

"Of course." Aidan planted a chaste kiss on Wyatt's lips and slipped out of his arms. "Wait here. I'll talk to him and then come tell you what he wants, okay? You don't have to see him if you don't want to."

Wyatt nodded. "Thanks."

"You're welcome." Aidan watched as Wyatt turned back to stare out at the city with his fingers clenched tightly around the balcony rail. He then slipped through the bedroom, shutting the door softly behind him.

DAMON stayed perched on the edge of the armchair, his fingers drumming on his knees, but he explored the apartment visually, carefully cataloging everything he could see from his position. The apartment was larger than he'd expected, the open living room leading to an eat-in kitchen and a hallway that clearly led to multiple bedrooms. As he waited, he took in the photos and knick-knacks, recognized his brother's touch in a few of them, and wondered if Wyatt was going to stay hidden the entire time he was here.

When he heard the bedroom door shut a second time, Damon sat up straighter, his eyes fixed on the shadowed hallway. He nodded as Aidan stepped into the room but kept his gaze glued to the shadows until Aidan had taken a seat and the silence made it clear that no one else was coming out.

Aidan watched Wyatt's brother for a moment, his unease growing as the silence stretched. Finally, when Damon's attention pulled away from the hallway and focused on him, Aidan cleared his throat and licked his dry lips. "So. You're Wyatt's brother."

"Yeah." Damon inwardly winced at the harsh tone. He'd expected it, had expected worse, but it grated on his nerves nonetheless. "And you are?" He knew the man's name but little else about him, and he had no idea why his brother was staying here when he'd been freed over five months earlier.

"Aidan Donecoff. His Bondmate."

Relief flooded through Damon, and he slumped back in the chair, his eyes closed and his muscles relaxed. "Thank heavens," he breathed, relishing the unexpected lightness that came with the knowledge that his brother had Bonded.

"What?" Aidan leaned forward, his brow furrowed and his body trembling with alertness at Damon's reaction. He had expected anger, frustration, perhaps even grudging acceptance, but relief was so unexpected, it left him waiting for the catch. "It's a legitimate, registered Bond."

"Which means that there's another layer of protection around Wyatt," Damon finished, smiling as Aidan's eyes widened. "I never agreed with what our parents did. Money was tight before, and then with Wyatt gone and payments coming in regularly, our standard of living went up, but it wasn't what I wanted. It wasn't worth it. I changed my major in college, became a lawyer, and only stuck around at home to make sure Tabatha was safe. I hadn't spoken to my parents from the day Tabatha moved out of their house until my mother called two weeks ago demanding to know if I knew anything about why their payments had stopped. I was lobbying for bills that would increase the consequences of doing what they did to Wyatt, so of course, she assumed I had something to do with it."

The coil in Aidan's gut loosened as Damon spoke, but it tightened again when Damon mentioned his parents' payments being stopped. He didn't know why it had taken so long, but now, five months after Wyatt had been dumped to die in an alley, people outside their circle of friends were becoming aware of Wyatt's newfound freedom. "How did you...." He swallowed, wetting his impossibly dry throat, and tried again. "How did you find us? Find him?"

"After my mother called, I remembered something Tabatha had said a while back." Damon pushed his hair back from his forehead and twined his fingers together in his lap, his eyes glued to his feet. "She had told me that our mother had called her, ranting about incompetent bankers and telling her she should switch banks. I guess the teller had asked if she had gotten the new car she was looking at, assured her that they'd verified her monthly deposits." He looked up, rubbing the back of his neck as he met Aidan's eyes. "She hadn't been looking at a new car. Neither had my father. I called in just about every favor I was owed and managed to trace the inquiry back to a Carina Orego. Then I found the paperwork she'd filed here."

"You found the paperwork for his residency here, but you didn't know we'd Bonded?"

Damon smiled sheepishly. "I stopped looking and got on the first plane out here once I got your address. Didn't even stop to pack a bag. I just really needed to see Wyatt, you know? Make sure he was okay with my own eyes."

"He thinks you're here to take him back to your parents, or that you're going to bring them out here, and that you'll try to make him go back to whoever was paying your parents."

"No." Damon shook his head emphatically, leaning forward and making sure he looked Aidan straight in the eyes as he spoke. He couldn't let Aidan think that, not when the opposite was true. "I'd like to tell Tabatha, if it's okay with Wyatt, but I have no intention of telling my parents. They don't have any right to know what he's doing. They lost that when they sold him." He practically spat the last two words.

Aidan nodded. He'd begun to suspect as much, but he'd had to ask. He didn't know what he would have done if Damon had answered differently, besides ask him to leave and do his best to keep him away from Wyatt, but Aidan was glad he didn't have to figure it out. "Good. I don't think he ever wants to see them again. He wouldn't let our lawyer file charges, even if prosecuting them was the only way to find out who they sold him to, because he would have to face them."

"I don't blame him. I don't have any desire to see them myself, and I'm not the one they sold." He looked down as he carefully considered his next words. "Do you think he'll talk to me now that you know I'm not out to take him away?"

"That's up to him," Aidan replied softly. "I should go tell him what you said. I'll ask him, but I'm not making any promises."

"Yeah. Okay." Damon nodded, and Aidan's heart twisted in sympathy at the guardedly hopeful expression on his face. If Wyatt said no—well, it was best not to think about it.

Unable to watch any longer and already feeling uncomfortable with the extended silence, Aidan stood and headed toward the hallway. "I'll be right back." He didn't wait for Damon to answer.

WYATT didn't turn as Aidan stepped back out onto the balcony. "Is he gone?"

"He wants to talk to you."

"No." Wyatt shook his head, his fingers clenched tightly around the wood of the rail. "I can't." It was a weak and pathetic-sounding protest, but it was true. He couldn't talk to his brother, couldn't think about what his brother really wanted, couldn't stand the thought of leaving his life—of leaving Aidan—because someone somewhere had been careless and now he was found.

He should have known the idea of having a good birthday was a preposterous one.

"Wyatt." Aidan could feel the fear ratchet up over their Bond. "He just wants to *talk* to you."

"How do you know?" Wyatt turned away and began pacing again, his long strides covering the length of the balcony in just a few steps, his hands balled into fists as he turned, and his whole body trembling with fear and anger. It was bad enough that Damon had shown up, but now Aidan wanted to give him a chance, wanted to expose Wyatt to him for more than a few seconds, wanted Wyatt to take a family member at his word. "He might have lied. He might be trying to trick us." His voice got louder with every sentence as he emphasized the points, angry that Aidan was siding with Damon against Wyatt. "He might—"

"Hey." Aidan grabbed Wyatt's shoulders, cutting off the suddenly frantic speech and stopping him just before he began wildly waving his arms. "Calm down. Listen to me." He waited as Wyatt slowly calmed and met his gaze with stunned eyes and a heaving chest. "If you don't want to see him, you don't have to."

"I don't."

"Okay."

Wyatt arched his eyebrow. "Really?" The quick turnaround was difficult to believe, and at the moment, Wyatt wanted a reason to stay angry. "Two minutes ago you were all in favor of the idea."

"Two minutes ago, I told you all Damon wanted was to talk. I told him I would pass the message along, that's it. I didn't promise him anything, didn't tell him you would come out." Aidan stepped forward and pressed his hand over Wyatt's heart. "If the answer is no, I'll walk back out there, tell him you don't want to talk, and make him leave."

"Promise?"

It hurt that Wyatt even had to ask, but Aidan ignored the pain and concentrated on giving Wyatt what he needed. They would worry about everything else later. "Of course."

"Then the answer is no. I don't want to talk to him. I can't."

"Okay."

This time, Aidan's simple, unquestioning agreement sent a surge of warmth and love through Wyatt, and he rushed forward, capturing Aidan's lips in a passionate kiss and wrapping him in a tight hug. "Thank you." It struck him again just how lucky he was that Aidan had been the one to find him in that alley all those months ago, and he wondered, as always, what he'd done to deserve such an incredible Bondmate. Damon's presence in the front room was distressing, and Wyatt knew he was going to keep worrying about what Damon really wanted, but here, with Aidan's assurance echoing in his ears, he could forget about Damon for a minute and relax in the safety and love of Aidan's embrace.

"You're welcome." Aidan slid his arms down Wyatt's back and tightened his grip briefly. "I'm going to go see Damon out, okay? Maybe help him get a cab and a hotel. It's late, and he didn't bring any luggage," he continued, rubbing his hands up and down Wyatt's back until the suddenly stiff muscles began to relax again. "He said he just flew out as soon as he figured out where I lived, so I'm sure he doesn't have a reservation anywhere. I would hate for him to have trouble finding a place to stay."

"I wouldn't," Wyatt muttered as he pressed his face against Aidan's shoulder, but even as he said the words, he knew they weren't true. Even with all his fears, Wyatt didn't want his big brother to have to deal with the issue of finding a place to stay this late at night. "Go," he said, stepping back and forcing a small smile.

Aidan hesitated. He hadn't missed Wyatt's reaction, but he didn't want to bring it up with Damon still waiting in the front room. He could push when he got Damon settled, or in the morning, if Wyatt was asleep by then. "I'll be right back."

"I know." Wyatt gently pushed Aidan toward the door. "Go."

Aidan glanced back once as he crossed the room, but Wyatt just made a shooing motion. He needed Aidan, but more than that, he needed to know that Damon had left and wasn't coming back.

Chapter Eighteen

WYATT turned the coffee mug between his fingers as he stared morosely into the dark liquid. Every time the bell above the door chimed, he would look up, his bottom lip caught between his teeth as he carefully watched the people enter and leave the café. Every time it wasn't the person he was waiting for, he would sigh, though he wasn't sure if it was with relief or disappointment.

Earlier, he'd gone by the hotel Damon was staying in and left a short note scrawled with a trembling hand on a piece of hotel stationary, asking Damon to meet him at this coffee shop. The note had said nine, and it was now almost ten, but Wyatt had no way of knowing if Damon had even received the message. He'd gotten the room number from Aidan but had been too afraid to knock on the door and had settled for slipping the note underneath and dashing off to the coffee shop before he could change his mind.

It wasn't ideal, but Aidan had told him Damon was planning on leaving soon—there wasn't any point in his staying around if Wyatt wasn't willing to see him—and as he'd lain in bed wrapped safely in Aidan's arms, Wyatt had decided he didn't want his brother to go back to Ambridia without at least hearing what he had to say. Wyatt would wonder forever if he didn't get answers, and this was the easiest way to get them.

Meeting in the coffee shop had been Aidan's suggestion. Wyatt hadn't wanted to go to Damon's hotel room, nor was he ready for Damon to come back to their apartment, but the coffee shop was neutral ground, and Wyatt hoped it would do as intended and put them both at ease. This conversation was going to be hard enough without the locale making it worse for either of them.

Aidan had offered to accompany Wyatt, and Wyatt had been tempted to accept, but he had ultimately declined. This was something he needed to do on his own. If Aidan came, he would run interference, and as alluring as that was, it wouldn't get Wyatt the answers he needed.

So here he was, by himself in an unfamiliar coffee shop, preparing to face his brother alone and doing his best to resist the nearly overwhelming urge to call Aidan.

The bell rang softly as the door opened, and this time when Wyatt looked up, he met the gaze of his older brother. He waited, his heart pounding heavily and his palms sweating against the warm mug, until Damon was only a few feet away. "Hey," he said.

"Hi." Damon pulled out the chair opposite Wyatt and sank into it wearily. He'd had a long, stressful day followed by a restless night of little sleep, and waking up to a note from the younger brother he'd been convinced had just excluded him from his life had thrown him completely off-kilter. "I wasn't sure you'd still be here." Until he'd walked into the café, Damon hadn't been sure it was Wyatt who had left the note. His handwriting had changed from the scribbles on the few cards and notes Damon had been able to scrounge up and save as their parents had purged Wyatt from their lives.

"I was going to knock." Wyatt looked back down at his coffee. "Aidan said I should talk to you. I just couldn't last night. And then, this morning, when I got to your room, I panicked." He looked back up and chewed on his lip. Damon would understand. He had to. "I couldn't talk to you in your hotel room."

Damon furrowed his brow as he tried to make sense of his little brother's words. Twelve years ago, he would have known exactly what Wyatt meant, but now he was clueless. "Why not?"

"I couldn't see you somewhere that private." He needed the buffer the other patrons in the café provided. He needed the knowledge that he was in a public place of his choosing to reassure him of his safety. "I'm not ready to talk to you without other people around."

"But you're ready to talk to me if they are?" Damon was going to take what he could get, but it was clear from Wyatt's body language that he didn't really want to have this conversation, despite the note he left and the words coming out of his mouth.

Wyatt shook his head. "Not really." Not at all, actually, but it was now or never, and he wasn't ready for it to be never, either. "I didn't think I'd ever see you again, Damon. When you showed up last night, I was scared. And angry. I didn't know what you wanted or how you found me. I thought you were going to…." He swallowed hard, his Adam's apple bobbing as he struggled to wet his suddenly dry throat. "I can't go back to that, Damon."

"I don't want you to." Damon reached across the table and patted Wyatt's forearm, withdrawing his hand quickly when Wyatt flinched. "That's not why I came. Even if it were, I don't think Aidan would let me even try. He was very protective of you when we talked."

"He loves me." Those words left a warm glow in Wyatt's chest and brought a blush to his cheeks, and he was glad he'd been looking down into his cup when he said them.

"I could tell." Damon rested his hands on the table and looked steadily at Wyatt. "I didn't mean to worry you, Wyatt. I honestly never thought about how you might react, and I should have. All I was thinking about yesterday was that I'd finally found you, and you were apparently okay, and I had to see it for myself." He shook his head. "You have no idea how upset Tabatha and I were when our parents did that to you."

Wyatt looked up, blinking curiously, but didn't say anything. He didn't trust that he wouldn't say something stupid or something he'd regret.

Damon waited, watching Wyatt's internal struggle. When it became clear Wyatt wasn't going to say anything, he reached into his jacket pocket and pulled out a manila envelope. He held it loosely between his hands, staring at it and contemplating what to do, before lifting his gaze to Wyatt once more. "I didn't even think about what day it was when I got on the plane. It was the first time in twelve years I hadn't thought about your birthday, but I didn't realize it was until I got to the hotel and saw the date on the ledger."

"That made it worse." Wyatt closed his eyes and slumped back in the chair, sliding down until his head rested on the top of the chair back. "I thought you'd come to bring me back to them and you were just rubbing it in by doing it on my birthday."

"I know. Aidan told me." Damon set the envelope on the table, flap down, and left it resting half on and half off the Formica. "You know I couldn't, right? Even if I wanted to, I couldn't make you come back to New Altz or to see our parents or to go back to whoever you were with." He slid his hand across the table again and gripped Wyatt's wrist loosely. "I don't want to, though. I never wanted you to go in the first place."

"Yeah, I know." Wyatt pulled his wrist free and again turned the coffee mug in circles with his fingers, taking comfort in the scraping sound it made against the table. "Didn't stop me from thinking it, though." He forced himself to meet his brother's eyes. "I was a prisoner for over eleven years, Damon. That kind of fear doesn't just go away because things get good. And then, it was my birthday, and it had gone so well, and when I saw you, I just knew I shouldn't have let myself think I was going to have a good birthday. I mean, why would I?" He laughed hollowly. "I've never had one. There's no reason for it to start now."

Damon leaned forward. He wanted to touch Wyatt again, to reassure him, but it was clear his touch did the opposite. "You should have more than one. Everyone deserves happy birthdays." He pushed the envelope forward, the clasp scraping across the hard surface, until it was just about touching Wyatt's cup. "I think you should see this." He tapped the envelope twice with his index finger before pulling his hand back. "I'm going to get a drink. Do you want anything?"

Wyatt shook his head. He wasn't going to eat or drink anything given to him by his brother. "I'm good. Had a muffin while I waited."

"Okay. I'll be back." He stopped a few feet away from the table and looked back, his heart clenching at the nervous expression Wyatt wore. "Look at what's inside the envelope, Wyatt. Please. It's stuff Tabatha and I have wanted you to see for a long time."

Wyatt watched as Damon got in line and waited with his back to the table and his attention fixed resolutely on the menu board behind the counter. When he was certain Damon was really going to be occupied with ordering, Wyatt let go of the coffee mug and slowly opened the envelope. Inside were twelve birthday cards, one dated for each year over the last twelve years, all signed by his brother and sister and each covered with short letters that occasionally spilled onto sheets of loose leaf paper stuffed inside.

Wyatt's hands shook as he opened the oldest one. He laid it flat on the table and bent over it, his hands wrapped around the coffee mug again as he peered at the notes scribbled hastily inside. The card itself was from Wyatt's sixteenth birthday and signed in large and exuberant script by both his siblings. The letters inside were dated two days afterward, and they were full of angry words and promises from Damon and Tabatha that they would do everything they could to make their parents change their minds and get Wyatt back. Tabatha's promises were full of hope and trust and childish naïveté that let her believe their parents hadn't really meant what had happened. Damon's were already cynical and threatening, any bit of trust he'd had in their parents destroyed two days earlier when they'd sold his brother.

The next card was much the same, though both letters expressed disbelief that it had already been a year. Tabatha was still full of hope and making plans for what she would do when Wyatt came home, though her trust in their parents was clearly diminishing. Damon was even more cynical and had pinned all his hopes and promises on what he could do rather than what he thought he might be able to convince anyone else to do.

As the years passed, the cards and letters stayed much the same, only the handwriting and day-to-day details changing as time went on. Tabatha's pre-teen loops turned into the smooth curves of an adult woman as her confidence in their parents faded year by year. Damon's plans grew more detailed even as he grew more frustrated with his failures. Repeatedly, they promised they would do anything they could to get Wyatt back, and repeatedly they expressed continual disbelief and frustration that they hadn't yet succeeded.

By the time Damon returned to the table, Wyatt was on the sixth card, the one that would have been for his twenty-first birthday. This card was happier than the others had been, and the letters seemed to presume that since

Wyatt was legally an adult, the agreement made with their parents would be voided and he would be able to leave. It was clear from the notes that neither of Wyatt's siblings truly understood at that point, but that rapidly changed. Postscripts added the next day showed their spirits dampened and their resolve to learn and do as much as they could strengthened. There was nothing upbeat about the cards after that.

Damon slowly pulled the card across the table so he could read it, his face falling and his heart clenching as he realized which one it was. "We never forgot," he said softly, folding the card back up and putting it carefully on top of the other ones Wyatt had read. "We never stopped hoping we'd find you some day or that our parents would tell us exactly what they'd done so we could fight it."

"I don't think you'd have been able to find me even if they had told you." Wyatt glanced briefly at Damon to make sure he was listening and then fixed his gaze on the edge of the table. He couldn't look at anyone while he said this. "I don't—" He sighed. "I don't remember much, and I don't know how much of what I remember is true. I was asleep the whole time, and everything they showed me was in the Dreamscape, using their memories. Or at least," he corrected with a rueful shake of his head, "what they told me were their memories. I didn't know anything about building dreams then, so it was what they chose to show me, not what I pulled from their thoughts."

He shook his head again, this time trying to clear the cobwebs of fading memories and half-forgotten dreams. "From what I could tell, though, it was pretty hush-hush. It would have to have been, since it was completely illegal." With a hard swallow, Wyatt looked up. "We don't know who had me. Our lawyer has people digging into it, but she says that even if we do find out what the company was, most of the people, even the higher-ups, aren't going to know anything about what they were doing to me."

It took Damon a few moments to process Wyatt's words. He hadn't known—hadn't asked—what had been done since Carina Orego had filed those papers he'd found. He'd assumed they'd known who had taken Wyatt, that the courts had known who had held him and that they were taking action against them. To hear otherwise required an entire adjustment in his thought process. "Do you know anything?"

"Just that some guy named Elliott was originally in charge of the program." The last word didn't feel right to describe what they'd done to him, but Wyatt had heard it used by his various handlers when they'd made him dream with them, and he couldn't think of anything else to call it. "He's the one who started my, um, training, I guess you'd call it."

"Training?"

Wyatt fought down hysteria. This was a very bad conversational turn, and if he didn't get the subject changed quickly, he was going to lose control, despite the public location and the crowd of people who would undoubtedly be watching the moment he began to panic. "At least I learned how to control dreams, right? It's a marketable skill. Not that they ever expected me to be free and alive to use it, but it worked out."

Damon gently took Wyatt's hands in his, stilling the frantic waving and willing his brother to calm down. "Take a deep breath, okay? That's it. In and out. Slowly." He breathed with Wyatt, demonstrating the relaxing breathing that had gotten him through so many stressful situations. Wyatt gradually calmed, his trembling limbs stilling. "Better?"

Wyatt nodded, his hands still gripping Damon's too tightly, but he wasn't on the verge of a breakdown anymore, and Damon would take what he could get. "Let's talk about something else, yeah? Tell me about your job. Aidan said you were working at the hospital with the kids? You like it, right?" He was babbling now, but if it would keep that haunted look from Wyatt's eyes, Damon would ramble on all day. "Aidan said you did, but I don't think he'd let me think you were anything other than deliriously happy, no matter how you actually felt."

"Yeah, I do," Wyatt replied, a small smile blossoming on his face despite himself. He hadn't thought it would be this easy to let go and push thoughts of "before" out of his head, but the idea of Aidan gruffly defending him and his happiness to Damon sent a swell of tenderness through him that dispelled the last of the lingering shakiness. "I love it."

Just like that, Wyatt was off, talking about his job and the kids he'd helped and some of the weird dreams he'd given them to keep them entertained and asleep. The conversation moved organically from there, with Damon talking about his job and then Tabatha's, telling stories about the times they'd gotten together recently and ragging good-naturedly on her Bondmate, a young man named Garrett who apparently made her very happy. Wyatt responded with tales about things he and Aidan had done and stories about their friends, focusing on the good parts of the past five months. They even touched on a few happy memories from their childhoods, though they were both careful to avoid any topics that included their parents.

Before they realized it, three hours had passed, and it was time for Damon to leave if he wanted to make his return flight to New Altz. "So, um," he said as he stood, holding out his hand awkwardly. "It was good to see you, Wyatt. I'm glad you're happy now."

"Me too." Wyatt looked at the extended hand and, in a snap decision he hoped he wouldn't come to regret, ignored the hand in favor of pulling Damon in for a brief hug.

Damon's eyes bugged out, but he managed to retain enough composure to return the embrace, and he patted Wyatt on the back as they pulled apart. "I'll come back in a few weeks, okay? Maybe bring Tabatha? I know she'll want to see you."

Wyatt consciously took a deep breath, again trying to make his suddenly racing heart calm. This was Damon, who he'd just spent several pleasant hours with, and he wanted to bring Tabatha, who felt the same way Damon did. There was no need to worry. "Just her. I don't—I can't—"

"I know." Damon clasped Wyatt's shoulder. "You know she'll have to tell Garrett where she's going though, right? He'll want to know what has her so excited, and she can't just disappear for a few days. He won't tell anyone else, I promise."

It was almost too much to ask. Damon's request wasn't unreasonable, but the more people in Ambridia who knew he was alive and free, the greater the chances that his parents or the people who had taken him would find out. "Only him." He let fear and desperation creep into his voice so Damon would know just how serious he was. "No one else can know. I can't risk *them* finding out."

"They won't. We don't want them to either." Damon didn't have to ask who *they* were. He already knew and felt the same way as Wyatt. There was no way he would let their parents or anyone else who might have had a stake in Wyatt's sale find out that he was free and doing well for himself. "Take care of yourself. And Aidan."

"I will. You too."

Damon squeezed Wyatt's shoulder one last time and pulled back. There was so much else to say and no time to say it, but at least he'd have the chance later. "I'll call you in a few days and let you know when we're coming."

"Okay." Wyatt stuffed his hands in his pockets and stood, feeling awkward and out of place, as Damon walked out of the café. When he was out of sight, Wyatt sank back into his chair, his shaky legs no longer able to support him. He needed to head home—Aidan was worried and that was where he felt safest—but he had to take a minute to compose himself before he gathered up the cards Damon had left and made his way to his car.

The morning hadn't gone as he'd expected, and while it was good, it was also terrifying. It had been nice to talk to Damon, to know that he and Tabatha supported him, but Wyatt's ability to trust had been ripped away twelve years earlier. Damon hadn't lied, but he also didn't know everything. Something was going to go wrong. Wyatt could feel it. All he could do was hope he was mistaken.

Chapter Nineteen

AIDAN'S parents lived in a moderate-size farmhouse surrounded by several acres of land, though the vast majority of the property had been sold off a few generations back when the family stopped making their money from farming and started earning it by working in offices. They'd kept the house, along with the lake at the back of the property and a few acres of what was now grass, and the result was an idyllic homestead close enough to the town of Montwick that it wasn't an inconvenience to get supplies or go to work, but isolated enough that neighbors seldom dropped by and the only noise was that of nature.

Wyatt could appreciate all this in a detached way, but all he could see when Aidan pulled the car into the driveway was the three people sitting on the porch, beers in hand, and the small child playing on the front lawn. They looked relaxed and friendly, but to Wyatt they were just as terrifying as Damon had been when he showed up three weeks ago.

He didn't want to get out of the car, but Aidan was already climbing out, a huge grin on his face as he walked around to Wyatt's door, and there was no way Wyatt could chicken out. Aidan would be too disappointed, and Wyatt couldn't do that to him.

Taking a deep breath, Wyatt climbed from the car and slid his hand into Aidan's. "They're just people," Aidan murmured as he closed his fingers around Wyatt's and squeezed, sending a surge of reassurance and love along their Bond. "And they've been looking forward to meeting you."

That didn't make Wyatt feel any calmer. It almost would have been better if they hadn't wanted to see him at all. At least then he wouldn't have to live up to any impossible expectations or make small talk with people he likely had nothing in common with except for loving Aidan. That was a decent starting point, he supposed, but it wasn't going to give them many conversation topics. So it was with great trepidation that he let Aidan lead him forward.

He needn't have worried. Before they'd gotten halfway to the porch, they were tackled by a whirlwind that had formerly been the child playing on the lawn. The boy attached himself to them both, wrapping one arm around

Wyatt's left leg and the other around Aidan's right as he gazed up at his uncle with his head tipped almost completely back. "Hi!"

Aidan ruffled his hair. "Hey, Nolan. How are you?"

"Good." Nolan immediately transferred his gaze to Wyatt's face. "Who are you?"

For a moment, Wyatt froze, ridiculously terrified of Aidan's small nephew, but then the skills that made him so good at working with the kids at the hospital kicked in, and he patted Nolan's shoulder with his free hand. "I'm Wyatt. What's your name?"

Nolan chewed on his bottom lip and looked back at Aidan for reassurance. When Aidan nodded, he grinned. "Nolan!"

"Well, it's nice to meet you, Nolan."

"You too!" Nolan quickly glanced over his shoulder before looking back up at Wyatt. He looked comical with his head tilted so far back that he would fall over if it weren't for his grip on his uncles' legs, and the serious expression on his face was at odds with his exuberant voice and relaxed posture. "You want to come and play with me?"

It was absolutely adorable, and Wyatt wanted to laugh, but he knew better and settled for sending a surge of amusement to Aidan. "I'd love to," he replied in all seriousness, "but I think your Uncle Aidan wants me to come with him first. Maybe when I'm done?"

"Okay!" And with that, Nolan was gone, dashing across the yard back to whatever had been amusing him before his uncles arrived.

After that, meeting everyone else was much easier. Aidan beamed as he introduced Wyatt to his mother, father, and brother, and then he stepped into the house calling for his sister and sister-in-law. Wyatt moved to follow, unsure about staying outside alone with Aidan's parents, but Sherilyn stopped him with a big hug. "Welcome to the family."

All Wyatt could do after that was hug her back. "Thanks."

AFTER a large, late lunch, Kaylee, Aidan's sister-in-law, took Nolan upstairs to put him down for a nap while the rest of the family moved out to the back porch. Wyatt settled next to Aidan on the swinging bench and sighed, his stomach full and his limbs heavy with post-meal sleepiness. He let the conversation flow around him, occasionally agreeing with something or elaborating on one of Aidan's comments, but mostly he dozed and stared out across the open grass to the trees in the distance.

All his worry about coming to visit seemed ridiculous now. Aidan's family had been more than welcoming, and the area was gorgeous with rich, green grass and tall, stately trees. It was peaceful out here, easy to relax even in the company of a half dozen near-strangers, and before long, Wyatt found his eyes drooping and his head tilting to rest on Aidan's shoulder.

Aidan pressed his lips to the top of Wyatt's head and flashed a fond smile at his parents. "Tired?"

"Hmmm." Wyatt wasn't, really, just content, lethargic, and feeling worn down by the self-inflicted stress of the morning. It was too much effort to move or keep up with the conversation.

"Go to sleep." Aidan shifted, bringing his arm over Wyatt's shoulders and supporting his neck, as he pulled his lover closer so they were sitting more comfortably. "No one will mind."

Wyatt did, but he was too relaxed in Aidan's arms to move at all, so he just hummed again and let his eyes drift fully closed. It was too much effort to keep them open, so while he wasn't going to sleep, he wasn't going to protest either. He would just listen to the conversation for now.

He'd only been drifting for a few minutes when Kaylee came back out, Nolan squirming in her arms and struggling to get down. "He won't sleep," she said in an exasperated tone as she handed the wriggling toddler off to her Bondmate, Jevon. "See what you can do. I can't even get him to lie down."

Jevon took him with a sigh, his hands wrapped fully around the recalcitrant three-year-old's waist. "Nolan. Listen to your mother."

"No!"

"Nolan...." It was an old argument, one that Jevon had gotten good at winning, but today Nolan wasn't having any of it. He was at his grandparents', and there was a new person here, and he wasn't going to be kept away from all the activity.

"No!" Nolan squirmed again, arching his back and kicking out his feet.

Jevon barely managed to pull him upright without dropping him to the deck. "Dammit, Nolan!"

At that, Wyatt pried open one eye. He didn't know Jevon well, but Aidan's surprise told him that this was an unusual occurrence. He glanced at Aidan, who nodded in response to Wyatt's unasked question, and then returned his attention to Jevon. "Do you, uh, want me to get him to sleep?"

All conversation stopped, and everyone on the porch except Aidan and Nolan regarded him with dubious looks on their faces. Aidan was amused and proud, and Nolan used the distraction to try to break free again.

Jevon hefted Nolan into a firmer hold. "He's kind of fussy," he said doubtfully as Nolan shrieked to emphasize his point.

"He's not very good with strangers," Kaylee offered at the same time, wincing as Nolan's scream interrupted her. "I don't think he'll go to sleep for you."

Wyatt raised his eyebrows but didn't move from his spot at Aidan's side. He could feel his lover's repressed mirth and did his best to keep it from creeping into his own voice. "Um. Dreamer." He smiled wryly. *"Everybody* goes to sleep if I want them to." It wasn't entirely true. There were a few people who could resist when a Dreamer tried to pull them into slumber, but even if Nolan were going to be one of them, he wouldn't be able to yet. "I can get him to sleep."

The sudden silence that followed the announcement was stifling. Wyatt shifted, sitting up and leaning forward so he could look down at his hands as he mentally cursed himself for making the offer. Aidan's family had been so friendly, and he'd had to go and remind them of how different he really was and ruin it all. He wanted to leave right then, but Aidan's arm was around his shoulder, and he had nowhere to go.

"Are you sure you don't mind?"

Kaylee's words were so quiet that Wyatt wasn't sure he'd heard them. He turned to her, only relaxing when he saw the hopeful expression on her face. "If you don't. I'm not exactly going to sing him a lullaby or give him warm milk, you know."

"Warm milk doesn't work anyway, and lullabies just make him want to sing along." Kaylee laughed nervously as she moved closer to her Bondmate and son. "He's usually really good about at least lying down for an hour or so, but I don't know what's gotten into him today."

"He's just excited," Jevon soothed, again shifting his grip on Nolan so the toddler wouldn't fall to the floor. "If you really don't mind," he continued, directing his gaze at Wyatt, "we'd appreciate it."

"It's no trouble." Wyatt patted Aidan's hand and stood, arching his back and raising his hands above his head to stretch his tight muscles. "Give him here."

Jevon held out Nolan, almost dropping him as he squirmed, and Wyatt took him, shaking his head at the child's antics. "Nolan, buddy," he warned, "don't make me drop you."

Nolan blinked up at Wyatt, but he calmed enough for Wyatt to pull him into his chest and wrap him in his arms. "Where's his room?"

"Upstairs on the left. I'll show you." Kaylee held the door open for Wyatt to step inside, ruffled Nolan's hair as she passed, and led the way up the stairs.

The room was obviously Nolan's every time he visited his grandparents. There was a child-size bed covered with a blue and green patterned duvet, posters of cartoon characters on the walls, and toys stacked in bins. The set of low shelves held more toys and age-appropriate books, and a rocking chair sat in the corner next to the dresser. It was a room Wyatt would have loved when he was Nolan's age, and it made him smile as he gently laid the boy on the bed.

Nolan immediately tried to get up, but Wyatt held him down as he settled on the floor next to the bed. It would have been easier to keep him in place if he'd been able to lie next to Nolan, but there was no way he would fit on that bed, especially not with someone else, even someone as small as Nolan. "Settle down," he soothed, adjusting his grip once he was seated on the floor, trying to ease Nolan into a reclining position. "I want to show you something."

Nolan stilled, but he didn't lie back. He'd been tricked too many times, and he wasn't going to fall for whatever Wyatt was trying. "What?" he asked, his arms crossed and his gaze defiant, though his tone was curious.

"I have to show you," Wyatt eased his grip and leaned back with his elbows on the carpet. "Lie down so I can, okay?"

"No."

Wyatt sighed. This was going to be harder than if Nolan had willingly cooperated, but Nolan was on the bed, and the rest would follow. "All right, but you have to stay right there, okay?"

Nolan glanced at his mother, then tightened his expression into a full-on scowl and nodded. "Okay."

Wyatt lay on his back, closed his eyes, and concentrated on the Dreamscape. He was asleep within seconds, an advantage of being a Dreamer, and immediately set out looking for the tiny spark that was Nolan's subconscious. It was easy to find, burning brightly nearby, and Wyatt fixed on it, coaxing it to come to him and shaping the Dreamscape with things he sensed would attract Nolan.

It was only a few minutes later that Nolan was sound asleep, his body materializing in the Dreamscape next to Wyatt, and his eyes wide as he took in the carnival that surrounded them. "This is where we went before!"

"Yep." Kids were easy; their wishes were always close to the surface and their ideal dreams were quite pleasant. It hadn't been hard to find Nolan's fascination with the carnival Jevon and Kaylee had taken him to the previous weekend, and it had been even easier to shape it into something nap-friendly. "I thought you might like to come back."

Nolan definitely did. His eyes were wide as saucers and his mouth hung open in awe as he bounced on his toes and tried to decide where to go first. "How'd you do that?"

"It's what I do. I can make you dream whatever you want to. See?" He concentrated again and materialized some cotton candy in his hand. Dreams were the best places to give things like that to children; the sugar high wouldn't affect them when they were awake, and it tasted every bit as delicious as the real thing.

"Wow!" Nolan immediately forgot his momentary confusion about Wyatt's explanation and focused on the cotton candy. He'd stuffed two sticky handfuls into his mouth before he remembered his manners and beamed up at Wyatt. "Thank you!"

"You're welcome." He waited until the rest of the fluffed sugar had been stuffed into Nolan's mouth and held out his hand. "You want to go ride something?"

"Yeah!" Nolan wrapped sticky fingers around Wyatt's and tugged. "Let's go!"

Wyatt let Nolan lead him into the carnival, dissolving the leftover sugar from both their hands as they walked. Their first stop was a ride that spun in circles. Nolan laughed and laughed as it spun around, insisting that they ride it again and again and never noticing that they never had to get off or wait in line. By the time Wyatt persuaded him to try something else, Nolan was hooked and ran ahead to the next thing that caught his eye.

Wyatt subtly changed the dream so that Nolan would feel safe despite the lack of supervision and carefully extracted himself, waking only when he'd fully pulled free of Nolan's dream. "He should sleep for an hour or so," he told Kaylee when he opened his eyes, stretching again as he climbed to his feet.

Nolan was curled up in a ball, his eyes closed and his breathing deep and even, just as Wyatt had known it would be. He pulled the blanket over the sleeping boy's shoulders and smiled at Kaylee as he left the room.

Everyone else was still on the porch and looked at him with expectant gazes as he settled back next to Aidan. Kaylee stepped onto the porch before he could say anything, though, slipping an arm around Jevon's waist and murmuring that Nolan was out for the count.

"What's he dreaming about?" Aidan asked as he wrapped his arm back around Wyatt's shoulders.

"The carnival he went to last week. The kid sure likes spinning rides." He shook his head. "I think I'm still dizzy."

Aidan laughed. "It's all in your head, you know."

"That doesn't make it any less real, just easier to control."

"I know." Aidan pecked Wyatt on the lips. "Go dream something you want to do," Aidan whispered as they pulled apart but left their foreheads touching. "I can tell you're tired."

Wyatt laughed low in his throat and leaned in so his lips were against Aidan's ear. "I need you there for that."

The surge of desire that raced along their Bond was exceedingly satisfying. "Later," Aidan promised as he pressed a quick kiss to Wyatt's cheek and settled back into the swing.

Wyatt twisted around and settled next to him, a contented smile on his face. That was a promise he was going to be sure Aidan kept.

Chapter Twenty

AIDAN shifted his grip on the wine bottle and plastic glasses so he could tuck the blanket more securely under his arm. The evening was cool despite the warmth of the day, and he knew Wyatt hadn't thought to grab one when he'd trekked out to the lake immediately after dinner. It had been warm then, and Wyatt had been so desperate to get out of the house that Aidan had been surprised he'd stuck around long enough to help clean up.

Dinner had been stressful, much more so than lunch. Aidan's sister, Isabella, wasn't feeling well and thus was quiet, and Blake watched his son's Bondmate with something that bordered on distrust despite his warm welcome when they'd arrived and the long conversation they'd had over lunch. It seemed that Wyatt's using his abilities was far different from Wyatt's having abilities that he theoretically used at some time but not where Blake could see them. Aidan was furious at his father, and his mother tried her best to mediate, talking so much to Wyatt and Aidan in an attempt to fill the void left by her Bondmate that Jevon, Kaylee, and Isabella were all but excluded as well.

Wyatt knew he was the cause of the tension and was quieter than Aidan had seen him in a long time. He shoveled food into his mouth as quickly as he could without being rude and responded only when Sherilyn's questions demanded it. Nolan was the only one unaware, talking up a storm to anyone who would listen, but directing most of his attention at Wyatt. Unfortunately, Wyatt was too aware of the unease emanating from Aidan's father to really respond properly, and not even the happy chatter of the three-year-old could lighten the mood.

By the end of the meal, Blake thawed a little bit under the pressure from his Bondmate, even making a few comments to Wyatt, but it was obvious to all of them that the way he felt about Wyatt had changed. Aidan only refrained from saying anything to keep the peace, such as it was, at the dinner table, and didn't hesitate to lay into his father the moment Wyatt fled the house in search of peace and solitude.

That had been hours ago, though, and Aidan had grown tired of waiting for Wyatt to return, so he gathered up a blanket, two plastic picnic-style wineglasses, and a bottle of red wine and headed out into the fields. It didn't take long to determine where Wyatt had gone—the only obvious destination was the lake, and when Aidan extended the extra sense that accompanied their Bond toward it, he could feel Wyatt sitting on the dock and worrying about the rest of their trip.

Aidan was determined to erase that worry.

He reached the lake a few minutes later and set his burden down near the shore before walking out across the dock to sit next to Wyatt. There were no boats moored—his parents' last boat had been sold a few years ago, and they had no intention of replacing it until Nolan was old enough to appreciate the experience—and the dock had been allowed to fall into disrepair. It was relatively solid, though, and Aidan sat on the edge so his feet dangled over the water. He slipped his hand into Wyatt's, squeezed tightly, and took as much reassurance from his lover's touch as he hoped he was giving.

Wyatt smiled and wrapped his fingers around Aidan's, drawing strength and comfort from his presence. "Hey."

"Hey yourself." Aidan nudged Wyatt's shoulder, rocking him slightly. "Are you all right?"

"Yeah." Wyatt managed a small smile. "It was just awkward in there, you know? I had to get away for a bit."

"I know. I was surprised that you stayed long enough to help clean up."

Wyatt laughed bitterly, the sound harsh as it carried across the placid water. "I didn't want to give your mother reason to stop liking me too."

"She wouldn't. And my father doesn't either," Aidan added, putting more conviction into his voice than he felt. "He just... needs a little bit of time to really get used to the idea."

Wyatt shook his head, dismissing the notion. "He knew I was a Dreamer when he met me. He was fine with it then." And that was the rub. Blake's reaction after he made Nolan nap was something Wyatt had experienced with some of the parents of the kids at work, and something he'd feared he'd experience elsewhere. He hadn't expected it from Aidan's family, not after their initial greeting. It stung more than he'd thought it would, and he was struggling to reconcile his feelings with the way Aidan felt about his father. "I guess he's just not fine with me using my abilities on his family. It's okay in theory, but in practice, I terrify him. He probably thinks I'm trapping you in horrible scenarios every night."

Aidan regarded Wyatt for a long, quiet moment, taking in his slumped shoulders and downturned lips that only reinforced the hurt, lost feelings echoing over their Bond. He ached to pull Wyatt into his arms, to whisper in his ear and promise that everything would be all right, that his father would come around and in time everyone would be simply grateful the kids slept so well and easily when he was there. He didn't know that it was true, no matter how much he hoped it was, and Wyatt didn't need reassurance. He needed distraction. "Well," Aidan said, amused, "the last few nights have been pretty horrible. I mean, we haven't done anything *fun* in nearly a week. I'm not sure how much longer I can hold out."

The words had the intended effect. Wyatt pulled away from Aidan, his mouth agape. "But—" All sorts of responses flashed through his head, but he was too shocked to give voice to any of them and had to settle for staring at his lover with wide, shocked eyes, his mouth opening and closing soundlessly.

Aidan grinned, his heart swelling as Wyatt's thoughts and feelings switched from upset and frustrated to shocked and intrigued. "What?"

"I. You." He pointed his finger at Aidan, waved his hand around, and had to settle for letting their Bond convey exactly how shocked he was at the idea of having sex at Aidan's parent's house.

"Relax. My parents won't know anything." Aidan wrapped his arms around Wyatt's shoulders and pressed his lips to Wyatt's ear. "Besides, it's a lovely night, I have a blanket, and no one is going to come looking for us for a few hours. Maybe we could solve that little problem."

Wyatt pulled back just enough to look in Aidan's eyes. "Oh? And how do you propose we do that?"

"Well." Aidan let his grin slide into a leer as his eyes roamed up and down Wyatt's body. "I seem to recall promising to make all *your* dreams come true earlier, so why don't you tell me? I have wine if you want to start there."

Wyatt decidedly did *not* want to start with any form of beverage. "Let's save that for later," he growled, yanking Aidan with him as he climbed to his feet.

Aidan slid his arms around Wyatt's waist, and they stumbled off the dock and over to the blanket, their legs tangling with every other step. Wyatt's hands were cool against Aidan's skin as he groped and fumbled, seeking more contact than the walking embrace and layers of clothing offered. Aidan barely managed to pull away when they reached the pile he'd left on the shore, and Wyatt was pressed against him again before he got the blanket fully spread out. "Hold on!" he exclaimed, gently pushing Wyatt away as he struggled to cover the sharp blades of grass. "I don't want grass stains on my ass!"

Wyatt fell backward and sprawled on the ground, the tension of the day evaporating as his whole body shook with uncontrolled laughter. "Who says you're going to be on the bottom?" he gasped between giggles, his chest heaving as he struggled to pull in enough air to form the words.

That got Aidan's attention very quickly, and he hurriedly finished before crawling over to Wyatt and pinning him down with his whole body. "Do you want grass stains on *your* ass, then?" he growled, his voice low and his eyes dark. "Is that your fantasy? Me taking you on the ground, hard and fast and dirty?"

The giggles died swiftly in Wyatt's throat as he stared up at Aidan with a lusty gaze. He'd never thought about it before, never fantasized about anything like that in all of their lovemaking, but the moment the words had left Aidan's mouth, Wyatt knew that was *exactly* what he wanted. "Yes," he managed, forcing the word past a suddenly dry mouth as he was overcome with desire.

Aidan felt the surge of *need* and *want* and *right now* and wasted no time in complying, yanking his shirt off before attacking Wyatt's, ripping the thin material when it didn't immediately slide up and over Wyatt's head. Pants were a little more complicated, the button nearly defeating him, but he managed to get it open and yanked, tugging jeans and boxers down in one go as Wyatt obediently lifted his hips and then his feet so Aidan could remove the confining material.

He stripped out of his own pants, kicking them away from the lake before pressing the entire length of his naked body over Wyatt's and swallowing the moan that escaped Wyatt's lips as their cocks rubbed together. Moaning with pleasure, he slid his hand between their bodies, stroking Wyatt into full hardness as his tongue delved into Wyatt's mouth, tasting and claiming. When Wyatt's hands began to roam over his body, Aidan grabbed them and pushed them above his head, holding Wyatt's crossed wrists with his right hand as he twisted his left around Wyatt's dick. "Keep them there."

Wyatt whimpered and nodded, turning his hands over so he could grip the grass and insistently pushing his hips up against Aidan. "Please," he whispered, sending a surge of desperate pleading along their Bond. "Need you."

"Soon." Aidan leaned into a bruising kiss before pulling back and slipping his fingers between Wyatt's lips. He slid them in and out of Wyatt's mouth and moaned with encouragement as Wyatt swirled his tongue, slicking the digits. "Ready?"

"Yes." Wyatt bent his knees and Aidan pushed one finger inside, then another, opening Wyatt as quickly as he dared, driven by the desire that echoed between them, pushing him for *more*.

Wyatt writhed and moaned, his fingers clenched in the grass, tugging at it and pulling tufts free as he struggled to keep his hands in place. Aidan's barely wet fingers made him ache and burn, but it wasn't anywhere close to enough, and he fought with desire to release the grass and encourage Aidan with more than sounds and surges along their Bond. "Dammit, Aidan, *now*."

Aidan couldn't resist the pleading and raw need, and he pulled back, fumbling in his discarded jeans for the small tube he'd tucked there when he'd headed out in hopes of a romantic encounter along the shore. It took far too long to open the cap, precious seconds during which Aidan was sure Wyatt was going to let go of the grass and take matters into his own hands, but Wyatt just lay there, exuding desire and looking fuckable.

The moment the cap popped free, Aidan poured the slick liquid over his cock and lunged, barely taking the time to be sure he was lined up properly before thrusting his hips forward, sheathing his entire length inside Wyatt in one go. "Oh *God*."

"*Move*." Wyatt wrapped his legs around Aidan's waist, using his legs to pull him closer. "*Now*."

Aidan was only too happy to oblige, pulling back and slamming forward into Wyatt, losing himself in the sensation. Wyatt writhed and moaned, struggling to keep his hands in place, his breath hitching as Aidan repeatedly hit that spot inside him, sending jolts of pleasure and pain through his body. All too soon, he was calling Aidan's name, pulling fistfuls of grass from the ground as he came hard and fast. Aidan followed, thrusting only once more before releasing himself inside Wyatt's body and then collapsing limply on top of him.

They lay there for several minutes, entwined together as they waited for their breathing and heart rates to return to normal. When he regained enough strength to move, Aidan pulled out and let Wyatt shift to a more comfortable position under him, but he made no effort to roll off or do anything about the sticky come drying between their bellies. "We should clean up."

Wyatt nodded. "In a minute." He sighed, dropping the long strands of grass he'd been gripping and stretching his arms up as he idly rubbed a few loose blades between his fingers. A wicked grin grew on his face as he grabbed a handful of ripped grass and, without warning, rubbed it down Aidan's back and over the curve of his ass.

Aidan yelped and rolled over, trapping Wyatt's arm beneath him. "What the hell!"

"Now we both have grass stains on our asses."

"I said I didn't want any!"

Aidan lightly smacked Wyatt's chest, but it only made Wyatt laugh harder as he rolled so he was the one pinning Aidan to the ground. "Tough. I happen to think grass stains are a very attractive look on you."

"You do?" Aidan arched an eyebrow and made an overstated come-hither face.

Wyatt ignored the expression and pressed a quick peck to Aidan's lips. "Yep. It makes me want to do all sorts of crazy things to you."

"Such as?"

Wyatt smirked as he leaned down until his mouth was only inches from Aidan's. "I think I ought to show you."

Aidan could definitely get behind that.

BY THE time they headed back to the house, the wine was gone and the stars had been twinkling in the sky for some time. The moon was surprisingly bright, making it easy to see the uneven ground as they trudged back across the field toward the lone lit window of the house.

"Do you think anyone waited up?" Wyatt asked as he slipped his hand into Aidan's and shifted his grip on the blanket to pull it tighter around his shoulders.

"Maybe?" Aidan shrugged. "I guess it depends on if they have anything they want to talk to us about or not. Mom was pretty upset with Dad for the way he acted at dinner, and I think she was planning on having a, ah, *discussion* with him about it."

Wyatt quirked an eyebrow. "I thought you already yelled at him." He wasn't sure how he felt about that bit of knowledge. It was nice that Aidan stood up for him, but he hated that he had to, especially to his own family.

"I did. But that doesn't mean she won't as well." Aidan nudged Wyatt's shoulder with his own. "She really likes you. You helped clean up dinner."

"Oh, is that why?"

"Well, it doesn't hurt." He flashed a quick grin at his lover and pulled their joined hands up to his mouth so he could kiss Wyatt's knuckles. "She liked you before that, but I think helping to clean up cemented your place as her favorite child."

"Favorite... child?" Wyatt's mouth dropped open. He'd never thought of it that way. This was *Aidan's* family, not his, and the idea that Sherilyn would consider him as a son had never crossed his mind.

"Well, yeah. We Bonded. That makes them your in-laws."

"But—" The idea of a family—of *parents*, even in-laws—that didn't hate him and think of him merely as a way to make money and support their *normal* children was mind-boggling. Blake was wary of his powers, sure, but being wary or even distrustful of him was completely different from selling him to the highest bidder just to get him out of their hair.

"What?" Aidan stopped and peered at Wyatt, trying to read his face in the dark, hoping it would help him make sense of the feelings echoing over their Bond.

"I just—" Wyatt waved his arm, nearly dropping the blanket, unable to put his thoughts and feelings into words. Finding out Damon and Tabatha didn't feel the same way as his parents had been a big shock he was still trying to fully process. The idea of anyone's parents thinking of him as a son whom they *loved* was too much to process. He had to stop thinking about it or his knees were going to give out. "I never...."

"Come on." Aidan tugged Wyatt forward, swiftly crossing the last few yards to the back deck. "Sit," he urged when they'd reached it, pushing Wyatt so that the backs of his knees hit the edge of the wooden planking and he sat.

Wyatt hadn't realized they were that close to the house. He found himself simply blinking at Aidan, still trying to come to terms with this new information. "Does she really think that?"

"They both do. Everyone does. You're part of this family now, Wyatt. I thought you knew that."

"I...." Wyatt shook his head, trying to clear the fog so he could find the words. "They're your family, not mine."

"They're *our* family," Aidan corrected firmly as he sat down next to Wyatt and slid his arm around Wyatt's shoulders. "That's part of what Bonding means, Wyatt. *We're* a family, which means that my family is yours and, as much as we might wish it weren't so, your family is mine."

Wyatt wasn't going to think about the last part. "But your father—"

"Doesn't hate you." Aidan put every bit of conviction he could muster into his tone. He wasn't sure what else his father was feeling or how he was going to react, but he was sure of that, and he had to do something to relieve the worry underneath Wyatt's awe and confusion. "It might take some time for him to get used to seeing what you can do, and maybe he never will, but he doesn't hate you."

"You don't know that."

"Yes, I do." Aidan pulled back a little and turned so he could look into Wyatt's eyes, cupping Wyatt's chin so he couldn't look away. "Do you know what he told me this afternoon? Before you went up to make Nolan sleep?"

"No." While Aidan had been talking to Blake, Wyatt had been talking to Sherilyn and Isabella and hadn't heard a word of the conversation between Aidan and his father.

"He said he was happy for me, and that he was glad I'd found someone who obviously cared so much. He'd barely met you, and he was already telling me that you seemed like a great person."

Wyatt let his eyes drop to the deck, his head falling as far forward as Aidan's hand would allow it. "That was before I dreamed with Nolan."

"He still knew you were a Dreamer. He just...." Aidan paused, waiting until Wyatt looked up to continue. "Everything is different when it happens to you or someone you love, that's all."

It made sense, but it didn't make Blake's rejection at dinner any easier to take, nor did it give Wyatt any confidence that Blake would come around. He leaned forward and rested his forehead against Aidan's. "I guess. I just—"

"I know. Just trust me, okay?" When Wyatt nodded, rocking both their heads, Aidan managed a small smile. "He'll come around. And even if he doesn't—"

"It's better than my parents?"

"That wasn't what I was going to say, but yeah," Aidan said wryly. "I promise, the worst he'll do is what he did at dinner, and if I know my mother, she's not going to let him get away with that either."

"Yeah, okay." Wyatt tilted his head up, pressing his lips to Aidan's in a gentle kiss. It was a lot to take in, and even though it was all good, it was draining to process. "Let's go to bed."

"Sure." Aidan climbed to his feet and held out a hand to help Wyatt up. "Do you want to try to sneak upstairs, or should we just walk through the kitchen?"

"Kitchen's fine."

"You sure? That's where they'll be if they waited up."

Wyatt pulled the blanket back around his shoulders and nodded as he took Aidan's hand in his once more. "Yeah. It's fine." And it was. Whatever was waiting inside—an empty kitchen or flustered parents—it was something he could handle, especially with Aidan by his side.

Chapter Twenty-One

WYATT dropped his duffel on the bed and flopped down on his back next to it so he was lying across the width of the mattress with his feet hanging off the side. "Is it just me," he asked, his eyes tracking Aidan as he moved around the bedroom, unloading his own bag and putting things away, "or did the trip back take twice as long as the trip up?"

"It didn't, but I think it always seems that way. It usually does whenever I go somewhere." Aidan sat down on the bed next to Wyatt's head and brushed a stray lock of hair away from Wyatt's eye. It seemed strange that Wyatt didn't know that, but then, this was really the first trip Wyatt had ever been on, not counting the one where he was hauled across the country while unconscious. "Glad to be home?"

"God, yes." Wyatt rolled over, resting his cheek on Aidan's thigh, his nose inches from Aidan's belt and his left eye closed so he could peer up at Aidan with his right. "It was kind of peaceful out there, though," he admitted after a moment. "Once your father stopped glaring at me, I mean."

Aidan laughed and nodded his agreement. "Well, yeah. I didn't think you meant *while* he was glaring at you."

Breakfast and lunch the day after Wyatt had put Nolan down for his nap had been decidedly awkward, with Blake alternating between distrustful glares and curious glances until finally Wyatt pulled him aside and asked what he had done. Wyatt's nerves vibrated for the entire first part of the conversation, but when it came out that Blake was concerned about what Wyatt had shown Nolan and worried about what Wyatt might have seen in his dreams, Wyatt laughed in relief, the tension fleeing his body so quickly he practically fell over.

Blake was rather confused at Wyatt's reaction, but then Nolan came up and asked if Wyatt could take him to the carnival again, which answered the first of Blake's questions, and Wyatt offered to bring anyone who was interested into the dream so they could experience for themselves exactly what he did. It was a rather interesting afternoon in the Donecoff household, with everyone except Aidan and Isabella taking Wyatt up on the offer.

By the time Wyatt got Nolan to sleep and woke everyone else back up, Blake was much friendlier. When he realized, thanks to Aidan's explanation, that Wyatt was much less likely to enter his dreams unbidden than Isabella's best friend, who was a Dreamer and had stayed over several times before she Bonded, he was downright apologetic. By the end of the night, he was just as friendly as when Wyatt first arrived.

The rest of the visit was much more pleasant and, now that they were back in the city, Wyatt realized he'd acquired a bit of a taste for the serenity of the countryside. "It was nice," he murmured, almost to himself, before he rolled onto his back, his head still resting on Aidan's thigh, and gazed questioningly at his lover. "You ever think about moving back out there? I mean, not necessarily out to where your parents live, but out of the city? Away from the noise and the crowds?"

Aidan shrugged, though he raised his eyebrow questioningly as he looked down at Wyatt. "Sometimes. But my friends are here, and so are my business contacts. I've never had a reason to seriously consider it."

"Would you, though? Consider it, I mean."

"Probably. If I had reason to." Aidan tested their Bond, wondering what was behind the line of questioning, but found only curiosity. "Do you want to move out of the city?"

"Maybe." Now it was Wyatt's turn to shrug. "I like it here, with you, and I like my job and all our friends, and I don't want to go so far that we have to leave all that, but it would be nice to be able to see stars instead of skyscrapers, you know?" Their apartment building was on the outskirts of Haverdsford proper, away from the towering skyscrapers, but they dominated the skyline, and even looking away from downtown, there were plenty of buildings and lots of light pollution that blocked out the stars.

Aidan made a noncommittal noise and began carding his fingers through Wyatt's hair. The repetitive motion soothed him, and Wyatt found his eyes drifting shut and the conversation drifting from his mind. He was half-asleep by the time Aidan spoke again.

"You'd have to get a new job." Aidan kept playing with Wyatt's hair, smiling down at him as Wyatt blinked his eyes open in surprise. "There are places that are basically out in the country and are close enough we'd still be able to see our friends and I'd still be able to drive into the city for an occasional meeting with a client, but they're all too far to commute every day. If we stay close enough for you to do that, we won't find any of the serenity or stars you're talking about."

Wyatt laughed and shrugged. He didn't particularly *want* to get a new job—he liked the one he had—but now he knew he could. He would go into any new job hunt with a work history and references, and he was almost certain he would find it easier to get a new job than it had been to get his current one. "I'm not suggesting we pack up and move right this minute," he said with a laugh as he pressed his head into Aidan's hand. He made a contented sound as Aidan's fingers flexed against his scalp. "It's just something to think about, is all."

"Duly noted. I'll ponder it in my free time." Aidan smiled as Wyatt rolled his eyes and shifted so he could again push his head into Aidan's hand. Aidan tugged lightly on the chestnut strands, and the feeling of contentment and love surging over their Bond reminded him so much of a cat purring that he had to laugh as he began running his fingers through Wyatt's hair again.

They stayed like that for some time, basking in each other's company and talking of things they might someday like to do. By the time their stomachs started rumbling, reminding them they hadn't eaten since breakfast, they were both sprawled out across the bed, their legs tangled together and Aidan's head resting on Wyatt's shoulder.

Wyatt's stomach growled first, making Aidan jump, though he laughed when his rumbled in reply. He blushed furiously, though he knew Wyatt was only fondly amused. "We should eat."

Wyatt laughed, the sound filling the room and the rapid shaking of his shoulders jiggling the mattress beneath him. "Probably." He propped himself up on his elbows and stared down at his stomach for a moment before turning his head to stare at Aidan's. "It's kind of amusing," he added as Aidan's stomach growled once again. "Almost like they're having a conversation."

It was impossible for Aidan to keep a straight face with Wyatt laughing and making outrageous claims like that, but he gave it a valiant effort before collapsing against his lover in a fit of laughter. "If they are," he managed to gasp out after a few minutes, "it's about how much they want us to put food in them."

"Then get off me and go fix us something." Wyatt shoved at Aidan, rolling him onto his side. He climbed to his feet, and when it became apparent that Wyatt wasn't planning to move anytime in the near future, he grabbed Wyatt and helped him up as well.

"Come on," he said, dragging Wyatt toward the kitchen. "You get to help."

"Oh lucky me."

AIDAN cooked a simple meal of pasta and red sauce while Wyatt finished unpacking and putting everything away. When he was done, Wyatt shuffled into the front room and collapsed on the couch where he lay with his arm flung over his eyes until Aidan came and shook him. "Dinner's ready," he said, his brow furrowed in concern and his hand remaining on Wyatt's shoulder as Wyatt sat up. "Are you okay?"

Wyatt shrugged and rested his forehead against Aidan's bicep. "Yeah. Just tired, I guess." When Aidan kept peering down at him with a dubious expression on his face, Wyatt forced himself to look up and smile. "You know I can't really hide anything from you. Nothing's bothering me. I just don't have much energy right now, that's all."

"All right." Aidan pulled Wyatt to his feet, concentrating on feeling everything he could through their Bond. Wyatt was tired, a little hungry, and bemused by Aidan's concern. Everything other than exhaustion was a bit muted, which seemed strange but could easily be explained by weariness from their trip, so Aidan pushed it out of his mind. "Let's eat, and then bed."

"Okay." Wyatt let Aidan lead him into the kitchen, where he sank into a chair at the table and began slowly and methodically pushing pasta into his mouth.

By the time Aidan was done eating, Wyatt's head was propped up by his free hand and his eyelids were drooping, but the bowl in front of him was empty, so Aidan snagged it on his way to the sink, pausing to kiss the top of Wyatt's head before walking away. "Why don't you head to bed? I'll be in shortly."

Wyatt stretched as he stood and came to stand behind Aidan, wrapping his arms around his waist and resting his chin on his shoulder. "I'll wait." The words were distorted by a yawn, but the gentle circle his arms formed around Aidan was unyielding, and Aidan didn't protest, just quickly rinsed the dishes so he could turn for a kiss before guiding them both to the bedroom.

They were in bed before Aidan noticed the blinking light on the phone. Usually people called their cell phones, so they hadn't thought to check for messages on the apartment line when they got home. It was only the darkness of the room that let him see the flashing red light.

Sighing, Aidan got out of bed and crossed to the bookcase. He smacked at the machine a few times, fumbling to find the right button in the dark. On his third attempt, a vaguely familiar voice began playing from the speakers. "Wyatt, Aidan, this is Zane from Carina Orego's office," it played, filling the room with the low baritone of the investigator's voice. "I have some information for you about the people who had previously held Wyatt. We need to talk to you as soon as possible. Please call me." He rattled off a phone number, and then the message ended.

Aidan swallowed hard, pushing down a surge of panic, flipped on the light with a trembling hand, and turned to look at the bed.

Wyatt was sitting up with his legs crossed in front of him. "Is it too late to call him back tonight?" His whole body ached with weariness, especially now that he'd teased it with sleep, but his mind was racing and he knew his eyes wouldn't stay closed until they at least attempted to find out what news Zane had for them.

"No." Aidan grabbed the phone from its perch on the bookshelf and carried it over to the bed, setting it down in front of Wyatt and sitting so they were facing each other. "Do you want to call or should I?"

They both looked a lot calmer than they felt, but Wyatt thought he'd miss every button if he tried to dial and he'd drop the phone if he got an answer, so he pointed his chin at Aidan. "You call. I'll listen."

Wyatt's nervousness was adorable, and if Aidan hadn't been feeling much the same himself, he'd have pulled Wyatt into his arms and kissed his nose, just because he could. As it was, he was too nervous to do anything other than concentrate on keeping his hand steady as he pushed the buttons, and activated the speaker. He held his breath as it rang.

Four rings later, the phone was answered with a click, and a pre-recorded message began to play, telling them Zane was unavailable at the moment. With a sidelong glance at Wyatt—this wasn't going to help either of them sleep tonight—Aidan left a short message, letting Zane know they were home and asking him to please call as soon as possible. After hanging up, he looked at Wyatt, silently asking what they should do next. Neither of them was going to get any sleep until they got answers, that much was obvious. Aidan was already beginning to wish he had never noticed the light on the phone.

Wordlessly, Wyatt took the phone from Aidan and quickly punched in numbers before holding it out so Aidan could activate the speaker. This time, it was answered quickly. "Aidan! How are you?" Carina's voice poured out of the speakers, sounding far louder than Aidan had anticipated.

He jerked in shock, surprised at who Wyatt had chosen to call, and blinked down at the phone for a few seconds before he found his voice. "Hey, Carina. I'm a little worried, actually."

Carina's voice immediately took on a note of concern. "Why? What happened?"

"Well, nothing. Yet."

Wyatt leaned in close to the speaker. "We got a message from Zane. He said he had some information for us about the people who, uh, had me, before."

"We haven't been able to reach him, though." Aidan picked up the thread of the conversation smoothly when Wyatt's voice faltered. "We were hoping you'd know what he wanted to tell us... or at least how we could reach him."

"Sorry." Carina sounded more worried than apologetic, and that sent a sharp stab of fear through Aidan's gut. "I talked to Zane yesterday, and he said he might have to leave town to look into something for another case of mine, but he didn't mention anything about having any news for you. What number did he leave?"

Aidan rattled off the number Zane had left. When Carina confirmed that was the number she had for him as well, Aidan's heart sank. "Well, if you hear from him, let us know right away. *Please*." He tried to keep his voice calm and his feelings under control. Wyatt's anxiety was mounting with each passing second, and one of them needed to keep a clear head long enough to finish the conversation with Carina.

"I will. And I'll check around to see if I can't find another number for him. I'll let you know as soon as I know anything." Carina paused, and the air in the room stilled in anticipation. "While I have you on the phone," she finally continued in a completely different tone of voice. She'd been confident, if worried, before, but this sounded hesitant and not at all like the Carina that Aidan was used to speaking to.

Wyatt noticed the uncertain tone as well, and his anxiety spiked as he leaned in closer to the speaker. "What is it, Carina?" He reached across the phone and took Aidan's hand as they waited for her to gather her words once more. Whatever she had to say, it didn't sound good, and he needed the physical contact with Aidan while he heard it.

"Your friends from back home are getting more aggressive, Wyatt." A little of the confidence returned to Carina's voice, and her words were soft and unhurried. "I'm worried that they'll attract attention from the wrong people if we don't do something."

"Like what?" Aidan was sure he already knew the answer, but he wanted to hear it said aloud so that neither he nor Wyatt could pretend Carina meant something else.

Surprising everyone, Wyatt got the words out before Carina could say anything. "You want to contact them, don't you? I think—" He swallowed hard, his mouth suddenly dry and his lips uncooperative. "I think you should."

"What?" The word came simultaneously from the phone's speakers and Aidan's lips, sounding equally shocked and amazed from both sources. "Are you sure?" Aidan continued, "You really didn't want to before."

"We will probably have to send them something directly from you, Wyatt," Carina cautioned, picking up immediately where Aidan had left off without giving Wyatt a chance to respond. "I doubt they'll believe anyone without something to prove they're speaking on your behalf... and at your request."

"I know." Wyatt smiled and squeezed Aidan's hand, taking comfort from his lover's presence. He needed it for what he was about to say. "Tell them...." He paused, sucking in a deep breath and concentrating so he could get everything out without stopping again. "Tell them I'd like to see them, if they can come here."

This time, both Aidan and Carina were stunned into silence. That was the last thing either of them had expected, and if Aidan hadn't been able to feel Wyatt's sincerity through their Bond, he wouldn't have believed it at all. He still didn't, not really. Only a few months ago, Wyatt had been terrified of the idea that his friends were looking for him, and now he was suggesting that they meet? His mouth fell open and he gaped at Wyatt, unable to find any words to express what he was feeling.

Carina found words before Aidan did. "Are you sure? That could be dangerous, Wyatt."

"No more dangerous than me sending something to them. At least if they see me, they'll know for sure that I'm all right." He shrugged as he scooted around on the bed until his shoulder pressed against Aidan's. "Then I know they'll stop looking."

Aidan slid his arm around Wyatt's waist. "But what if they tell someone? Are you positive you want to risk that?" he asked in a worried voice.

Carina echoed the sentiment over the phone line. "If they tell the wrong person, or say the wrong thing on their site, your parents could find out. The people who held you could find out."

"I know," Wyatt replied, feeling contented as he realized he really was. There was a tiny tingle of doubt in the back of his mind, but he pushed it aside, holding on to the gut feeling that it was the right thing to do. "I think we can trust them. They were good friends when I was younger, and they obviously care."

"If you're sure."

Carina's agreement sounded dubious at best, but Wyatt ignored it and nodded as he rested his head on Aidan's shoulder. "I am."

"All right." Carina sighed. "I'll start looking into contacting them in the morning. And I'll see if I can find anything about what Zane wanted to tell you as well."

"Thanks, Carina."

"Anytime."

Aidan hung up the phone and looked from it to the head of the bed where their mussed pillows lay, looking tempting. Wyatt was limp and heavy against him, exhaustion forcing his eyes mostly closed despite the worry he still felt about whatever it was Zane had called to tell them. It was adorable but problematic, and Aidan needed him to wake up enough to lie down properly. "Hey," he said, gently nudging Wyatt with his shoulder. "Let's lie down, okay?"

Wyatt lifted his head, blinked sleepily, nodded, and slowly began crawling back toward his pillow. It hurt to move. Every muscle in his body ached with the need to sleep, and even when he collapsed onto his stomach, his face buried in the pillow, the hurt didn't fully go away. "Are you coming?" he asked, turning his head a little and peeling one eye open to search for Aidan. He wasn't going to fall asleep tonight without Aidan curled up at his side.

"Of course. Just let me put the phone back and get the light." Aidan brushed his hand across Wyatt's cheek and neck as he climbed out of bed.

"Okay." Wyatt leaned into the touch, making a contented sound, then reburied his face in the pillow. He was hardly aware when the light switched off and only noticed the dipping of the bed because it was followed by a warm body wrapping around his. As soon as Aidan relaxed against his side, Wyatt slept, his body too exhausted for him to dream.

Chapter Twenty-Two

AIDAN couldn't move. His limbs were heavy, weighted down by some unseen force, and the more he thought about it, the harder it became to draw in air. His eyes would have been wide with panic, but they were stuck in a half-lidded position. He didn't dare attempt to close them, out of fear he would succeed and wouldn't be able to get them open again. He tried to lick his lips and swallow to wet his painfully dry mouth, but his tongue and throat were just as resistant to movement as the rest of his body, and the effort left him with dry lips and the taste of granite on his tongue.

He was lying on his back in what appeared to be an opulent bedroom, though it was all done up in shades of gray and the air was strangely calm. The bed, or whatever it was he was on, seemed to be relatively high, and his head was propped up with what he assumed were pillows, giving him a perfect view of closed ornate double doors.

When he got past the initial panic of his limbs not responding, Aidan realized that, because his head and eyes were positioned so he couldn't actually see his body, he had no idea what he was wearing or if he was wearing anything at all. The last thing he remembered was curling up in bed, naked, and falling asleep while holding Wyatt. Now, he couldn't feel sheets or clothes or anything over his body. Come to think of it, he couldn't feel anything under his body either, though he assumed there had to be something there. He felt far too heavy to be floating.

There was something about the situation he felt he ought to recognize, but his brain was responding slowly, too, as though it was also weighted down by whatever was making it impossible for him to move and difficult for him to breathe. He couldn't think of whatever it was he was supposed to remember. He knew that ought to disturb him, but the panic was just as slow in coming as his thoughts were in processing.

He lay there, not trying to move any more, strangely lethargic as his limbs grew heavier and heavier. His eyelids drooped slightly, cutting a few feet of the wall out of his vision. As they moved, he thought that perhaps he should try to push them back open, just in case they closed all the way, but before he finished the thought, they'd stopped, the extra weight apparently balanced out by the position of his head. It was just as well; trying to force them open would have involved caring, and Aidan didn't. He didn't think. He didn't feel. He didn't do anything except lie there, perfectly still and completely unaware of anything except the wall and doors his gaze was pointed toward. Even they were fading away, becoming blurry and indistinct until he could hardly make them out at all.

The doors crashed open with a blur of movement and a strangely muffled thud. Now there was a darker area in Aidan's vision, still blurry and indistinct, but a change in surroundings he'd already come to accept as unchangeable. He would have frowned if he'd been able to and cared enough to do so. He didn't, though, and the dark hole stayed where it was as his vision began to blur further. Soon the wall and doors were a haze of gray, and the change no longer mattered at all.

Something not-gray moved into his field of vision. Pink, his brain supplied, though slowly, and not until his entire view was blocked by something round and pink with bits of brown at the top and round greenish circles in the middle. Aidan's brain supplied the adjectives slowly and unwillingly, and he knew without thinking that none of them belonged in this place. It was gray and still here, and that was all it was ever supposed to be. Color and movement did not belong.

Nor did sound, but there was some, soft and urgent in his ear. When he concentrated, Aidan could make out words, strung together and spewed out in a panicked tone that made no sense to him.

"Oh, God, Aidan. No. This shouldn't— You can't— Oh God!"

Something stirred within Aidan, and he knew he should recognize the voice, knew the words should mean something, and knew there was something he needed to say, something he needed the blur of color and motion and sound to do. It didn't matter, though, because he couldn't remember, couldn't speak, couldn't care, and soon he wouldn't be able to hear or see to do so anyway.

The voice continued, but the words ran together until it was just sound. The colors and shapes faded until they were distorted and indistinct. And then, they were all gone, and there was nothing.

WYATT ran blindly through the hallway, doing his best to stay in the center as he careened around corners and clomped down stairs. The floors were getting sticky and hard to move over, but in the middle, they were relatively solid, and if he pushed himself he could run and only leave faint impressions of his shoes behind. The walls were melting, though: doors, lockers, and pictures dripping down into grotesque parodies of what they used to be. The floor near the walls was liquefying, puddles of goo that refused to support any sort of weight without completely sinking into itself and trapping whatever pressed on it.

Wyatt had almost been caught once, when he'd stumbled toward a door he was certain led back into the room he had been in only a second earlier. One moment, he'd been sobbing as he'd watched Aidan complete the final transformation from flesh to granite, becoming stone just like the rest of the spaceship he was trapped on, and the next he was in the hallway of what looked to be his old school, facing a set of double doors that had already started to melt. He had lunged forward, desperate to get back to Aidan, desperate to hold on to whatever remained of his Bondmate, and sank into the floor as the door had melted around his hand.

As he'd struggled to get free, Wyatt heard a voice he didn't recognize calling his name and had doubled his efforts, straining against the hot, sludge-like material until he tumbled back into the center of the hallway, covered in goo but otherwise unencumbered. His shoe had come off his foot as he pulled, and he was now running lopsidedly with his sock hanging off his toes. It made moving awkward, but he didn't dare stop to fix it or take off his other shoe. He had to get out of the building before it melted completely, and he had to do it while avoiding the person he could hear moving behind him. Whoever it was kept calling his name, asking him to wait, begging him to listen, but he couldn't listen. Stopping would be deadly, so he just ran.

The floor beneath his feet grew softer as he moved, stumbling through the hallways and only finding more stairs. There seemed to be an endless supply of them, and there were no windows or room numbers or anything else to indicate what floor he was on or how many more flights of stairs he had to make his way down before he could find his way out of the building. Every so often, the stairs he was on would come to an end, and he'd go in search of a door out but only find melting walls and more stairs. It was then that was the most dangerous, for the person chasing him had a straight shot, and if he looked back, Wyatt knew he would see whoever it was.

He didn't look, he just ran and ran, his legs aching and his lungs burning as his eyes searched frantically for a window or a door or even a thin spot in the melting wall. Anything that would lead him outside where he could find help, get away from the person chasing him, and get off the endless supply of stairs.

AIDAN picked up speed as the floor beneath his feet suddenly became solid again. Ahead, he could see Wyatt launching himself from a window, and he followed without hesitation, his foot hitting the windowsill as he launched himself into the air. Wyatt landed in a second-story window of the next house over, so Aidan angled his body so that his jump would take him to that spot.

Behind him, he could hear the wolves and pumas and knew that anyone who remained in the house they'd just left had been devoured by the beings that used to be their pets.

He felt a brief pang of regret for whoever they were, but there was no time to mourn them. The animals were following him, and he had to catch up to Wyatt and convince him to wake them both up. It was time he called Kyler—Wyatt had fought a mild fever for five days, but now it had reached dangerous levels—but he couldn't while he was trapped in a series of bizarre nightmares brought on by a fever that had spiked sometime during the night.

At least in this dream and the one before it, he knew what he needed to do and was able to move to do so. He never, ever wanted to repeat the dream about the stone room that wanted him to be a permanent part of it.

Now if he could just get Wyatt to stop running from him.

He landed in the window, startling an already surprised girl, and dashed past her without so much as a by-your-leave. "Get out of here!" he called back as he flew out of the room, hoping he wasn't too late to see which way Wyatt went and breathing a brief sigh of relief when he saw Wyatt disappear through a door down the hall. He followed, flinging the door open and cursing under his breath as he saw Wyatt jump out the wide-open window and sail into the air.

There was no time for regrets. He could hear the animals snapping and snarling behind him, their yips and growls punctuated by screams of pain and terror that made him cringe, and Wyatt was floating off, soon to be lost in the myriad of houses that dotted the landscape. Aidan jumped, hoping the girl who had occupied the room he'd landed in had managed to get out before the animals came, even as he wondered if she was at all real or just a figment of Wyatt's fevered imagination.

They hopped from house to house, Wyatt always managing to stay just ahead of Aidan and never looking back to see that it was his Bondmate behind him. The pack of animals chasing them grew with each house they landed in, their presence apparently enough of a catalyst to turn any domesticated animals in the houses into their wild counterparts. Occasionally, Aidan would see other people floating away after jumping out of the houses' other windows, but mostly the people inside died screaming. He did his best to block the sounds from his mind, reminding himself that the sooner he caught Wyatt, the sooner the whole thing would stop.

WYATT landed in a bedroom and dashed through it, not even checking to see if there was a person inside. When he reached the hallway, there were stairs in front of him and he ran down without thinking, forgetting about the need to jump from the windows or the person chasing him or the pack of wild animals chasing him. He had to get to the kitchen. Salvation would be found in a bowl of cake batter.

The kitchen was easy to locate at the back of the house near the stairs, but once Wyatt reached it, he realized he had no idea how to bake a cake. The kitchen was stocked with everything he could need, he was sure, but despite the numerous bowls and mixing utensils on the counter and the state-of-the-art oven on one wall, there was nothing, anywhere, to give him a clue what needed to be done.

It wasn't fair. They'd rarely had cakes when he was a child, and when they did, his mother didn't let him or his siblings anywhere near the kitchen. The chances that Wyatt especially would mess something up, ruining the family treat, was great, and she hadn't been willing to take that risk. Aidan hadn't shown him, either, making the cakes for Wyatt's and Nolan's birthdays while Wyatt was at work, and the only other cake they'd had was bought from a bakery instead of homemade. Why anyone would even think Wyatt would know what to do was beyond him, and as he stared at the stainless steel appliances and myriad of ingredients, Wyatt clenched his fingers into fists and pressed his lips together as he blinked back tears.

The whole situation was completely unreasonable. If it was so important that this get done, Aidan ought to have been around to do it, so Wyatt wasn't saddled with a completely impossible task. Aidan wasn't around to do anything anymore, though, so it was up to Wyatt.

His hands shaking with grief, frustration, and barely suppressed anger, Wyatt began digging in the cupboards, hoping to find a box of mix or a cookbook that could give him instructions. There wasn't much time, that had been made painfully clear, and if the cake had to bake for any length of time whatsoever, they were screwed. *He* was screwed.

It had also been made clear that Wyatt was the one solely responsible for meeting these demands. Nothing would change that, and if he wanted Aidan back, he had to do this and do it right.

There had to be something that could help him, something that would let him figure this out enough that he could at least have started when time ran out, but there was nothing, only raw ingredients that made it clear he was expected to make this thing completely from scratch and without a recipe.

He couldn't. He didn't even know where to begin, and as he stared into the cupboard, it dawned on him that he was so close to everything he ever wanted and he was going to be thwarted by something as stupid as a cake. Tears began to fall from his eyes as he cursed his parents and Aidan and anyone else who could have taught him how to bake. After struggling to overcome so much, he'd failed because of this one thing, and now he was trapped alone in this kitchen with no one to help, no one to comfort him, no one to care.

He sank down to the floor, pulled his knees up to his chest, and buried his face in his arms.

AIDAN skidded to a halt as he entered the kitchen. Wyatt was curled up on the floor, his back pressed against the oven, his face red and streaked with tears. Aidan's heart constricted at the sight, his whole body momentarily freezing at the anguish he felt through their Bond. As soon as he was able to move, he crossed the room and knelt by Wyatt's side, gently placing one hand on Wyatt's shoulder as he wondered what could possibly have upset him in the normal-looking kitchen.

With a tender touch, Aidan stroked his fingers over Wyatt's cheek, brushing his knuckles over the tear tracks as he softly called his Bondmate's name. "Wyatt? Come on, it's time to wake up." He wasn't sure what sleeping inside the dream meant, but he knew it couldn't be good, and though he kept his voice soft and his motions smooth, the sense of urgency he felt grew to almost unbearable levels.

Wyatt stirred, making a soft noise as he nuzzled into Aidan's hand. He didn't open his eyes, but Aidan could tell Wyatt was waking up, so he kept talking, his voice soft and low. "Wyatt? Come on, that's it. Open your eyes for me, okay? Can you do that?"

Wyatt didn't want to, but the voice sounded so worried that Wyatt knew it would hurt him just as much to stay asleep as to wake up, so he shifted and slowly blinked, not quite ready to leave the blessed oblivion that had enveloped him. "Aidan?" he asked, disbelief coloring his tone as he rubbed at his eyes, clearing the bleariness from them and blinking again when the sight didn't change.

Aidan was staring down at him, his green eyes worried and his body composed very much of warm flesh instead of cold granite. It was the most beautiful thing Wyatt had ever seen.

He surged upward, wrapping his arms around Aidan and burying his face in the crook of Aidan's neck. Aidan embraced him, and they stayed like that for several moments, their bodies pressed close together, Wyatt thrilled Aidan was alive and Aidan relieved Wyatt had finally stopped running.

When Wyatt started to relax, Aidan pulled back a little bit, resting his forehead against Wyatt's and looking into his eyes. "Hey." He kissed Wyatt softly, though he pulled back before it turned into anything more than a gentle press of warm lips. "Listen to me, okay?"

Wyatt nodded, loosening his grip slightly and shifting into a more comfortable position. His eyes never left Aidan's, and his hands roamed over Aidan's back as he sought to reassure himself that no part of his lover was made of stone. "Okay."

Aidan took a deep breath and kissed Wyatt again. "I need you to wake me up."

The words took a moment to penetrate Wyatt's brain. When they did, his eyes widened in panic, and he shook his head frantically. "No." Even now, with the sudden reminder that he was dreaming and that Aidan had never been in any real danger, he couldn't bear the thought of the separation that would result if he woke Aidan. Even if he immediately followed, there would be a few seconds where he was here alone, and he couldn't stand that, not with the memory of Aidan turning to stone fresh.

"Wyatt, please." Aidan brushed his hand across Wyatt's forehead, wincing when he realized that it was warm, even here. "I need to call Kyler. You're sick."

"No." Wyatt shook his head and clung tighter. It didn't matter what was happening in the real world or why his dreams were so weird right now. Aidan was here, holding him, and nothing was going to convince Wyatt to let that go.

"Please." Aidan watched as the kitchen walls started to crumble around them, his stomach dropping further with each piece that broke away. "Wyatt, this dream is falling apart, and I don't know where we're going to end up next, or if we'll be together. I *need* to call Kyler." He grabbed Wyatt's shoulders. "You can pull me back to you as soon as I'm done, or I can try to wake you up if you want. Either way. But you *have* to wake me up so I can call Kyler or we're going to be stuck in these nightmares until something really bad happens."

The desperation in Aidan's voice matched what Wyatt was feeling. He hated the sensation, but he hated even more that Aidan was feeling it, so as he took in the rapidly crumbling walls and the darkness that lay beyond, he nodded. "Yeah, okay. Try to wake me?" He tried to keep his desperation out of his voice, but it was pointless. Even if he succeeded and Aidan wasn't able to feel it through their Bond, Aidan would feel the desperation in the way Wyatt kissed him, hard and fast and with no thought for finesse.

When Aidan nodded, Wyatt looked at him, smiled wanly, and pushed. With a soft pop, Aidan vanished, leaving Wyatt alone in the rapidly disintegrating room.

AIDAN rolled out of bed and stumbled toward the phone as soon as his eyes snapped open. He grabbed it from the bookcase, dialing Kyler's number from memory as he returned to the bed and began shaking Wyatt's shoulder, silently praying he would wake quickly. His skin was like fire under Aidan's palm, and he hadn't stirred at all by the time Kyler answered, sounding horribly groggy.

"Wyatt's sick. *Really* sick." Aidan flopped down on the pillow, his eyes sliding closed as Wyatt started to pull him back into the Dreamscape. He struggled against it as he begged Kyler to come quickly, explaining that he couldn't wake Wyatt and detailing the horrible nightmares he'd just escaped.

"I'm on my way. Try to stay awake."

The phone call ended with a sudden click, and Aidan's last thought was that there was no way he could comply with Kyler's request. Wyatt wouldn't let him. They were both trapped in a nightmare, too busy trying to escape the room of flesh-eating bugs to be aware of the phone that lay beeping between them or the frantic worry of their friends.

Chapter Twenty-Three

THE man crawling on the ceiling looked like an old-school horror movie vampire, complete with bald head, wrinkled skin, and horribly elongated fangs descending from a mouth full of pointy teeth. He was dressed in rags and clung to the ceiling with filthy, clawlike fingernails that he swiped ineffectively downward with every forward movement. It should have been ridiculous, and if Aidan had been watching it on television, it would have been, but while he was trapped in a dingy cellar with Wyatt unconscious at his feet, he could only be thankful the creature above him was moving slowly.

He backed up farther, crouching low so he could drag Wyatt along the dirty floor with him. After spending so long chasing his Bondmate through the Dreamscape, Aidan was glad they were together, even if Wyatt had fallen unconscious almost as soon as they'd ended up in this rundown room. He wasn't about to let anything except genuinely waking up separate him from Wyatt now.

When his back hit the wall, Aidan knelt, hoisted Wyatt into a sitting position, and began shaking him gently. "Wyatt, come on. You have to get us out of here." He wasn't sure another dream would be any better, but the creature was getting closer and looking more and more menacing with each passing moment.

Wyatt stirred. "Aidan?" He groped blindly, strong fingers finding Aidan's shoulder and squeezing as his gaze locked on the thing crawling across the ceiling. "What's going on?"

"Change the dream, Wyatt."

For a long moment, Wyatt just blinked, his eyes never leaving the creature and his fingers digging harder and harder into Aidan's shoulder. Then, without warning, the room changed around them. The walls became sleek, curved metal and the creature disappeared as the ceiling changed to finish the curve started by the walls. The corner where Aidan cowered vanished just as he and Wyatt began to drift up, floating to hover in the middle of the room.

Wyatt stared at him; the surprise reflected there also echoed over their Bond. "I don't think I can change it again. Not yet." He tightened his fingers briefly around Aidan's shoulder before letting them relax to the point that his hand almost fell free. He didn't have the energy to hold on any longer.

"We're fine." Aidan took Wyatt's hand, wrapping Wyatt's long fingers in his slightly smaller ones and forcing his lips up into a smile that would have hidden his worry from anyone other than his Bondmate. "I don't see anything dangerous here. We don't need to move just yet."

"Good." Wyatt let himself calm down. Letting his eyes drift shut, he leaned back into the air as though it were a current of water.

Aidan shook him. "Don't sleep. We're already dreaming and I need you... aware." Wyatt could theoretically do anything he could imagine in the Dreamscape, but the fact that he kept sleeping, or trying to, was worrisome. There were times his body needed more rest than actively dreaming could give him, but he wasn't supposed to be in the Dreamscape when he sought extra rest. His body only appeared here when his consciousness was present. He should have vanished when he went deeper, not curled up into a ball with closed eyes and loose muscles.

They floated together for an indeterminate amount of time. Aidan kept shaking Wyatt awake while keeping a sharp eye out for any indication of danger. None appeared, though, and the room remained unchanged, seemingly warm and safe despite the fact they were floating in the middle of it.

It was strange, and it took Aidan what felt like forever to relax.

His limbs had just started to loosen when the walls of the room shook, vibrating with horrible force. A sharp rapping noise—loud and fast, almost like a knock—accompanied each rattle. There was another sound, too, almost like muffled voices, but Aidan couldn't hear it clearly, so he tuned it out, concentrating on Wyatt and the room. Wyatt looked back at him, silently asking if they needed to go.

Aidan was just about to tell him to change the dream when the walls shook again. This time the rapping noise took on a familiar pattern. He rolled himself over in the air so he was more or less upright and took Wyatt's face in his hands. "Wake me up."

"But—"

"Wyatt. That's Kyler knocking." He hoped it was, anyway, because if someone else had interrupted them today, he wasn't going to be happy. This was the most peaceful dream they'd been in since Wyatt got sick, and Aidan was going to lose his mind if he didn't get some real rest soon. "You have to wake me up so I can let him in." When Wyatt nodded, he kissed him gently. "Try to wake yourself up, too, okay? Kyler's going to want to talk to you, and he can't do that when you're asleep."

"I could bring him here."

"He can't treat you here." Aidan smiled sadly and brushed the backs of his fingers over Wyatt's cheek. "Besides, we need to rest. I'm a little exhausted from dealing with melting buildings and evil pets and all the other things your fevered brain cooked up for us."

"I'm sorry." Wyatt looked down and held back the tears stinging his eyes. He wasn't going to give into them, not even if he was sick and exhausted and beyond confused by all the crazy things his mind kept throwing them into. "I don't know why I can't control it."

"It's all right. Just wake me up." The less they said about Wyatt's attempt to control the Dreamscape right now, the better. Wyatt had tried to regain control right after Aidan's phone call to Kyler. Aidan hadn't been able to wake him and Wyatt hadn't been able to stop himself from pulling Aidan back into the Dreamscape. Everything he'd tried to do had ended up twisted, and Aidan didn't even want to think about the way the sand of their favorite beach turned into hundreds of thousands of tiny creatures that tried to devour them or how the sun had fallen toward them in a fiery ball when they tried to watch it set from the balcony of their apartment. Aidan had insisted Wyatt stop trying to control things, and they had ended up in the dingy room with the vampire-thing crawling on the ceiling.

It had been a slight improvement anyway, and Wyatt's efforts at changing the dream had been more successful, if a little weird. Now, however, Aidan needed out so he could let Kyler in and hopefully end this entire ordeal with a night of restful sleep.

"Okay." Wyatt leaned in and gently kissed Aidan, then closed his eyes and concentrated. He didn't bother to open them once Aidan was gone, just lay back and drifted. He didn't have the energy to try to wake himself.

"SPECIAL delivery, sir. A rush."

Elliott motioned the mail clerk into his office and looked up as she placed a small package wrapped in plain brown paper on his desk. There was no address on it, just his name written in block letters. He quirked an eyebrow as he looked at it. "Who's it from?"

"I'm not sure, sir. It was dropped off at the front desk, and they called and asked me to deliver it." The clerk shrugged as she held out a tablet with the delivery queued up on the screen.

"I see." Elliott pressed his thumb to the tablet, signing for the package. "Thank you."

The clerk nodded and left, her gaze fixed on the floor and the tablet clutched to her chest. Elliott followed her to the door, watching until she disappeared around the corner before shutting it firmly and returning to his desk with a smile on his face.

His heart beat in a rapid pitter-patter as he opened the package with steady hands, resisting the urge to tear into it. If it contained what he thought it did, it was too valuable to just rip the paper off. Carefully, he folded back the brown wrapper to reveal a slip of plain white paper with "5:00" written on it in the same block style as the outer wrapper. Under it was a black plastic box that opened easily when he pressed his thumb against the latch to reveal a glass vial nestled in a bed of foam. Elliott lifted it free carefully, smiling as he read the word written in black ink across the glass.

Vinculex. If the note meant what he thought it did, in just three hours, Wyatt Mettler would be his again.

AIDAN yanked the door open, the words of greeting dying on his lips when he saw who was standing there. Instead of the eccentric doctor he'd expected, he found himself faced with Wyatt's brother and a slender brunette woman who looked enough like Wyatt and Damon that she had to be Tabatha. Aidan leaned heavily against the door, blinking and trying to figure out what was going on. "Damon?" He briefly squeezed his eyes shut and sucked in a deep breath, trying to fortify himself. He was too tired to fight Wyatt's pull for long. "What are you doing here?"

"Visiting Wyatt?" Damon looked Aidan up and down, frowning as he took in the dark circles under Aidan's eyes and the pale pallor of his skin. "We talked about coming today, remember?"

"Today? Fuck." Aidan tried to sort out dates and times in his head but found that if what Damon was saying was right, he was definitely missing a day or two. "It's already the fourth?" Another wave of exhaustion washed over him, and he slumped against the door, his eyes falling shut as he struggled to keep himself awake.

"Yeah." Damon stepped forward, catching Aidan by the shoulders as he slipped farther. "Are you all right?"

Aidan didn't want to lean on Damon. He barely knew the man, and there was still the possibility Zane's message involved him in some way. But his grip was strong, and if Aidan didn't lean on someone, he was going to fall asleep where he stood. "Wyatt's sick," he managed, struggling to straighten his knees. "Fever dreams are not restful."

"Okay, so why are you—?"

Damon cut his sister off with a sharp look. "They're Bonded, Tabatha," he hissed before returning his attention to Aidan. "How long? Has he seen a doctor?"

"Couple days. I think." He really wasn't sure anymore. He had thought it was the first or second of Mago. To find that it was already the fourth was worrisome. "Doctor is on his way. Made Wyatt wake me up 'cause I thought he was at the door." He slumped more even with the added support of Damon's hands on his shoulders. There was no way he was going to make it much longer before Wyatt succeeded in pulling him back to the Dreamscape. "He's trying to pull me back in." More likely Wyatt just wasn't coherent enough to fight it, as he had to make a conscious decision not to pull Aidan into the Dreamscape when he was there. It was up to Aidan to fight it now.

Yet Aidan wasn't sure he wanted to. If he didn't need to be awake to open the door for Kyler, he'd stumble to the nearest soft surface and give in to the tempting pull of sleep. His body needed the rest, and sharing nightmares with Wyatt would be far less awkward than conversation with a brother-in-law he barely knew and a sister-in-law he'd just now met.

Tabatha looked from Damon to Aidan. Her mind was still reeling from the knowledge that Wyatt was alive and free and apparently doing well. She had not expected to be greeted by *this*. It was almost too much. "Is there something we can do?"

"Wake him up," Aidan managed as he forced his body to straighten and turned himself toward the couch. If he was lucky, he would make it that far. There was no way he was going to make it to the bedroom. As it was, he was going to have to hope Damon would catch him and keep him from hitting his head on anything if he fell asleep midstep. "Then wake me up." He gestured with one arm toward the back of the apartment so she would know where Wyatt was and took one staggering step forward.

Damon barely caught him before he hit the ground.

IN ALL the times Tabatha Alders, née Mettler, imagined reuniting with her older brother, the scenario she faced never crossed her mind. Wyatt was sprawled out on a large bed, the covers tangled around his legs and one foot hanging off the side. She could see the flush of his skin even from the doorway, and from the restless manner in which his head and limbs moved, it was apparent he wasn't sleeping comfortably.

She wanted to go in and wake him as Aidan and Damon told her to, but she found she couldn't set foot inside the room. The mere sight of Wyatt—taller and bulkier than she remembered and with a slightly different haircut and a few extra wrinkles—was enough to freeze her limbs. This was why she had flown across the country, lying to her boss about where she was going and swearing her Bondmate to secrecy, but now that she was here, she couldn't take that final step.

Damon came up behind her, laid his hands on her shoulders, and she twisted her head to look at him. She felt as though she should say something to explain why she was hovering in the doorway watching Wyatt toss and turn in the rumpled bed, but she couldn't find the words and ended up just gaping at him, her mouth opening and closing like a fish's.

"I know." Damon squeezed his sister's shoulders and stepped around her into the room. "It's hard to believe, even when he's right there." He was doing a little better than Tabatha was because he'd seen Wyatt a few weeks earlier and had spoken to him on the phone since, but this was still hard to take. Aidan's appearance had rattled Damon, but Wyatt's had his gut in knots. He could only imagine how Tabatha must feel, to have *this* be her first sight of Wyatt in over twelve years.

It didn't matter, though. If they were going to get the answers they needed to pass along to the doctor when he arrived, they had to wake Wyatt up, and now. Damon shoved down the misgivings he felt at invading his brother's bedroom and crossed the floor with swift steps. Wyatt's bare shoulders were frighteningly hot when Damon touched them, and he winced. "Wyatt," he said, keeping his voice low as he began gently shaking his younger brother. "Time to wake up."

Wyatt shifted and made a soft sound in protest, but his eyes remained closed. Damon shook harder, raising his voice slightly. "Come on, Wyatt. I need you to wake up for me."

Again, Wyatt made a soft, unhappy sound but didn't stir. His nose scrunched a little and his eyes tightened, but he gave no other indication he was at all affected by what Damon was doing.

Damon cast a worried glance at Tabatha, who had stepped a few feet into the room and stood peering at the bed, ready to bolt if something happened, though she wasn't sure if she would move toward Wyatt or out the door. She doubted she would know until she moved.

"Wyatt!" Now Damon was yelling, the sound horribly loud in the silent room, and he was shaking Wyatt hard enough that his head started to rock on the pillow as Damon jerked his shoulders back and forth.

This time, the noise of protest that escaped Wyatt's lips was accompanied by an uncoordinated bat of his hand toward Damon's arm, and he peered up at his brother through slitted eyes. "Damon?" he slurred, not sure he was actually seeing his brother standing over him. "What're you doin' here?"

Damon let out a relieved laugh as he grinned down at his brother. "You invited us, remember?"

"Us?" Wyatt rubbed his eyes and blinked. He could only see Damon, but he didn't dare turn his head as the room spun.

"Yeah. Us." Damon brushed the sweat-slick hair back from Wyatt's forehead and stepped back a little so he was no longer blocking Wyatt's view of their sister. "Tabatha's here too."

When Wyatt lifted his head a little and peered at her, Tabatha waved back awkwardly. "Hey, Wyatt."

Only the good manners Wyatt learned as a small child let him respond in kind. "Hey." He let his head fall back to the pillow and looked up at Damon again. He wasn't entirely sure this wasn't another dream he couldn't control. "Where's Aidan?" His Bondmate had been with him, a warm and comforting presence at his side in the wind-whipped void he'd been floating in before he'd opened his eyes to find his brother staring down at him with a worried look on his face. He didn't like having his siblings present without Aidan there.

"Asleep on the couch." Damon shook his head, a fondly amused smile on his face to mask the worry he felt when he thought about how Aidan had collapsed. "He barely managed to let us inside before you pulled him back into the Dreamscape. I had to carry him to the couch. He told us to wake you up so you can both talk to the doctor when he gets here."

"Kyler?"

"I guess? Aidan didn't say before he fell asleep." Damon slid a hand under Wyatt's back, barely hiding a wince when his hand brushed against the sweat-wet sheets. "Can you get up? We should probably all wait out in the front room."

"Maybe?" Wyatt struggled to sit up and found himself grateful for Damon's hand before he was halfway there. The world tilted ominously, rocking back and forth and threatening to dump him off the bed, and it was only Damon's support that kept him from toppling over or falling back. "No."

"All right, just lean on me, okay? Move your feet and let me do the work." He pulled Wyatt's arm around his shoulder and heaved, dragging his brother out of the bed and up into a mostly standing position. "You good?"

The noise Wyatt made wasn't one of assent, and he buried his face in Damon's shoulder, but Damon started moving anyway. Wyatt would likely fall asleep before he felt ready to move, and Damon wasn't going to let that happen.

When they reached her, Tabatha ducked under Wyatt's free arm, taking some of his weight off Damon. Wyatt tensed a little at having the sister he hadn't seen in so many years pressed close to his side, but he lacked the energy and coordination to pull away, so the three of them made their way down the hall, Damon and Tabatha awkwardly dodging pictures and doorframes as their shoulders brushed against the walls.

They dumped Wyatt on the couch, and Damon shook Aidan until he slowly opened his eyes and shifted enough that he was sort of sitting up. Tabatha took a seat in one of the chairs, eyeing her brother and his Bondmate with a curious expression, but Damon stood in front of the couch, his calves pressed against the coffee table and his arms crossed over his chest as he waited. It only took a minute before Aidan slumped to the side, his shoulder hitting Wyatt's, and Wyatt's head tilted to rest against the top of Aidan's.

Damon poked them both in the shoulder. "Stay awake. The doctor will be here soon."

Aidan rolled his head against the back of the couch so he was peering at Damon through heavily lidded eyes. "Yeah, okay." He let his head fall back to the side and his eyelids droop. "Bastard better get here soon."

Fortunately, there was a knock on the door before Damon could come up with an appropriate response. He rushed over and yanked it open to find a casually dressed man with tousled hair and startlingly blue eyes. "Are you the doctor?" he asked, leaning against the door and blocking most of the entrance with his body.

"Yeah. And you are?" Kyler pushed past Damon and headed straight to the couch, pulling out a tablet and a thermometer as he walked.

Damon swiftly secured the door and hurried after him. "Wyatt's brother."

Kyler kept his back to Damon and stuck the thermometer in Wyatt's ear, swearing under his breath when he saw the readout. "Right. He mentioned you."

Damon shifted awkwardly, wondering what, exactly, his brother had said, but Kyler ignored him, checking Wyatt's pulse and breathing. He frowned at his tablet. "Hey," he said softly, gently tilting Wyatt's head so he could look in his eyes. "How long have you been feeling like this?"

"We got home on the twenty-eighth," Aidan answered for him, forcing his eyes open. "I think it started then."

Wyatt managed to nod before a cough that started deep in his chest wracked his whole body. He wrapped his arms around himself and doubled over so his shoulder rested against Kyler's thigh. "Shit. Can you...?" He waved one arm back and forth until Kyler got the idea and pushed him up to lean against the back of the couch.

Ten minutes later, Kyler started digging in the bag he'd dropped on the coffee table when he'd first arrived. "You," he said, looking at Wyatt, "have pneumonia. And you,"—he transferred his gaze to Aidan—"are exhausted, and I wouldn't be surprised if you ended up with pneumonia."

"Not my fault." Aidan shifted into a slightly more horizontal position, his head pillowed on Wyatt's shoulder. "Wyatt's crazy fever dreams aren't exactly restful."

"No, I don't imagine they are." Kyler carefully maneuvered Aidan off Wyatt's shoulder and chuckled when Aidan sleepily glared at him. "Let's get you both back to bed." They opened their mouths to protest, but he silenced them with a stern look and a pointed finger. He angled it at Wyatt first. "*You* are going to take something so you sleep deeply enough that you don't dream. And then we'll see how quickly *you* fall asleep," he finished, pointing at Aidan.

There was a tense moment during which Kyler worried Wyatt would complain, but Wyatt simply nodded and let them help him to his feet.

Aidan followed along under his own power, though barely, and watched through heavy eyes as Kyler pressed a syringe against Wyatt's neck and released the sedative with the push of a button. He drifted, not quite awake but unwilling to fall asleep until Kyler laid a hand on his shoulder.

"He's out," Kyler said. "Go to sleep."

Aidan did, his body immediately falling into a deep, dreamless slumber.

Chapter Twenty-Four

AIDAN wasn't sure what woke him—Damon frantically shaking his shoulder or the sudden feeling of *wrong* he got over his Bond with Wyatt. They happened simultaneously, jolting him into awareness with an abruptness that left his head spinning. He blinked in the unexpected light as he rolled over, propping himself up on one arm to look at Wyatt and then Kyler before his vision fully cleared. "What happened?"

Kyler draped his stethoscope around his shoulders and poked some buttons on the screen of his tablet. "He needs a hospital. He's worse than I thought."

Wyatt was still deeply asleep, but his face was scrunched in pain, and his breath came in heavy, painful-sounding gasps. Aidan took his hand and frowned when Wyatt's fingers remained limp in his. Even when he was deeply asleep, Wyatt *always* responded when Aidan laced their fingers together. Aidan had spent several late nights testing the theory before wrapping himself around Wyatt and giving in to the siren's call of sleep and pleasant dreams. Wyatt's complete lack of response worried him almost as much as the labored breathing.

"How long…?" He shook his head, uncertain if he was asking how long Wyatt had been struggling to breathe, how long he'd been asleep, or how long it would take to get to the hospital. Possibly all three. The exhaustion weighing down his limbs clouded his brain, and he was practically trembling with the effort it took to keep himself upright.

"Ten minutes, maybe. You haven't been asleep long." Kyler clicked off the tablet and began packing his bag. "He just started having trouble breathing, but I don't want to wait. He needs the hospital now."

"Should I call?" Aidan gestured to the phone on top of the bookcase, though he knew Kyler had one in his pocket and he could see one clipped to Damon's belt.

"It'll be just as fast to drive him."

"Yeah. Okay." Aidan let his head fall back to the pillow. He knew he needed to get up, to put on some clothes, and to make himself presentable enough for the trip, but he was totally drained of energy.

A T-shirt and a pair of loose pants landed on his chest and he wondered how they'd gotten there.

"Put those on." Damon emerged from the closet, holding clothes that should fit Wyatt, and crossed to the bed to help Kyler manhandle Wyatt into them, curious if they'd have to dress Aidan as well.

They did. He dropped back to sleep without responding to Damon's command, and Damon decided without consulting anyone that it would be easier to dress him and then wake him again rather than trying it the other way around. Wyatt was sick, but Aidan was clearly almost as bad, and his complete exhaustion gave Damon a little bit of insight into what his parents had feared when they'd seemed almost desperate to get a teenage Dreamer out of the house.

It made him angry all over again.

AIDAN could barely keep his eyes open as he followed Kyler and Damon, who carried Wyatt between them. A large part of him wanted to jump forward, push Damon out of the way, and take up the burden himself, but the heavy weariness in his limbs and the phantom bricks hanging from his eyelashes overrode that desire.

They were halfway down the hall when the door started rattling with the thud of a heavy fist against it. Kyler looked back at Aidan. "Were you expecting anyone else?"

"No?" He shook his head, wishing he could remember. He didn't *think* he'd called anyone else, but he'd lost track of several days and hadn't been expecting Damon and Tabatha either, so it was possible he'd forgotten a phone call he'd made. Or perhaps one of their other friends had decided to stop by. "I don't think so. It could be Ratri or Olin or someone, though."

Tabatha popped her head into the hallway from where she'd been waiting near the door. "Should I open it?"

Aidan didn't really want her to, but they had to open it to get Wyatt to the hospital, and there wasn't much sense in delaying the inevitable. "Yeah, go ahead." They could send whoever it was away and get going without a long conversation right at the door. "Tell them... I don't know. Just, go ahead and open it." He'd make himself move around Kyler and Damon once there was room to pass so he could deal with whoever it was.

Tabatha scurried out to the front just as the banging got louder. "Hold on a minute! I'm coming!" It took her a few moments to fumble with the complicated lock Kyler had secured after they'd originally gotten Wyatt into bed, and the banging picked up again before she got it open.

When she did, she wished that she'd taken longer.

Eight people clustered on the other side of the door. Two wearing suits stood at the front of the group, surrounded by four burly men and two lithe women, all wearing dark blue uniforms and looking exceedingly serious. "Is this Wyatt Mettler's residence?" the man wearing the light gray suit asked, his face twisted into a frown as he tried to peer around Tabatha into the apartment.

"Who's asking?" She shifted subtly, trying to block the view and keep them from seeing Kyler and Damon carefully setting Wyatt on the loveseat.

The other suited man stepped forward, pulling a sheaf of papers from the inside pocket of his navy jacket. "My name is Crispin Aller. I'm here on behalf of Reyes Frontier Incorporated. We've obtained proof that Mr. Mettler was permanently assigned to us as a slave." He handed the forged papers to Tabatha and pushed his way past her into the apartment. "I'm sure you'll find that everything is in order there."

Aidan stepped forward at the unexpected threat to Wyatt, drawing on reserves of energy he didn't know he had. He crossed his arms and stopped in front of the man, their toes practically touching, and looked down into his eyes. He'd never been more grateful for his above-average height. "Get out of my apartment."

Crispin raised his eyebrow as he looked up. "And you are?" He suspected he knew. He'd anticipated the protest, calling in several favors to earn the paycheck Elliott was giving him.

"Aidan Donecoff. This is my apartment." It took a lot of effort, but he managed to keep his voice and body steady. "I need you to leave."

"Just as soon as Wyatt Mettler agrees to come with us, we will." Crispin snatched the papers from Tabatha and shoved them at Aidan, then pushed past, practically knocking Aidan over as he shoved against him with his shoulder.

On a normal day, his push wouldn't have even rocked Aidan, but shock and exhaustion had him staggering backward. He caught himself with a hand on the wall and twisted to follow without glancing at the papers. "You need to leave *now*. Without Wyatt." He'd told Wyatt again and again that no one was going to come and get him and that they *couldn't* take him by force. He wasn't going to let that be a lie. "Get out of my apartment or I'll call the police."

"We brought the police with us." The smaller man in the light-colored suit stepped into the apartment, gently pushing Tabatha aside. She went without resistance, too stunned to do anything else. Her feet moved almost of their own accord, shuffling just enough to keep her body upright.

The men and women in the dark blue uniforms poured in behind the guy in the gray suit just as soon as Tabatha was out of the way, forming a semicircle that blocked all access to the door. Crispin grinned as they stopped, their poses casually threatening, the guns on their hips apparent. "As you can see, the police are already here, and they're on our side."

Crispin's tone was so casually smarmy that Aidan wanted to deck him. His fingers clenched into a fist, but Kyler stopped him from going any further with a light hand on his shoulder. "You won't help him by getting out of control, Aidan."

"What am I supposed to do?" he hissed, not caring if any of the men or women could hear. It was all he could do to keep his gaze from falling on the loveseat and revealing Wyatt's not-too-hidden position and obvious vulnerability. "I'm not letting them take him!"

"I already called Carina. She's on her way."

That calmed Aidan a little, as did the fact that Damon and Tabatha had moved to flank him. Kyler stepped up to his right side, putting Tabatha farthest away from any immediately apparent danger, and together the four of them formed their own wall between the men in suits and the loveseat.

Unfortunately, their four-person wall couldn't block eight people simultaneously. Both of the men in suits managed to slip around them as the policemen and women stepped forward in a more obvious assault, and they found Wyatt quickly. Crispin tucked the holograph back into his suit jacket and motioned two of the burlier men forward. "James, Trevor. Scott and I will need your assistance with this."

The two men stepped forward, and the other four officers moved to fill in their places. The walls were evenly matched now, but Aidan wasn't at all concerned with that. All he saw was four strangers hovering over Wyatt, threatening to take him away and discussing him as though he were a *thing* and not a person. Both Kyler and Damon held Aidan's upper arms, and it was only the pressure of their fingers digging into his flesh that kept him from throwing himself forward and blindly attacking the men circling his Bondmate.

"You can't take him."

"On the contrary, Mr. Donecoff, I can. I have papers from the courts that say so. Wyatt Mettler belongs to my company. You'll find that the courts back us up." He looked down his nose as he spoke, tilting his head back so he could address the three taller men.

"My brother isn't a *thing*." Tabatha took a small step forward, her hands clenched into fists at her side, but ducked back behind Kyler when Crispin's appraising gaze swiveled to her.

"Your brother, is he? I don't suppose you have the same talents?" He looked up and down her body and then shook his head. "No, I suppose not. I know it was made quite clear to your parents that we were very interested in any Dreamers they could convince to take our offer. If you were one, too, well, you wouldn't be standing here."

Damon's hand fell from Aidan's arm, and suddenly Aidan found himself in the position of having to hold Damon back rather than being held back by him. "He didn't take your offer!" Damon strained against Aidan's grip, almost slipping free as the adrenaline began to leave Aidan's body and his grip weakened. "Our parents sold him! Illegally! You can't have him back, and you can't have her either!"

It was tempting to let go and see what Damon would do to the oily man for saying things like that about his brother and sister, but Aidan wasn't going to risk the others carrying Wyatt out while they were distracted with harming Crispin. "Don't," he said in a low voice, his hand resting lightly on Damon's bicep. "Not yet."

"You heard—"

"I know." He'd seen the fear in Tabatha's eyes, and worse, he could hear Wyatt's labored breathing from halfway across the room. He sounded terrible, felt worse, and both the sound and the sensation echoing over their Bond made Aidan desperate to get him to proper medical help. He never thought he'd regret listening to Kyler, but right at that moment, he wished they'd called the ambulance. Paramedics interrupting this little scene would be a perfect distraction and give them time to figure out what to do. The paramedics would probably insist on taking Wyatt to the hospital, and even if the police posted a guard outside his room, he'd still be somewhere *safe*, not dragged off where Aidan couldn't reach him. "We have to time this right."

"Yeah. Sure. Get Kyler ready."

The odds weren't good. There were four officers behind them, four men in front of them, and they were the only people in the room who weren't armed. Still, the men seemed pretty serious—Scott had gone so far as to *touch* Wyatt while inspecting the thin scar around his wrist, the only vestige of the slave bracelet Kyler removed—and Aidan couldn't stand waiting anymore. He was about to drag Damon and Kyler forward with him, consequences be damned, because he was *not* letting them take Wyatt without a fight, when he remembered something. "You can't take him," he said again, forcing his body up straighter and silently cursing the fog enveloping his brain that kept him from remembering this crucial fact until just now. "He's my Bondmate, registered and everything. You can't take him, not without my consent, and I won't give it."

Crispin looked annoyed for a brief moment, but then smiled, his lips curling up in a way that made Aidan's stomach churn. "I have papers that say otherwise. Read them. You're going to have to fight this in court."

Aidan wouldn't do that. Wyatt was *not* leaving with these men, and it didn't matter what he had to do to stop it. They could fight in court to get him—though he was sure they would lose—but they weren't taking him. Neither of them would survive that, especially not with Wyatt so sick. "No. He's my Bondmate and he's staying with me."

"That's cute." Crispin stepped back around the loveseat and stroked the back of his fingers down Wyatt's arm in a gently possessive gesture that made Aidan's blood boil. "Trevor, if you and your people could take care of this, I think Scott, James, and I can handle Wyatt here."

Aidan saw red and surged forward, adrenaline and anger pushing his limbs beyond their limits as he struggled to get to Wyatt. Damon and Kyler were right behind him, but before they made it halfway to the loveseat, they were yanked from behind, pulled from their positions at Aidan's shoulders and forced to the ground with guns in their faces. One of the female officers slammed Tabatha against the wall and pressed her there with her entire body while the other held a gun to her temple, the dial clearly set in the lethal red zone. Aidan managed two more steps before he hit a brick wall in a blue uniform, and his arms were twisted behind his back as he was forced to his knees.

"Get off!" He bucked wildly, kicking his legs out behind him in a futile attempt to knock Trevor off his feet and break free. Trevor gripped harder until Aidan cried out in pain and then dragged him over to the loveseat. He shoved Aidan against the back of it with his arm still twisted behind his back and the cold metal of a gun jammed up underneath his chin.

It was torture, being this close to Wyatt, separated by less than a foot of padding and fabric, and unable to touch him, reassure him, or do anything to stop the men scooping him up in a gross parody of the gentle way Damon and Kyler had carried him out from the bedroom. Scott took Wyatt's legs, James grabbed him under his arms, and Crispin walked with them, smirking down as Wyatt's breathing hitched, his wheezing getting worse with the new position.

Aidan's chest burned in sympathy, and he bucked again, drawing on the last remnants of his adrenaline in an effort to get to Wyatt. Trevor laughed, digging a knee into his back and pressing the gun tighter against his skin. "Patience. I'll let you up soon."

Soon wasn't what Aidan wanted, but the formerly cool metal of the gun was now hot against his skin, and he could feel the muscles in Trevor's hand shift as he flipped the setting higher and changed his grip on the trigger. If he moved now, the last thing he would ever see would be Wyatt being carried away from him. He'd end up a slave again, and it might not be possible to rescue him without the protection of a Bondmate. Their friends would try, Aidan was sure, but he had to be there to help them and to support Wyatt when they won, which he had to believe they could do.

All that ran through his mind with astonishing clarity and swiftness as he followed Wyatt with his gaze. It hurt to watch, both because Wyatt was being taken from him and because the pain echoing along their Bond worsened every time Wyatt was jostled, but he made himself watch until the two suits and their lackey stepped out the door with their precious cargo.

Then, as Trevor pulled the gun away from his chin, Aidan moved, rushing toward the door with speed that should have been impossible. He made it past Damon and Kyler, past Tabatha, close enough that his fingertips brushed the cool metal of the doorknob before he was jerked back by his collar and slammed hard into the wall.

As Aidan slid down, blood already dripping into his eyes, he looked on as his lover's captors walked out the door, their guns tucked back into their holsters and satisfied expressions on their faces. Trevor was the last to leave, and as the door closed behind him, Aidan's vision grayed and then blacked to nothing.

Part Three

Chapter Twenty-Five

AIDAN woke to stabbing pain and a bright light shining in his eyes. He whimpered as he tried to twist his head away and found his chin held in a hand far too small to be Wyatt's. "Stop." He tried to bat at the light, but his arms were heavy and didn't want to cooperate, and he only managed a little wave of his hand.

Another hand landed on his shoulder and a vaguely familiar voice chuckled in his ear. "Easy, Aidan. I think he got you pretty good."

"What?" He licked dry lips and blinked again as the light switched off, revealing Kyler and Damon peering down at him with concerned expressions on their faces. When he turned his head a little, he could see Tabatha sitting on his other side, her lip caught between her teeth, and she wrung her hands together in her lap. "What happened?'

"What do you remember?" Kyler tucked the light back in his pocket and dabbed at the cut on Aidan's forehead with a damp cloth. It looked worse than it really was, but the rapidly growing bump under the split skin concerned him, and he wasn't going to let Aidan up without discovering how he'd been affected by his impact with the wall.

"We were, um…." Aidan squeezed his eyes shut, wishing he could let his head fall forward, but Kyler was still gripping his chin, keeping it firmly in place. "Hospital. We were going to the hospital. And then—" The memories rushed back. "People came and, oh God, Kyler!" He pushed at his friend. "They took Wyatt!"

Kyler struggled to keep his voice calm and his hand steady as he brought a bandage up to Aidan's forehead. "I know." It worried him more than he was willing to admit, but he had to deal with what was in front of him or he'd go crazy trying to figure out the could haves and should haves.

"So why aren't we…? We have to—Kyler!" Aidan pushed again, batting Kyler's hand away. "We can't—why aren't we following them?"

"They knocked you out, Aidan, and held us all at gunpoint. What were we—" Tabatha choked back a sob. "What were we supposed to do? There were eight of them and they had guns and they really wanted to shoot us!"

Damon put his hand on his sister's shoulder, pulling her close and tucking her head under his chin. "We would have ended up dead if we'd done anything else."

"Well, they don't have guns on us now." Aidan pushed himself up, ignoring Kyler's protests and keeping his back against the wall until he found his balance. "Let's go."

"We can't. Carina is coming and we need to—"

"We need to get Wyatt back before they drug him and lock him away somewhere to keep him dreaming their bidding for the rest of his life!"

"Aidan."

Kyler put a hand on Aidan's shoulder, but Aidan swiveled around, flinging it off. Wyatt was in trouble, in danger, and sick on top of that, and if Kyler wasn't going to help rescue him, he was the enemy right now. "We have to go get him, *now*. Are you going to help me, or not?"

Kyler closed his eyes, licked his lips, and swallowed hard. "No."

"Then get out of my way."

"I can't." He stepped forward a little, one hand outstretched. "Aidan, we'll get him back. I promise. But we have to be smart about it. Be patient."

Patience was not an option. Aidan pushed past Kyler in much the same way he'd shouldered past the men who had been there earlier, with determination backed solely by adrenaline. He had to go after Wyatt, had to do it right then, and if Kyler wasn't going to help, Aidan wasn't going to waste precious minutes trying to convince him. There wasn't time. Every minute Wyatt spent with those men was a minute too long.

Kyler staggered backward as Aidan shouldered by, stepping awkwardly to the side as he struggled to keep his balance. "Aidan!"

He didn't look back, just kept plowing toward the door. "I'm not stopping!"

"Yes, you are." Damon grabbed both of Aidan's shoulders and pulled him backward, wrapping his arms around Aidan's torso and holding him close to his chest, his muscles straining as Aidan struggled. "You can't just run after him."

"Yes, I can!" Aidan twisted and bucked, trying every trick he knew to break free of Damon's strong grip. It was hard and tight, and Aidan found himself wracking his brain as he struggled, trying to remember what his sister had learned in the self-defense classes she had taken as a teenager. She'd showed Aidan—by demonstrating *on* him, unfortunately—but he couldn't remember anything she'd done, just that it caused quite a bit of pain.

He jabbed his elbow backward, hitting Damon hard in the solar plexus, and took advantage of Damon's momentary discomfort to twist free. He managed two steps before he was grabbed again, and Damon and Kyler pulled him back into the room. Kyler kicked out with his foot, knocking Aidan off balance. He stumbled, his feet catching on each other, and suddenly found himself being dragged, his toes in the air as his heels scraped against the carpet.

He kept thrashing and bucking, trying to get his feet back under him, but failed, and found himself pinned to the couch just as someone knocked on the door. "Let me up! I have to answer that!" Whoever it was could come in as he ran out.

"I'll get it." Tabatha yanked open the door to reveal a slender, dark-skinned woman. "Please tell me you're the lawyer."

Carina Orego blinked at the young woman in front of her. "Yes. And you are?" She'd never seen her before, and was far from who she'd expected to find opening Aidan's door.

"Tabatha Alders. Wyatt's sister." She stepped back to let Carina in and locked and bolted the door behind her. "You're a little too late," she continued quietly, "but I think they could use your help with Aidan."

Carina's eyes got wide as she took in the scene in front of her. Kyler and a man she'd never seen were holding Aidan down on the couch, talking to him in low voices she couldn't quite understand. "What the...? Aidan?"

"Carina!" Aidan lifted his head and redoubled his struggles to get free. "Tell them to let me go!"

"Uh...." She looked at Kyler with one eyebrow raised, hoping he would take the hint and fill her in on what was going on. She didn't know the other man holding Aidan down—though given the fact that the woman was Wyatt's sister, she could guess—but she trusted Kyler and knew there had to be some logical reason behind his actions.

"The men I called you about took Wyatt. Aidan's trying to run after him." Kyler leaned forward as Aidan squirmed. "He won't listen to reason."

"You're not being reasonable." Aidan bucked again, kicking his legs futilely as he tried to roll out from under the two men. "Tell him, Carina."

"I actually think I agree with Kyler on this one, Aidan." She moved around the couch slowly, trying to process the information. She caught Kyler's eye and then her gaze landed on the bag that had fallen to the floor in the earlier struggle. "I didn't see anyone outside, so whoever was here is gone. Running after them won't do any good."

"It would have if they'd let me leave right away," Aidan muttered, and a lot of the fight left him. His struggles became less desperate and more a matter of principle. "I could have caught up then."

"And done what?" Carina kneeled by Aidan's head and nodded at Kyler, who slowly pulled back as Carina moved forward. She tried to keep the movement as stealthy as possible, acting as though she was leaning in to give Aidan a hug before abruptly switching to take Kyler's place. The betrayed look on Aidan's face cut straight to her heart.

"I don't know." Aidan turned his head toward the back of the couch so he wouldn't have to look at Carina. Kyler's refusal to let him leave was bad enough, but he'd known Carina longer than he'd known Kyler, and he'd thought that if anyone would be willing to help, it would be her. "I just... I have to get to him, Carina."

"I know you do." It took every bit of willpower to keep her voice steady, and she threw a desperate glance at Kyler, silently asking him to hurry, before returning her attention to Aidan. "You will. We'll get you to him. I promise."

Kyler bit his lip as he dug in his bag, frowning at the contents before pulling out a syringe and a vial. It wasn't what he wanted to use, but he hadn't come prepared for everything that had happened over the past hour, and he needed to give Aidan something to keep him calm. This would do for now.

He swiftly loaded the syringe and then kept it tucked behind his back as he returned to the couch and smoothed his hand over Aidan's forehead. Aidan squeezed his eyes shut, refusing to look at him, and Kyler wasn't sure if that made it easier or harder to poke the syringe into Aidan's arm. The sedative released with a hiss, and Kyler pulled back, unable to meet the hurt gaze Aidan directed at him.

The drug hit Aidan quickly, making his limbs relax against his will and his eyes droop despite the effort he put in to keeping them open. As his body loosened, his captors eased off, and there was a brief minute where he was completely unrestrained. The thought of making a break for the door flashed across his mind, but even curling a finger was beyond him at that point, and he ended up giving in to the fog soon after, his eyes falling the rest of the way shut and his breathing evening out.

"He'll sleep for a while." Kyler sank to the floor next to the couch, leaning against the arm where he could still watch Aidan.

Carina sank back into one of the chairs and raised her eyebrows. "Did you have to put him to sleep?"

"I didn't have anything else. I didn't exactly come prepared to keep Aidan calm after Wyatt was kidnapped." He shot Carina the expected withering glance. "Though I'm not sure it would have mattered. He was exhausted enough that anything might have put him out."

"So, then, what do we do?" Damon asked.

"We wait." Carina leaned forward, resting her elbows on her knees, and looked at Damon. "And try to figure out as much as we can while Aidan is sleeping. I need to know exactly what they said so I can check on it, and then we'll see."

"But we're going to get him back, right?" Tabatha hugged her arms to her chest and leaned her head on Damon's shoulder. "We're not going to let them keep him, are we?"

"No." Kyler shook his head and managed a small smile.

"But we have to do this the right way so we can be sure it never happens again."

"Yeah, okay." The Mettler siblings sat down next to each other on the love seat, Tabatha pressed close to Damon, and looked across the room at the lawyer. "What do you need to know?"

AIDAN woke slowly. His eyelashes were sticky, but it was too much effort to raise a hand to rub at them, so he just let them be, his eyelids drooping heavily as he looked around the room.

It was slightly more crowded than when he had been knocked out, and it took him a moment to recognize Hunter and Brianna as the two people squashed together in one of the armchairs, Brianna balanced on Hunter's lap. Wyatt's brother and sister sat on the love seat, Carina perched on the edge of the armchair closest to the couch, and Kyler sat cross-legged on the floor, his head tilted to the side as he peered at Aidan.

"How are you feeling?" he asked, reaching out to brush some of the gunk from Aidan's eyelids with a damp cloth.

"Um." Aidan wanted to flinch away from the fingers gently swiping under his eyes, wanted a drink to clear the cotton from his mouth, wanted to get up and run after Wyatt. At least, he felt like he *should* want all that, and on one level he did. It was strange, though, with the remains of the sedative coursing through his system, it felt more as if he were floating and watching the scene on the television or a movie screen. He *knew* he wanted those things, but he didn't really feel them, not in the desperate way he'd felt like running after Wyatt earlier. Now it was more like watching a show or reading a book and wanting something for one of the characters.

"Aidan?" Carina leaned over and brushed his hair back from his forehead. "Are you back with us?"

"Uh." His vocabulary certainly wasn't. "Maybe?" He blinked a few more times, clearing his vision now that Kyler had removed the gunk from his eyelashes. It was still hard to focus, and he wasn't sure he was up to any of the questions Carina was sure to ask. "Thirsty."

Brianna slid off Hunter's lap, headed to the kitchen, and returned a moment later carrying a glass of water. She stepped over Kyler to sit on the edge of the couch next to Aidan and held the glass out above him. "Drink slowly."

Aidan struggled to push himself upright but ended up with his head and torso supported by Kyler as Brianna held the water. When he was done drinking, he let his head fall back against Kyler's hand and barely resisted the urge to let his eyes close again. "Thanks."

"You're welcome." Brianna set the glass on the coffee table and returned to Hunter's lap, wrapping her arms around his neck and resting her head on his shoulder. Her gaze remained fixed on Aidan.

Carina looked at Aidan. "Are you ready to talk?"

Aidan wasn't, not really, but the little voice in the back of his head told him that it was best to do this now while he still felt mostly detached from everything that was happening. If he waited until the drugs wore off, they were likely to have to sedate him again, and he didn't want his friends to have to do that any more than they wanted to do it. "Probably," he offered, rolling onto his side so it was easier to look out into the room. Sitting up was still beyond him, and he didn't want to have this conversation while propped up by one of his friends.

"We can wait, if you need to." Tabatha shrugged and flashed an uncomfortable smile as all the eyes in the room swiveled to look at her. "Damon, Kyler, and I already filled Carina in on most of what happened."

"Why are you still here, then?" Aidan tilted his head so he could direct an accusing stare at Carina. "Shouldn't you be out doing all those legal things they wanted me to wait for? I mean, that's why you drugged me, isn't it? So you could do this the *right* way?"

"I drugged you so you wouldn't hurt yourself," Kyler corrected, but Aidan wasn't listening to him. His eyes were focused on Carina, and Carina alone.

"I've already left another message for Zane. He's back in town, and he'd filled me in a little on what he left that message about, but I want him to come here and tell us the whole story. I think they might have some clues that will help us find Wyatt."

"There were papers." Aidan tried to look for the bundle of papers Crispin Aller had thrust into his hand, but he didn't see them. "He gave me papers that said he had the legal right to take Wyatt. At least, that's what he told me they said. I didn't read them."

"We found them. And I've already called my contacts at the courthouse about them too. They're being looked into, I promise."

It seemed wrong to Aidan that Carina was sitting in his living room when he didn't have any answers. "But—"

"Aidan." Carina angled her head so she could meet Aidan's eyes and make sure he was really listening. "It's easier for me to be here. Everyone has my number, and no one will expect me to rush right over or wait around for them if I'm doing this over the phone. Besides," she added, her lips turning up into a fondly exasperated smile. "Did you really think I was going to leave when you were so upset you had to be drugged?"

"I was kinda hoping you wouldn't bring that up."

Hunter snorted. "Seriously? You really thought that we wouldn't? Come on, man, you know us better than that. Well, most of us, anyway," he added, his eyes briefly flickering to where Damon and Tabatha sat on the loveseat, watching the proceedings. "We're worried about you, man."

"Worry about Wyatt."

Brianna laid a hand on Hunter's arm, stopping him from spewing out the words on the tip of his tongue. "We're worried about both of you, Aidan. We all want to get Wyatt back as much as you do."

That wasn't possible, but Aidan didn't have the strength or inclination to argue. "Okay." He shifted around a little, getting more comfortable. "So what do you need me to tell you?" If his friends were going to sit here and worry about him, he was going to make sure they were productive while doing so.

"Anything you can remember. We have a company name and address from the papers they gave you, and I'm sure Zane has more information, but every little bit could be helpful. We'll find him, Aidan. I promise."

"Right." He believed Carina; he just wasn't sure they'd find Wyatt soon enough, and that was what worried him the most. "If you say so."

"I do. Now are you going to help, or mope?"

There really wasn't a choice there. The drug-induced detachment was fading, and if Aidan wanted to stay sane, he had to do something. It was better to get the talking part out of the way while he still lacked the energy for action, so he carefully rolled a little bit more and forced his eyes open. His memories of the past several days were hazy and fuzzy, but he would tell Carina every detail he could remember if it would help find Wyatt faster.

Chapter Twenty-Six

WYATT woke gradually. He became aware of scents and noises first, and they slowly eased their way into his consciousness, drawing his curiosity. Clicks and beeps and a muted buzzing he didn't recognize filled the room he was in, and the scent was too sterile and antiseptic to be home, but it didn't smell like the hospital either. The strangeness of it set alarm bells ringing in his brain, but his limbs felt heavy enough to be made of stone, his eyelids felt as though they were glued to his cheeks, and it was so hard to draw air that it felt like an elephant was sitting on his chest.

He wanted to return to the senseless oblivion of sleep, but his body wouldn't cooperate and his brain began to filter more and more information to him. He lay still, listening and smelling, trying to process what he was sensing. There was something familiar about it, something he felt he should recognize, but he couldn't place it and wasn't sure he wanted to.

His nose started to itch with a tiny tingle that grew as he focused on it until it was nearly unbearable and demanded he scratch it. Moving still seemed like too much effort, but eventually Wyatt's need to soothe the itch outweighed his lethargy, and with great reluctance, he struggled to move his painfully heavy arm.

It wouldn't budge. Frowning, Wyatt tried again, and when that failed, tried his other arm and his legs. Nothing would move, but it wasn't the heavy torpor that made a fraction of an inch seem like several feet. This was different: bands of pressure over his forearms and legs kept him from achieving even that little bit of movement.

Wyatt's eyes snapped open again when he realized what it was, and he struggled to lift his head to visually confirm what he suddenly feared. It was difficult. His head seemed to weigh twice as much as the rest of his body, and his eyes were watering from the light before he'd managed to move even a few inches. When he did finally manage to lift his head, he found that not only could he not provide any leverage with his arms since they were strapped to the bed with padded restraints in two places, but also that he couldn't sit up at all because there was a band across his chest as well.

It prevented him from doing more than tilting his head forward until his chin touched his chest and peering down his body, but that was enough. He could see the restraints strapped over his arms and chest and a bit of experimental wiggling left him fairly certain that his legs were restrained as well. He could move his feet back and forth and wiggle his fingers, though it took a lot of effort, but actually lifting any part of his body other than his head was impossible.

It hurt to breathe, sharp stabbing pains like knives plunged into his lungs every time he inhaled. He couldn't stop himself from hyperventilating, though, his breath coming fast and shallow in his panic. This wasn't right. He would never dream himself into this position, not even in the horrible nightmares brought about by the fever wracking his body. The nightmares he'd shared with Aidan had been terrifying, but he'd always been safe, even when it hadn't felt that way. This wasn't safe, not even close.

As he struggled to keep his breathing under control, Wyatt looked around the room, his eyes acclimating to the brightness a little. He could tell he was in a small room with a low, white ceiling and beige walls. The doors and molding were stained dark wood, and along the wall opposite the bed stood a chest of drawers stained the same color as the molding. The table near the bed matched as well, though it appeared a bit more battered and, unlike the chest of drawers, had items on it, not that any of them would be helpful to Wyatt. On the side of the bed opposite the table sat an upholstered chair, and another chair with a lamp behind it occupied one of the corners.

With the exception of the restraints strapping Wyatt to the bed and the bits of medical monitoring equipment he could see if he tipped his head back as far as possible, it was a nice-looking room. Not home, but a place he could have been comfortable visiting if he'd come of his own free will.

Other than the restraints and the monitoring equipment, nothing appeared at all out of place, and nothing tingled Wyatt's senses the way the keys to changing other people's dreams often did. The clock on the bedside table kept the same time when he closed his eyes and opened them again, and there was nothing in the room that didn't exist in the real world. There wasn't much he could do, but every test he performed indicated he was actually awake and this was real.

It made him feel sick to his stomach. Bile rose in his throat and burned in the back of his mouth. His memories of getting here were hazy, and he had no idea who held him.

When he got his stomach mostly under control, Wyatt resumed his visual exploration of the room, peering at everything as best he could. His vision began to swim and his head started to pound, but he kept attempting to focus despite the pain and the way it began to feel like he was floating on water instead of lying strapped to a firm and immovable bed. He only made it halfway around the room again before it got to be too much, and he had to close his eyes and spread his fingers out, pressing his hands against the mattress as he tried to focus on it and stop the room from spinning.

It was still moving when the door creaked open. He opened his eyes, twisted his head to look at the door, and immediately regretted it. Every bit of stability he'd gained immediately vanished, leaving him feeling as though he had just spent hours on the spinning carnival ride he'd dreamed up for Nolan. It was nearly impossible to get his eyes to focus on the person who stepped through the doorway.

The sight wasn't worth the effort, far from it, and with a groan, Wyatt slowly turned his head back so he would have been staring at the ceiling had he left his eyes open. Closing them didn't help much against his persistent dizziness, but it did mean he wasn't forced to look at the last person he ever wanted to see.

Elliott smiled as he walked around the bed and settled in the chair on the other side. "I trust that you're more awake this time, Wyatt?" It was a rhetorical question—the monitors above the bed gave him an accurate reading of Wyatt's state of consciousness—but he tilted his head to the side to peer at his subject anyway. He was curious to see if Wyatt would respond.

He didn't. Not quickly enough for Elliott, anyway, and Elliott reached out, took Wyatt by the chin, and turned his head so they were facing each other. "I know you're awake, Wyatt. Open your eyes and look at me when I'm speaking. Please. I don't want to make this more unpleasant than it already is."

Wyatt doubted that very much, but he also didn't want to find out what ideas Elliott had in mind, so he slowly eased his eyes open one at a time and directed them in Elliott's general direction. He didn't attempt to focus on the man's face. Merely having his eyes open was bad enough to make the room spin and his stomach rebel. He was afraid that if he focused on anything right then, especially Elliott, he would end up sick again, and this time he didn't think he would be able to hold it back. As tempting as the idea of throwing up on Elliott was, Wyatt doubted he'd be able to reach him unless he managed some magnificent projectile vomiting, and even that wouldn't be worth the consequences.

"Good boy." Elliott grinned and pulled his hand back to his lap, much to Wyatt's relief. His skin was crawling where Elliott had touched it.

"What do you want?" Wyatt was certain he didn't really want to know, but anything was better than this game Elliott seemed to want to play, acting as though he cared even though Wyatt was strapped to a bed and completely incapable of doing anything to defend himself. He was completely at Elliott's mercy, and if it was going to stay that way, he wanted to know why.

Elliott adjusted his appraisal of the young Dreamer who had caused so many problems for him over the past few months. "I have a proposition for you."

Wyatt was certain he would reject Elliott's proposal on principle alone, but he raised one eyebrow in what he hoped came across as a gesture of curiosity. If Elliott was talking, he wasn't doing anything else to Wyatt, and feigning interest in his offer was the only way Wyatt was sure he could keep him talking.

"You're going to work for us again."

"That's not a proposition." Wyatt struggled to keep his expression calm. "And it's not going to happen."

"It will." Elliott leaned forward so his face was only inches from Wyatt's and smiled at the terrified look in Wyatt's unfocused eyes. "There is no question about you working for me. It's a matter of how."

"I won't do it. No matter what you offer. You can't make me."

"Wyatt, Wyatt, Wyatt." Elliott shook his head and clucked his tongue in mock sadness. "You're here, aren't you? We can make you do whatever we want. You can't leave." He let his eyes flicker down Wyatt's pajama-clad body, taking in the multiple restraints. "You can't even sit up without assistance."

Wyatt growled low in his throat and moved to sit up without thinking. The restraints jerked him to a sudden stop, bruising his arms and making his head lash back and thud against the mattress with enough force to set the world twirling around him again.

Elliott laughed, a low chuckle in Wyatt's ear he couldn't block out even when he concentrated exclusively on calming his roiling stomach. He doubted he'd be able to sit up unaided even if he hadn't needed someone to remove the restraints, but he couldn't let Elliott know that. He wouldn't give the man anything else to use against him.

"I want to make this easier on you, Wyatt." Elliott brushed strands of tangled, sweat-slick hair back from Wyatt's forehead and left his hand resting on Wyatt's brow in a gesture that would have been caring coming from anyone else.

Coming from Elliott it was creepy and worrisome, and Wyatt would have turned his head away had he possessed the presence of mind to remember he could. Instead, he shut his eyes tighter and hoped he could fall back asleep so he could escape this waking nightmare.

The hand slid down Wyatt's cheek to his chin. "Are you listening to me, Wyatt? I don't want to have to repeat myself."

Reluctantly, Wyatt directed an unfocused gaze at Elliott's blurred figure. "Yes."

"Good." Elliott slowly turned Wyatt's head back and forth, watching as Wyatt's flushed face blanched and noting how he struggled to keep his eyes fixed on a single spot.

"Just tell me, please." He couldn't keep this up much longer. Elliott's touch was making him queasy and the constant movement of his head was going to force him to expel anything that remained in his stomach after days of not eating. The way things were, it would definitely get on Elliott's hand at the very least, but that was small consolation for the way Wyatt felt at the moment. He would much rather the whole thing just stop.

Elliott held Wyatt's head still and leaned closer to peer directly into his fever-bright eyes. "You're going to work for us again, doing the same thing you did before. We've been looking for someone to replace you, but...." Elliott trailed off, grinning in a way that left Wyatt certain his nausea wasn't solely a result of too much movement. "Let's just say that we've had a hard time finding anyone as cooperative as your parents were. We need you, Wyatt, and we're willing to offer you a compromise. Work for us willingly, dreaming when and what we need you to, and the rest of the time will be yours. We'll let you wake up if you want, give you a nice apartment in our building, get you access to a fitness center, a spa, and any delivery service you want. We'll even pay for premium cable packages so you can watch whatever you'd like on television. Or you could spend your time dreaming with that graphic designer you Bonded with, if that's what you really want to do."

He said the last bit in a tone that implied he found the mere idea ridiculous, but Wyatt didn't take the bait. His mind latched on to the mention of Aidan, and he couldn't focus on anything other than that. "Aidan?" he asked hoarsely. "Where's Aidan?"

"Not here. And he never will be, just as you'll never leave. But we'll let you visit him in your dreams if you cooperate."

"I want to see Aidan."

Elliott pulled back, settling in the chair with his legs crossed and his hands folded in his lap. "You can see Aidan if you cooperate with me. Can you do that, Wyatt?"

"Can't." Wyatt let his eyes close and his head fall to the side as he shifted, trying to get more comfortable under the restraints holding him securely to the bed. "Need Aidan."

Elliott leaned forward again, but Wyatt was asleep, his breathing even, his face flushed with fever, and his eyes moving rapidly under their lids—a sure sign he was dreaming. The monitor beeped above his head, making Elliott frown as he glanced at it and read the bad news it was transmitting. He couldn't give Wyatt more drugs, not yet, but perhaps the fact they hadn't finished their conversation would be for the best. Wyatt was surely seeking out his Bondmate, and Elliott would get to rip him away again, promising that a reunion, even a dreamed one, would be all the sweeter.

Yes, this would work out well.

Elliott turned to leave the room. When he reached the door, he turned back, casting one last look at the sleeping man on the bed. "Enjoy the dream, Wyatt. It's the last one you'll ever have with him unless you cooperate." Then, smiling at a job well done, he walked out of the room, closing the door behind him and leaving Wyatt to his dream. Elliott could use a bit of rest himself. Shattering Wyatt's world was going to take quite a lot of work, even if the young man did eventually cooperate.

Chapter Twenty-Seven

AIDAN was dozing when Carina got the call from her contacts at the courthouse, so she took the phone and stepped out onto the balcony, leaning on the rail as she listened. After a few minutes, she stepped back inside, grabbed a notepad and pen, and went back out so she could sit at the picnic table and take notes. She wanted to write all of this down. They'd need records later.

By the time she was ready to come back inside, her hands were shaking, the notepad was rumpled from being clenched tightly, and she owed Aidan a new planter, as she'd kicked one on the balcony so hard it had fallen over and shattered. The news was not good, and while Carina couldn't blame anyone for how they'd reacted when Wyatt was being taken, the information she'd just received made the entire situation a hundred times more frustrating... and yet also managed to give her a small bit of hope.

She took a deep breath before limping inside, held the air in her lungs and then let it out with a deep sigh that relaxed her all the way down to her toes. It wasn't perfect—she'd be tense again in a second if she really started to think about things—but she had to remain calm enough to give the news to Aidan and the others, calm enough that Kyler wouldn't think she needed any help relaxing. Carina agreed with Kyler's decision to sedate Aidan, but she didn't need him to start thinking anyone else should be sedated, especially not if that someone was her.

Everyone looked up expectantly when Carina walked back in. They sat in the exact spots she'd left them in but now watched her with raised eyebrows and knowing looks, and for a moment, she was afraid Kyler was going to lunge for his bag and stab her with a needle before she reached her chair. It was an absurd thought, and she forced herself to shake it away as she sank into the plush chair, but given the events of the day, she supposed she could be forgiven a few irrational moments, especially with everyone looking at her as though she held all the answers.

She wished she did. Instead, she had more questions and bad news she would give anything to avoid sharing. The thought of how she was about to break Aidan's heart was enough to break her own as she leaned down and gently shook his shoulder.

Aidan squinted up at Carina. "Hmm?"

Carina opened her mouth and found she lacked the words to convey any of the thoughts rolling around in her head.

It was Brianna who came to the rescue. "Did the planter do something to you, Carina?" she asked in a teasing tone that only sounded slightly forced despite her worry and the tenseness pervading the room.

Carina smiled wanly in thanks for the distraction but didn't give it a response. Usually, she would joke, telling Brianna she was imagining the planter had been her face or something equally ridiculous they would both know wasn't true, but the situation was too serious for that. "The police never came for Wyatt," she said softly, her eyes never leaving Aidan's prone form. "And no papers were filed with the courts."

Aidan practically fell off the couch as he scrambled to sit up. "But we saw them!"

"Did you get badge numbers? Call to verify? If a real policeman was here, I need to know so I can tell my contact, but no one was officially sent."

Aidan slumped over, falling limply onto the pillow he'd been resting against until he'd heard Carina's news. "No. I was too, um, overwhelmed, I guess. I don't know. They came in, and they had the uniforms on, and that Crispin guy gave me papers, and they looked official and—" He broke off, barely choking down a sob.

"They played it well, and I'm sure they planned on you being too overwhelmed to check. I doubt they gave you time to check either."

"Real police would have given me time," Aidan answered in a dull monotone. "I should have known that, should have checked, or called, or done something besides let them walk out of here with him. He couldn't even—" Aidan choked back a gasp. "He was sedated, Carina!" He punched at the couch cushion, slamming his fist into it repeatedly before throwing it across the room, narrowly missing the television. "I should have stopped it!"

"You couldn't have, Aidan."

"Is that supposed to make me feel better? That I was helpless and too overwhelmed and out of it to even think to make a fucking phone call that would have saved Wyatt? At least if they'd been real police, I genuinely wouldn't have been able to do anything. With this, I should have and I didn't."

Kyler gently laid a hand on Aidan's knee, moving slowly and taking care to avoid Aidan's flailing arms. "Aidan, you were exhausted and not thinking straight *at all*. The rest of us were far more coherent than you were, and we didn't think to call." He caught Aidan's gaze and looked him straight in the eyes. "*I'm* the one who said we didn't need to call the paramedics. If they'd shown up, they would have insisted that he go to the hospital, and we would have had time to stop this. Hell, I should have known that they weren't real when they didn't insist on calling the paramedics themselves. No real police officer would just carry an unconscious person off. There's too much of a lawsuit risk."

"So, what? I should blame you and not me?" When Kyler nodded vehemently, Aidan let out a dry, hollow-sounding chuckle. "It's not your responsibility to keep him safe."

"It's not yours either." Damon slumped a little on the loveseat when all the eyes in the room turned to look at him. Most of them had forgotten he and Tabatha were there, and their surprise at his audacity was clear on all their faces. He almost wished he hadn't said anything, but it was too late to change that, and the words needed to be said, so he barreled forward. "No offense, Aidan, but my brother is an adult. I know that you helped him a lot when you first met him, and anyone can see how good you two are for each other—even people who don't really know you—but Wyatt is twenty-eight. He's responsible for taking care of himself." Damon leaned forward, his eyes seeking Aidan's. "Isn't that the point? Isn't that why you all have fought so hard to make sure he's free? So he *can* stand on his own?"

"That doesn't mean I can't take care of him," Aidan countered. Nothing anyone could say would make him feel better or any less guilty. "That's how a relationship works. We take care of each other."

"But it doesn't mean you're responsible for everything that happens to him."

"If you want to blame someone, blame me. I'm the one who opened the door."

Aidan looked over to Carina and then back to Tabatha. "What is this? Let's all blame ourselves for what happened?"

"Will it make you feel better? I mean, Brianna and I weren't here when it happened, but I'm sure I could come up with something if I tried hard enough." Hunter leaned around his Bondmate to flash a cheeky grin at Aidan. It fell short when Aidan directed a lost gaze in his direction.

"The only thing that will make me feel better is getting Wyatt back." The words came out biting and much harsher than anyone in the room deserved, but Aidan couldn't help himself. Everyone was sitting around, trying to take the blame that clearly rested on his shoulders, and none of them were doing anything to fix the situation. "Why don't you focus on that instead of making up some stupid lie about how it's your fault when it's not?"

The sudden silence was deafening. Everyone looked at Aidan with eyebrows raised and mouths hanging open. It was Kyler who dared to break the silence, sucking in a deep breath and again laying a hand on Aidan's knee. "Um, Aidan? That's why we're all here."

"Really? It seems like you're here to drug me and stop me from going after Wyatt, and Carina's here to give me bad news and make me feel worse than I already do, and they're here to... I don't even know." He dropped the hand waving around, vaguely indicating everyone else, and rested his head against the back of the couch and let his eyes slip closed. He was exhausted and the constant arguing was just draining him, far more than he would have thought possible, but maybe it was the lingering drugs in his system. They were still keeping him calm and detached, far less worried and frantic and angry than he would have been otherwise, so it was entirely possible they were making him tired as well. He couldn't think of any other explanation for why his eyelids felt as though there were weights attached to them and his limbs suddenly felt like they were made of iron. He just wanted to curl up and sleep, but he couldn't, not with his friends trying to take the blame and no one doing anything about getting Wyatt back.

"We're all here to help, Aidan." Carina scooted so she was sitting on the edge of the chair. She was tempted to move to sit on the couch next to him, but she wasn't sure how well that would be received, and Aidan had other friends here. He needed Carina present as his lawyer first and his friend second, especially given the news she'd received out on the balcony. "There isn't much we can do right now, though. The cops—real ones—are on their way to take statements from everyone who was here."

Aidan forced his heavy head upward so he could look at Carina with a disbelieving expression. "And what are they going to do? Tell me that they can't act on anything because we don't have any evidence and we let him in?"

"No. They're going to take your statements and get officers investigating immediately. Wyatt was taken against his will when they had no right to do so. That isn't something that the police are going to take lightly."

"Sure." Aidan didn't believe it and wouldn't until he saw the evidence of an investigation with his own eyes, but he didn't have the energy to argue.

The room went silent again for a minute, a more comfortable one this time, and Aidan had just about drifted to sleep when Tabatha sat up straighter on the couch and looked around at everyone. "So, is there anything we can do until the police get here? Or until your investigator friends get here? Should we call anyone else or, I don't know, figure out what we're going to do when they come?"

"It's hard to know what we're going to do without knowing what Zane has to say." Carina rubbed a hand over her face and shook her head, trying to keep her brain in lawyer-mode. "Most likely we'll simply pass the information on to the police at this point. It would be counter-productive to work independently now."

"It's not always counterproductive," Damon mumbled, his gaze dark and his arms crossed over his chest as he looked at his brother's lawyer. "Sometimes that's the only way to get things done." He had plenty of experience with that back home. Though he worked with the authorities when it was possible, often working against them was the best way to change people's minds.

"No, it's not, but in this case it is. Trust me, I know the people down at the station. This is something they'll act on."

"So then, what? We just sit around and wait? There's nothing we can do now?"

Carina tore the pages she'd written on out of the crumpled notebook and passed it to Aidan. "Write down what you remember happening. Everything you remember. It'll help when the police come." She looked around, making sure to meet the gaze of everyone else who had been present when the men had come and taken Wyatt. "You all should. It will be easier to think of things now than when the police are questioning you and making you nervous. That way they can focus on asking questions that will lead you to remember more, rather than trying to figure out what you remember."

Aidan tore a few sheets of paper from the notebook and passed it over to Kyler. "Pen?" he asked, looking up at Carina. He didn't *want* to think about what had happened, didn't want to have to go over it anymore, but if Carina was right and this was the best way to help Wyatt, he'd try. Assuming someone gave him a pen, of course, because there was no way he was getting off the couch.

Carina grumbled something about it being Aidan's apartment but went into the office down the hall and returned with several pens and a few more notebooks that she passed out to Kyler, Damon, and Tabatha. "Write down every detail you remember, no matter how insignificant. You never know what might help."

"Should we discuss it?"

"No." This time it was Damon who answered his sister. "If we discuss it any more than we already have, we'll start to get confused about what we remember and what we were told, and we want to give the police as many unbiased views as possible. If they're going to be able to do anything, they'll need it." The last was said in a tone that clearly conveyed his doubt about their ability to do anything, but he dutifully began to write in the notebook he'd been given anyway, starting with the moment he'd arrived at the apartment and been greeted by a half-asleep, desperate Aidan.

As he wrote, a thought occurred to him. "Is the front door to your building usually open? When I was here back in Glio, I had to follow someone in through the front door, but when Tabatha and I arrived earlier, it was open. I wasn't really thinking about it then, but it seems odd now."

"It *is* odd." Aidan dropped the pen on top of the papers he was writing on, left the whole stack on the coffee table, and turned to look at Damon while he propped his chin up on one hand so his head didn't fall forward. "It's a secure building. The door is supposed to be locked, but during the day if it were propped open, it's doubtful anyone would notice. Most of the tenants work day jobs, and those that don't work from home like I do. There's not much traffic through the lobby on a weekday." He paused, blinked, and turned to Kyler. "It is a weekday, right?"

"No, but yesterday was."

"Good." He really couldn't remember what day it was, though he was pretty sure someone had told him, probably when he'd let Damon and Tabatha in. It was too difficult to remember right now, though. Remembering was work, and Aidan didn't have the energy for that.

He slumped back against the couch again, forgetting all about his half-finished recount of the day's events, and let his eyes close. Maybe if he just rested for a minute things would be better when he opened his eyes. If his friends would just stop talking, maybe he'd be able to get enough rest to clear his brain and function. He was going to need to do that later, he knew that much, though at the moment the reason why was escaping him.

"Aidan!" Kyler shook Aidan's shoulder once, making his head flop, and waited to see if the other man was going to open his eyes. "Wake up!" Aidan shouldn't still be falling asleep, not from the drugs, and for him to have drifted off that quickly, even after his earlier outburst, was worrisome. The last thing they needed was for something to be wrong with Aidan as well.

"Don't want to," Aidan mumbled, barely cracking his right eye so he could look at Kyler. "I'm tired. 'S your fault anyway."

"The drugs should have worn off by now, Aidan." Kyler unabashedly laid his hand across Aidan's forehead and used his thumb to pry one eye open. It dilated properly, so that was one worry eliminated, but Aidan's clear exhaustion was still bothersome. He was about to reach for his tablet and run a quick diagnosis on Aidan when Brianna and Hunter came and sat next to him, one on each side.

"I'm still not feeling everything as strongly as I would, so they have to be in my system some," Aidan mumbled.

"They are, but they shouldn't be doing this. You'll feel detached for a while before they've fully worn off, but there shouldn't be enough left in your system to put you to sleep. It could make it *easier* for you to sleep, but it couldn't *make* you."

"Then what is?" Aidan rolled his head so it was resting against Hunter's shoulder. "I just want to sleep and I can hardly keep my eyes open and everyone wants me to think about things and do things and I can't stay awake."

Hunter shifted slightly so Aidan's head fell into a more comfortable position. "Maybe you should stop trying."

"What good will that do?"

Brianna turned so she was sitting sideways on the couch and took one of Aidan's hands in hers. He didn't squeeze back, but he didn't protest either, and she kept her gaze on his limp fingers as she spoke. "Well, for one, you'll be better rested when the police arrive, which will be helpful." She bit her bottom lip and looked up, taking in Aidan's closed eyes and pale pallor. "But more importantly, if the drugs Kyler gave you aren't making you this tired, do you think maybe Wyatt is?"

"Wyatt's not here. That's the problem."

"I know he's not here. But you're Bonded, so if he's dreaming, he can find you, no matter how far apart you are. Maybe he's trying to pull you in with him. This might be good."

"Really?" That idea hadn't occurred to Aidan. He knew Dreamers could dream with their Bondmates no matter the distance between them, but he and Wyatt had never had the opportunity to test that, and in all the panic, it hadn't occurred to him to try. If Brianna and Hunter were right, though, it could be very, very good.

"Really," Brianna confirmed, grinning at him.

Aidan grinned back, smiling for the first time in what felt like forever, and nodded, his eyes already slipping closed again. "Well, that's easy enough."

He didn't wait for anyone else's opinion. Brianna and Hunter knew best, and if they thought Wyatt was trying to pull him in, that was good enough for Aidan. He let his body relax, getting comfortable on Hunter's shoulder, gave in to the exhaustion pulling at him, and drifted off to the low sounds of his friends' discussions.

Chapter Twenty-Eight

IT TOOK Wyatt some time to realize he had fallen asleep, because in his dream he was in the same room, still strapped to the bed, and still terrified that Elliott was going to walk back in at any moment and enact his plan to keep Wyatt from Aidan forever. It was only when he unconsciously shifted his arms as he tried to get more comfortable that he noticed he *could* move them. It wasn't enough for him to get free, but it was enough for him to realize he was in the Dreamscape, and that this was a nightmare.

The thought simultaneously terrified and calmed him. Given that he was dreaming the same thing happening in the real world, he wasn't sure he could manipulate the Dreamscape. But if he could, then he might be able to find help. He might be able to find Aidan.

There was only one way to find out.

Wyatt closed his eyes, reached out with his mind, and pushed.

The world twisted around him, and when it stopped moving, Wyatt cautiously moved his limbs and sighed in relief when nothing stopped him from lifting them. He was obviously no longer in that horrible room, but he was just as obviously not where he'd tried to go—the beach where he often brought Aidan. The material he lay on was too hard to be either the bed or sand, and he couldn't tell what it was by feel alone, so it was with great trepidation that he slowly opened his eyes.

Disappointment flooded through Wyatt when he saw a red ceiling that seemed to be miles above his head. The flying buttresses looked oddly familiar, and with a sinking stomach, he recognized the giant spaceship he'd been trapped on during his feverish nightmares. It wasn't a pleasant memory—the dream had led him to an adjoining ship where Aidan slowly turned to stone before his eyes—and he shuddered as he rolled over and deliberately navigated his way to the edge of what appeared to be a giant table.

Carefully, Wyatt lowered himself to the ground, dangled by his hands from the table, and dropped to a chair. He then repeated the process from the chair to the floor. The room he was in was gigantic, and when he climbed to his feet, Wyatt found that short of learning to fly—which didn't seem to be part of this dream—there was no way he was getting back up on the table. For that matter, anything that might help him leave the room by walking out of it was so far above his head that he couldn't imagine a way to reach it. He was going to have to twist the Dreamscape again.

This time Wyatt tried a new strategy and didn't focus on a specific place. Instead, he directed his thoughts to Aidan, trying to will himself to wherever in the Dreamscape Aidan might currently be, while at the same time trying to pull Aidan into the Dreamscape if he wasn't there already.

The scene began to blur around him, and Wyatt squeezed his eyes shut against the unusual swirling accompanying the scene change. It was dizzying and worrisome, but he did his best to ignore it and push through. If it continued, he'd worry about it later, but he had more pressing issues at the moment.

When Wyatt opened his eyes this time, he was on a beach, but not the isolated one he frequented with Aidan. Motionless bodies lay stretched out in rows under the midday sun. At first, they looked like sunbathers, and Wyatt instinctively started to try to find the one real one among the thousands of dream creations, but as he approached, he realized that none of the people lying on the beach were alive. The sand was covered with bloated, decaying corpses that stretched for miles and miles.

Nauseated, Wyatt stumbled to some nearby rocks and was promptly ill, coughing up the little bit in his stomach as the scent of decay permeated his airways. As soon as he finished retching, he closed his eyes and twisted again, leaving fate to decide where he ended up. He was so desperate to get away that he didn't care where or with whom he landed next.

Anything and anyone was better than this. He'd even take Elliott if he had to.

The next dream was a carnival fun house, one filled with distorted mirrors and a clown that jumped out from behind a mirror and tried to stab him. Startled, he twisted again without thinking about it. Next was a long hallway of doors, none of which opened, and then an auditorium full of naked people telling him to get up on stage and strip as it was his turn.

He twisted several more times, taking himself through dream after dream, losing track of where he was going and where he'd been, his search for Aidan the only constant. Every time he paused, he reached out for his Bondmate, searching the Dreamscape and feeling along their connection to try to bring them together.

It wasn't until he'd gone through more than twenty different dreams that Wyatt caught sight of a figure off in the distance, and his heart leapt. He dashed forward, moving as quickly as he could, yelling and waving his arms, but Aidan never noticed, never saw him, and never got any closer. Wyatt's muscles ached and his lungs burned as he ran, but he couldn't stop moving or he'd lose sight of Aidan—and then he'd have to find him all over again. Wyatt wouldn't stop, not for anything, not even if he had to run all night.

Then, just as suddenly as he'd located Aidan, Wyatt found himself only feet away and stumbled to a stop, collapsing into the sand at Aidan's feet. "Aidan," he breathed, blinking dazedly up at his lover and trying to draw on his ability to change the dream to help him regain his breath.

For a minute, Wyatt feared Aidan was a manifestation of his imagination, a picture he could look at and maybe touch but not interact with, but then Aidan looked down. His reddened eyes widened as he fell to his knees and his hands pawed at Wyatt's shoulders eagerly. "Wyatt!" he sobbed. "Oh, God, Wyatt."

It didn't matter that Wyatt couldn't breathe. He wouldn't have been able to anyway, not with Aidan clutching him so desperately and his body responding in kind. He said nothing, just surged up, his mouth meeting Aidan's in a frenzied kiss. Their lips clashed, and when their tongues met it was more of a fight than a dance. It didn't matter, not so long as they could touch each other, feel each other, and revel in each other's presence.

Aidan lowered Wyatt to the sand, stretching out on top of him as he continued to plunder Wyatt's mouth. His hands roamed, tugged at Wyatt's shirt and belt, and finally he pulled back, his lips hovering just inches from Wyatt's and their noses practically touching. "Off."

It took Wyatt three tries to successfully remove their clothing, and Aidan echoed the flash of worry he felt because of the difficulty along their Bond, but then they lay naked in the sand. Aidan slipped his hand down to stroke Wyatt's cock, and Wyatt bucked as he strained to increase the contact. His hands roamed over Aidan's back, slid down to cup his ass, and he pushed one finger into Aidan as Aidan flicked his thumb over the tip of Wyatt's cock.

They moaned together and swallowed the sounds with yet another intense kiss. Wyatt rolled them over, pinning Aidan to the sand, his finger still in Aidan's ass as he pressed their groins together, wrapped his other hand around their cocks, and stroked them slowly and languidly. Aidan's breath hitched in his throat, and he whimpered as he tried to jerk up and down simultaneously.

Any other time, Wyatt would have teased Aidan, pointing out that even in the Dreamscape, he couldn't move his hips in two directions at the same time. But this time he was too desperate to think about anything other than how turned on Aidan was and how gorgeous he looked laid out on the sand beneath him. He pulled his finger almost all the way out and slid another in beside it, scissoring them as soon as they slid all the way into Aidan's ass. He could simply will Aidan stretched the same way he willed his fingers to be slick enough that they didn't hurt, but his control was shaky and this was much, much more fun. There was nothing in the world like Aidan writhing on the sand beneath him, and he wouldn't give this up for anything.

Aidan pushed against Wyatt's finger, scratching Wyatt's back. Wyatt pumped their cocks, and the sensations running through them and echoing over their Bond nearly overwhelmed them, so by the time Wyatt pulled his fingers out and lined himself up, Aidan was nearly spent. Only by desperately focusing on coming with Wyatt inside him did Aidan manage to hold back.

Wyatt pushed in with one forceful thrust, bottomed out before pulling back, changed the angle slightly, and thrust in again. He was hot and slick and filled Aidan completely.

They came together, calling out each other's name as their orgasms rocked the whole Dreamscape. Then they collapsed on the sand, boneless and sated and completely content for the first time in days.

They lay still for some time, basking in each other's presence and clinging tightly. Though they'd been literally joined together only moments before, it wasn't enough, couldn't possibly be enough until they were reunited outside of the Dreamscape, and they both knew it. The knowledge weighed on them, dragging them down and ending the peaceful moment far sooner than it otherwise would have.

Aidan broke the silence first. "Where are you?" he asked in a soft, almost broken voice. "In the real world, I mean."

"I don't know." Wyatt closed his eyes to regain his composure. "Back with whoever had me before, but I don't know who they are or where they took me. The only person I've seen is Elliott, and I still don't know his last name."

"But you were awake, right? They haven't—" Aidan broke off and waved his hand, knowing Wyatt would understand what he meant and why he couldn't say the words.

"I don't think so." He managed a small smile. "I'm pretty sure Elliott would have found a way to make me dream with him just so he could rub it in. I was awake when I talked to him. Sort of, anyway."

Aidan's eyes widened with concern. "What do you mean, 'sort of'?"

"I was awake," Wyatt hastened to reassure Aidan, then calmed him with a chaste kiss. "I just wasn't very coherent. I mean, I'm sick, right?"

"Yeah. We were taking you to the hospital when—" Aidan swallowed hard and gathered his courage so he could force the words past his lips. He didn't want to say this at all, but if anyone had the right to hear directly from Aidan exactly what had happened and exactly how badly he had messed up, it was Wyatt. "Two men showed up with what they told us were policemen. They had papers and guns, and they took you, and I didn't stop them. I tried, but I couldn't, and then Kyler drugged me so I couldn't run after them to get you back." He let his head fall back against the sand and squeezed his eyes shut. "I'm sorry."

Wyatt closed his eyes as well and leaned forward to press his forehead to Aidan's. "For what?"

"For not stopping them! For not knowing that they weren't real policemen or real court papers! For not fighting harder when Kyler tried to drug me and they tried to keep me away from you! They came into *my* home, and I just... I just let them take you when you'd already been drugged unconscious!"

"Aidan." Wyatt pulled back some and rubbed his thumb over Aidan's cheek. "Look at me." When tear-filled green eyes met his, Wyatt leaned forward, kissed Aidan's freckled nose, and gazed down at him. "The last few days, I guess it is, are really hazy, but I remember some of the nightmares I had. And I remember that you were in every single one of them. And I remember agreeing to let Kyler drug me so that *you* could rest. If this was right after that, Aidan, there's no way you could have done anything. And if they had guns, I'm glad you didn't try any harder than you did."

"I should have done something."

"What? Aidan, listen to me." Wyatt said softly. "There is nothing you could have done. Anything you might have tried would have just ended up in you getting hurt. They outnumbered you, right?" He waited for Aidan's nod and then continued. "So you were outnumbered by people who had guns who you thought were the authorities. I'm *glad* you let them take me."

Aidan swallowed hard as irrational fear spiked through him. "But—"

He silenced Aidan's pending protest with a swift kiss, then said, "I'm not glad I'm stuck where I am. I don't enjoy being strapped to a bed any more than I enjoy being away from you. But I'm *fine* where I am right now. They're not hurting me. I'll be okay for a few more days while you find me and get me out."

"How do you know we will?"

It hurt to ask, but Aidan had to. He could feel Wyatt's confidence in him, but he couldn't understand it. It was as though his whole world had been ripped apart, and he only felt even remotely complete here in this dream. He knew Wyatt felt the same way. The confidence didn't make sense.

"Because I know you." Wyatt's smile widened into a more genuine one. "And I know our friends. I bet that I had so much trouble finding you because you were trying to stay awake to strategize with them, and that our apartment is full of people who are just dying to do something to the people who showed up and took me away."

Aidan had to smile at that too. "Yeah, okay. You're right."

"Of course I am. Did you call Carina? Is she keeping everyone in line?"

"Kyler called her while they were taking you. I guess he hoped that Carina would arrive and be able to do something legally, but she didn't." Aidan shook his head. "Carina got mad when her contact confirmed that there were no policemen or official papers, and took it out on our planter. She owes us a new one."

"If whatever plan she's come up with for getting me back works, I say we forgive her and replace it ourselves." Wyatt followed the comment with a deep kiss, this one not at all chaste, and Aidan moaned into it, tangling his hands in Wyatt's hair as they lost themselves in the taste of each other.

When they finally broke apart, Aidan hummed in agreement, encouraged by the thought of getting Wyatt back home safely. "Yeah, she can break as many planters as she wants if she manages to get you home. Of course," he continued, assuming a mock-pensive look, "her plan mostly involves using the courts and doing this the legal way, so I'm not sure how much credit we're going to really be able to give her."

Aidan reached up and stroked Wyatt's cheek with the back of his fingers. "I love you."

"I love you too." Wyatt mimicked Aidan's gesture, then lowered his head for another kiss. He nuzzled Aidan's nose and rested their foreheads together, his eyes closed as he forced the next words past the sudden lump in his throat. "I don't know when they're going to wake me up. I'm sure they're going to want to try to *persuade* me again."

"Persuade you?" Aidan gasped. "To do what?"

"Work for them, uh, *voluntarily*," Wyatt said in a scathing tone. "At least, that's what they called it. Elliott said that if I cooperated with them, he'd set me up in a luxury apartment in their building and I'd be allowed to wake up between times they needed me to dream for them. He said they'd even *let* me dream with you, if I wanted." He let out a hollow laugh, his breath warm against Aidan's cheek. "I wouldn't be allowed to leave, of course, or actually see you while I was awake, but he'd let me have any other luxury I could imagine."

"And he really thought that would convince you?"

"I don't know. He said he was willing to compromise with that because it was better for the bottom line. I guess it's expensive to keep me drugged for years at a time." Wyatt laughed again as hysteria threatened to overwhelm him. "I think I fell asleep before I could answer him, but I wouldn't have accepted. I can't stay there."

"I know." Aidan fought to keep his voice steady as anger, fear, and frustration threatened to overwhelm him again. "We should make plans."

"I don't know when I'll be able to sleep, either."

"But you can pull me in, right? I mean, that's why I couldn't stay awake when you were sick and why I kept falling asleep before I ended up here, right?"

"Yeah." Wyatt nodded, rocking his head against Aidan's. "It was hard, though, and I don't know if it was because you were fighting it or because I'm sick or both."

"Well, I won't fight it next time. If I'm feeling at all like I need to sleep, I will, I promise. No arguments, no struggling to stay awake, just giving in, okay?"

"Yeah, but—"

Aidan cut him off. "But nothing. If you fall asleep, you pull me in, understand? Even if you haven't figured anything out or can't give us any information, you still pull me in. I might have news for you, and even if I don't, I still want to see you. I *need* to see you."

"But what if you can't sleep?" Wyatt's voice came out soft and quiet. He didn't want to ask the question, but he had to know. He couldn't risk pulling Aidan into the Dreamscape if he was driving or walking through a crowd or something.

"I'm not going to go anywhere that I can't be pulled into the Dreamscape, I promise. Even if I have to go to the courthouse or police station, I'll make Kyler or Carina or someone drive, okay? *Pull me in if you fall asleep.*"

He was so adamant about it that Wyatt could only nod and agree. "All right. Anytime I fall asleep, I'll pull you in, even if it's just to say hi."

"Thank you." Aidan pulled Wyatt down for a final kiss. "You should probably send me back now, though. I should pass what you told me along to everyone else." He didn't add that he didn't want to be here when Wyatt woke. It would knock them both out of the dream—he knew that much from experience—and he didn't think he could handle the abrupt transition in his current emotional state. Having Wyatt send him away would hurt, but having Wyatt suddenly torn away again would hurt more.

Wyatt nodded slowly, licking his lips. "Yeah, okay. I'll try to see what I can figure out myself."

"Good."

They lay quiet for a minute, neither of them wanting the time together to end, but eventually Wyatt woke Aidan. The sand was soft underneath him, but unwelcome after the hard planes of Aidan's body, and he wasted no time enjoying the scenery. He had just sent away everything he wanted, so there was no reason to remain here. With a sigh, he closed his eyes, reached out, and twisted.

When he opened them again, he was back in the room he'd started in, once more strapped firmly to the bed, and all too aware of the harsh reality of his situation.

Chapter Twenty-Nine

AIDAN woke with a smile on his face, but it faded quickly when he realized nothing had changed. Wyatt was still being held in an unknown location and, aside from confirming his suspicions that the people who took him were the same people who'd held him before, Aidan had learned nothing. Now he was separated from Wyatt again, unable to even talk to him until Wyatt pulled him back into the Dreamscape. It was enough to make him want to go back to sleep in the hopes that Wyatt was still there, but he'd promised he'd pass on the little information he knew, and his presence would be needed when the police arrived.

Kyler leaned over the arm of the couch and peered down at Aidan, a curious look on his face. "You awake?"

It was clearly a rhetorical question, as the answer was obvious, but he replied anyway, groaning and throwing an arm over his face. "No."

"Awesome." Kyler gently lifted Aidan's arm, noting with approval that the circles under his eyes were looking less pronounced and that his irritability was far closer to his usual early morning grumpiness than to the exhausted disorientation he had exhibited earlier. He laid Aidan's arm back down and resettled onto the floor. "Did you find Wyatt?"

Even with his eyes covered, Aidan knew every person in the room turned to look. He could feel each gaze land on him, making his skin tingle until he felt like he was going to jump out of it. Cautiously, he shifted his arm so he could peer around his elbow, and found that he was correct: his friends formed a ragged semicircle around the room and were all focused on the couch—on him.

With difficulty, he forced himself to sit up, swing his legs to the floor, and push with one arm until he leaned back against the couch in a mostly upright position. He was still exhausted but wasn't feeling an overwhelming need to sleep.

"I did," he said. It occurred to him to wonder how he ended up lying down in the first place—the last he remembered he was sleeping on Hunter— but there were more important things to focus on at the moment. "Or rather, he found me." He let his mind drift back to the early moments of their encounter, and smiled to himself.

"And?" Tabatha leaned forward from her position on the love seat, scooting all the way to the edge of the cushion.

Aidan blushed as he mentally reviewed his meeting with Wyatt, and Hunter groaned, throwing his head back against the chair and rolling his eyes. "Don't tell us about *that* part."

Aidan's blush deepened and he looked down, no longer able to meet any of his friends' eyes. Of course, Hunter *would* pick up on *that* aspect of his visit with Wyatt. "Wasn't planning on it," he muttered, shaking his head as he tried to get his brain back on track.

Carina shot Hunter an annoyed look and turned back to Aidan. "Does Wyatt know anything? Has he even woken up?"

"Yeah." Aidan pulled a couch cushion up to his chest, hugging it tightly. "It's, um." He looked at Damon through brimming tears, every bit like a lost little boy instead of a self-sufficient thirty-two-year-old man. "It's the same people who had him before I found him. He, uh,"—and here he had to look away again—"he said when he woke up, he was strapped to a bed and Elliott, the guy who *trained* him when he was first taken, was there."

The entire room erupted into angry murmurs, but Aidan ignored them, keeping his eyes on his fingers and his back stiff as he waited for them to calm down. He couldn't answer their questions, couldn't listen as Brianna softly explained to Damon and Tabatha what little they knew about the people who had taken Wyatt when he'd been sold by their parents, couldn't let himself feel the outrage permeating the gathering. All he could do was wait, the pillow still hugged tightly to his chest and his mind focused strictly on the information he needed to convey without thinking at all about what it meant.

When the murmurs quieted, Aidan swallowed hard and picked up where he'd left off. "He said they tried to bribe him into agreeing to be their slave. Elliott told him that they would let him wake up and let him dream with me if he dreamed what they wanted when they wanted... and if he realized that he was never ever going to leave their building."

No one asked if Wyatt had agreed, which was a good thing because Aidan probably would have lost it if they had. Instead, they all sat in stunned silence, waiting for Aidan to continue.

After a long pause, Kyler placed a gentle hand on Aidan's shoulder. "Was there anything else?"

"No," he managed, shaking his head. "We arranged that he would pull me into the Dreamscape the next time he falls asleep, so I need to stay where I can fall asleep immediately, but that's it. I had him wake me up so I could pass the information along to you guys and—" He didn't finish the sentence, but everyone in the room nodded sympathetically anyway.

"We'll figure this out, Aidan. The police should be here any minute and—"

The door shook as someone pounded on it, and they all exchanged glances, wondering if speaking of the police had somehow summoned them. Everyone looked to Aidan, expecting him to answer or at least to indicate that someone should, but he couldn't make himself move at all. The mere idea that he would have to again recount what happened left him trembling in his seat, and he was sure he was going to shake apart at any second.

Kyler squeezed Aidan's shoulder, crossed the room, checked through the peephole in the door before rolling his eyes, and stepped back as he pulled it open. "Afternoon, gentlemen."

Ratri and Olin rushed into the room, practically tripping over each other and Kyler in their haste to get inside. They barreled to a stop just inside the living room, staring at Damon and Tabatha Mettler. Ratri's eyes narrowed. "Who are you?"

For a moment, everyone tensed and wondered who exactly should introduce Wyatt's siblings, but then Damon stood, holding out his hand. "Damon Mettler, Wyatt's brother. And this is our sister, Tabatha."

The temperature in the room seemed to drop. Ratri looked from Damon's outstretched hand to Aidan and back again, one eyebrow cocked as he raked his gaze up and down Damon's body. "You're who?"

"Wyatt's brother?" Damon said slowly, holding his ground admirably despite the very strong urge he felt to step back. "We came out to visit Wyatt and Aidan. We got here just before…." He trailed off, swallowed hard as he shifted uneasily under Ratri's stern gaze.

"So what?" Ratri asked in a low voice, stepping into Damon's personal space and glaring up at him despite his disadvantage in height. "You led them here? You found out your brother was free and thought you'd do something about it? Didn't you think he'd been hurt enough? What do you get out of this? Are they going to start paying you now too?"

Damon staggered back, blinking as he tried to process Ratri's rant. "I— We—"

"We didn't *lead* them here." Tabatha jumped up from the couch and pushed between her brother and Ratri, standing toe to toe with the shorter man. "We didn't *want* Wyatt taken back to wherever he is. We never wanted it to happen in the first place! I was twelve years old and had to watch my parents just give my big brother away! How could I possibly want that, or anything that came with it?"

"I'm sure your life got loads better afterward. Your mommy and daddy could afford to dote on you then."

"I would rather have had my brother!" She clenched her hands into fists and drew herself up to her full height. Tabatha was the shortest of the Mettler siblings, but she was still taller than Ratri, and she held herself like she knew what she was doing. "I never wanted this to happen, and I was *thrilled* when Damon told me that Wyatt had gotten free. We were both thrilled that he'd Bonded with Aidan, because that meant that they weren't supposed to be able to do this to him!"

"Then why did they show up right after you did?" Ratri drew himself up as well, glaring at her with fire in his eyes. "Why was he safe for *months* and then as soon as you found out, they come and rip him away? Hmm? How do you explain that?"

"I don't know." Tabatha's voice got low and dangerous as she balled her fists tighter, preparing for the fight clearly brewing. "Maybe someone else found out at the same time. Maybe that's how long it took them to track him down. Maybe they found a neighbor or a coworker who was willing to turn him in."

"And maybe you led them here."

"If we did, it wasn't intentional. Damon and I did *everything* we could to make sure that no one back home knew what we were doing. I *lied* to my boss about where I was going and why."

"And your parents?"

"We don't talk to our parents." Damon put a hand on his sister's shoulder and pulled her back some, but she shrugged it off, moving closer to Ratri.

"He's right. We avoid them as much as we possibly can and have since I moved out and actually could. We didn't like what they did then, and we don't like what's happening now. All we want is for Wyatt to be okay, and if you can't believe that...." She clenched her teeth as she glared at Ratri. Her muscles were taut and she balanced on the balls of her feet, ready to spring forward at a moment's notice. If he didn't believe her, it wouldn't be pretty. Tabatha had grown up in a rough neighborhood, and even after the family's financial situation improved, she had continued to fine-tune the skills she'd had to master at a young age. She was reasonably confident she could take Ratri, and it showed.

"I don't."

Tabatha lunged forward, growling low in her throat. Her arms were around Ratri's neck before anyone else managed to move. "Take it back!"

Ratri leapt back, flailing ineffectively against Tabatha's shoulders and sides, wanting to force her to let go but still too much of a gentleman to do anything that might be considered untoward. "You're lucky I don't hit girls."

"I'm not a girl." Her knee swung up and the room exploded into action. Kyler and Olin pulled Ratri back at the same time Damon grabbed Tabatha around her waist and lifted her away from Ratri. She shrieked and kicked out, almost hitting Ratri anyway and nearly making her brother drop her. By the time Damon staggered back to the couch and sank down with Tabatha still struggling in his lap, Hunter, Brianna, and Carina had rounded the coffee table and positioned themselves between Ratri and Tabatha.

"Stop it, both of you!"

The entire room froze after Carina's authoritative bark. Even Aidan looked up, blinking at the scene in front of him as he tried to drag his mind back to the here and now.

Tabatha squirmed, trying again to get free of Damon. "Not until he takes it back!"

"I won't." Ratri tried to push past the wall of people separating him from Tabatha and Damon. "She shouldn't be here! Neither of them should!"

"I have as much right—"

"I said stop!" Carina's voice echoed throughout the room, silencing everyone. "You're not helping Wyatt, either of you. Tabatha and Damon didn't lead anyone here, Ratri." She stared hard at him before swiveling to direct her gaze at Tabatha. "And he's just trying to protect your brother. So both of you, cut it out and focus on what's important."

Tabatha scowled as she slumped back against her brother. "Fine."

"Yeah. Fine." Ratri relaxed his tensed muscles enough that Olin and Kyler loosened their grip, and he shook off their arms, rolling his shoulders and continuing to glare at Wyatt's siblings but otherwise behaving. "I won't say anything else." He stalked across the room, Olin on his heels, and sank onto the couch next to Aidan, his arms crossed over his chest and a scowl etched on his face.

"Good." Tabatha said flatly. "You shouldn't have said anything in the first place."

Aidan let his head fall forward. The world of what ifs and should haves he'd been wandering in prior to Carina's bark seemed more and more attractive with each passing moment, and he couldn't take any more. "Guys, please, drop it," he begged without looking up. "All of you. That's not what's important right now."

"It is if they're the ones who led those people here," Ratri growled.

"They didn't, okay?" Aidan knew he should have said something earlier instead of letting Carina do it, but he was too worn down. Even now it was too much effort to glare at Ratri and he settled for clenching the cushion tighter, digging his fingers into the plush fabric hard enough to leave marks. "We've been talking to them for weeks, Ratri. This isn't the first time they've seen Carina and *we* invited them out here. They aren't their parents, okay?"

"So why is this the first time *we've* heard of them?"

The scorn in Ratri's tone made Aidan turn and stare incredulously at his friend. "Because Wyatt wanted to introduce them in person, all right? He was afraid you'd go all caveman if he told you he'd been talking to them, and with good reason!"

"I wouldn't be all caveman if Wyatt hadn't been taken."

"We weren't exactly planning on that, Ratri." Aidan practically spat the words out, and if he'd had more energy, he'd be copying Tabatha and trying to strangle his friend. "And they weren't either, all right? Just trust me and drop it. I don't need this right now."

Ratri visibly softened, and he stared at Aidan apologetically for a moment before sliding an arm around his shoulder and pulling him close. "Sorry, man. I get a little overprotective, sometimes, you know that."

Aidan relaxed against his friend. "I know. But they're not the bad guys, I promise."

"Yeah, all right. Sorry."

"But hey!" Hunter added as he and Brianna returned to the chair they'd been sitting in. "When we find out who the bad guys are, we'll point you in the right direction and let you go as caveman as you like!"

It was a ridiculous comment, especially since they really couldn't if they wanted to do this the right way—the police tended to frown on vigilante-style justice—but it broke the tension, and after a nervous chuckle, everyone started to calm down and drift back to where they'd been before Ratri and Olin had arrived.

Carina was just catching them up on what they'd learned so far—which was really nothing, though she managed to draw it out far longer than Aidan hoped she would—when there was another knock on the door. Kyler stood without looking at Aidan and opened it to let Zane in.

"Took you long enough," Aidan said coldly.

"Yeah. Sorry about that." Zane stood awkwardly in front of the television, completing the circle of people in the room, his hands shoved in his pockets and a sheepish expression on his face. He shifted from foot to foot as he talked, looking absurdly like a schoolboy called in front of the teacher for bad behavior. "I was investigating some pretty intense leads, and I didn't get the message that you'd called back."

"You should check your messages more often," Aidan said with a scowl.

"I know. I'm sorry." Zane shrugged apologetically. "The good news, however, is that I know who took Wyatt and how they found him."

That got everyone's attention and the entire room sat up straighter. Even Aidan managed to stop leaning against Ratri, though the look he directed at Zane lacked the rapt fascination of Tabatha's or the curiosity of Olin's. "Well? How?" He leaned forward, resting his elbows on his knees. "And who?"

"And do you have proof?" Carina added before her employee could answer. "We've already contacted the police, and we can't give them speculation. We'll need facts we can back up."

"I have proof," Zane confirmed. "It was a little hard to follow at times, and it's a convoluted trail, but we have proof." He held out the briefcase clutched loosely in his left hand and set it on the coffee table. "There should be enough in there to get a warrant at least."

"Good." Carina grinned, flashing an appreciative smile to him before letting her face fall into a more somber expression. "Now that we've established that, would you care to share what you learned?"

Zane looked embarrassed, cleared his throat, and stepped forward a little. "I followed the money trail, which is why it took so long. The funds being deposited into Ursula and Lorne Mettler's account were coming from a dummy corporation, and I had to trace it back to the real corporation."

"Which is?" Aidan didn't care *how* they'd found the answer, only that they had, and he wanted to know what it was right then. If Zane didn't tell him soon, he would likely use the last of his energy to deck him.

"Right." Zane bent down, pulled a data pad from the briefcase, and began scrolling through it, his eyes quickly roaming over the information on the screen.

Aidan leaned forward, growing more and more impatient and chewing on his bottom lip as he willed Zane to read faster. He was perched on the edge of the couch when sudden pain shot through his entire body. He tumbled forward, hit his head on the coffee table, and landed in a heap on the floor, where he curled into a ball and willed the agonizing burn to stop.

It ripped through him, feeling like a fire consuming him from the inside out. The agonizing sensation jumped from nerve to nerve, shooting down to his fingers and toes and setting off a cacophony of pounding inside his skull. He was vaguely aware of hands stroking along his skin, the cool touches doing nothing to soothe the pain, and voices talking around—or possibly to—him, but he couldn't respond. The searing agony was too great for him to do anything other than lie there, whimpering, until it became too much for his body to handle and he passed out.

Chapter Thirty

MOANING, Wyatt turned his head from side to side as his body fought his return to wakefulness. He tried to stretch, only to have his arms caught by the restraints locking him to the bed, and he opened his eyes as everything came flooding back with startling clarity. He lifted his head as far as he was able and looked wildly around the room, scanning rapidly as he tried to determine if anything had changed while he'd been asleep.

The only new addition was sitting in the same chair he'd occupied earlier, his hands clasped beneath his chin and his expression thoughtful as he watched Wyatt struggle awake. "Did you have pleasant dreams?" Elliott asked in a soft voice, leering at Wyatt.

"You don't get to know about my dreams," Wyatt ground out through clenched teeth, again straining against the restraints. Each yank hurt more than the last as he tugged hard enough to leave bruises despite the padding encircling his limbs.

"I'll know all about them soon." Elliott wrapped his hand around Wyatt's arm and sent tremors of terror and disgust racing through him. "You're going to be dreaming what I want you to dream, when I want you to dream it. There's no point in trying to hide from me now."

"No, I won't. There is *nothing* you can offer me that will make me willing to work for you. *Nothing*." Wyatt turned his head and twisted his shoulders as far as he could in a futile attempt to escape Elliott's touch. His skin burned everywhere his captor's stubby fingers had been, painfully intangible reminders of his position and what he was forced to endure. "I already have everything I want, and you can't take that away." He set his jaw. "I won't accept your offer, Elliott, and you can't make me."

"Just think on it, Wyatt." Elliott brushed his fingers over Wyatt's cheek and stepped back from the bed. "You don't have everything anymore, and I promise, my offer is the best you're going to get. If you enjoy the life you've made at all, I strongly recommend you take it. It's the only offer that will let you hang on to anything you found." He turned and walked from the room, pulling the door fully shut behind him and leaving Wyatt once again alone in his nightmare.

The silence filling the room in the wake of the door thudding shut deafened him. Wyatt was tempted to yell and scream, to make as much noise as possible, just to prove he *could* still make noise, to prove he could still *hear* it and that Elliott's words weren't the last thing he would ever hear. It took great effort to keep his mouth firmly shut and test the theory by yanking hard on the restraints. The buckles clicked and the cloth snapped as he tugged and pulled. They were simultaneously the best and worst sounds he'd ever heard. The best because they were a sound that wasn't Elliott's voice; and the worst because they meant he was securely strapped down and had no hope of breaking free.

With Elliott's parting words echoing in his head he worked himself into panicked exhaustion. He didn't stop struggling until the room spun horribly around the bed, making him feel as though he was going to throw up or fall off. Neither was a pleasant prospect—he wanted to leave, but he didn't want to be flung off the bed to do so—and so he let his head fall back against the mattress and squeezed his eyes shut. The sensation of movement didn't fade, but at least this way, Wyatt wasn't confused by his brain telling him one thing and his eyes another.

He tried to sleep, to call upon that innate ability to drop off at any moment, figuring that if he was dreaming, he wouldn't feel so dizzy and disoriented. But he couldn't make it work. Every time he tried to access the part of his brain that allowed him to enter the pleasant oblivion of the Dreamscape, it slipped away, leaving him thrashing and whimpering. Nothing he attempted worked, and by the time he gave up on the idea, he was hyperventilating, panicked by his inability to do something he had been able to do for as long as he could remember.

When he opened his eyes again, the room was hazy, like everything was obscured by fog or underwater. He blinked and jerked against the restraints until he remembered that he couldn't lift his hands to rub his eyes, and then blinked more, struggling to clear his vision so he could see what, if anything, had changed.

The room was hot, and for a minute, Wyatt had the crazy idea that maybe the haze was caused by heat. He was roasting in the loose cotton pants and thin cotton shirt he wore, and at that moment, if he could move at all, the first thing he would do would be to strip, freeing himself from the sticky clothing. The places where the restraints pressed against his skin burned and chafed. They felt worse than the dry mouth and cracked lips that had tormented him since he woke up.

There were shadows in the room now, stretching out from corners and from under furniture, slowly moving to take over the room. They grew even as Wyatt watched them, sending tendrils out one bit at a time, always crawling closer and closer to the bed, converging around it in an arc that left no room for escape even if Wyatt had been able to get off the bed. They were after him, trying to torment him into agreeing to what Elliott wanted.

If they didn't back off, he might.

Wyatt squeezed his eyes shut and silently chanted that it wasn't real. He told himself it was a dream, or a hallucination brought on by the fever still racking his body and the dehydration that had to be setting in after hours of nothing to eat or drink. It wasn't real; shadows didn't just spring from walls and attack people, and Wyatt knew it, but every time he opened his eyes they were there, inching closer and closer to the bed and covering the room with darkness.

He began thrashing, trying to get free, his fear of the shadows adding to his desperate need to get out of this place and back to Aidan. He yanked and tugged, straining against the padded cloth and leather, twisting until his wrists were raw and his breath was labored from the effort. Still the shadows crept closer, and no matter how much he screamed, no one came to see why.

When the door finally opened and the overhead lights flicked on, driving back the shadows, Wyatt felt nothing but relief. He barely bit back the grateful thanks that threatened to gush from his lips as Elliott came into view, smiling his sickening smile down at Wyatt and brushing a bit of stray hair that had fallen into Wyatt's eyes off his forehead. The touch broke the spell, and Wyatt tried to jerk his head away as he swallowed back everything he'd been about to say. "Don't touch me," he croaked, his voice hoarse from screaming.

"You're not exactly in a position to be making demands, Wyatt." Elliott pulled up the chair and sat close to the bed, his legs crossed and his hands folded neatly in his lap. "I believe I am the one holding all of the cards here." He leaned forward, smirking. "The only thing you get to decide is how painful this will be for you."

Wyatt narrowed his eyes as he tried to focus on the man sitting next to him. He squinted more than glared, but he fought against the spinning room and his roiling stomach to keep his expression adamantly angry. "Let. Me. Go."

"That isn't an option, Wyatt," Elliott said in his smooth voice. "You belong to me, and you always will." He laid his hand on Wyatt's forehead and tutted. "We really must do something about this fever, my boy."

"I'm *not* your boy, and I don't belong to you. I don't belong to anyone." Wyatt said without moving his head. Elliott's hand felt slimy and made Wyatt's skin crawl, but the clammy coolness of it felt good against his fevered skin, and he was reluctant to give up even that little bit of comfort.

"That's where you're wrong. You are mine; you have been since your parents sold you to me, and that will never change." Elliott settled back in the chair, rested his elbows on the armrests, and steepled his hands. "You're sick, you're dehydrated, and your blood sugar is dropping. Even if I were inclined to let you continue to resist, you wouldn't be able to hold out much longer. Your body is going to give out soon without water and medical treatment, and I'm the only one who can provide that right now." He leaned closer, pulling Wyatt's eyelids open with his thumbs. "You are completely at my mercy."

Elliott's expression suddenly turned serious, all traces of mirth disappearing as he pulled a syringe from his jacket pocket, holding it up and looking at it fondly as he turned it so the overhead light best hit the gleaming metal and sparkling liquid. "I really, really wished that we could have done this another way, but you've made it clear that you're not going to cooperate, so I'm afraid you leave me no choice. You will never dream with Aidan again."

"If you drug me to sleep, I'll just dream with Aidan. I won't dream with anyone else." Wyatt was frantic now, his eyes fixed on the syringe as Elliott carefully prepared it, knocking his fingernail against the side as he coaxed the air bubbles to the top and squirted them out. "It won't do you any good to force me to sleep."

"That, Wyatt, is where you're wrong." Elliott sounded almost sympathetic, and his expression bordered on kind as he tore an alcohol-soaked bit of gauze out of its wrapper and swiped it along Wyatt's arm. "This," he said, holding up the needle, "contains more than just the starter dose of the drugs we kept you on the last time you were here. I've added Vinculex. I'm sure," he added, his face twisting from sympathetic to malicious, "you know what that does."

"No." Wyatt shook his head as he frantically prayed that it wasn't true. "You can't! It—it won't—"

"It will." Elliott placed the tip of the syringe against Wyatt's arm, holding the limb steady with his other hand. "This is your last chance, Wyatt. Agree to work with me and you'll get to dream with your lover again."

Even thinking about it left Wyatt feeling like his heart was being ripped out through his chest, and for a brief, fleeting second, he contemplated agreeing, thought that maybe he could bide his time, learn more about Elliott and his colleagues and pass the information on to Aidan, but as soon as the thought crossed his mind, he knew he couldn't go through with it. He couldn't do it, no matter what the consequences. "No."

"I had really hoped it wouldn't have to be this way, Wyatt." Elliott's expression was again sympathetic as he slowly pushed the needle into Wyatt's vein and pressed the plunger. "I do hope you'll be more cooperative when we speak tonight." He tucked the syringe back into his jacket before he turned to leave, flashing one last, regretful look at Wyatt before he slipped through the door, closing it gently behind him.

Wyatt didn't answer, he couldn't. He could feel the drug as it surged through his system, and then he was overwhelmed by a sudden, intense pain like he'd never felt before. He tried to curl up into a ball, to hug his stomach, but the restraints prevented that, and he could only lie there, moaning as his body trembled. When the other drugs kicked in, sending him down into a sleep so deep he had no hope of even dreaming, much less visiting the Dreamscape, it was a relief, and Wyatt gave into them without a fight.

Chapter Thirty-One

EVERY bit of Aidan's body hurt. Fire raced along his skin, drums pounded in his skull, and needles stabbed into his eardrums. His muscles spasmed as though electricity raced through them, contracting and expanding too quickly for him to control his limbs and hurting so much it made his bones ache. His stomach roiled, clenching as it sent conflicting messages of nausea and extreme hunger to his brain. Even his lungs were in on it, wrapped tight in steel bands and making it agony to draw even the tiniest of breaths.

Tears leaked out from under his eyelids as he struggled to fight through the fog in his brain and gain some sense of place and time. He could feel the cushions beneath him, their soft padding doing nothing to ease the pain, and heard voices but couldn't make out individual words. It was all just noise that grated on his sensitive ears as they spewed meaningless babble.

A hand landed on his shoulder and he twitched, trying futilely to get away from the added pressure, a tiny whimper escaping his lips when he completely failed to move.

"Aidan?" Kyler leaned down close, keeping his voice low as he tried to catch Aidan's attention. "Can you hear me?"

He could, but he couldn't answer. His voice wouldn't respond any more than the rest of his body, and he longed to return to the oblivion of unconsciousness. All he could do was groan as Kyler brushed the tears from his cheeks with a gentle hand.

"He's waking up."

Brianna inched closer, trying to peer over the shoulders of the people crowded around the couch. "Is he…?"

"I don't know." Kyler frowned down at his patient, his expression growing more worried as Aidan continued to whimper and twitch but failed to give any sort of coherent response. He'd bandaged the cut on Aidan's forehead as soon as they'd gotten him on the couch, but there was something off in the readings he was getting, something he couldn't treat if his suspicions were right. "Aidan," he tried again, this time running his thumbs just below his friend's eyes. "Can you open your eyes?"

This time, Aidan managed to make a sound that resembled disagreement. He fought hard with his eyelids, but they wouldn't budge, wouldn't even flutter, and he didn't have the energy to keep up the battle. It was all he could do to remain focused on Kyler's voice, and even shaking his head was out of the question.

Kyler frowned at the noise Aidan was making and moved his hand to rest against Aidan's forehead. It was warmer than it should have been, and his frown deepened as he tried to figure out exactly what the problem was and what he could do about it. His tablet only confirmed what his eyes had already told him—Aidan was in agony, but with no discernible physical cause. "Calm down," he whispered gently, stroking his hand over Aidan's sweat-slicked forehead and exchanging worried glances with their friends.

No one spoke for several minutes, the silence only broken by Aidan's piteous moans and the soothing noises Kyler made as he tried to keep Aidan calm. Everyone else hovered awkwardly, feeling like they should do or say something, but lacking any idea what.

It was just beginning to get awkward when Carina cleared her throat, breaking the growing tension. "What's happening to him?"

"I don't know." Kyler kept his voice soft and gentle because Aidan was responding a little to his tone, though not his words. "Physically, he's fine, except for the cut on his head, but he's in anguish." He stroked Aidan's forehead once again, gently rubbing his thumb along the length of the bandaged cut. "I suspect it has something to do with his Bond and whatever those people are doing to Wyatt, but without both of them here, I can't confirm anything."

"Is there anything you can do?"

Kyler shook his head, letting his concern show as he watched Carina complete the switch from lawyer to worried friend. "Muscle relaxers might help, or at least stop the spasms, but I don't have any with me. I don't want to give him painkillers without talking to him first, and I'm reluctant to give him another sedative. The last one only wore off a few hours ago."

Brianna circled around to the back of the couch and peered over it at Aidan and Kyler. "Do you have muscle relaxers you can go get?"

"Yes. Why?" Kyler directed his curious gaze toward Brianna, taking his eyes off Aidan for the first time since he'd fallen and hit his head. "I don't think it's a good idea for me to leave while he's like this."

"What if he were asleep?"

"Possibly," Kyler allowed, his tone hesitant. "I don't want to drug him, though, and I don't know how successful you will be at keeping him asleep in this state. The pain he is in will wake him up."

"Hunter and I can keep him asleep, at least long enough for you to go get the muscle relaxers. We can talk to him, too. Maybe he can tell us something about what's going on."

Kyler thought about it for a moment, frowning down at his patient and weighing the pros and cons of leaving. Part of him feared Brianna and Hunter would not be successful and that something worse would happen while he was gone, but if he went, he could bring back more supplies and be better prepared to deal with a turn for the worse, should one occur.

Aidan shifted under his watchful gaze, moaning lowly and scrunching his face up in pain. His eyelids fluttered, and for a very brief moment, he gazed up at Kyler with the most pain-filled look Kyler had seen in his years as a doctor. He immediately stroked Aidan's forehead, carefully pressing his eyes closed and softly shushing him. "Okay." He couldn't watch Aidan suffer any longer.

Brianna patted him on the shoulder and held out her hand to her Bondmate as she circled the couch, pushing the coffee table back a little farther after stepping over Olin and Carina to reach the open area in front of it. When Hunter joined her, they settled down together, curling up on the carpet, each of them reaching up to gently take Aidan's hand. "We'll keep him asleep until you get back," she promised, giving Kyler the most reassuring smile she could manage and then letting her eyes close.

All three of them were soundly asleep within seconds.

AIDAN looked around, frowning as he recognized his apartment. He was still lying on the couch, sprawled over the cushions, but now, instead of overwhelming pain and a cacophony of voices grating on his overly sensitive ears, there was peace and silence. His body didn't hurt at all, and he marveled at the lack of pain as he slowly sat up, scanning the room for a familiar face.

The room was empty, and he was about to get up and search the rest of the apartment when Brianna stepped in from the kitchen, carrying a glass of water. Her presence hit Aidan like a punch to the gut, and he fell back onto the cushions, only then realizing what he had missed while marveling at the lack of pain.

He couldn't feel Wyatt.

Brianna settled next to him, grimacing as she put the glass of water on the coffee table. "Aidan? What's wrong? Do you still hurt?"

"He's not here."

"Who's not?"

"Wyatt. H-he's not here." He tapped his temple.

"Of course he's not, honey. He's probably awake. You were hurting so much, though, that Hunter and I—"

"No!" Aidan cut her off, shaking his head violently. "He's not *here*." He jabbed his finger emphatically into his forehead, hitting the spot where he was cut in the waking world. "I can't feel him. *At all*."

Her eyes widened as understanding dawned, and she sucked in a startled breath, covering her open mouth with dainty fingers. "You're sure?"

Tears welled up in Aidan's eyes as he nodded. "Yes. I can't. It's not— it's empty, where he usually is. There's nothing, at all, not even an echo."

"Oh God. Hunter!" She turned toward the kitchen as she called for her Bondmate. The plan had been for him to stay back, just providing support while Brianna kept Aidan calm, but this was too big for either of them to handle alone.

Hunter popped his head through the doorway, his expression a combination of worried and curious. "What's wrong?"

"Wyatt's not... I can't...." Aidan couldn't say it again, and he cast a desperate glance at Brianna.

"He can't feel Wyatt. At all."

"Fuck." Hunter quickly crossed the room and sank to sit cross-legged on the floor next to the couch, looking up at his Bondmate and his friend. "Nothing?"

"No," Aidan protested. The physical pain was nothing compared to this and in a way had been a blessing. At least it had kept him too out of it to be aware of the hole in his head... and his heart. "Not even an echo, like there is when one of us is asleep and the other isn't. Just... nothing."

"We have to tell Kyler and Carina."

"Yeah." Hunter exchanged a wordless glance with Brianna. "I'll go tell them. You stay with Aidan."

"No." Aidan forced himself to sit up. "I don't want to stay here. I *can't*. Wake me up."

Brianna gently laid her hand on Aidan's shoulder. "Aidan, honey, we can't. You're in too much pain when you're awake."

"This is worse." Aidan put every bit of the agony he was feeling into his voice and choked back a sob as he tried to continue. "That kept me from feeling *this*. At least then I couldn't tell that Wyatt is j-just gone."

Hunter awkwardly patted Aidan's knee. Comfort was definitely more his Bondmate's forte, but he couldn't just sit there and do nothing. "Aidan, man, I get it, but—"

"No! You don't!" Aidan jerked his knee away as he cut Hunter off. "You can't! Brianna is *right there!*" He jabbed his finger toward her emphatically. "I can't feel Wyatt *at all*! I can't even tell if he's *alive!*"

"Aidan." Brianna squeezed his shoulder gently. "I'm sure you would be able to tell if he were... were dead." The last word came out as barely a whisper, like saying it any louder would give weight to the possibility.

"How?" He turned toward her, blinking back tears as he met her eyes. "How would I possibly know? There's just a hole where he used to be. I can't tell if they did something to him so that I just can't feel him or—" He swallowed hard, hardly daring to think it, much less give voice to it. "Or worse."

"I think you would know," Hunter said softly, folding his hands in his lap and tilting his head so he could meet Aidan's eyes straight on. "Even if they are blocking you, I think you would still feel it. Besides," he added, looking back down at his hands as he twisted them in his lap, "it wouldn't make sense. They can't make him dream for them if he's dead, and that's what they want, right? It's in their best interest that he be alive and healthy."

Regardless of what the men who took him wanted, Wyatt wasn't healthy, hadn't been when he was taken, and Hunter's words offered scant comfort. Aidan looked back at him with a hollow gaze and slumped further into the couch. "Then what are they doing to him? Why can't I feel him?"

"I don't know, man." Hunter shrugged and offered an apologetic smile. "Wish I did." He pressed his lips together and shifted restlessly, putting his palms against the floor and curling his legs under him. "I'm going to go, all right? I need to at least tell Carina about this, and see if Kyler's back yet."

"No!" Aidan shot upright, shrugging off Brianna's restraining hand and leaning forward with a desperate look in his eyes. "You *have* to wake me up."

"Aidan—"

"*Please.*" He took Brianna's hands in his. "It *hurts*, Briana. I c-can't keep feeling this. I'd rather be in physical pain than this."

"Aidan, honey, you didn't see—"

"I felt it, okay!" He was yelling now, but he didn't care. He couldn't bear this hollow ache. "I didn't need to see because I *felt* it. I know what that felt like and I know what this feels like, and I would rather feel that."

"No." Hunter's voice was soft but firm, and he shook his head as he looked at Aidan. "You looked like you were going to hurt yourself. More, I mean, and I think Kyler felt the same way. We're not waking you up without his okay."

Aidan sucked in a shaky breath, sprang to his feet, and began pacing the room. He clenched his hands into fists so tight that his nails cut into his palms. He hated this, hated being trapped here, completely at the mercy of the two Dreamers who controlled the environment. When he was in the Dreamscape with Wyatt, it was fun and exciting to see how Wyatt would change the world to suit their mood, but Wyatt always woke Aidan when he asked. Hunter and Brianna were keeping him here, and for the first time, he understood the fear some people had of Dreamers.

"Wake. Me. Up," he insisted, emphasizing every word as he shook with frustration and fury.

"No." Brianna circled the couch and positioned herself directly in Aidan's path so he had to stop short to avoid running her over. "You need to rest, Aidan."

"This isn't restful." It was anything but.

He moved to step around Brianna, but she stopped him with a hand on his arm. "What if I sent you deeper?"

"What do you mean?" He tilted his head to the side and frowned at her, forcing back the hope that she'd come up with an agreeable solution.

"I won't wake you up, and Hunter won't either. We can't watch that, and Hunter's right, Kyler was worried." Brianna held up a hand to forestall Aidan's protest. "I *will* put you into a deeper sleep, though, if you want. I can make you sleep so deeply that you won't dream at all."

"How will I know what's going on?" Aidan wouldn't care while he was asleep, he knew, but even the idea of being out of touch with the effort to locate and free Wyatt made him ill. The idea of not feeling any pain—mental, emotional, or physical—was tempting, but he couldn't let Brianna do that to him if it meant he was stuck asleep without any idea what was going on until Wyatt was rescued. He just couldn't let everyone else do everything. Wyatt was *his* Bondmate, *his* lover, *his* responsibility.

"I'll wake you up—*all* the way up—as soon as Kyler is back and gives you whatever medicine he thinks you need. I promise." She slid her hand down Aidan's arm and wrapped her fingers around his hand. "I know you need to know what's going on. I would if it were Hunter," she added with a faint smile, "and I'm not going to deprive you of that. But I can't sit back and let you be in that much pain, Aidan."

"I'm in that much pain here, too, Bri. It's just a different kind of pain."

"I know." Brianna tugged gently on Aidan's arm and led him back to the couch, pushing him down and curling up next to him, her head on his shoulder and her legs practically in his lap. She pressed close, her arms slipping around his waist and her hands resting loosely on his far hip.

Aidan wrapped his arm around her, instinctively holding her close as though she were the one being comforted, and sighed as he rested his chin atop her head. "Do you promise you'll wake me up when Kyler gets back? No matter what he says about it?"

"Of course"

"We both will," Hunter added, again resting his hand on Aidan's knee. "You just have to get some rest, man, okay? I promise we'll wake you up as soon as Kyler gets back, and we'll make sure you're awake to hear any news we get."

"I need to hear what Zane has to say." He wouldn't rest easy if he didn't, no matter what Hunter or Brianna did. "I have to know who has Wyatt."

Hunter patted Aidan's knee. "We know. And you will. I promise."

Aidan closed his eyes and held Brianna tighter. It didn't ease the ache in his heart or fill the hole left by his inability to sense Wyatt anymore, but it was comforting nonetheless, and he took everything he could from the feeling of a warm body in his arms, even though it was too soft and too small to be the one he wanted to be holding. "Okay."

Brianna pulled back just enough that she could look into Aidan's eyes. "You're sure?"

"Yeah." He nodded. "Just be sure to wake me up when it's time to talk to Zane again, okay?"

"We will, I promise." Brianna kissed Aidan's cheek and then cuddled up close again. "Just close your eyes, okay?"

Aidan nodded as he relaxed back into the cushions, his eyelids slipping shut almost of their own accord. He could hear Hunter and Brianna conferring quietly, and then everything faded away, cocooning him in darkness, silence, and peace.

Chapter Thirty-Two

WYATT could feel the heavy weight of plush covers draped over his body and a fluffed pillow beneath his head. Even without opening his eyes, though, he could tell it wasn't *his* bed. It wasn't cozy enough, the covers were a little too heavy, and most importantly, it didn't smell right. Wyatt's bed, the one he shared with Aidan, always had a fresh, spicy scent, a mixture of fresh breeze from their detergent and the cinnamon discs Aidan always sucked on while he was working. Even when the sheets were fresh out of the laundry, the scent didn't fade entirely, and all Wyatt usually had to do to feel comforted was roll over and bury his face in the pillows, even if it was just the dream version of their bed.

This bed lacked any sort of distinctive scent at all, and that was the first clue that Wyatt wasn't where he wanted to be. As he moved his arms—and said a silent thank you that he actually *could*—he noticed the sheets were too rough as well as too heavy, and though he might have once thought them luxuriously soft, he didn't anymore. Aidan didn't spend the money he'd earned from the novels he'd illustrated as a side job often, but when he did, he spent it well, and extremely high thread count sheets were one of his indulgences. It was an easily justified one, considering how much time they spent in bed, given that Wyatt was a Dreamer, but it had left Wyatt spoiled.

When he had made all the observations he possibly could while lying mostly still, Wyatt opened his eyes and slowly blinked them against the dim light of the room. He'd suspected what he was going to see, but it was still disappointing to have his suspicions confirmed. The room was the same one he'd first come to awareness in after that fateful last meal with his family, identical down to every detail. The only thing that had changed was Wyatt himself, and the age of the man sitting in front of the window. There was more gray at Elliott's temples than there had been the first time Wyatt met him, and the wrinkles around his eyes were deeper and better defined. He looked the same as he had just a few hours earlier, sitting next to the bed he'd strapped Wyatt to, but the differences between his appearance now and his appearance when Wyatt had first met him were more obvious here, enhanced by the way the room hadn't changed one iota.

Slowly, Wyatt sat up, looking around and noting the position of everything in the room before leaning back against the headboard. Where

Elliott's dream-room had once seemed luxurious, it now seemed cramped and shoddy, the product of someone who wouldn't know quality if it were shoved in his face. "I'm still not going to do whatever it is you want me to, Elliott. And you won't impress me with this display of... whatever this is." He waved his hand around to encompass the room and all of its contents. "I'm not a poor boy who hasn't had anything nice in his entire life anymore."

"The point isn't to impress you, not this time." Elliott twisted the switch on the lamp, brightening the room. "The first time I brought you here, it was, you're right, but not anymore. Now it's about... other things." He smiled in a way that made Wyatt's whole body shiver with revulsion.

"What other things?"

"Power, mostly." Elliott smirked as he watched Wyatt try not to squirm under his gaze. "I know you would never come here if you had a choice, so I brought you here to remind you that you don't."

Wyatt lifted his chin as he glared back at his captor, putting every bit of hatred he felt for him into his gaze. "I'm not going to cooperate with you, no matter how much you threaten me."

"I'm doing more than threatening, Wyatt." Elliott stood and crossed the room until he was standing by the bed, again looming over Wyatt. "You are mine, and the sooner you accept that, the better things will be for you. I gave you the opportunity to have a good life, and you rejected it. Now you're going to live the one I choose."

Wyatt fought the urge to slink down into the bed and forced himself to climb out of it. Standing, he was taller than Elliott, and he couldn't keep the evident pleasure off his face as Elliott had to look up to meet his gaze. "Only for a little while, and not without a fight. My friends will find me, *Aidan* will find me, and you *will* lose."

"And how is your precious Bondmate going to find you, Wyatt?" Elliott asked as he traversed the room and sank back into the chair. He crossed his legs, resting his right ankle on his left knee, and held the tumbler loosely between his fingers. "He's probably far too occupied with other things."

"Like what?" Wyatt leaned against the wall where the door would be if the room had one, his arms crossed over his chest and his legs crossed at the ankles. He couldn't imagine anything else that would possibly be on Aidan's mind, but he was curious about where this line of taunting was leading. If he could get Elliott to reveal even a part of his plan, it could be useful.

"Agonizing pain would be my first guess. Or perhaps his friends have already dragged him to a hospital where they've drugged him insensible. Either way, I doubt his mind is on you right now."

Wyatt's heart lurched in his chest at Elliott's words, and he couldn't stop himself from leaning forward a little as concern and curiosity forced him to drop his aloof attitude. "Why would he be in pain?"

"Come sit down and I'll tell you." Elliott gestured to the chair opposite his once more. "We'll have a little chat, and then I'll explain what your Bondmate is likely going through."

"Tell me now, and I'll sit down and listen to whatever it is you have to say," Wyatt countered, again leaning back so his head was against the wall. It was sheer bravado, and possibly a stupid move as he had absolutely no power here and knew it, but he wasn't going to give into Elliott's demands without a fight. He couldn't, not if he wanted to stay sane until Aidan found him.

Elliott raised his eyebrows and they disappeared under the bushy white of his hair. "Are you so naïve as to believe that I'm going to simply acquiesce to your demands or are you trying to fight me? I'm not telling you anything until you sit and we talk."

"Believe what you want." Wyatt shrugged, leaned his head back against the wall, and let his eyes slide closed. His stomach churned with worry, and there was a niggling feeling at the back of his mind telling him he should know what was wrong with Aidan, but he couldn't put his finger on what and he wasn't going to give in to find out. Not yet. "I'm not sitting down and talking with you until you tell me."

Elliott didn't dignify that with an answer, just settled back into his chair and watched Wyatt curiously. His gaze was hard and sharp and made Wyatt's skin tingle as he felt it on him, but neither of them was willing to give up their perceived advantage. The minutes stretched out without either of them moving, and the tension mounted in the room until the Dreamscape manifested it as thick cords of reddish brown arching between them. The taut lines creaked and groaned as they undulated, rippling up and down until they snapped, exploding into tiny flakes that settled over the room like ash. As time dragged on, the cords grew thicker and tighter and exploded more rapidly, leaving no surface in the room untouched by flecks the color of dried blood.

Still, neither of them moved.

Wyatt thought about manipulating the Dreamscape, of making the flakes disappear, taking them both somewhere else, or even seeing if he could break free of this dream altogether, but he wasn't ready to fail, so he didn't try. Instead, he glowered at Elliott, barely resisting the urge to smirk when the flecks settled inside Elliott's cup and his expression turned horribly sour.

When the entire surface of the drink was covered in reddish brown, Elliott set the glass on the table. "Vinculex destroys Bonds, but it only works right if both partners are given a dose. When only one partner gets it, it's horribly painful for the other one. Right now, your Bondmate probably feels as though his internal organs are being ripped out, and he will, until they give him a dose as well."

"And if they don't?" Wyatt's eyes bored straight into Elliott, and his expression and tone said clearer than any words could express that he wasn't going to argue this one. "What happens to him—to us—if they don't give it to him?"

"I don't know. If they give it to him, it will stop the pain but finish the process of destroying your Bond. If they don't...." He shrugged as he gestured for Wyatt to come closer and continued when Wyatt pushed himself off the wall. "No one has ever let it go long enough to determine what would happen if only one partner ever received a dose. No one has ever been willing to endure the pain long enough to find out. It is, I hear, indescribably excruciating."

Wyatt sat in the chair Elliott had indicated, moving slowly as he brushed the reddish brown flakes from the seat so he wouldn't shake with fury. "So if they take Aidan to the hospital...."

"The doctors will eventually figure out what is causing the pain and give him a dose as well." Elliott folded his hands together in his lap and regarded Wyatt with a satisfied expression. "And then it will all be over. He has no reason to come for you anymore, Wyatt. Your Bond may already be irrevocably destroyed, and if it isn't, it will be soon. You're on your own, and you belong to me."

Wyatt's stomach turned, and it was only because he retained some control over the Dreamscape that he managed to keep whatever was in it down. "That's not true," he argued, but even as he said it, he knew the words were false, and that Elliott was at least partially right. He had been too wrapped up in Elliott and his schemes to notice, but now that he was looking for it, the spot where he could always feel the vibrant hum of Aidan was empty, gaping and aching instead of filled with the love he'd come to rely on.

"We both know it is. Can you feel him at all?"

He didn't want to answer, but Wyatt found himself shaking his head before he'd even thought about it, and the quiet "No" that escaped his lips was beyond his control.

"I didn't think so." Elliott leaned forward, his expression smug as he looked at Wyatt. "You do realize, don't you, that even if your dream scenario comes true, and your supposed friends do somehow find a way to save you, that you may never feel him again? That there may not be a way to stop his pain without giving him Vinculex as well? That he may already be irrevocably damaged by the pain he's experiencing? Do you *really* want to go back to him if that's the case?"

"I love him." Wyatt lifted his chin and met Elliott's eyes with defiance. His gut clenched and his heart ached at the thought of any of the things Elliott suggested, but he wouldn't let Elliott know that.

"But will you still? And will he still love you?"

"Of course I will, and so will he." No matter what Elliott said, Wyatt wouldn't doubt that. He couldn't. It was all he had to hold on to.

"And you're certain of this?" Elliott sounded sympathetic as he shook his head sadly. "Oh, Wyatt. You are still so young, and so naïve. Most people wouldn't be able to stand being around someone who reminded them so much of what they'd lost and who had caused them so much pain. Your Aidan may want his dose even if they do pull off a miraculous rescue."

"He won't." Wyatt thrust his chin out further, his mouth set in a thin line. "And you're the one who is causing us pain."

Elliott settled back in his chair, watching as Wyatt struggled to maintain his composure. Wyatt wanted to leap across the table separating them and wring Elliott's throat, but just as he had the first time he'd been in this room, he knew that attacking Elliott would only go poorly for him, and so he managed to keep his seat and his fortitude—barely.

"I'm only doing what I have to. You were given the chance to cooperate."

"You kidnapped me and wanted me to agree to be your slave and help you in your unethical and illegal business practices," Wyatt replied in a flat voice. "That's not offering me a chance to cooperate."

"See it your way. You're here now, and I told you what you wanted to know, so now it's time to listen." Elliott reached into his jacket pocket and pulled out a slip of paper, which he set on the table.

The visible manifestation of their tension had stopped once Elliott had begun his explanation of how Aidan was being affected by what was happening to Wyatt, but the flecks that had settled over everything remained, and the slip of paper sank into them and was quickly buried.

"You're going to want to take that," Elliott told him once the paper was almost completely covered, only one small spot of white showing where it was.

"No, I'm not. If you want me to do something, you can tell me." He didn't add that he would still refuse. He didn't need to. They both knew it. "I'm not going to read anything. This is a dream. Your books don't have any words in them. Why should I believe that paper will say anything or that it won't change the minute I read it if it does?"

"It won't, but suit yourself." Elliott stood, straightening his jacket and brushing the flakes that had landed on his legs and shoulders to the floor. "I thought you might want to be prepared when we send you into a dream, but if you think you can figure it out, then, by all means, don't read it. You'll have time, I suppose. My staff has told me that we must cure this pneumonia of yours before we ask too much of you." He shook his head in mock sadness. "Just another reason you never should have left, Wyatt. We never let you get sick."

Wyatt didn't know what he meant. "What do you—?" he started, but Elliott vanished, popping out of the dream without a sound and leaving Wyatt alone in the dirty room. He looked around, searching for a clue other than the piece of paper Elliott had left for him, and frowned with disgust at the flakes that covered everything. His vision wavered as he concentrated on them, willing them to vanish, and a few of the flakes wavered, flashing out of existence before appearing again. "Dammit!"

If he couldn't do this, he would never break free.

He tried again, and again, and in the end, his head hurt and he couldn't tell if his inability to control the dream was caused by whatever drugs Elliott and his people were pumping into his body, the fever that still ravaged it, or both. Neither helped, he was sure, but in the end, it didn't matter. Both meant he was stuck here, unable to get to Aidan, unable to even clean up the mess that surrounded him.

With a sigh, Wyatt settled back in the chair, letting his head fall forward as he watched the flakes that dotted the arm of it. He had brushed off the seat when he'd sat down the first time, but flakes still covered the arms and back, and some of them stuck to his skin and sleeve. Now they threatened to fall on him once more and dirty the only relatively clean place in the room, sullying it with a tangible reminder of Elliott's presence that kept Wyatt from concentrating on what he needed to do.

They were keeping him from Aidan, and the anger he felt at that thought sent energy surging through his body. As he directed every bit of his anger toward them, they wavered and vanished, leaving the arm of the chair pristine once more. This sparked an idea in Wyatt's head. Careful to keep hold of his frustration, he focused his attention on another small area of flakes and ignored them everywhere else.

Slowly, they began to disappear, vanishing in tiny chunks. Wyatt cleaned the bed first, then the chairs, and then moved to the other furniture and the floor. With each area he managed to clean, his hope and confidence grew. He wasn't ready yet to rebel: there wasn't any point in trying to wake up while he was still held prisoner in the real world, and he wasn't strong enough to try to find Aidan, even if he could feel him. This, however, was something he could do, and it gave him hope that when Elliott shoved him into another dream, he'd be able to manipulate it for his own means.

Anything he could do to make this better was a small step in the right direction.

When the room was clean, Wyatt picked up the paper Elliott had left, climbed onto the bed, and lay across it diagonally. He folded his hands loosely over his stomach with the paper clasped under them, and let his eyes close. He would look at the paper later, but for now, he was going to rest and see if he could will himself from dreams into oblivion.

Chapter Thirty-Three

AIDAN watched through heavily lidded eyes as Zane cleared his throat, waiting to get everyone's attention so he could resume his explanation of what he had found about the people who took Wyatt. They'd been trying for over ten minutes now, and Aidan *really* wanted them to hurry, but every time they tried to start, something would come up, delaying the explanation—and Aidan's return to the oblivion of dreamless sleep. Every delay was legitimate, but Aidan *hurt*, and he didn't know how much longer he'd be able to hold out.

When Brianna had woken him, every bit of Aidan's body had been in excruciating pain, despite the muscle relaxer that left him feeling loopy and floppy. His muscles hadn't been trembling, so he'd been able to summon enough coherency to actually talk, but that had been the only difference between then and when he'd first felt the agonizing pain. Every other bit of torture was still present, even after Kyler injected him with the strongest painkiller he had access to.

He had just gotten settled in an upright position, leaning drunkenly against Ratri's shoulder so he could listen to what Zane had to say, when a knock on the door heralded the arrival of Gwendolyn and Misty, two of Wyatt's friends from work. They were friends with Brianna as well, had heard about what happened through the hospital grapevine, and had rushed over as soon as they'd been able. Their presence was welcomed, particularly by Hunter and Brianna, who were relieved to have other Dreamers to help them. But their arrival necessitated a delay while they were caught up on the entire situation thus far.

That was five minutes ago, and Brianna was almost done with her succinct explanation, but Aidan was afraid something else was going to come up and delay them yet again. "Are we ready?" he asked, his voice a hoarse croak, barely audible over the hushed conversations of his friends.

"We should be," Ratri said, moving Aidan into a slightly more comfortable position. "Come on, guys," he yelled, drowning out all other conversations in the room. "Let's not make this take any longer than we have to. People are waiting on this information."

The room immediately quieted and all eyes turned to Zane, who shifted a little as he looked around. "Are we ready?"

"Please, Zane, proceed." Carina nodded at the private investigator, once again in full lawyer mode and ready to act on whatever information Zane had collected.

"All right, well." Zane sucked in a deep breath and released it slowly. He pulled a sheaf of printouts and data cards out of his briefcase, handed them to Damon along with a portable drive, and picked up his data pad. "The company depositing money into Ursula and Lorne Mettler's account was a dummy corporation. It only existed on paper, and its ties to the parent company were hidden well. We had to trace through four layers of companies before we got to a real one, which is why it took so long."

"Okay, and?" Tabatha leaned forward, resting her arms on her knees, and waved one hand in a circular motion that impatiently signaled for Zane to get to the point.

"The first company we found was Fabrisystems, a manufacturing company that specializes in low-end electronics."

"What do you mean, the first? Isn't that the company who took Wyatt?"

Zane shook his head. "No. We thought it was, at first, but their operations haven't changed at all since Wyatt got free. In fact, they're doing better, so they clearly haven't lost any inside advantage, and they're not really in a cutthroat market. A room full of Dreamers wouldn't be able to do much for them, much less one."

"So then what?" Hunter scooted to the edge of his chair, only held back from springing up to pace the room by Brianna's hand on his arm. "You said you had something?"

"I do." Zane scrolled through the screen of his data pad, pursing his lips until he found what he was looking for. "We were stumped for a while, but Fabrisystems is a subsidiary of Reyes Innovations. Now, Reyes Innovations doesn't have any products that they sell themselves, but they do have several other subsidiaries, one of which *is* in a cutthroat market and *has* lost market share in the months since Aidan found Wyatt. It's called Lumoinnovations, and *it* is the company that has been paying Wyatt's parents. A man named Elliott Sloan is the head of their Market Research Division, and we have good reason to believe that he is the person who spearheaded the project."

Aidan struggled to sit up straighter, fighting back the pain to join the conversation. "Wyatt mentioned a man named Elliott when he was telling me about what his parents did, and when we met today in the Dreamscape. He said he was the one who, uh, trained him."

"That would make sense," Zane acknowledged with a nod. "From what we could find on him, he's a Dreamer, but with very little ability. He has to augment his abilities with drugs to do more than watch someone's dreams, and he can't even do that if they're not practically in the same room with him."

Misty plopped one foot heavily on the ground to keep herself from falling off the arm of the couch. "The guy is a *Dreamer* and he did that to Wyatt? How? I mean, it was bad enough when I thought it was someone who didn't really understand, but if he can do it too...." She shuddered and trailed off, completely at a loss for words.

"The psychological profile that Lumoinnovations did on him when he was hired indicates that he has great animosity toward Dreamers," Zane responded in an uncertain voice. "I can only assume that he is bitter about his lack of abilities. He's strong enough that he was classified as a Dreamer once he hit puberty, but he doesn't have the ability to do anything with it. He probably resents those of you who can."

"Okay, that sucks for him," Gwendolyn said, scooting over so Misty could squeeze between her and the arm of the couch, "but that doesn't give him the right to do what he did. I mean, if his abilities are so weak, most people wouldn't even know he had them. No one is going around branding Dreamers or anything."

"We could be here all day if we try to figure out the workings of that man's mind," Kyler reminded them as the conversation swelled with speculation. "We don't need to know why he did what he did, just where. So long as we have proof of that, the rest of it doesn't matter."

"Oh, we have proof." Zane gestured to the stacks of information he'd given to Carina. "Most of the Market Research Division at Lumoinnovations is engaged in legitimate activities. They run polls and focus groups and whatever else they do to find out what type of marketing is most likely to get people to buy. There is one small department, however, that was formed about a year before Wyatt was taken. They have an unusually large budget for a department that consists of only eight people, and they had extremely high turnover in the first six months following Wyatt's arrival there." He paused and looked around the room. "None of the people who left are still alive. They all died within two months of leaving Lumoinnovations."

Aidan's head snapped up at that revelation. "You mean he had people *killed*? Because they didn't agree with what he was doing to Wyatt?" He wanted to disbelieve with his entire being, but he remembered what Wyatt had told him about the man, and when he thought about it at all, it didn't seem that far-fetched.

"It seems that way," Zane agreed, "though I don't have any proof of that."

"We don't need proof of *that*," Carina pointed out. "We need proof of what they're doing now. We can worry about what they did in the past later, after we get Wyatt back."

"Besides," Brianna added, her arms still slung around Hunter's waist, "while that's horrible, I don't see how it implicates them in having Wyatt, even back then."

"That in itself doesn't, no, but on the first business day of every quarter, that department bought a very large amount of goods and services from Fabrisystems. The same amount each time. Apparently, their low-end electronics broke. *A lot*," Zane added wryly. "Or at least, they used to. Amazingly, all their repair bills went away at the same time Fabrisystems stopped paying the Mettlers."

"How much were they paying them?"

Zane slid a piece of paper across the coffee table to Tabatha. She picked it up, her eyes widening as she showed it to Damon.

"Our parents were getting that much a quarter because they *sold* Wyatt?" Damon's mouth dropped open as he clutched at Tabatha's arm. Their standard of living had improved once Wyatt had been taken away, but he didn't remember it improving *that* much.

"Tax-free too," Zane added. "Fabrisystems reported it as a payout for a settlement—damages awarded for pain and suffering, or something."

"Yeah, they suffered, all right." Tabatha rolled her eyes as she sank back on the couch and crossed her arms. "What else did those assholes get our brother into?"

"That is actually most of the proof against Lumoinnovations. It's in greater detail in the documents we provided." Zane gestured to the stack in front of Damon. "But that sums it up. The only other thing we have against them is how they found Wyatt again. It's not completely conclusive, but it should be enough, when coupled with what we've already told you, to get a warrant."

"How did they find him?" Aidan managed to ask. He'd been drifting on a wave of pain ever since sitting up, and it was getting harder and harder to concentrate on the conversation, particularly when it deviated into side topics. He didn't really care how much Wyatt's parents had been paid to sell him. He only cared that they managed to get him away from the people who currently held him—legally or not.

"It's a matter of public record. Wyatt has a driver's license. You registered your Bond. The address isn't hard to find with that." Zane pushed his hair back from his forehead and sighed. "They knew to look because a clerk at the courthouse told them to. I can't prove anything, but there's one who got a large deposit into his account right after Wyatt registered for residency here, and again after you registered your Bond."

"So why wait so long?" Aidan struggled to straighten. As the muscle relaxers and painkiller worked their way through his body, he was becoming more and more lethargic and slumping harder against Ratri. He wasn't sure he could really lift any of his limbs, and yet he still wanted to curl into a ball so he could clutch at his agitated stomach and claw at the fire that raced along his skin. The more the drugs were absorbed into his body, the less effective they were, and his pain levels were practically what they had been before Brianna had put him to sleep. "We registered our Bond five months ago."

"Red tape?" Zane shrugged. "There were people watching Wyatt's parents in Ambridia, but they stopped around the time Damon came out here."

Ratri cast a dark look toward Damon. "So he did lead them here."

"Doubtful." Zane cut off Damon's protest before it took form. "More likely, it was determined Wyatt's parents weren't going to do anything drastic about their funding being cut off, and they weren't needed anymore."

"So why'd they show up now, on the same day Wyatt's brother and sister did?"

"Coincidence." Zane quieted Ratri with a glance. "There's an investigator working for Lumoinnovations by the name of Crispin Aller."

"That's the man who took Wyatt!" Aidan sat up straight, shock and adrenaline giving him temporary muscle control the relaxants had taken away. "He's the one who shoved those papers into my hand!"

Zane's face darkened, his suspicions confirmed. "He's known in certain circles for operating outside the law. My guess is Elliott Sloan wanted him to get something that would help him keep Wyatt, maybe even break your Bond, and he had to wait for that."

Aidan collapsed back onto the couch, his temporary strength draining away at the reminder of what he was missing. "Would someone really do that?"

"Crispin would." Zane turned off his data pad and tucked it in his pocket. "I worked with him before he decided the ends always justified the means and started breaking the law to solve cases. I didn't want to have anything to do with it, and we went our separate ways."

"Good. You know what he's capable of." Carina gathered the papers together. "I'm going to take this down to the police and see if I can get something moving. I'll call as soon as I know anything for certain." She stopped in front of Aidan after she crossed the room, laying a hand on his shoulder and squeezing gently. "We're going to get him back."

Aidan couldn't hold back the wince that the added pressure from Carina's hand elicited, but he managed a nod anyway. "I know." For the first time since this nightmare had begun, he believed it.

As she left, Zane on her heels, Kyler moved over to the couch and put his hand around Aidan's shoulder. "Hey." He rested his free hand against Aidan's forehead and frowned at the elevated temperature. "How much pain are you in right now, Aidan?"

"On a scale of one to ten?" He kept blinking, hoping that eventually his vision would clear, but it remained hazy, and though he thought he saw Kyler's lips curve up into a tiny smile at the question, he couldn't be sure. "About a hundred."

Immediately, Kyler began digging in his bag. "Do you need another painkiller?"

"Doesn't really help." Aidan tried to draw his knees up to his chest, but his muscles wouldn't cooperate and he ended up twitching a little as he leaned over so far he was practically lying in Ratri's lap. "Nothing does, not really."

Kyler slid his hand over to the side of the bag and fingered the pre-loaded syringes he'd tucked into the pocket. "Do you want a sedative?"

"No." Aidan shook his head; his eyes squeezed shut against the pain. His body felt like it was trying to turn inside out, every cell afire with agony, but he couldn't give into unconsciousness. Not when they were this close. He had to hold on.

"Aidan...." Kyler cast a desperate glance around the room, silently begging their friends for help. He knew why Aidan didn't want to be sedated, and was in truth reluctant to do it, but something had to be done to relieve Aidan's pain, and if the muscle relaxers and painkillers weren't doing so, then he wasn't left with any other option.

Aidan scooted a little bit farther away from Kyler. He only managed to move a couple inches, but it made the point. "No."

"*Please.*"

Aidan was about to protest again when Misty and Gwendolyn broke off from talking to Hunter and Brianna and knelt in front of the couch. Two manicured hands gently touched Aidan's shoulder, and he opened his eyes to see the women staring down at him with identical expressions of concern.

"Come on," Misty said gently. "Let us help you sleep. We'll let you know anything Carina says and wake you up as soon as anything happens. I promise."

"I can feel him missing, even when I'm asleep." He blinked slowly, wondering if the slurred words had really come out of his mouth. "I can't feel it as much when I'm in pain. It's good."

"Maybe if you're asleep, he'll be able to find you."

"No. It's not...." Aidan shook his head, trying to clear the cobwebs so he could string his disjointed thoughts into a coherent sentence. "I don't think he can get to me. He would've pulled me to sleep if he could. I think whatever they're doing to him, it's keeping him from me. That's part of it."

"So we'll make sure you don't dream." Gwendolyn brushed her fingers over the hair at the nape of Aidan's neck and tucked the tag of his shirt back inside. "You can't keep doing this to yourself, Aidan. It won't do Wyatt any good if you're a wreck when he's found. He's going to need *you*, and if you're sick and weak because you wouldn't let us help you, how are you going to be able to help him?"

"Come on, Aidan, you know Wyatt," Misty said, picking up where Gwendolyn had left off. "If you're hurting, he's going to try to take care of you, even if he needs to be taking care of himself."

"Let them help you, man."

Aidan twisted his head a little so he could glare up at Ratri. "You too?"

Ratri held up both hands in a gesture of surrender. "Hey, when they're right, they're right. And I'm not getting into an argument with them." His expression sobered as he let his hands fall back down, sliding one of them over to squeeze Aidan's bicep. "Seriously, Aidan. There's nothing you can do, and it's killing us all to watch you like this. Let us help you."

Aidan could feel his resolve weakening with each of his friends' arguments. "But what if something comes up?" he asked, desperate to find a reason to cling to consciousness. If he were asleep, he might miss something, and that would be unforgivable.

"Then we'll take care of it." Olin twisted around from his position on the floor to look at Aidan. "That's what friends are for."

"We'll wake you up if you're needed, I promise."

There was no way Aidan could resist the combined power of all his friends, especially not when Misty used that tone on him. "Yeah, all right," he agreed, shifting a little so he could lie down fully. Four sets of hands stopped him, and he blinked in puzzlement. "I thought you wanted me to sleep?"

"In your bed," Misty said firmly, pointing one manicured finger toward the back of the apartment.

"But why?" He'd taken several involuntary naps stretched out on the couch since this nightmare had begun, and he couldn't understand what was wrong with taking a voluntary one there now.

"You're not sleeping with your head in my lap, for starters," Ratri said as he continued to ease Aidan upward. "And I ain't moving."

Gwendolyn rolled her eyes. "You'll be more comfortable in the bedroom. The couch isn't exactly big enough for you to stretch out."

She had a point, though part of Aidan was tempted to lie down right where he was just to irritate Ratri. It wouldn't do him any good in the end, however, so he let his friends help him up. With his arm slung over Gwendolyn's shoulder and Misty's arms wrapped around his waist, he began the long, arduous trek back to the bedroom.

Chapter Thirty-Four

THE house resembled the one Wyatt remembered from his childhood. The layout and decorations were completely different, but the aura of determined pride and making do with very little was familiar. Back when Wyatt was a child, still happily living with his family, his mother had done the same thing: arranging cheap knick-knacks and homemade facsimiles of more expensive décor around to the greatest advantage. If anyone looked at all closely, it was clear none of it was the real thing, but it was also clear it had been arranged with pride.

The surge of fond nostalgia he felt upon noticing the similarity surprised Wyatt. He had thought he'd left all fondness for his former life behind when he was sold by parents more interested in money than the welfare of their middle child.

The setting wasn't really the point, however, and Wyatt didn't stay to reminisce or linger over the ceramic figures dotting the shelf above the stairs. He'd been sent here to get specific information for Elliott, so he needed to get out of the house and situate himself somewhere there would be no risk of stumbling across it accidentally.

Wyatt might not have a choice about what dreams he visited at the moment, but he did control how he acted in them, and he wasn't going to use his time in the Dreamscape to do Elliott's bidding. He would spend it searching for Aidan or one of his other friends, not digging up secrets for the man trying to take away his freedom once again.

The house was missing all its windows and doors, leaving Wyatt with no easy exit. Clearly, whatever Elliott wanted him to find—Wyatt didn't know what it was because he hadn't read the paper left for him—was supposed to be in this house. That meant Wyatt wanted to be out of it.

As he staggered around, searching for a way out or a place he could create one, Wyatt leaned heavily on the walls and banisters and cursed Elliott again. The more he tried to move, even here, in the Dreamscape, the more obvious it became that Elliott hadn't taken the advice of his staff and let Wyatt recover from the disease ravaging his body before attempting to use him. Wyatt wasn't surprised—Elliott wasn't exactly the most honest or caring person he'd ever met—but it did make him wonder how long he'd been trapped. It felt like a day, maybe a little more, but between being trapped in the Dreamscape and the fever wracking his body, he had little sense of time.

It could have been a day. It could have been ten.

After searching for what he knew were minutes but felt like hours, Wyatt found the foyer and stared hard at the blank wall where the front door would have been had the house possessed one. It should have been easy to imagine a door and make one appear, but the wall didn't ripple, didn't even shimmer, and Wyatt frowned as he shook his head and focused his gaze to try again.

Sharp pain shot through his skull, and he staggered backward to the stairs, gasping for breath and rubbing at the bridge of his nose as he tried to will the pain away. It just got worse, transforming from a single point of pain to multiple spikes that spread out until it felt as though a legion of little creatures was stabbing ice picks into his head from every angle. He doubled over, wrapping his arms tightly around his stomach as he tried to fight the nausea threatening to overwhelm him.

It didn't work. Wyatt leaned over and spit the meager contents of his stomach onto the floor at his feet, gagging around the bile and wondering in the back of his mind how he had anything in him to spit up. He hadn't eaten while awake in a few days, he was sure, and in the Dreamscape, nothing like this ever happened. It wasn't supposed to, and the fact that it did set his stomach churning again, this time with terror.

The acidic taste lingered in his mouth, and he spat again, futilely trying to rid himself of the sour flavor. When it still remained on his tongue after he'd added several gobs of spit to the growing brown mess on the floor, Wyatt concentrated on willing the taste—and the mess—away.

The pain in his head spiked, the ice picks turned to jackhammers. He swayed, coming dangerously close to collapsing face-first into the glop at his feet, and only avoided falling flat by desperately gripping the banister.

It took some time for the dizziness to pass, and Wyatt couldn't tell if it was minutes or hours later, even in dream time, that he was finally able to lift his head from his arm and focus on anything other than the insides of his eyelids. The whole foyer slid in and out of focus as the air shimmered and thickened, leaving Wyatt peering through haze as he tried once again to concentrate on the blank wall.

He could handle the smelly pile at his feet and the sour taste in his mouth, but he *had* to get out of this house. The only thing that mattered was finding Aidan, and he couldn't do that trapped here.

With his thoughts focused on Aidan, Wyatt closed his eyes, braced himself, and mentally reached for that place that let him twist the Dreamscape. Even brushing against it sent a wave of pain through his body, but he ignored it, mentally steeling himself as he grabbed and twisted.

Wyatt had never felt such excruciating agony before. It made the pain he'd felt when he and Aidan had delayed consummating their Bond feel like a single fresh paper cut. The burning he'd felt then was merely the heat of a fever compared to the flames licking at his skin now. He curled into a ball and tumbled forward without thought for where or how he would land. He was only aware of the pain coursing through his body and rippling over his flesh, getting worse and worse. He hit the floor, hard, another wave of agony rolled over him, and then everything faded away.

COLD water splashed all over Wyatt, soaking him and leaving him coughing and sputtering as he tried to blink the drops out of his eyes and focus on the figure looming over him. When the man finally came into view, Wyatt shut his eyes and groaned. "Leave me alone."

"You didn't get the information I needed."

"I'm not going to get the information you need. There is *nothing* you can do that will make me cooperate."

Elliott set the bucket down and crossed his arms, watching his charge with an elegantly arched eyebrow. "You will."

"No." Wyatt opened his eyes and did his best to glare defiantly at Elliott. It wasn't easy; Elliott stood behind his head, which made the angle exceedingly awkward, and Wyatt was soaking wet, which diminished the effect.

"You can't do anything else." Elliott cocked his head to the side and let his lips curl up slightly. "Every time you try to do something other than what we want, you'll just end up right back here." His smile grew. "And then I'll just send you back out again."

Wyatt jutted his chin out. "Then I'll be in here a lot."

"I doubt that. You'll give in sooner or later."

"No, I—" Wyatt stopped as Elliott disappeared, leaving him on the wet bed in soggy clothes with a head that ached too much to think about trying to change anything.

The minutes passed slowly as Wyatt waited to be sent somewhere else. He was sure Elliott would force him out, but it never happened, and eventually, he moved on the bed, got off the water-soaked covers, and lay on the floor, staring at the ceiling as he wished he was dry and his head would stop hurting.

When his clothes mostly dried out and felt stiff against his skin, he cautiously sat up, moving with care to avoid jostling his aching head even more. The room was unchanging, full of the all-too-familiar furniture that had seemed so opulent and impressive once upon a time, still pristine and unlived in, and still—and now *with* a door.

Slowly, Wyatt climbed to his feet and crossed to the door. It fit seamlessly into the room, with color and molding that matched the furniture and a shiny, ornately curved silver-colored handle. It was tucked into a corner. If Wyatt hadn't spent countless hours trapped in this elaborate cell, he might have believed he'd missed it on his previous visits, but it was clearly new, despite the fact it looked as old as everything else in the room.

His hand shook as he gripped the handle. It was cool under his hand, almost cold, and when he turned it, he felt an arctic blast rush through the slowly widening crack. He could hear the wind howling, but that didn't stop him. Whatever was on the other side had to be better than being stuck in that room for the foreseeable future.

The wind howled again, sounding worse this time, and a scream accompanied it. Wyatt jerked the door open, acting on instincts that overrode his desire to be smart and cautious, and jumped through the doorway.

Snow piled high, blowing and drifting into miniature hills in the bleak landscape in front of him. The slick and shiny pure ice in the valleys between the snowdrifts glinted in the late afternoon sun. Barren trees stood in the distance, but something hung from the closest one. A sickening feeling grew in Wyatt's gut, and he turned to retreat as his mind processed what he was seeing.

He had barely turned around when the door slammed and vanished, cutting him off from the suddenly welcoming prison Elliott had trapped him in, and then, without moving at all, Wyatt found himself once more facing the tree. This time, he was much closer and had a painfully clear view of what hung from the lowest limb.

Wyatt squeezed his eyes shut. "It's just a dream," he whispered, repeating it like a mantra as he slowly forced tense muscles to relax and gathered the courage to open his eyes. The sight was no less gruesome or heart-wrenching on a second look, and Wyatt had to swallow bile several times as he forced his unwilling legs to carry him across the frost-covered ground to the gnarly tree. The body hanging from it was clearly dead, though freshly so, and Wyatt couldn't help but remember the scream that had propelled him through the door and wonder if he would have been in time had he moved sooner.

He knew the answer was no, just as he knew this wasn't real, but when he looked at Aidan swinging in the breeze, none of that mattered. All he could see was his lover, dead, and all he could think about was how it was his fault. He should have cooperated with Elliott, should have done something differently so that he wouldn't be faced with this.

It was the worst thing he could possibly imagine.

With trembling hands, Wyatt gently cupped Aidan's cheek. "I'm sorry," he whispered, pressing his face into Aidan's chest. He tried to tell himself the cold was strictly from the wind and snow, but even as he thought it, he knew this kind of cold didn't come from weather. This kind of cold only came from within.

Minutes or perhaps hours passed before Wyatt moved again. He was freezing in his icy clothes, his hands and face completely exposed to the elements, but he didn't care. He couldn't care, not with Aidan's body dangling in front of him, a rope taut around its neck and its head tilted at an awkward angle that could only be the result of a snapped spinal cord.

When Wyatt finally pulled away, he harshly wiped at the tears running down his cheek and freezing as they dropped onto his clothes. It was with determinedly dry eyes and surprisingly steady hands that he struggled up the tree, hitching his way up the rough bark by sheer strength of will, and inched his way out onto the branch Aidan dangled from.

The branch creaked and groaned under their combined weights, bending farther and farther with each inch Wyatt moved, but it didn't break, and Wyatt eventually closed his fingers around the knot that secured his lover to the tree. The binding was tight and Wyatt's fingers were frozen, but he was determined not to leave Aidan hanging there and didn't give up until the rope moved and the knot slowly came undone.

Lowering Aidan to the ground by the rope tied around his neck was horrifically painful, but Wyatt couldn't let him fall and there was no other way to get him down. Aidan's knees bent gracelessly as he hit the ground, and he ended up lying awkwardly on his side, looking more like a dead body than he had while hanging. Now he bent weirdly, his stiffening joints not letting him sprawl like he should. The rope fell on top of him in a way Aidan never would have tolerated.

The first thing Wyatt did when he reached the ground was untie the rope from Aidan's neck and fling it as far away as he could. Then he fell to his knees and pulled Aidan into his arms with a harsh sob. As Aidan's head fell back in a way that it never could have if he'd been alive, Wyatt's control broke, and he screamed and yelled, cursing everyone and everything as he rocked back and forth and sobbed brokenly into Aidan's shoulder.

The wind howled around them, but Wyatt paid it no mind until a splatter of something wet hit his cheek and then his hand. Slowly, he lifted his head, peering through bloodshot eyes at the changed landscape. Gone were the drifts of snow and stark trees, and in their place were a hangman's noose and an axe. Bodies were piled under the open trapdoor and scattered haphazardly on both sides of the cutting block. So many of them, and Wyatt recognized every one.

The pile of heads was the worst. Ratri and Olin stared at him with unblinking eyes, Kyler's mouth was partially open with a drop of blood on the chin, and Carina's nose pressed into the ground. Hunter's head was missing from the pile, as was Damon's, but he recognized their headless bodies in the pile on the opposite side of the chopping block. Beneath the gallows, Brianna, Misty, Gwendolyn, and Tabatha all twisted together in a way that made it difficult to see where one ended and the other began.

Wyatt didn't even have the strength to sob. He buried his head against Aidan's shoulder again, shaking as he hugged the cool body close, and whispered, "It's not real," until his mouth refused to form the words any longer.

A strange moaning and shuffling caught his attention not long after his voice gave out, and he looked up again to see the bodies moving. He thought it an illusion at first, a hallucination brought on by too much grief, perhaps, but then Brianna sat up and carefully extracted herself from the other women. Her head hung at an odd angle, flopping too far to be supported by an unbroken neck, and there was a feral gleam in her eyes that sent a feeling of dread straight to the pit of Wyatt's stomach. Her mouth gaped, but the words that came out were understandable. "Hello, Wyatt."

Just moments earlier, Wyatt had thought this nightmare couldn't possibly get worse. But this was. He gulped back a cry that surfaced a moment later as Aidan stirred in his arms, grinning grotesquely as he sat up and pulled himself free. Wyatt moved away hastily, scooting backward as fast as he could manage and desperately trying to put distance between himself and the now moving bodies all turning toward him.

"Aren't you happy to see me, Wyatt?" Aidan's head tipped even further to the side, and he haltingly shifted his expression into one that resembled confusion. "I thought you would want to see me."

"Yes, Wyatt," the women chorused from underneath the gallows. "Aren't you happy to see us? We're here because of you."

"No." Wyatt shook his head frantically as he kept backing away. "No you're not. You're not here. This isn't real. It's a dream. Just a dream." His voice broke on the last words, and he stopped moving, pulled his knees to his chest, and hugged them close as he sobbed into the cold denim of his jeans. "It's just a dream."

"It's never just a dream, Wyatt, you should know that." Hunter stumbled over and picked his head up out of the pile. "If it were just a dream, you'd be able to control it, to make us go away, but you can't, can you."

"It's because of Elliott. He's doing something, giving me drugs or... I don't know. He's controlling it somehow." Even as Wyatt said it, doubt crept into his mind and his voice, and he had to focus hard on repeating and believing his mantra. "It *is* a dream, just not one I can control. That's all!"

"We're here because of you, Wyatt." The voices of his friends formed a strange chorus. "We died because we became friends with you."

"We died because we're related to you," Damon and Tabatha added, leaning against each other in the empty space between the gallows and the chopping block.

"I died because I Bonded with you," Aidan finished, taking a shambling step forward and reaching out to Wyatt with both arms. "It's all your fault." His lips curved into an eerie imitation of a smile as his fingers brushed Wyatt's knee. "And now you're here, and we can have our revenge."

"For what?" Wyatt tried to scramble away, but Aidan fastened surprisingly strong fingers around his calf. "I didn't *do* anything, to any of you!"

"You didn't have to." Olin hefted his head, holding it as high as he could so he could look straight into Wyatt's eyes. "We died just because we knew you. You're dangerous to be around, dangerous to know."

"This is all your fault," Kyler added, his head still on the ground and his body crouched over it. "I don't think we can forgive that."

"No. We can't." Ratri raised his head above his shoulders and heaved. It flew through the air, laughing maniacally, and landed at Wyatt's feet, where it rolled until it looked straight at him again. "You have to pay, and I'll make sure that you will." The head rolled again, and its teeth fastened into Wyatt's ankle.

Wyatt kicked and screamed, tears running down his cheeks as he frantically tried to free himself from both Ratri and Aidan. Neither gave at all, and when Wyatt looked up, he saw the rest of his friends advancing toward him. "Stop! Please!" He grabbed at Aidan's sleeve, begging him to stop, to reconsider, to intervene, but Aidan shook him off and pushed him to the ground, pinning Wyatt flat with unnatural strength and leaving him completely helpless.

The others continued to advance, circling around him like sharks, closing in slowly and cackling and jeering the whole time. Soon, other hands were on him, tearing at his clothes and his skin, ripping pieces of him off as they all yelled that he had to suffer for their deaths and for the trouble he'd caused when they'd been alive. Aidan leaned over him, his grin wide and horrible, and stroked a hand over Wyatt's forehead. "Time to die."

The last thing Wyatt saw was Aidan's dead green eyes as he leaned in to take a bite.

Chapter Thirty-Five

CARINA didn't bother to knock when she returned to Aidan's apartment. She just walked in, frowning slightly at the unlocked door, and shut it hard enough to gather everyone's attention, flipping the lock as soon as it was closed. When all eyes were on her, she smiled grimly. "They got a warrant."

The room immediately filled with questions as people talked over each other until it was impossible to understand anything. Carina didn't make it fully into the living room before Tabatha and Brianna dashed to her, bouncing on their toes as they asked for more information. Hunter and Ratri started yelling, each screaming his questions louder and louder in an attempt to top the other and get his question answered first.

As the yelling reached near-deafening levels, Kyler caught Carina's eye across the room, then stood, stuck his fingers in his mouth, and let out a piercing whistle that drowned out every voice. "Let Carina talk! She's not going to tell us anything if she has to yell over this din."

It was so un-Kyler-like that everyone stared at him in shock for some time before they nodded and settled back into their seats. "Sorry, Carina," Ratri said, looking appropriately abashed as Olin tugged him down and hissed a reprimand in his ear.

"Yeah, sorry."

The apologies chorused around the room as Carina walked over to the chair she'd sat in earlier. She made herself comfortable before continuing her narration. "We took the evidence down to the police station I'd contacted earlier, caught Charlie and his partner as they were heading over here to come take statements, and—"

"Wait." Kyler cut Carina off with an apologetic look. "Should we wake Aidan up? He needs to hear this."

"We did promise that we'd let him know as soon as anything happened," Brianna added hesitantly. She bit her lip and worried it between her teeth for a moment before continuing. "Maybe you should tell us, and then we can go wake Aidan and you can tell him."

"Do you *really* think that's going to go over well?" Damon asked with raised eyebrows. He'd been mostly quiet as his brother's friends took care of the situation. He felt very much like the outsider he was, but even he knew Aidan wouldn't take that well, and he felt compelled to defend Wyatt's Bondmate since Wyatt couldn't.

"No, but...." Brianna sighed. "He needs rest. And really, unless Carina has some awesome news for us beyond what she said when she came in I don't think that it's necessarily worth waking Aidan for. He's going to be in pain, and when we tell him that a warrant has been issued, I don't know that he'll let us put him back to sleep. He's going to want to be a part of all of this, no matter how much it hurts him."

"Brianna is right," Kyler agreed. "I don't know that I can agree to wake Aidan until something happens." He turned to look at Carina. "Nothing has happened, right?"

"They'll call when something does." Carina patted the phone on her hip. "Charlie said that they'll be sending a team out within the hour; they just have to assemble everyone first. They're moving fast, both because Wyatt might be in danger and because they don't want Lumoinnovations to get wind of the warrant and move the evidence."

"Do you really think they would?" Tabatha had returned to her seat next to her brother, and now pressed close against Damon's side as she peered at everyone else. "I mean, how could they?"

"I don't know, but if they can, they will. You have to remember, these people didn't stop at kidnapping or illegal slavery. I doubt they'll let a warrant stop them from doing what they want either."

Tabatha turned wide eyes to Carina. "But—"

"Don't worry about it," Carina soothed, rubbing her hand over her face as she spoke. "The judge is issuing it while Charlie assembles his team. They'll be moving before the ink is dry."

"And when will we know anything?" Ratri's voice was rough, deeper than normal as he tried to keep a tight leash on his emotions. Lashing out was the last thing Aidan needed him to do, but it was Ratri's instinctive reaction, and he was having difficulty sitting on it.

"Charlie said he'd call as soon as they found anything, but that could be hours. Lumoinnovations is a big place, and it will take them a while to find anything that's there. Assuming that there *is* something there, of course."

That got everyone moving again. They exploded into a cacophony of angry voices, upset by the mere suggestion that they might not find anything.

Carina waited patiently for the noise to die down. "They may have other offices, other buildings they own or rent, and Wyatt might be in one of those.

I hope he's in their main headquarters, but if he isn't, we might not find him today."

"Please don't say that." Brianna's voice was soft, and it was only because the room had quieted completely that anyone heard her. "I have to believe that he's there, you know? And do you really want to tell Aidan that we have a warrant, but that it might not do any good because despite all the evidence, Wyatt might not be there after all? I don't want to be around when you do, that's for sure."

"I don't want to tell Aidan anything yet. I don't think we have enough information to merit waking him."

"What information?" Misty appeared at the entrance to the hallway, rubbing her eyes as she struggled to focus on Carina. "What don't you want Aidan to know?"

"That they got a warrant and the police are moving in to try to find Wyatt as we speak."

Misty's voice was cold as she spoke. "And you don't want Aidan to know this?"

"It's not that I don't want him to know," Carina started, looking down as Misty began moving toward her. "I just don't think I have enough information to merit waking him up. Not with all the pain he was in."

Misty clenched her hands into fists. She was barely taller standing than Carina was sitting, but Misty didn't let that stop her from stopping in front of her, mouth set in a thin line. "We *promised* that we would let Aidan know *anything* that happened. That's the only reason he agreed to let us help him sleep to begin with, and now you think that we shouldn't tell him? You're going to wake him up anyway, with all this yelling." She whirled around, directing a glare at each person in turn. "Gwendolyn and I have been fighting to keep him asleep, and you managed to wake both of us up with the noise. We can't fight against him *and* outside interferences. It won't work!"

Kyler stood and gently took Misty by the shoulders. "Let's go wake him up, then."

"You're sure?" Despite her protests, she was genuinely surprised at Kyler's agreement and could only blink and let him guide her back to the bedroom.

"Yeah. I don't like the idea, but you're right. He's going to wake up, and he's going to be upset if we keep things from him. So we won't."

When they reached the bedroom, Kyler stopped in the doorway to let his eyes adjust to the dim light. Aidan lay tucked under the covers, his expression peaceful in deep sleep, though every so often a flicker of something far from peaceful passed over it. Next to him, Gwendolyn lay on top of the covers, her red hair spilled out over the pillow sham and her expression twitching a moment after Aidan's did, every time.

"He's still fighting her." It wasn't a question. Kyler didn't have to be a Dreamer to know something about how it worked, and this was a lot like a coma victim trying to wake up, except they wanted Aidan to stay asleep.

"Yeah." Misty sighed and sat down next to Gwendolyn. "Let me go in and let her know to bring him up. It's going to take a few minutes."

Kyler nodded and started to settle himself in a chair to watch, but before Misty closed her eyes he jumped up again and grabbed her arm. "Wait."

She gave him an exasperated, impatient look. "What?"

"Can you—" He stopped, rubbing the back of his neck as he thought about what he was about to ask. "Can you and Gwendolyn bring Aidan and me into the same dream? So we can talk to each other that way?"

"I *could*, but...." Misty bit her lip. "He doesn't want to be in a dream. We have him sleeping deeply enough that he's not dreaming right now. He said that when he's in a dream, he can feel Wyatt not being there, I guess." She let out a short, exasperated laugh. "That sounds horribly awkward, but I'm not sure how else to describe it."

"Yes, I know what you mean. If we keep him in a dream, he won't be in physical pain, though, right?"

"No, but—"

"And it will be easier to put him back down deep enough that he's not dreaming?"

"Yeah, but—"

"Then that's what we need to do." Kyler put a hand on Misty's arm. "I'll explain to him why. You and Gwendolyn just make sure we're both in the same dream, okay?"

Misty looked at Kyler for several moments as she agonized over his suggestion. There really wasn't much of a choice when it came down to it, so she eventually nodded. "Make yourself comfortable. I don't want to do this with you flopped onto the floor or sprawled out over us."

Kyler gave her a grateful grin before stretching out on the couch tucked into the corner of the bedroom. He was tempted to find room on the bed, but with Aidan in the middle and Misty and Gwendolyn on either side of him, there wasn't much space, and the couch was easier, if less comfortable. "I'm ready whenever you are."

Misty settled on top of the covers next to Aidan and pushed herself into the Dreamscape. Gwendolyn was easy to find, though less easy to convince of the merits of Kyler's plan. In the end, however, she gave in, simply because she didn't want to see her friend in that much pain either, and she agreed that Aidan needed to be given this bit of news. It wasn't as insignificant as Kyler had made it sound. It was real hope, the first bit they'd had since Wyatt had been taken, and that was worth waking Aidan, at least partially.

Once Gwendolyn agreed to the plan, the women shaped the Dreamscape together, creating a peaceful coffee shop in an effort to keep Aidan as removed as possible from things that reminded him of Wyatt. When it was built, complete with the scent of coffee brewing and lattes that were to die for, they went to get their respective charges.

Kyler arrived first and wasted no time fixing a chai tea latte. He was seated at one of the tables, sipping on the perfect drink, when Aidan arrived, falling into the chair across from Kyler, his features twisted in agony. "I hate it here," he whispered, clenching his fingers around the edge of the table. "I can feel Wyatt—" He shook his head. "I mean, I can feel where Wyatt is supposed to be, and…." He turned his desperate gaze to Gwendolyn and Misty, who hovered just to the side of the table. *"Wake me up."*

"No." Kyler put a hand on top of Aidan's and squeezed. "I know you don't like this, but it's better for you than waking you up. We need to keep you asleep so you're strong enough to come with us to the hospital when they bring Wyatt there."

"What?" Aidan sat up straighter, pushing all thoughts of the agony he was in out of his mind. "They found him?"

"Not quite." Kyler held up a hand to forestall any protests. "Carina came back and said that they issued a warrant to search Lumoinnovations. The evidence Carina and Zane provided was enough for the judge, and they're heading over there now."

"So if he's there," Misty said in a gentle tone, "he'll be rescued soon."

"And if he's not?"

The pained look on Aidan's face was almost enough to break Kyler, but he squeezed Aidan's hand again, hoping to take some of the pain away, and kept his voice firm. "Then the search will lead us to where they *do* have him. Lumoinnovations is a big company, which means there are records. If Wyatt isn't there, they'll find something to tell them where he is."

"But they don't have him yet." Deflated by the knowledge, Aidan slumped in his seat. He so desperately wanted to hear that Wyatt had been rescued that this tiny bit of hope was almost worse than having none at all. Every molecule of Aidan's body ached to be reunited with his Bondmate, and he wasn't going to be satisfied until that happened.

"No, they don't," Kyler admitted calmly.

Aidan nodded, his eyes on their joined hands. "Do you really think it will be today?" he asked in a small voice, without looking up.

Misty stepped closer and slung an arm around Aidan's shoulders. "I'm counting on it."

"We all are," Gwendolyn agreed, slipping around to Aidan's other side and pressing a kiss to his cheek. "I doubt that Lumoinnovations would keep Wyatt anywhere other than securely locked in their home office. They think he's too valuable of a resource." She spat the last word, her pretty face twisting up in disgust.

Aidan shuddered at the word and accepted the women's embraces, grasping Kyler's hand more firmly. It didn't begin to heal the hole left by Wyatt's absence, but it felt good nonetheless, and he relished the contact for a few minutes. "They'd better find him."

"They will." Kyler stood and walked around the table, never pulling his hand from Aidan's, and crouched down so he was looking up at the others. "Even if it's not in the first place, they won't stop looking, and they'll find him. Besides," he added with a grin that was only partially forced, "Gwendolyn's right. The chances are very good that he's being kept in the home office. As much as I hate that they think of him as a 'valuable resource', it may work to our advantage in this situation."

"Yeah. It might." Aidan managed a small smile for his friend and twisted to look at Misty, then Gwendolyn. "Can you, um, send me back? So I'm not dreaming anymore?"

"Of course." Misty shared a look with Gwendolyn before taking Kyler's hand and leading him away from the table. As she started to wake Kyler, Gwendolyn concentrated on sending Aidan back into deeper sleep. She then woke herself, joining Misty and Kyler in the bedroom where Aidan slept soundly.

The three of them sat up. The dream had only felt a few minutes long, but more than two hours had passed in the real world, and Kyler was sore from lying on the slightly small couch for so long. "Do you think they've learned anything else?" he asked as he stood, lifted his hands above his head, stretched up on his tiptoes, and bent forward at the waist. He looked ridiculous, practically folded double with his hands extended above his head, but it felt good, and he didn't care.

"Maybe." Misty shrugged as she climbed from the bed, stretching a little herself before crossing the room. "Let's go see."

They didn't have to. Before any of them reached the door, it burst open and Hunter and Brianna dashed through. They skidded to a halt when they saw three of the room's four occupants awake, but the surprised silence didn't last long.

"Wake Aidan up," Hunter commanded, already heading to the bed to do just that.

"Wait!" Gwendolyn screamed as she, Misty, and Kyler reached out to stop Hunter. "What happened?"

Brianna gently untangled Misty from Hunter so he could move to the bed. "They found Wyatt."

Chapter Thirty-Six

WYATT gasped for breath as his eyes sprang open.

His whole body trembled and his chest heaved as he looked around the room with wide eyes, trying to calm his rapidly beating heart and ground himself. He'd never thought that he'd be *glad* to be here, in Elliott's room, but now, after that horrible nightmare he was sure would haunt him for years to come, he was. It was familiar and comfortable to an extent, and while what he really wanted was to wrap himself in Aidan's arms and bury his face against Aidan's shoulder, this at least was something he knew and understood.

This was a nightmare he could handle.

It was several minutes before Wyatt settled enough to try to sit up, and when he did, he was unsurprised to see Elliott sitting in his usual chair, hands folded in his lap and expression detached as he watched Wyatt struggle to come to grips with what he'd witnessed. He said nothing as Wyatt flopped back down on the bed.

This time Wyatt let his eyes close and his arms fall out to the sides. "What do you want now?" he asked in a resigned voice. He already knew the answer.

"The same thing I've wanted every time I've spoken to you, Wyatt." Elliott didn't move from the chair, but he still managed to convey the impression of looming. "Did you enjoy the little dream we cooked up for you?"

"It was *fabulous*." Wyatt pushed himself up onto his elbows and glared across the room at his captor. "I've always wanted to participate in a zombie flick, and you just made it real. So, thanks." It was hard to keep the bravado in his voice, but he couldn't consider letting it fade. Elliott may have seen how upset he was when he brought him out of the nightmare, but that didn't mean Wyatt would give him any more ammunition.

"That wasn't the impression I got when you arrived here."

"Yeah, well, I was playing my role of terrified victim." Sarcasm was good. He could hide behind sarcasm.

"Somehow, I doubt that." Elliott shifted, crossing his legs and letting his right ankle rest on his left knee. "You don't strike me as the type of person who doesn't care about his friends. Why would those children you knew twelve years ago still be looking for you otherwise?" He shook his head sadly, clicking his tongue in dismay. "It's a pity, really. It makes you so easy to manipulate."

"And the alternative is better?" Wyatt pushed himself all the way up into a sitting position and rolled his eyes. "Going through life without anyone caring about you at all? Without caring about anyone at all? No thank you."

"Friends are a weakness, as you just learned." Elliott pressed his fingertips together just under his chin. "I don't burden myself with such things."

"More like you wouldn't know how to make a friend or what to do with one if you were handed written instructions." Wyatt climbed off the bed and went to sit in the chair opposite Elliott. It surprised the other man, and his eyebrows twitched as Wyatt leaned forward, putting his face closer to Elliott's than he ever had before. "That's why you're going to lose."

"I highly doubt that."

Wyatt sat back in his chair with a smirk. "Well, you'd be wrong. That's what you don't understand. Friends aren't a weakness. They're a *strength*."

Elliott scoffed. "They leave you vulnerable."

"They protect your back." Wyatt laughed as Elliott raised an eyebrow in disdain. "Do you really think that cutting off my contact from Aidan was going to make him give up? Make any of them give up? It's going to make them fight *harder*, and no matter how many resources you have at your disposal, they'll find a way to locate me, and they *will* get me away from you."

"Your Bondmate," Elliott replied, sneering, "will be so insensible with pain that he won't be able to function, much less do anything to rescue you. The only way he'll be able to do that is if he lets them give him the other dose of Vinculex, and then what will the point of finding you be?"

"Love." Wyatt let out a soft huff of laughter and shook his head. "You really don't get it, do you? Aidan and I aren't just connected by our Bond. We *love* each other, and nothing you can do will ever change that."

"You really are idealistic, aren't you?" Elliott asked with an incredulous expression. "It's amazing that you can still feel that way, after everything I've done to you."

"It's who I am. Besides," Wyatt continued maliciously, "what you and my parents did to me before your people messed up, that's what led me to Aidan. You used me, and abused me, and brought me to the people who made me happier than I ever imagined I could possibly be. Thanks to *you*, I met the love of my life and made friends who I *know* will stand by me no matter what."

Elliott's smug expression faded at little, but he puffed up his chest and pushed his nose in the air. "I think you're going to be sadly mistaken in that, my boy."

"I'm not your anything, Elliott. And we'll see, won't we? Someday soon, I'm going to see you in the real world and you'll get what's coming to you."

"The only thing coming to me is wealth and increased market share!"

"Maybe in *your* dreams." Wyatt rose and went back to the bed. He lay down diagonally, his hands behind his head and his feet crossed at the ankles. He spent a minute staring up at the ceiling before letting his eyes fall closed.

Elliott fumed for a minute and then stalked over to stare down at Wyatt. "This conversation isn't over."

"It takes two people to have a conversation, Elliott, and I'm done talking, so I guess it is over."

"You listen to me, you brat." Elliott knelt on the mattress and jerked Wyatt up by the collar of his shirt, holding him at an awkward angle while he pushed his face very close to Wyatt's. "You *will* listen to me, and you *will* do what I tell you to do, or I'll throw you right back into that nightmare. You owe me everything and you *will* pay it."

Wyatt's stomach clenched at the mention of the nightmare, but he managed to keep his expression stoic as he met Elliott's gaze. "I don't owe you anything," he said in a calm, clear voice completely at odds with what he was feeling. "You owe me twelve years of my life, however, and I *will* collect on that debt."

"You can't." Elliott dropped Wyatt and stood up, looming over Wyatt from behind his head. "You will never get those years back."

"No, I won't," Wyatt agreed in a steady voice. "But I can make sure that you don't have a future."

The room shimmered, the walls fading to translucent before darkening again, and some of the furniture flickered in and out of existence. "Not from in here you can't."

"But I will from out there." Wyatt rolled over, sat up, and stared Elliott down. "You don't seem to understand. My friends are going to find where you have me, and they are going to get me out of here, and I *will* do whatever it takes to make sure you're punished."

"Then I'll make sure you can't." The room shimmered again and all the furniture vanished.

Wyatt fell hard to the floor, landing on his hands and knees and wincing in pain. Before he could get up, Elliott was on him, grabbing him by the collar and shoving him headfirst into the flickering wall. He cried out in pain, his hands up to ward off the further blows Elliott tried to land on him, but Wyatt could do little other than struggle weakly.

"If I can't have you working for me, I'm going to make sure you can't harm my operation." He pounded Wyatt's head into the wall again, somehow timing it so that Wyatt's hands went through but his head met a solid surface. "I'm going to make sure you don't ever wake up, one way or another."

Wyatt twisted and struggled, kicking out as he tried to attack Elliott from below. His feet mostly skidded against the suddenly slick floor of the room, but he kept trying. "You're not going to win this, Elliott," he protested, squirming in Elliott's grip and contorting his body in ways he'd never imagined possible. "No matter what you do here, you're going to pay."

"Not if you can't testify." Elliott stopped thrusting Wyatt into the wall and pulled him up so they were face-to-face. "If I hurt you enough in here, you'll never wake up—no matter what they do—and you won't be able to hurt me."

"My friends will, no matter what you do." Wyatt took advantage of his new position and swung his leg, hooking it around Elliott's and pulling. They landed in a heap on the floor. Elliott momentarily lost his grip on Wyatt's shirt, and Wyatt scrambled free, taking up a position in the far corner of the room. After his experience in the house earlier, he wasn't going to risk trying to change the Dreamscape, but that didn't mean he was without recourse. A kid didn't grow up in the neighborhood he came from without learning a few tricks, and twelve years spent mostly asleep hadn't lessened his memory of any of them.

"Your friends won't have the power that you would." Elliott panted as he gained his feet. "*You* are the only one who can do real damage, the only one who knows exactly what happened."

"I shared the memories with Aidan. And my brother and sister are here too. They'll testify about what our parents did. You're going down, Elliott."

"I am not!" Elliott dashed forward, his shoulders lowered as he prepared to tackle Wyatt into the wall. Wyatt waited, balanced on the toes of his feet, and stepped aside at the last minute, grabbing Elliott's arm and twisting it behind him as he rushed by.

This time, it was Elliott's head that hit the wall, and hard. Wyatt rammed him into it a couple of times before letting him drop to the floor where he lay, panting, his suit disheveled and his face flushed with anger.

"You're not going to win."

It took Elliott some time to stand, and when he did, he leaned against the wall, one hand bracing him as he staggered a little, searching for his balance. Wyatt was across the room by the time he found it, but Elliott didn't charge again. Instead, he walked with slow, measured steps to the center of the room, where he stood, his arms crossed and his body swaying slightly, and glared. "Don't push me, Wyatt."

"Or what?" Wyatt wrapped his arms around himself protectively. "What could you possibly do to me now? I'm not going to let you hurt me, and you know it's only a matter of time before you're found out. I can handle whatever nightmares you throw at me until then."

"Don't be so sure." Elliott advanced again, not quite running, but with quick, purposeful steps. The heels of his shoes clicked on the floor of the room, their staccato rhythm increasing as Wyatt slid along the wall, moving to keep the maximum distance between himself and Elliott. He was confident in his ability to fight back and win any purely physical altercation, but that didn't mean he wanted to risk it. The longer he kept Elliott here, trying to hurt him, the less time he would spend trapped in the horrific nightmare he never wanted to visit again.

The first obstacle appeared before he was halfway around the room, a low wall jutting out in front of him and forcing him to step closer to Elliott to move around it. The next obstacle pushed him away from the wall before it retreated with surprising speed, and the third cut the room in half. It did not go away. Elliott's smirk widened as Wyatt clenched his hands into fists.

"You're not going to win," Wyatt repeated.

"I think I will. One way or another. I always do."

"Not this time." Wyatt charged, taking Elliott by surprise as he tackled him around the middle and bore him to the ground, hard. "I'm not going to let you."

The floor tilted under them, and Elliott used the sudden incline to roll them over and pin Wyatt down. "You can't stop me. There is *nothing* you or your friends can do." He put his hands around Wyatt's neck, squeezing hard and pushing him down into the floor—it gave around Wyatt, seeping up over his neck to take the place of Elliott's hands. Other bits of melted floor slid over Wyatt's limbs, gluing him to the floor as effectively as he'd been strapped to the bed in the waking world.

Elliott stood, looking down at Wyatt's struggling figure. "Get out of that, if you can."

Wyatt couldn't, but that didn't stop him from struggling, pulling at his arms and legs in the hopes that the floor would give and let him free. He thrashed his head, desperately trying to relieve the pressure on his throat, but every time he moved, it squeezed tighter and tighter, cutting off his oxygen and leaving him desperately gasping for air.

"That's what I thought." Elliott pulled a bit of the floor up and smirked as it formed into a thick stick in his hands. "Now I can make sure that you'll never wake up." He swung the stick down, hard.

Elliott's aim was off, just a little, and Wyatt twisted his head to the side at the last second. He had just enough mobility to dodge the blow, but as soon as he did, the band over his neck tightened, securing him in place and making it impossible for him to draw in any air but the thinnest whiff. Spots danced in front of Wyatt's eyes, and he didn't see the second swing as it came down, hitting him in the center of his forehead and making the world spin around him. "Stop!"

"No." Elliott raised the stick again. "You will *not* ruin me. Not after everything I put into you."

Wyatt could barely see anything now, and he'd ceased struggling to free himself in favor of struggling to breathe. His vision narrowed to a thin tunnel and he closed his eyes. He didn't want to have the slightest hint of when the blow was going to fall. He didn't want it to be the last thing he ever saw.

It never fell.

After a long moment fraught with terror, Wyatt cautiously opened his eyes again, reluctantly abandoning the memories of his time with Aidan and half expecting to see the weapon just inches from his face. Instead, he saw Elliott flickering in and out of existence, struggling to stay in the Dreamscape. The stick had already vanished from his hands, and as Wyatt lay there, struggling to breathe and to make sense of what he was seeing, the bonds holding him in place loosened and collapsed. Slowly, he sat up, looking around in shock as the room crumbled around them.

"You!" Elliott lunged at Wyatt, though he ended up falling to the floor, missing Wyatt completely as he sprawled flat. "What did you *do*? You shouldn't be able to do this!"

"I'm not." Wyatt scooted away from Elliott, his eyes wide as he watched what was left of the room vanish. Piece by piece it crumbled away, turning to dust that disappeared as it fell and leaving only the unformed Dreamscape in its place. "I'm not doing anything."

"Then who is?" Elliott pushed himself up onto his hands and knees and lunged again, flickering and missing once more.

"I don't know," Wyatt said as he looked around in wonder.

As soon as the room had completely vanished, Elliott let out a pained scream. He flickered once, twice, and then he was gone with a pop that echoed through the emptiness, leaving Wyatt completely alone.

Cautiously, he stood, his eyes wide as he searched for something to indicate that he'd been shoved into another dream or that he'd just imagined Elliott disappearing, but the Dreamscape remained the same, blank and gray, ready to be built on just as soon as Wyatt could.

Chapter Thirty-Seven

AIDAN groaned as Kyler swung the car around a corner, taking it so fast that Aidan was flung against the passenger side door. The seatbelt pulled tight, cutting across his chest and rubbing against his cheek, adding to the agony he already suffered, and he wasn't able to hold back the pained noise that slipped from his lips as he pressed his forehead against the cool glass of the window.

"Aidan, are you all right?" Brianna leaned forward from the backseat and frowned when Aidan flinched at the light accidental touch of her fingers on his shoulder as she curled them around the front seat. "Are you sure you don't want Kyler to give you something else?"

"I'm *fine*," he managed, though he was anything but. Each passing moment made the pain coursing through his body worse, and the knowledge that he would be reunited with Wyatt soon wasn't as calming as he thought it should be. He couldn't let himself really believe it until it actually happened. "It'll get better soon, anyway."

Kyler shifted awkwardly in the driver's seat as he stopped the car at a light. "It might not." He bit his lip and ran a hand through his already disheveled hair. "We don't know for certain what cut off your Bond, Aidan. If it was something they gave him, you could stay cut off until it leaves his system." He left the possibility that the Bond might never return unvoiced.

"Then I'll wait." Aidan ground out the words as he hunched over, tugging at the shoulder strap of his seatbelt and trying to curl up into a ball. "I don't want to be drugged when I see him."

"You might need to be." Kyler eased the car forward and pressed hard on the gas as soon as the light turned green. "The doctors are going to want to see you. Police too. It could be a while before you get to see Wyatt, and if his doctors have any idea how much pain you're in, you won't get a choice. They'll drug you as a condition of getting to see Wyatt."

"Can they really do that?" Hunter asked.

Aidan looked at Kyler in astonishment. "They can't, can they?"

"Yes," Brianna answered for Kyler. "They can. They'll say something about it potentially distressing Wyatt and how if Aidan isn't taking care of himself then he's not going to be good for Wyatt. With the amount of pain Aidan's in, taking care of himself definitely involves taking painkillers."

"They don't help. Nothing does." Aidan twisted in his seat. "All they do is make me drowsy, and I can't be there for Wyatt if I'm drugged asleep."

"No, but—"

"You'll have to hide it," Kyler said flatly as he turned into the hospital parking garage. "Brianna is right, they will say exactly that and either make you leave or make you take drugs. And I honestly don't want to think about what drugs they'll give you," he added in a quieter voice as he leaned out the window, swiped his ID badge at the ticket machine, and waited for the gate to rise.

"What do you mean?"

Kyler swung the car into a parking spot, keyed it off, and turned in his seat to look at Aidan. "If you aren't going to be able to hide this, you need to tell me now. I have some suspicions about what they gave Wyatt, and you do *not*, under any circumstances, want them to give you what they'll think you need."

"What do you think they gave him?" Hunter asked, leaning forward and pushing his head between the front seats.

"Vinculex."

"Fuck." Hunter sat back heavily. "Really?"

"Yes. I hope I'm wrong, but I'm not aware of anything else that could do this."

"So you think they gave Wyatt a dose and if they give Aidan one...." Hunter shook his head. "Aidan, man, you have to pretend. If you can't, we gotta take you home."

Aidan didn't know what they were talking about, but at the moment, he didn't care. Whatever Wyatt had been given, the doctors would fix it. "No. I need to see Wyatt."

"Then pretend." Hunter opened his door and climbed out. "No matter how bad this is," he added, leaning back into the car, "what they'll want to do is a million times worse. Don't let them know how much pain you're in."

"Can you pretend?" Kyler put a hand on Aidan's arm, watching carefully for his reaction. When there wasn't one, he nodded. "Good. I'll do my best to get you in quickly and keep the doctors away, but I don't work here, I just have rights. Wyatt will have another doctor assigned to him, and you can't let him notice how you're feeling."

"I won't." Aidan climbed stiffly from the car. He had to brace himself on the door as he stood, waiting for the graying of his vision to clear before he steeled himself and stepped away from the support of the vehicle. He couldn't move quickly as each step was agony, but he managed to take small, steady steps without wincing or groaning, and by the time he'd made it to the end of the car, his head was held high and his face was composed. "Will this work?"

"If you can hold it," Hunter acknowledged, waiting at the end of the car for the others to join him.

Brianna took the long way, slipping past Aidan to close his door after slamming her own, and then slid under Aidan's arm, wrapping herself around his waist. "You can lean on me a little. They're going to expect you to be upset."

Aidan just shook his head. "I need to do this by myself." It wasn't something he could explain, not even to himself, but he needed to walk through those doors completely unsupported. To do otherwise would jinx the entire day.

"All right." Brianna squeezed briefly and pulled away, taking Hunter's hand as they all walked into the elevators together.

AIDAN shifted awkwardly in his chair, trying his best to make it look like it was just the hard seat and his impatience making him uncomfortable. Several police officers stood down the hallway, chatting with men in white coats, but no one was talking to Aidan, not even his friends. Damon, Tabatha, Gwendolyn, and Misty had arrived not long after he had, following at a slightly more sedate pace than the one Kyler had used. Carina, Ratri, and Olin came a few minutes behind them, having taken the time to straighten and lock up the apartment. It had seemed like a silly idea at the time, but Kyler'd assured Aidan he'd appreciate it when he came home after seeing Wyatt.

Assuming, of course, that he actually *got* to see Wyatt.

He'd been here for more than twenty minutes, and except for a curt acknowledgement of who he was, neither the doctors nor the police had paid him any attention. Brianna had directed him to the chairs, and the others joined him when they arrived, but no one was talking, and it was about to drive Aidan mad.

"What's taking so long?" Tabatha asked, sliding down in her seat and crossing her arms as she voiced the words Aidan didn't dare to. "Why can't we see him?"

"He might not even be in a room yet." Brianna shrugged when everyone's eyes turned to her. "I'm sure they're evaluating him and running tests and all sorts of crap. Those doctors are probably letting the police know what they found." She nodded at the group clustered down the hallway just out of hearing range.

"When are they going to tell us?"

"They'll let Aidan know as soon as they know anything." Misty patted him on the knee, reminding him exactly how much he hurt and making him fight back a wince.

"Which will be?" Tabatha looked and sounded younger than her twenty-four years, but her petulant expression and defiant posture vanished as a doctor headed their way, followed by a police officer.

The doctor headed straight to Aidan. "Mr. Donecoff, if you'd like to come with us?"

Aidan blinked stupidly for a moment as his brain fought to process the doctor's words through his haze of pain. "Yeah, sure," he said once he'd caught up with the conversation, pushing himself up slowly before he'd finished talking. "Lead the way."

Brianna laid a hand on his arm as he passed. "Do you want one of us to come with you?"

Aidan glanced at the doctor and the cop, both of whom had carefully neutral expressions on their faces. He couldn't tell if they approved, but neither actively objected, so he nodded. "Just you." He could acknowledge that he needed the support, but he didn't want everyone with him. That would just get too overwhelming, and he'd broken down in front of his friends enough since Wyatt was taken. They didn't need to see it again. Not when they were so close to good news.

The doctor led them into a small room and gestured for Aidan and Brianna to take seats on one side of the small table. He took the chair directly opposite Aidan while the police officer took the chair across from Brianna, and they both pulled out data pads.

Aidan swallowed hard.

IT FELT like Dr. Brunner had been talking for hours. Officer Martin Sanchez, the partner of Carina's friend Charlie, had quickly summarized what they'd found at Lumoinnovations—Wyatt floating in a tank of liquid, hooked up to more wires than they could easily count, with IVs feeding drugs and nutrients into his body and computers monitoring his vital signs. He'd asked Aidan a few questions about how they'd obtained the information Carina had handed over and about what had happened when the men from Lumo-innovations had come and taken Wyatt, but then he'd sat back and let Dr. Brunner take over. That had been at least twenty minutes ago, though to Aidan's aching body and heart, it felt like forever.

The information Dr. Brunner shared wasn't as simple or straightforward as that from Sanchez, and Aidan's head was spinning. He really only understood one word in five, but what it boiled down to was that Wyatt was unconscious with so many drugs running through his system that the doctors couldn't do anything but keep him comfortable and wait for his body to metabolize them. They didn't know when—or if, but Aidan was trying *really* hard to ignore that part—Wyatt was going to wake up.

"It could be tomorrow," Dr. Brunner said, scrolling down on his data pad, "but it isn't likely. He's essentially in a drug-induced coma, and we can't tell what the ultimate results of the cocktail he's been given will be."

His tone was gentle, but the words bit nonetheless, and Aidan couldn't look up when he nodded. "I understand. Is that all?"

"Ah." There was an awkward pause as the doctor scrolled further through the data pad. "There is one other thing. You were his Bondmate, yes?"

"Were?" Aidan looked up with wide eyes and met the doctor's sympathetic gaze with his surprised one. "I *am*."

"And do you still feel the Bond?"

"What does what Aidan can feel have to do with how Wyatt is doing?" Brianna jumped to her feet, pushing her chair back as she leaned on the table. "Isn't that what we're here to discuss?"

"It is, but as I'm sure you know, ma'am, the health of one Bondmate can affect the other. Based on what we've determined they gave Mr. Mettler, there is a drug I'd like to give Mr. Donecoff as well. I think it would benefit them both, and could speed Wyatt's healing."

"If you're talking about what I think you are, the answer is no."

"With all due respect, ma'am, you don't get to decide." Dr. Brunner turned his attention back to Aidan. "Mr. Donecoff, I can see that you're in pain. You'll be far more comfortable if you let me administer this to you," he said in a soft voice. "Wyatt will be as well," he added in an even softer tone.

"Aidan, no." Brianna grabbed Aidan's arm before he had a chance to open his mouth. "You can't let him give you that. It's what Hunter was talking about in the car!"

"But—"

"*Please.*" She clutched harder, sending waves of pain through Aidan's body that he tried hard to ignore. "At least wait until after you've seen Wyatt."

The idea of being pain-free was tempting, but Brianna had a point, and Aidan was smart enough to know she was referring to what Hunter had said rather than what Kyler had said for a reason. He wasn't going to make any decisions without talking to his friend and doctor about it. "Let me see Wyatt. I'll decide after that."

"It would really be in your best interest to do this now."

"No. I want to see Wyatt. We're not going to discuss anything else until I do."

"Mr. Donecoff, I'm afraid—" Dr. Brunner began, but he stopped as the door opened, admitting Kyler.

"I need to borrow Aidan and Brianna for a bit, if that's okay." Kyler left the door open as he crossed the room and stopped behind Aidan. He laid a hand on Aidan's shoulder as he turned to the doctor. "We've gotten Wyatt settled, and I know they're both anxious to see him."

"Dr. Jedry, I really must insist that we be allowed to finish this conversation."

"Come on, Bill." Kyler straightened his lab coat as he stepped around the table toward Dr. Brunner. The coat, along with the stethoscope draped around his neck, made Kyler look different, like the doctor he was instead of the way Aidan usually saw him, as the goofy friend who just happened to be awesome at medical things. It was weirdly reassuring.

Dr. Brunner tried to protest, but Kyler stopped him. "Let them have five minutes. It'll make everyone happy, and then you can finish telling Aidan all the gritty details. I won't even try to steal your thunder," he added with a cheeky grin before stepping back.

"Very well. Please seriously consider what I told you, Aidan."

"Of course." Aidan nodded as he let Kyler pull him to his feet. It was a good thing he did, because the sudden change in altitude had him fighting back an unexpected wave of dizziness and he probably would have fallen if not for Kyler's restraining hand on his arm.

"You all right?" Kyler whispered as he and Brianna guided Aidan from the room.

"Yeah. Just dizzy for a moment."

They stepped into the hallway and Brianna pulled the door shut behind them, using just a little bit more force than was necessary. "Good timing, Kyler."

"Hunter said something was up. What happened?" Kyler led the way to a bank of elevators and pushed the call button. "All he could tell me is that you were suddenly worried."

"The good doctor was trying to get Aidan to take Vinculex."

"Dammit!" Kyler hit the wall hard. "You didn't agree, did you?"

"No, but—" Aidan shook his head, trying to clear it. It was getting harder and harder to focus through the pain, and if he were completely honest, he'd have to admit that the idea of something that could relieve him of it was very tempting. "He said it would take care of the pain I'm in."

"It would."

"Then why don't you want me to take it?"

The elevator arrived, and Kyler led them inside and pushed the button for the tenth floor before answering Aidan. "It would permanently sever your Bond with Wyatt. You're in pain because the dose they gave Wyatt is blocking your Bond. Giving a dose to both partners irreparably severs it. You wouldn't be in pain anymore because your body wouldn't be trying to feel something that isn't there."

Aidan's blood ran cold. "Why would he want me to take something that does that?"

"He probably believes that it's the only recourse."

"And is it?"

"Maybe." Kyler sighed and rubbed his hand over his face. "I don't know what's going to happen since Wyatt was given a dose of it. Giving one to you as well might be the only thing we *can* do, but it's not something I'm willing to do just yet. We at least need to wait until Wyatt wakes up."

Aidan swallowed hard. "And then?" he asked in a soft voice, the words almost catching in his throat. "What happens if he wakes up and I still can't—?"

"That won't happen." Brianna looked over at Aidan sympathetically as the elevator doors opened, and she stepped through, waiting just outside as Aidan turned to Kyler.

"Kyler?"

"*If* that happens, we'll deal with it then." He, too, patted Aidan's arm. "For now, let's just assume Brianna is right, okay?"

"Yeah. Okay." Aidan nodded as he followed Kyler out of the elevator and down the hall. The three were silent as they passed the nurse's station and a row of open doors Aidan couldn't look through. He didn't want to see anyone but Wyatt.

Finally, after a journey that seemed much longer than it actually was, Kyler stopped in front of an open door and gestured toward the room. "He's in there." He smiled slightly as Aidan looked at him in askance. "Go on. We'll be right here."

It was harder than it should have been to walk through the door. The bed wasn't visible until Aidan was fully inside the room, and he almost didn't want to go any farther. If he didn't see Wyatt, he could imagine how he was doing, and Aidan was almost afraid his imagination was better than reality.

The first bed Aidan saw was empty, and his heart skipped a beat as he was momentarily afraid that Kyler had brought him to the wrong room or that Elliott's men had returned and somehow managed to whisk Wyatt out of the hospital despite the policeman talking to the nurses down the hall and the slew of doctors and technicians looking at Wyatt until just a few minutes previous. The empty bed mocked him, and he almost lost his balance as his knees weakened, making him stagger and turn to catch himself. The twist left him facing another bed, this one occupied, and his knees almost gave out again.

Wyatt lay on his back with his head slightly elevated, a sheet drawn up to his waist, and his arms resting at his sides. A single IV was inserted into the back of his right hand, secured with tape, and a pulse oximeter was clipped to the end of his right index finger, but there was nothing else attached to him. If Aidan tried, he could almost imagine Wyatt was simply sleeping, despite the paleness of his skin and the unnatural stillness of his limbs.

Aidan made his way to Wyatt's side, where he stood, waiting for Wyatt to move the tiniest bit. He didn't. Only the slow rise and fall of his chest and the constant beeping of the monitors attested to the fact that he was alive, and Aidan found himself blinking back tears as he struggled to make his mouth work. "Hey." He lowered the rail on the side of the bed and slid his hand along the sheets to find Wyatt's. "You have to wake up, okay? I can't—"

Intense pain shot through him as he curled his fingers around Wyatt's. It felt like a bolt of lightning hit him, setting fire to every muscle in his body and causing him to stiffen before every muscle relaxed completely, sending him sliding to the floor as darkness rushed up to meet him.

Chapter Thirty-Eight

WYATT cursed in frustration as spikes of pain shot through his head again. The Dreamscape was still the flat gray of unformed dreams, and despite his best efforts, Wyatt wasn't able to manipulate it. He'd been at it for hours or perhaps even days—time was impossible to track here—and still nothing, even though the unformed Dreamscape was the easiest to manipulate. He couldn't even build one tiny thing, much less weave the complex dreams he was used to creating.

Lacking anything to throw, he kicked and stomped, growling when he found it no more satisfying than the empty throwing motions. Kicking and stomping only worked as stress relief when there was something to kick and stomp. Though he was able to stand or sit however he wanted, there was never any resistance except what was required to support his body, which left him feeling like an idiot instead of making him feel better.

Close to the end of his rope, Wyatt dropped, kneeling with his head resting in his hands. If he could only manipulate one tiny thing, he could be patient as he worked on expanding his abilities. He could hope. As it was, he could do nothing, so he sat and wondered when and if his abilities would return.

KYLER eased the hospital room door shut and stood just inside the threshold shaking his head at the scene in front of him. It was an unusual one, and he was sure they would never have gotten away with it if several of them hadn't been hospital employees. Wyatt and Aidan were in the hospital beds, on their backs with IVs in their hands and monitors attached to their chests. Hunter and Brianna curled up together on one of the two trundle beds normally used by the hospital's Dreamers, Misty lay on the other, and Ratri and Olin stretched out in the uncomfortable plastic chairs Sacred Heart provided for visitors. Only Damon and Tabatha were awake, perched on the side of their brother's bed and carrying on a quiet conversation. It was crowded, and they wouldn't all have fit if the room hadn't been designed to allow the hospital's Dreamers to sleep comfortably next to the beds of the patients.

Tabatha looked over when Kyler stepped farther into the room. "Nothing's changed."

"I didn't think it would." Kyler moved to stand by Aidan's bed and checked his chart, noting the readings on the monitors that indicated he was dreaming. "Gwendolyn stopped by before she left for the day, said she couldn't find Wyatt anywhere in the Dreamscape."

"Misty said that Aidan still can't feel him either," Damon added. "Do you think—" He swallowed hard. "Do you think he's going to wake up this time?"

"I hope so." Kyler put Aidan's chart back on the hook at the foot of the bed and picked up Wyatt's. It didn't tell him anything he didn't already know, but it let him feel like he was doing something useful, so he flipped through it as he spoke. "If anyone can," he said, hating the cliché but knowing it was true in this instance, "it's Wyatt."

"Are you sure?" Tabatha's voice was barely a whisper. She looked and sounded horribly lost as she squeezed Wyatt's hand and regarded Kyler with hopeful eyes.

Kyler hung up Wyatt's chart so he could devote his full attention to Wyatt's siblings. "When Aidan found Wyatt, he was almost dead. The people at Lumoinnovations had thought he was, and they'd literally thrown him out like trash. They left him behind a dumpster in the snow, and he would have died if Aidan hadn't found him when he did. Wyatt came back from that. It wasn't easy, for any of us, but he made it. If he can survive that, he can survive this."

"He had Aidan then."

"He has Aidan now." Kyler smiled softly at Tabatha. "I know you don't know either of them very well right now, but do you really think that Aidan will give up on Wyatt? Or that Wyatt will give up on Aidan? He didn't really have Aidan the first time he was freed; they hadn't Bonded yet. Now they have."

"And those *people* blocked it." Damon somehow managed to give the word the same tone most reserved for disgusting trash.

"That's just going to make them fight harder." Kyler shook his head fondly as he recalled what he'd been told by the other Dreamers. "Aidan is spitting mad, and he's only not demanding to be woken up because Misty convinced him that Wyatt might be looking for him and that the best place to find him was in the Dreamscape. He's going to do everything he can to be there for Wyatt, I promise you that."

"I know." Tabatha managed a small smile. "It's just, he's been gone half my life, and we finally find him again, and then this happens. It's not fair, you know? And then sometimes I feel like maybe I shouldn't feel this upset because—you're right—I don't know him anymore, not at all."

Damon hugged her close. "That doesn't mean you can't worry. We've been worrying for twelve years, Tabatha. It's okay to keep doing so."

"I know, I just…. I don't know."

Kyler squeezed her shoulder. "No one thinks badly of you for worrying or being upset, Tabatha. They'd think less of you if you weren't."

Tabatha wiped her eyes with the back of her hand and managed another smile. "Yeah, okay." She blinked a few times, clearing the tears away, and looked back down at Wyatt. "So you really think he'll wake up?"

As a doctor, Kyler wasn't supposed to give assurances like that, not unless he was absolutely certain they were true, but Wyatt and Aidan were his friends, as was everyone worrying about them, and vague assurances that didn't really say anything weren't what he wanted to say. "I'm sure he will. Just give him some time to find his way back."

MISTY sat cross-legged on top of a flat rock, her hands resting palm-down on her knees as she looked out over the landscape. She'd chosen a beach this time, and below the high outcropping she sat atop, a strip of white sand lined the shore and brilliant blue waves tumbled in and rolled out, leaving their mark a little bit higher each time as the tide came in.

She watched for a minute, basking in the serenity of her private place. She could always relax here, no matter how bad things got in the real world or in the dreams she walked, and she desperately needed this now. They had been trying to find Wyatt for five days now, and still there was nothing, not even the tiniest glimmer of his presence in the Dreamscape.

Once she'd found her center, Misty closed her eyes and let her senses extend beyond the edges of the dream she had created for herself. Her mind brushed against all sorts of dreams—the sick grandmother envisioning a day at the park with her grandchild, an injured man imagining what he'd do when he was well enough to be with his Bondmate again, and young twin Dreamers happily playing together in the Dreamscape despite the illness ravaging their bodies in the real world. She brushed by all of them without stopping. No one needed her assistance, and she had far more important things to do.

When she found Aidan's dream, she stopped in briefly, letting Gwendolyn know she was busy searching the Dreamscape for Wyatt and giving Aidan a hug. He was despondent and only mechanically hugged her back, but she just squeezed harder and kissed his cheek before resuming her quest.

The dreams she brushed against varied as much as the people having them, but none of them led to Wyatt, and Misty was forced to retreat to her personal haven before she'd made any progress at all.

"So I was thinking," Gwendolyn said, appearing suddenly in Misty's dream, "maybe we're not finding him because he's not actually dreaming."

"But he should be. I mean, Kyler said that his brain activity is just like it is when he's dreaming. Why would it do that if he's not?"

"Maybe he's trying."

"What?"

"Look." Gwendolyn sat down next to Misty, mimicking her pose. "Wyatt was able to dream with Aidan when he was first taken, right?"

"Yeah."

"Okay, well, what if the people who had him realized what he'd done and did something to stop it? I mean, there are drugs that can affect a Dreamer's ability to control the Dreamscape, right? We give them to patients here sometimes, when their dreams get out of control and we can't spare the staff to sit with them all the time."

"Yeah, but they're temporary. The longest I've heard of a dose lasting is somewhere around twelve hours. Wyatt's been here for *five days*, and he had to have been given the last dose sometime before he was rescued. Why would they still be working?"

"They gave him a lot?" Gwendolyn shrugged. "The police said they had him on multiple IVs, right?"

"I think." Misty shrugged sheepishly. "I wasn't really paying all that much attention. I didn't want to hear it, you know? Things are bad enough without being able to vividly imagine them."

"I know." Gwendolyn shuddered delicately. She didn't like being able to picture it either. "But what if they were continuously giving it to him? I mean, they'd probably do whatever they thought was necessary to keep Wyatt under control, right? So long as it wasn't going to kill him, why wouldn't they just keep pumping it into his body? It would mean that he couldn't do anything they didn't want him to do."

"Maybe." Misty chewed on her bottom lip as she thought about it. "You could be right. Wanna go tell Kyler?"

"No. You go ahead. I should get back to Aidan before he goes nuts. He about panicked when I left, but I didn't want him to hear this theory until I'd discussed it with someone else."

"Good call." Misty stood and stretched, lifting her hands above her head and arching her back as she pushed up on to her tiptoes. "I'll go talk to Kyler. You get back to Aidan." She waited for Gwendolyn to vanish and then concentrated, letting the dream fade away as her mind slipped back to reality.

CARINA stopped Kyler in the hallway outside of the room Wyatt and Aidan shared with a hand on his bicep. "Any changes?"

"No." Kyler shook his head. "Any news?"

"Hardly. They're waiting to set a date for the trial until we can give them a more firm diagnosis, but they're not going to be able to wait too much longer." Carina rubbed at the back of her neck. "Charlie thinks that things will go through okay with just the testimony of the officers who found Wyatt and the evidence Zane collected, but I'd be more comfortable if at least one of them could take the stand as well."

"And if neither of them can?" Kyler didn't like asking, but it had been six days, and he had no idea when Wyatt or Aidan would wake up.

"They'll be convicted—there's too much evidence for them not to be— but it'll lose a lot of the human element, and they might get off a little lighter than they otherwise would have."

Kyler sighed and stared hard at the wooden door he'd shut behind him. "Brianna and Hunter are dreaming with them now. Everything that we can test indicates Wyatt should be somewhere in the Dreamscape, but no one can find him."

"What about Gwendolyn's theory?"

"It's a good one, but it's not really very helpful. If she's right, it's going to be next to impossible to find Wyatt. Without a dream to anchor him, he could be anywhere, and the unformed Dreamscape is a big place. They can't just go there and expect to find Wyatt; even if two people go at the same time, unless they travel together there's no way to be sure they'll end up in the same place. It's tricky."

"It's dreams." Carina shook her head. "They're not supposed to make sense. None of mine ever do."

"Mine either."

Carina smiled grimly. "I have to go back to work. You'll let me know if anything changes? I need to keep Charlie informed."

"Of course." Kyler managed to match Carina's smile. "I hope something does before it's too late."

"Me too." With a pat on Kyler's arm, Carina stepped around the doctor and slipped inside the hospital room.

WYATT flopped onto his back, flung his arms out to his sides, and stared up. The "sky" was the same gray, and only his personal sense of orientation made it truly "up." If he wanted, he could roll over, making up down and down up, but he'd long since grown tired of that game and now just wanted to be able to do something with the unformed matter that had once so easily yielded to his wishes.

His last attempt ended in a horrible headache that sent him fleeing to the deep dreamless sleep that was his only rest. He'd hoped that when he woke he would be able to manipulate the Dreamscape, but since he wasn't actually *in* a dream, he was afraid to try.

Still, nothing ventured, nothing gained, or whatever the latest cliché on the matter was, so after staring aimlessly upward for some time, he sat up, held his hands in front of him, and concentrated.

A dull ache immediately began at the back of his skull, but this time it was accompanied by a slight shimmering between his palms. His heart rate sped up as he concentrated harder, ignoring the growing pain in his head as the shimmer slowly solidified, turning into a perfectly formed bar of chocolate. "Holy shit."

It was with something approaching reverence that Wyatt peeled back the wrapper and slowly lifted the bar to his mouth. It *looked* right, and smelled right, but that didn't mean it *was* right. There was only one way to determine that, and as Wyatt slowly sunk his teeth into the soft candy, he knew that he had formed it correctly. This wasn't going to provide him any nourishment in the real world, but it tasted damn good in the Dreamscape, and it took an enormous amount of willpower to hold back as he ate, swallowing each bite before shoving the next one into his mouth.

When it was done, Wyatt concentrated again, this time not bothering with cupped hands. He ended up doubled over in pain as ice picks stabbed through his skull, but when he managed to uncurl, there was a whole basket of food in front of him. Fruit and vegetables spilled out around sandwiches, and in the bottom, when he dug down deep enough, there was candy. With a delighted sound that made the pain in his head worse, Wyatt grabbed an apple and a sandwich and dug in with gusto.

It was sometime later before he dared try to manifest anything again. The food was delicious, but the headache didn't fade as fast as he'd hoped, and he didn't want to risk any setbacks by being too aggressive. It was enough for the moment to know he was able to manipulate something again. He could be patient for the rest of it.

To an extent, anyway.

He probably didn't wait long enough before trying again, if he was going to be perfectly honest, but there were only so many ways he could entertain himself in this gray void without actually attempting to manipulate it, and once he'd consumed all the food, he'd run out of them all. For the sake of his pounding head, he did wait after he'd finished the food, but his headache wasn't completely gone when he finally stretched out on his back and closed his eyes.

This time, he wasn't going to try to *make* something; he was going to try to *find* something.

At first, this attempt went like all the others that had preceded it, with the pain in his head deepening as he searched futilely for a dream he could touch. The pressure behind his eyes grew, making his head pound in rhythm with his heartbeat, and he squeezed his eyes shut as he forced himself to continue searching. Just as he was about to give up, he touched something.

It was only the faintest of brushes, but it was there, and he latched on with every bit of strength he possessed, drawing himself closer to the dream as he tried to figure out whose it was and what he could do with it. He didn't recognize the person—a thirtysomething homemaker from the looks of things—when he got close enough to actually peer inside the dream, but the fact that it was an actual dream and not just more formless gray void gave him hope that even the ability to manifest something hadn't. If he could find dreams, he could find Aidan.

The woman's dream resisted all of Wyatt's attempts to slip inside it, and it vanished as she woke up before he was able to figure out how to get inside, but when it was gone, he lay on his back, grinning like a loon despite the pain in his head and the ache deep inside him that could only be equated with exercising muscles that hadn't been used in far too long. He had to wait again.

The next time he searched for a dream, he found a child's, and then an elderly man's. Neither of them were people he'd ever seen before, and both dreams resisted his attempts to enter them, but he was able to find them both before he had to stop because of the pain, and that was enough. He might not be able to find Aidan or any of his other friends yet, but he was getting closer, and it was looking more and more likely that he would eventually be able to succeed.

The third time he found the dream of someone he recognized, though not someone he knew well. Marissa Waters was a patient at the hospital, one he'd dreamed with as she had a minor operation, and the surge of emotion he felt when he recognized not only her, but the room he'd dreamed into existence for her, was indescribable. He'd found someone he knew, which meant he was getting closer. He was going to find Aidan soon—he knew it with every fiber of his being.

The next time he ventured out, he found him.

Wyatt almost didn't believe it at first, almost dismissed the dream as one he wasn't interested in and passed on to the next he could locate, but then he realized he recognized the place and looked closer.

His heart jumped in his chest, and he faltered, almost losing track of the dream. But he managed to hold on, just barely, and peered inside, hoping against hope it wasn't a hallucination and that this time, his attempts to enter the dream would be successful.

Wyatt didn't try at first. He watched, basking in the glow of seeing their apartment, of seeing *Aidan*. He sat on the couch with Hunter and Brianna and looked horrible, far too thin with glazed eyes and sunken cheeks, but right then, it seemed like he was the most wonderful thing Wyatt had ever seen. It was Aidan, really truly Aidan, and simply seeing him was enough to drive away Wyatt's headache and leave him feeling as if he were on top of the world.

Finally, when he'd basked in the glow of success for so long that he knew he had to do *something* or he'd lose his chance, Wyatt slid his eyes shut and concentrated. He'd entered Aidan's dreams hundreds of times before, but it had never been this difficult, not even when they'd first met, before Wyatt had really woken up for the first time. There had never been this resistance before.

It didn't take long for him to reach the point where he'd stopped before, with his muscles and head aching and his whole body hovering on the verge of complete exhaustion. This wasn't just anyone's dream, though, it was *Aidan's* dream, and Wyatt was willing to do *anything* he could to be reunited with his Bondmate, including push himself beyond anything he'd imagined he could possibly do. One look at the way Aidan huddled on the couch, one glance at the lost expression on his face, and all of Wyatt's resolve returned. He closed his eyes once again and *pushed*.

The result was not what he expected. Instead of pushing himself into the dream, he pulled things out of it. Three books he recognized as being among Aidan's favorites appeared in a haphazard pile at his feet. With a frown, Wyatt tried again, pushing harder this time, but all he ended up with was more books and one dragon figurine from the top of the bookcase.

Shaking with frustration and impatience, Wyatt tried again, and again, taking more books, more figurines, and even a picture, but he was never able to breach the barrier going the other direction and put anything into the dream, not even the things that had come out of it. He hissed and cursed, kicking at the books in irritation and yelling his anger to echo through the void.

It was the worst kind of torture, and when he had half the contents of the bookcase lying at his feet, Wyatt was almost ready to give up. He didn't have the energy to do more, but when he glanced into the dream and saw Aidan's face, he gathered his strength and closed his eyes. He only had one more try, so it had to be good.

Chapter Thirty-Nine

AIDAN walked the length of the couch, running his hand along the back of it, and turned when he reached the end to retrace his steps. The room was much bigger than just the length of the couch, and Brianna had remarked several times that if he was going to pace he ought to do it properly and stride across the entire room. But Aidan wanted to keep his hand on the soft fabric of the furniture. It wasn't his real couch—just a dream version of it—but touching it grounded him and he desperately needed that.

"How long has it been?" he asked as he slid his left hand along the cushioned surface and began slowly moving forward again.

"A week," Brianna said quietly, pulling her knees up to her chest as she sat on the love seat and watched Aidan pace. "It's been a week."

"And he hasn't woken up yet?"

"Aidan, you would know." She smiled and shook her head. "You'll probably know before anyone else, even whoever is awake in the room with you two. Once whatever it is they gave him wears off, you'll know."

"Then what's taking so long?" He swung around the end table and dropped onto the soft cushions, letting his head fall back as he sprawled. "Shouldn't things have worn off now?"

"We could always—"

"No!" Aidan lifted his head and shook it emphatically. "You said that he's more likely to find me if I'm here, in the Dreamscape, right?"

"Yes, but—"

"Then I'm staying." His tone left no room for argument. "I have to be where he can find me, Bri."

"I know." She moved from the love seat to the couch, sprawling next to Aidan. "You sure you want to stay here? I mean, we could go somewhere else, if you wanted. The others would still be able to find me."

"Would Wyatt?"

"If he's looking for us, yes."

Aidan wavered. They'd originally formed the dream version of his apartment because it was familiar and everyone felt comfortable here. Keeping it constant was much easier than having four Dreamers attempting to maintain the same fantasy none of them had reference points for, and it was too painful for Aidan to let any of them take him to the places Wyatt usually formed for him. His apartment was the last place he'd seen Wyatt, and even though he wasn't here, his presence still lingered in Aidan's mind, making it a little easier to bear. "No," he finally said. "I'll stay here. You can go if you want. I don't need someone with me all the time."

"Yes, you do." Brianna leaned over and hugged Aidan. "I heard how much you freaked out when Gwendolyn went to talk to Misty, and she was only gone for maybe ten minutes. I'm not leaving you alone."

"Who said anything about leaving him alone?" Hunter appeared near the front door, then immediately crossed the room and flopped onto the couch next to his Bondmate. "Why would we want to leave Aidan alone?"

"We don't."

"I was just saying that I don't need a babysitter all the time."

"'Course you do, man. I mean, I get it, so don't take it the wrong way, but none of us are going to leave you alone for a minute until Wyatt wakes up."

"And if he doesn't?"

Brianna laid a hand on Aidan's arm. "He will."

"You don't know that."

"Yeah, man, we do." Hunter grinned cockily, his mouth stretching farther than should be possible. "I mean, come on, Wyatt's the most stubborn person I know. He's gonna wake up, even if it's just to prove those bastard doctors wrong."

Aidan smiled at the memory. The last time Hunter had been in his dream, he'd been ranting and raving about how Dr. Brunner said it was now unlikely Wyatt would ever wake up and how a few other doctors apparently agreed with him. It had taken both Kyler's and Carina's influence to get them to leave, and Hunter had immediately gone into the Dreamscape where he could express his anger without doing any real damage. He'd still been ranting about their incompetence when he'd shown up in Aidan's dreams hours later, and Aidan had been too amused by his antics to worry about what the prognosis meant for Wyatt.

"Yeah, you're right," Aidan admitted. "If he knows what they said, he'll wake up soon."

"He's going to wake up soon anyway, Aidan." Brianna formed a cup of coffee from the fabric of the Dreamscape and handed it to Aidan. "He'll figure out how soon."

"I hope—" Aidan stopped as books began to disappear from the shelves he'd been staring at blankly. "Are either of you doing that?"

"No," they said in unison, their eyes as wide as Aidan's. More books vanished, and then a few trinkets from on top of the bookcases.

Hunter stalked over to the bookcase and stared hard at it for a minute. One of the books flickered and blinked out of sight and Hunter swung around to look at Aidan and Brianna. "Someone's pulling them out of here. I'm going to—"

He grabbed a wavering book and disappeared along with it, leaving Aidan and Brianna gaping in astonishment.

BRIANNA dashed to the bookcase and ran her hands over the spines of the remaining books. "Dammit, Hunter!" she exclaimed as she yanked and tugged at the covers, tearing at the dust jackets in a way that made Aidan very glad this was the dream version of his apartment and not the real one.

It hurt to see his books treated like that.

Aidan approached her slowly, his arms outstretched and his movements deliberate so he wouldn't startle her. The girl could pack a punch, and though being hit here wouldn't physically hurt him in the real world, he'd definitely feel it until he woke up. He didn't want to risk it. "Bri?"

She whirled toward him, a book in one hand and a picture from the top of the case in the other. "It stopped. They're not disappearing anymore!"

"I know." Aidan took another step forward and gently took the items from her hands. "Hunter probably stopped it."

"But he's not here!"

Aidan barely had time to set the book and picture down before Brianna collapsed against him, her whole body shaking as her breath hitched. "Shh," he whispered, sliding his arms around her and holding her close. "It'll be okay. I'm sure he'll be back."

"But what if he's not? What if someone wasn't just pulling them out of here? What if they just don't exist anymore or—Oh God!—are being destroyed?" Her whole body went limp as her eyes rolled back in her head, and Aidan barely stopped her from crashing to the floor.

"Dammit, Brianna." He scooped her up in his arms and carried her over to the couch, where he gently laid her down and brushed her hair back from her forehead as he knelt next to her. "Come on, don't do this to me. I need—" He sucked in a deep breath and let it out shakily. "I don't know if I can do this, Bri. I'm kind of messed up right now. Please wake up?"

He kept brushing his hand over her cheek and forehead until her eyelids fluttered and she blinked at him. "Aidan?"

"Hey." He managed a shaky smile as he sank back to sit on his heels. "You okay now?"

"I think." Slowly, Brianna sat up and looked around the room. Her gaze lingered on the ravaged bookcase, and she let out a tiny whimper as she turned her gaze back to Aidan. "He's really gone, isn't he?"

"I'm sure he's fine," Aidan assured her, hiding his own anxiety. "This is *Hunter* we're talking about, remember? Come on, how much trouble could he get in that he can't get out of?"

"He does have a lot of experience getting out of trouble."

"Exactly. So he'll be fine. I promise."

Brianna leaned over and wrapped her arms around Aidan's shoulders, hugging him tightly. "Since when are you the calm and logical one in this situation?"

"Since you decided to faint on me?"

WYATT heard three more books land at his feet as he sagged, falling to land on the pile he'd dragged out of the dream. There was no way he could try again, not for some time, and he wasn't even sure if he'd be able to keep track of Aidan's dream in the time it took him to regain his strength. Likely, he'd have to find it again, and assuming Aidan hadn't woken up, that was still going to be a difficult task. If he lost it, it could be anywhere, and until he was able to better extend his senses and find people he knew, the chances that he'd stumble across Aidan's dream again were practically nonexistent.

He doubled over as his eyes watered, bending so far that his forehead rested on the pile of books, and he wrapped his arm around them, clutching the vestiges of Aidan he had. He was squeezing them tightly when a warm hand touched the back of his neck.

"Wyatt?"

Sucking in a shaky breath as he attempted to regain some semblance of control, Wyatt slowly turned his head, blinking hard when he saw the figure crouched next to him. "Hunter?" He stretched out a trembling hand and gently touched Hunter's arm, gasping when his fingers met solid flesh. "I'm not hallucinating, am I?"

Hunter laughed loud and hard as he pulled Wyatt in for a tight hug. "No, man, I'm really here. Hitched a ride on those books you were dragging over."

Wyatt laughed as he buried his face against Hunter's shoulder and wrapped his arms around his friend, clinging. "How'd you know I was the one taking them?"

"Didn't." Hunter shrugged. "I mean, I kind of hoped, but I really had no idea where they were going. I was actually just trying to see if I could figure it out; I didn't know I'd come with. It's a complete accident that I ended up here."

Wyatt pulled back enough that he could look Hunter in the eyes, shaking his head and laughing at the absurdity of the situation. "Only you, man."

"Yeah, well, I finally found your ass. We've been looking for over a week."

"A *week*, really?" Wyatt swallowed hard. He knew that it had been a while since Elliott had been pulled out of the Dreamscape, but there was no way to judge the passage of time here, especially without dreams to help mark it. Time passed oddly in the Dreamscape regardless of form, but it was slightly easier to measure in actual dreams than in the unformed Dreamscape.

"Yeah." Hunter sobered as he pulled back farther, sliding his hands up to Wyatt's shoulders and holding him at a slight distance. "You're in the hospital. Zane was able to follow the evidence they'd been gathering, and they led the police straight to the people who had you. We've been waiting for you to wake up for a week now."

"What about Aidan? Is he there? They didn't—" He swallowed hard. "They didn't give him any drugs, did they?"

"Aidan is, uh, sharing a room with you." Hunter didn't quite meet Wyatt's eyes. "He collapsed in pain several hours after you were taken and said he couldn't feel your Bond anymore. We were keeping him asleep as much as possible, but when he got to the hospital and touched you, he collapsed again. Kyler admitted him, and we've been keeping him under."

"And what about drugs?"

"Nothing. I promise. Someone has been awake in your room the whole time. Kyler insisted."

"Thank God." Wyatt slumped as a weight lifted from his shoulders. "At least they didn't give it to him."

"Yeah, um." Hunter rubbed his hand over his neck. "Wyatt, Kyler says—"

"Keeping Aidan asleep, is that why you and Brianna were dreaming with him?"

"Yes, but—" Hunter cut himself off, distracted from the news he didn't really want to give by Wyatt's question. "Wait. If you could see that we were there, why didn't you come in? Why were you pulling things out?"

"I didn't mean to. I was *trying* to go in, but I couldn't. Elliott gave me something, and it messed everything up. It hurts to manipulate the Dreamscape, and half the time I still can't do what I want to do." He slumped down, burying his face in his hands. "That's why I'm here. I can't get into any dreams, or wake myself up, or anything."

"And that's why we couldn't find you," Hunter added, almost to himself. "We've been looking everywhere, but it's not as simple as just going into the void."

"I know." Wyatt sagged against the pile of books. "It's only been recently that I was able to even find dreams, and I was so afraid that I'd lose Aidan's and never find it again when I couldn't get in."

"Well, you found me. I'm almost as good."

Wyatt couldn't help but smile as he halfheartedly smacked Hunter on the upper arm. "You wish."

"I am so! Just maybe not to you," he admitted as he stood and held out a hand to Wyatt. "Come on, let's get you reunited with Aidan."

"How?"

"It's time to wake up."

Wyatt pulled his hand back from Hunter's. "I can't. I've been trying, but it doesn't work. I can't just—"

"You can't," Hunter corrected, grabbing Wyatt's wrist, "but I can. Let's go." Before Wyatt could protest, Hunter closed his eyes, grabbed the fabric of the Dreamscape, and twisted.

Chapter Forty

HUNTER scrambled to his feet, staggering the two steps from the trundle bed he shared with Brianna to Wyatt's bedside before he was fully awake. He leaned heavily on the bed, staring down at his friend and muttering under his breath as he waited for Wyatt to move. It should have worked. It *felt* like it had worked, but until Wyatt opened his eyes, there was no way to know for certain, and as he stared down at Wyatt's still form, Hunter was half-convinced he'd failed.

Kyler, Misty, Ratri, and Olin looked at him curiously, wondering what was going on, but he couldn't explain. It would only raise their hopes, and unless Wyatt opened his eyes in the next few seconds, Hunter would have to try again. If he could even find Wyatt.

"Come on, man," he whispered, barely resisting the urge to shake Wyatt's shoulder. "I know I dragged you out of there."

Misty came and stood next to him, placing her tiny hand atop his. "What happened?"

He opened his mouth, but he didn't have the chance to answer.

Wyatt made a soft, distressed sound, the first noise he'd made since being rescued, and everyone in the room clustered around the bed, pressing close and watching avidly as his eyelids fluttered open. They closed again almost immediately, and he turned his head, whimpering at the light, but it was enough, and suddenly he was being jostled from all sides and smothered by five foot two inches of excited brunette.

"Wyatt!" Misty climbed onto the bed, plastering herself to him and peppering his cheeks and forehead with kisses. "You're awake!" She wriggled around so she sat next to him, her body blocking some of the light, and cupped her hands around his chin. "We were so worried!"

"Um." Wyatt slowly raised his hand to rub at his eyes and blinked more as he looked around the room. "Aidan?" There was a crowd of people around his bed, almost everyone he could possibly want to see right now, but not the one person he *needed* to see. "Where's Aidan?" he asked again, this time letting the panic creeping over him seep into his tone as he forced the words out through his sore throat.

"Sleeping." Kyler shooed people away from Wyatt so he could see Aidan lay sleeping, held in the Dreamscape by Brianna and Gwendolyn, who were asleep on the trundle beds in the middle of the room.

Wyatt immediately tried to get up, ignoring the protests of his body in his desperation to get to Aidan.

"Easy." Kyler gently pushed on Wyatt's shoulder and his body gave in to the light pressure, his elbows buckling as he flopped back down on the pillow. "You need to stay right there."

"But—" Wyatt looked up at Kyler with pleading eyes. Hunter had promised he'd be reunited with Aidan, and merely being in the same room wasn't enough. Not when Aidan was still asleep and Wyatt didn't know if the faint awareness he could feel in the back of his mind was because of physical proximity or because their Bond was reasserting itself.

"I'm going to get him now." Hunter squeezed Wyatt's shoulder and settled on the trundle bed with Brianna. "I'm sure Brianna is worried sick about me too."

"Hurry?" Wyatt couldn't stop staring, his gaze never leaving Aidan's slumbering form as he waited impatiently for him to wake up. He rolled onto his side so he could get a better view, but it wasn't enough.

"Of course." Hunter grinned as he closed his eyes, but before he fell asleep, Ratri grabbed the bottom of his bed and yanked, startling him. Hunter flailed as the trundle bed slid across the tiled floor. "What the hell, man?"

"Hold on a sec." Ratri started directing people around the room, instructing them to stand in corners or move closer to the door. "If we move the trundle beds to this wall, we can push the other beds together, and then we don't have to worry about these two trying to sneak out of bed to get to each other."

Wyatt had never liked Ratri more than he did in that moment, and he smiled his thanks before returning his gaze to Aidan, almost content to watch him sleep while his friends set about finally reuniting them.

AIDAN was engaged in a staring contest with both Brianna and Gwendolyn when Hunter arrived in his dream. The girls had their hands on their hips and their mouths set, while Aidan's arms were crossed and his eyes were narrowed. It would have been a close contest if Aidan hadn't been outnumbered two to one.

Hunter approached them from the side, moving slowly and doing his best to keep his eyes on all three of them. "Um, guys?"

"Hunter!" Brianna broke away from the contest to pounce on her Bondmate, jumping up and wrapping her legs around his waist as she squeezed him tightly and caught his lips in a deep, passionate kiss that lasted for several seconds before she pulled away. "You made it back!"

"Um, yeah." He shifted his grip on Brianna's lower back. "Sorry."

"Well, maybe *you* can tell Aidan here that he needs to stay asleep," Gwendolyn interrupted before Brianna could go off on a tangent about how irresponsible Hunter had been.

"I don't!" Aidan stalked over so he could look pleadingly at Hunter. "I can *feel* Wyatt again. I need to be awake so he can—"

"That's what I came to tell you."

"Thank you! See?" Aidan whirled to glare at Gwendolyn. "Hunter agrees—" He froze for mere seconds and then swiveled back to Hunter. "Wait. What?"

"When I uh, left—"

"*Vanished*," Brianna corrected as she dropped back to the floor.

"Fine. When I *vanished*, I went with the books. Turns out Wyatt was in the void, and he was trying to get into your dream, but he couldn't. Every time he tried, though, he brought stuff out, and I hitched a ride with the last bit." He stuffed his hands in his pockets, rocked back on his heels, and grinned. "Once I convinced him I wasn't a hallucination, I woke him up."

Aidan's heart thudded in his chest and his hands began to shake as hope flooded through him. "Wyatt's awake?" he asked in a squeaky voice, barely able to say the words for fear that saying them would make them untrue.

"Yep."

It took a few breaths for that to penetrate, but when it did, Aidan very calmly stepped up to stand toe-to-toe with Hunter. He looked Hunter straight in the eye and, with great effort, kept his voice steady as he asked, "Then why am I still asleep?"

Hunter swallowed hard, put his hand on Aidan's shoulder, and grinned. "You want to take care of that?"

AIDAN'S eyes snapped open and he was halfway out of the bed before any of the Dreamers were fully awake. It hurt to move and his head spun, but he could see Wyatt in the other bed, grinning at him, and Aidan wasn't going to let anyone keep him away.

"Whoa!" Olin grabbed his shoulder, firmly pushing him back down on the bed. "You need to stay there."

"No! I need—"

"See? I told you!" Ratri said to the room at large, cutting Aidan off as he added his hand to Olin's, with the added insult of standing directly in Aidan's line of sight to Wyatt. "You need to stay put," he added, giving Aidan a stern look. "Give us two minutes and we'll have your beds pushed together. You think you can do that?"

It was tempting to say no, but Aidan knew Ratri would find a way to keep him in bed if he didn't agree, so he nodded. "Yes. Now can you move?" he added with a glare, batting at Ratri, who laughed and stepped away to resume moving the now empty trundle beds.

It was actually less than two minutes, but it seemed like much longer. Kyler briefly checked Aidan over while Ratri and Olin moved the cots and Misty asked Brianna and Gwendolyn what happened. Aidan's eyes never left Wyatt's until their beds were pushed together and the rails between them lowered. Then it wasn't Wyatt's eyes he was interested in anymore.

He rolled across the gap between their beds before the wheels had been locked in place, pushing the bed back into Ratri and Olin, but as he landed on top of Wyatt, he didn't care, and Wyatt's lips muffled Aidan's perfunctory apology at their cries of pain. Wyatt raised his arms and wrapped them around Aidan, squeezing him tight, and when they finally broke apart, gasping for air, it was impossible to tell whose smile was bigger.

"Hi," Aidan whispered, resting his forehead against Wyatt's and rubbing their noses together.

"Hey." Wyatt slid his hands up to the nape of Aidan's neck and pulled him down for another kiss, slipping his tongue inside Aidan's still parted lips.

It was magic.

Their hands roamed as their tongues danced, Aidan sliding his fingers along Wyatt's sides, and Wyatt scratching his way down Aidan's back. They moaned as their tongues curled together and slid apart, chasing each other from Aidan's mouth to Wyatt's and back again. Aidan's eyes slid shut as he lost himself in the taste of Wyatt, relishing the spicy, fruity flavor he hadn't savored in far too long.

"Love you," Wyatt whispered, pulling back just enough to talk before sliding his tongue back into Aidan's mouth and rubbing it along the ridges of the roof as he swallowed Aidan's moan. He tightened his grip around Aidan's back and was about to roll them over when a hand landed on his.

"All right guys, that's enough."

Aidan bit back a laugh, resting his forehead against Wyatt's again as he fought to keep his shoulders from shaking too badly. "Forgot we had an audience."

"Don't really care," Wyatt replied, tipping his chin up and pressing his lips against Aidan's.

This kiss was brief and almost chaste, but Aidan opened his mouth a little and tugged on Wyatt's bottom lip with his teeth as he moved so he lay next to Wyatt rather than on top of him. "We'll indulge your kink for exhibitionism later," Aidan replied sarcastically as he let Kyler help him settle next to Wyatt and put the IV he hadn't noticed losing back in his hand.

"Not while you're in the hospital under my care, you won't," Kyler admonished with a stern look as he looked them over again, and making notes on both charts. "How are you feeling, by the way? Besides…." He quirked an eyebrow and waved his hand. "Are you in any pain still?"

"No," Aidan said, then repeated it with wonder as it really sank in. "No. Not at all."

"And your Bond?"

"It's back." Aidan didn't try to keep the smile from blossoming on his face as he focused his attention inward for a moment, lightly brushing against Wyatt's presence in his mind. "Feels like it was never gone, to be honest."

Wyatt didn't wait to be asked. "I feel it too." He tugged Aidan a little closer and squeezed, needing the physical reassurance in addition to the love echoing along their Bond. "Just like it was before—" He stopped and swallowed hard, grateful he didn't actually have to say what had happened.

"How?" Aidan asked as he rolled over farther, taking care not to pull any of the tubes and wires free as he rested his head on Wyatt's shoulder and slid his arm over Wyatt's waist. "When we were, um, coming up here, you said that it might not come back."

"Elliott told me the same thing," Wyatt admitted softly as he shifted so he could more comfortably wrap his arms around Aidan. "He said that Aidan would be in a lot of pain—"

"I was."

"And that he'd have to have a dose, too, in order to make it stop."

Kyler hung the clipboards back up and took a seat on the foot of Wyatt's bed. "I'm just guessing here, but it might have worn off."

"What do you mean?" Ratri asked as he settled in one of the chairs next to Olin. "Why wouldn't you know?"

"Honestly, we don't know much about how Bonds work. There's something in our brains and bodies that let us form them, and we can identify someone who has one based on certain chemicals in their blood, but we don't know what causes them, or what makes two people right for each other, or why about fifteen percent of people never form them. One theory is that they originated with Dreamers, since a Bond lets them sleep in peace and enjoy their own dreams if their Bondmate is awake, but there are far more Bonded pairs than Dreamers, and not all Dreamers Bond either. The truth is, everything we think we know is a guess, and we don't know much about how dreaming really works either."

"So, what? We're all medical mysteries?" Brianna grinned at her Bondmate. "I mean, I knew Hunter was, but—"

"Hey!" Hunter jostled her with his shoulder, but they settled quickly at Ratri's stern look.

"Shut up. We want to hear this."

"Basically, yeah," Kyler answered. "Vinculex blocks the chemicals that can indicate a Bond. If both partners get a dose at the same time, the Bond is dissolved and it doesn't reform. If one partner gets it and the other doesn't, it causes extreme agony, as Aidan found out."

"Extreme agony is a bit mild," Aidan muttered as he squeezed Wyatt tightly and burrowed closer. "I'm not sure words exist to adequately describe it."

"I'm sorry," Wyatt whispered as he pressed a kiss to the top of Aidan's head. "I didn't want—"

"You didn't ask for it." Aidan tipped his head up so he could look at Wyatt. "It's not your fault."

"I know. I just… I feel bad."

"Don't." Aidan lifted his head and gently kissed Wyatt, sliding his tongue across Wyatt's closed lips and slipping it inside when Wyatt obligingly parted them.

Kyler cleared his throat. "As I was saying," he said pointedly, waiting with a raised eyebrow until Aidan pulled back and settled his head on Wyatt's chest once again. "Vinculex is mostly used in cases of abuse. If one partner harms the other, mentally or physically, the injured partner can request that the Bond be forcefully dissolved."

"Who would hurt their Bondmate?" Brianna asked as she scooted a little closer to Hunter. "You feel *everything* they feel. What kind of sick person *does* that?"

"It happens more than you'd imagine," Hunter said in an uncharacteristically somber tone. "A lot of times when one partner is a Dreamer and the other isn't, the one who isn't acts on their prejudices because they think the Dreamer will want the protection of the Bond too much to say anything."

"I'd like to know where Lumoinnovations got it, though," Kyler added. "It's a highly controlled substance, and Lumoinnovations doesn't have any contracts with the companies licensed to produce it. There's not much floating around either. Courts can order it to be administered in cases of abuse, or a couple can request their Bond be dissolved, but they have to both agree and petition the courts for it to happen."

"People actually do that?" Wyatt tightened his arms around Aidan, squeezing him hard and vowing to never let go.

"It's rare, but it does happen. I only know of two instances where it took place, but I guess Bonding gets it wrong sometimes."

"I can't imagine wanting that." Olin squeezed Ratri's knee and subtly moved their chairs closer together.

There was a chorus of agreement around the room, and Aidan tilted his head so he could kiss the underside of Wyatt's jaw. "I *never* want that," he whispered. "This was bad enough, and not being able to feel you was worse than the pain."

Wyatt just smiled, letting his agreement flow along their Bond with a surge of affection and love.

"Okay, all that's fascinating, and we agree, but how does that explain what happened with the lovebirds over there?" Ratri waved his hand at the beds and mock-scowled at the way Wyatt and Aidan cuddled together.

"The point I was trying to make," Kyler continued in an exasperated tone, "is that it's always administered in pairs. Even in the few cases I've read about where someone managed to get a dose via the black market, their partner would be at a hospital begging for it within hours. No one I'm aware of has ever gone this long, and it's possible that it just worked its way out of Wyatt's system." Kyler shrugged, tilting his head to the side as he looked at his friends. "You both sure you feel all right?"

"Well," Aidan murmured, his lips brushing Wyatt's neck, "I could use some alone time, but other than that I'm good."

Wyatt buried his laugh in Aidan's hair. "Me too."

"Guys." Kyler lightly smacked their calves to get their attention and gave them his best stern glare. "Seriously. I'm asking as your doctor here."

"I'm *fine*, Kyler," Aidan replied with a sigh, shifting to look at him. "I'm tired, and a little sore like, I don't know, I used my muscles too much or something, and I would *really* like a few minutes to catch up with my Bondmate without everyone watching, but other than that, I'm good. Honestly."

"Me too," Wyatt added, giving Kyler a contrite look. "My wrists are a little sore from when I was strapped to the bed, but I'm good. *Really.*"

Kyler nodded, but before he could say anything, the door flung open, hitting the stopper with a dull thud as Tabatha tore through it and skidded to a halt at the foot of the joined beds. She stood completely still, her eyes wide and her mouth hanging open as she stared at Wyatt.

"Tabatha?" he asked incredulously, shifting in the bed a little so he could see her better.

She didn't answer, just made a squeaking sound, covered her mouth with her hands, and kept staring.

"Um." Aidan tried to sit up but was stopped by Wyatt's arms. "Is she okay?"

"She's *fine*," Damon said as he entered at a more sedate pace, stopping next to his sister and shaking his head as she squeaked again. "She's just overwhelmed, I think. She didn't exactly have a chance to talk to you when we got here," he added, glancing at Wyatt and taking in the pushed-together beds with a raised eyebrow. "How are you feeling, anyway?"

"Well, um, she's kind of creeping me out, and I'm a little tired, but other than that I'm good," Wyatt said softly.

Damon laughed as he squeezed Tabatha's shoulder. "You can talk to him, you know. He doesn't bite."

Aidan bit back a laugh and pressed his face into Wyatt's neck as Wyatt muffled his giggles in Aidan's hair. Their shoulders shook, and mirth echoed back and forth along their Bond, making it harder and harder to keep the laughter in, but neither said anything. They didn't have to for everyone to get the point.

"He's awake," Tabatha said softly to Damon, her eyes widening further at the display.

"Yeah." Damon glanced at his sister and continued in the tone perfected by older siblings everywhere that let their younger brothers and sisters know exactly how burdensome they were being. "That was the whole point of the call we got, remember?"

Wyatt lifted his head slightly. "She, uh, didn't get any smarter, did she?"

"Nope. Sorry." Damon grinned. "She still takes a while to grasp the obvious."

"I hate you both."

"No you don't," Wyatt replied, easily falling back into banter that was familiar more than twelve years later. "You *love* us."

"Yeah, okay." The response was right, but her tone was shy, and she shuffled her feet and ducked her head as she inched forward, curling her fingers around the rail at the foot of the bed and watching Wyatt through lowered lashes.

It was Wyatt who finally broke the ice. "If you want a hug, you're going to have to come to me. I get yelled at if I try to get up."

A smile blossomed on Tabatha's face as she dashed around the bed and leaned over, grabbing Wyatt tightly enough that she practically dislodged Aidan, making him squawk. "I missed you," she whispered as she kissed his cheek.

"Yeah," Wyatt agreed, squeezing back. "I missed you too."

Aidan gave them a second and then shoved playfully at Tabatha's arm. "Get off. He's mine."

Tabatha laughed and slid her arm so she was hugging Aidan as well. "Like anyone could take him from you."

"I sure as hell hope no one else tries," Ratri muttered. "I do *not* want to go through that again."

Everyone agreed, and Aidan rolled his eyes. "Right. 'Cause it was so bad for all of *you*."

"Hey now!" Gwendolyn stood, her hands on her hips and her eyes narrowed playfully. "We had to take care of *you*, and trust me, it was not a walk in the park for any of us."

"Yeah, yeah." Aidan waved her off, the teasing tone of his words lost behind the yawn that immediately followed. "I know. I'm a terrible baby."

"All right, that's enough." Kyler started shooing people from the room. "That's enough excitement for now. It's time to let them get some real rest."

Tabatha kissed them each on the forehead and then joined the trail of people leaving the room. Damon followed, and soon only Kyler and Misty were left.

"What's she doing?" Aidan asked with another yawn as he burrowed in closer to Wyatt and let Kyler arrange and check their IVs and monitors one more time.

Misty looked up from where she sat on one of the trundle beds. "After everything that just happened, you don't really think we're going to let the two of you wander in the Dreamscape without *someone* there, just in case? I'm not going to dream with you," she added with a laugh at their horrified looks, "but I'll be close enough in case something happens."

"Thanks, Misty." Wyatt relaxed back into the pillows, his eyes closing immediately. It had been too long since he'd been able to do this, and despite everything that had happened, he was looking forward to it. A good night's sleep and pleasant dreams with Aidan was all he'd wanted for a long time.

It wasn't long before everyone was asleep, leaving Kyler standing in the middle of the room, smiling down at his patients tangled together on the joined beds, their breathing and heart rates matching exactly as they slipped off together into the Dreamscape. "Sweet dreams," he whispered, flicking the light switch off as he slipped out of the room.

Chapter Forty-One

AIDAN grinned at Carina as he locked the door and rearmed the alarm. With the apartment secured, he returned to the love seat, sat down next to Wyatt, and made a contented noise when Wyatt's arm slipped around his shoulders. Even now, their first day home after spending more than week in the hospital, he found it difficult to be out of physical contact with Wyatt, and Wyatt felt the same way. It was as though they were trying to make up for their forced time apart.

Soon they would have to learn to let go of each other again, but they were going to enjoy the opportunities for closeness while they could. Soon they'd have to return to work, and hours of any kind of separation weren't at all appealing. They wanted to stock up on time together while they could.

Carina sat on the couch, her briefcase at her feet, and watched as Wyatt pulled Aidan closer. "You two capable of separating?" she asked drolly, with a pointed look at the entire free cushion.

"Why would we want to do that?" Wyatt tilted his head to the side and managed to look genuinely curious for about thirty seconds before he burst out laughing.

Aidan shrugged. "Is there a problem with us sitting like this?"

"Not at all." Carina lifted her briefcase to the coffee table and opened it. "I just wanted to make sure it wouldn't be an issue at the trial. We've scheduled a date, and you're both being asked to testify." She set two sheets of paper out on the glass surface.

The temperature in the room seemed to drop ten degrees. Wyatt stiffened, making his back ramrod straight, and his fingers stilled on Aidan's shoulder. "Is Elliott going to be there?" he asked in a low tone.

"Elliott Sloan's trial is the one you are being asked to testify at, so yes, he will be there. The other cases will likely be dependent on the outcome of the Sloan trial, so they're being held later."

"Good." Wyatt nodded, relaxing a little and pulling Aidan close again. "I want to make sure that bastard gets what's coming to him."

Carina's eyebrow quirked, but she ignored the comment. "Your brother and sister have agreed to testify as well, and your friends are probably going to also. I haven't gotten a full list yet, but I suspect that everyone who was here will be on it. I've asked that they send everything for the two of you through me."

"Thanks, Carina." Aidan took one of the sheets of paper from the table and glanced over it. "I'd rather get any news from you than through the mail, and I'm *not* letting anyone I don't know in our apartment."

Wyatt shuddered and nodded his agreement. "No kidding."

Their friends had helped get a new alarm system installed while they had been in the hospital, but neither of them really felt safe, even on the high floor and with all the doors and windows secured and monitored. Wyatt had been taken from right where they were sitting, and despite the way everything had turned out, it was going to take them some time to feel comfortable in their home again.

Carina laughed. "Oh, I'll be well compensated. I'm billing you for this, you know."

Aidan waved her off. "I wouldn't expect anything less. You charge me, Kyler charges me...." He shook his head as he trailed off. "Sometimes I wonder why I'm friends with the two of you."

"I could start charging you for your pleasant dreams," Wyatt whispered.

"I'd like to see you try." Aidan laughed. "Besides," he added as he slid his hand across Wyatt's thigh toward his groin, "I think you get plenty of compensation."

"Maybe I want more," Wyatt teased, slouching in his seat so that Aidan's fingers rested on the fly of his jeans. "I don't think I've been compensated enough recently."

"We haven't exactly had a lot of *time*," Aidan growled, but before he could move any further, Carina cleared her throat. "Yes, Carina?" he asked.

"Just pointing out that you aren't alone."

"I know." Aidan smirked as he squeezed Wyatt's hand. "Was there anything else?"

"Actually, there is." She pulled another sheet of paper out of her briefcase and placed it face down on the table while she closed the briefcase and returned it to the floor. "The information Zane passed along to the police and courts included the names of the friends from Ambridia who are still looking for you, Wyatt. I had contacted them just before you were taken, and the police contacted them for their statements, so they've come out here. They've asked to see you."

Wyatt stilled, the movement of his fingers against Aidan and the twitching of his foot stopping as he sucked in a deep breath. "Lilly and Quinton?" he asked, the words catching in his throat and grating against his suddenly dry mouth. "They're here?"

"They're staying in a hotel downtown." Carina handed the paper to Wyatt. "They left their contact information yesterday, and I told them I would pass it along."

"Thanks." Wyatt picked up the paper and slowly pulled it back toward his body, but he didn't turn it over. "Do you think—?"

"It's up to you, Wyatt," Carina said calmly as she grabbed her briefcase and stood. "They seemed sincere, and they've been very helpful in passing along all the information they had gathered over the years, but I think they'll understand if you're not ready to meet with them yet. I didn't promise them anything other than to pass along the information."

Aidan squeezed Wyatt's hand again before disentangling himself so he could let Carina out. "Will they testify?"

"It's possible, but not likely. Their information has all been submitted into evidence." She headed for the door, Aidan following, and stopped with her hand on the knob. "Don't let him do anything he's not comfortable with, Aidan. I really think his friends will be okay if they just know that he's all right."

"I don't think we need to worry," Aidan said as he turned off the alarm. "He won't call them if he doesn't want to. Trust me, he's stubborn like that."

"Yeah, I know." Carina shook her head fondly as she looked over at Wyatt still slumped on the couch. "Go take care of him. I'll call when I learn something new."

Aidan looked over at Wyatt as well. "I will." He shut the door behind her, locked it, and was turning to the alarm panel when Wyatt came up behind him, wrapped his arms around Aidan's waist, and set his chin on Aidan's shoulder.

"What did she tell you about me?" he asked softly, sighing as he molded his body against Aidan's.

"Just that I should take care of you and make sure you don't do anything you don't want to do." Aidan twisted around so they stood chest to chest and held Wyatt close. "I told her no one was going to make you do anything you didn't want to do."

"That doesn't stop them from trying, though." Wyatt sighed, closing his eyes. "It's the story of my life."

"Hey." Aidan pulled back a little, waiting for Wyatt to reopen his eyes before speaking. "Your life is this, here, with me. It's whatever *we* make of it, you got that?"

Wyatt nodded, smiling faintly. "Yeah. I just—" He shrugged. "I felt like I was on top of things, you know? I was in control of my own life for the first time ever, and then…." He trailed off with a sigh, slumping forward to rest his forehead against Aidan's.

"I know. But we got through it. And we're going to get through this trial and come out on top, and then there's not going to be anything that can stop us from doing whatever we want."

"You really think so?"

"I know so." Aidan tilted his chin up, pressed his lips gently against Wyatt's. "No one is ever going to make you do anything you don't want to again."

"Except testify?"

"Do you really not want to?"

"I'm not looking forward to it."

"But?"

"But I want to make sure they get what they deserve," Wyatt admitted with a shrug. "So I guess I do want to testify. I'm just not excited about it."

"Yeah, well." Aidan grinned. "I'm not exactly jumping for joy over here."

Wyatt smiled briefly before he sobered again. "What about Lilly and Quinton, though?" he asked, immediately pulling his bottom lip into his mouth and chewing nervously on it.

"What about them?"

"Should I see them?" Wyatt stepped away, his hand coming up to rub at the back of his neck, and he shifted nervously, turning so his back was to Aidan as he fidgeted. "I don't want to upset them, but I don't know if I'm ready for that, especially after everything else. There's so much going on right now and—"

Aidan cut Wyatt off by copying their earlier pose with their positions reversed. "Lilly and Quinton know what happened. They won't be upset if you can't see them yet, I promise."

"How do you know?"

"Well, Carina said they'd be happy just knowing you were okay, for one."

Wyatt turned in Aidan's arms, leaning to the side and tipping his head so he could look Aidan in the eye. "I thought you said she just told you to take care of me and not let me do anything I didn't want to do."

"Do you expect me to believe that you wouldn't feel like you had to go meet them if I hadn't told you that?"

"No," Wyatt admitted with a wry smile that quickly turned impish. "So now that you've taken care of making sure I don't feel that I have to do something I don't want to, how are you going to take care of *me*?"

Aidan grinned as he slid his hands down Wyatt's torso. "Oh, I can think of a few ways."

"And what," Wyatt asked as he backed Aidan against the wall, his heart racing in anticipation of *finally* getting to really touch Aidan again, "if I want to take care of you?"

Aidan's breath hitched as Wyatt squeezed him through his jeans. He could feel Aidan's desire along their bond and his heart sped up in response. "I think that would be acceptable."

"Acceptable?" Wyatt growled as he lowered his head to suck on Aidan's earlobe. "I'll show you acceptable," he added, moving his hand under the waistband of Aidan's jeans and slipping inside his boxers to circle his cock.

"M-more than," Aidan stuttered, thrusting his hips forward as Wyatt gripped him. He struggled to think of the right word to describe his feelings and decided to use all of them. "Marvelous. Fabulous. Outstanding, even."

"That's more like it." Wyatt licked around the shell of Aidan's ear and sucked the lobe into his mouth as he flicked open the button of Aidan's jeans and dragged the zipper down. The fly parted easily, and he pushed Aidan's jeans to the floor as he moved his lips to Aidan's neck, savoring the salty taste of his skin. He lifted his hands, yanking and tugging at Aidan's shirt, and shifted away just enough to pull it over Aidan's head. Then he paused to take in the sight.

Aidan leaned against the wall, his head tipped back, his face flushed, and his mouth open just slightly. His eyes were closed and his hands hung loose at his sides, his fingers twitching as he waited for Wyatt to step close again. His freckles stood out against his flushed skin, a smattering of them covering the bridge of his nose and his cheeks and a few more dotting their way down his neck and torso. They gave out completely by the time his chest gave way to sculpted abs, but the firm line of muscle continued all the way down to Aidan's groin, where his cock arched up from a bed of curls and his balls nestled between the spread of his legs. His thighs were parted slightly, just enough that Wyatt would be able to slip a hand between them, and his jeans and boxers pooled around his bare feet, the splashes of blue and black contrasting with the rosy wood of the floor and the bronze tan of Aidan's legs.

Wyatt *wanted*, more than he'd ever wanted anything, *ever*, and his grin broadened as he recalled this was his for the taking. Aidan belonged to him just as he belonged to Aidan, and this latest ordeal had proven that was never going to change. He could have this, all of it, everything Aidan was offering, and the knowledge made him giddy with pleasure.

He was only able to hold back for a few seconds before he pounced, cupping his hands around the curve of Aidan's ass as he slowly dragged one finger along the crack.

Aidan made an incoherent noise, his eyelids fluttering as he pawed at Wyatt's shirt. "Off," he managed, lifting his chin to look Wyatt in the eyes. "Lube."

Wyatt cursed under his breath as he flung open the coat closet door and started digging frantically in the bags on the floor. Aidan stepped up behind him, reaching around Wyatt's waist and flicking at the button of his jeans. By the time Wyatt found what he was looking for, his pants and boxers lay at his feet and Aidan's hands had slipped under his shirt and pushed it up to his shoulders.

He twisted as he stood, letting Aidan pull the shirt over his head with practiced ease. As soon as he was free of the restrictive material, he turned and pushed Aidan against the wall once more, this time with his back out and face pressed to the plaster. Wyatt made short work of the package he'd located, ripping and tearing at plastic and cardboard until he'd freed the bottle, and he wasted no time in pouring the slick, cool, liquid over his fingers and handing the bottle to Aidan.

Aidan took it with trembling fingers, holding it tightly with one hand as he grabbed Wyatt's chin with the other, pulling him in for a soul-searing kiss. The pleasure echoed along their bond, leaving them both panting and desperate. He pushed his hips back as Wyatt pressed one lube-slicked finger inside him, and they moaned together, losing themselves in the feeling of being physically connected after so long apart.

Wyatt twisted his finger, making Aidan's hips buck, and it wasn't long before Aidan was begging him for another finger and then another. Wyatt stretched Aidan as quickly as he could, twisting his fingers to make it as pleasurable as possible, but neither of them wanted to wait, and the next thing Wyatt knew, Aidan was pressing the bottle of lubricant back into his hand.

"Hurry," Aidan growled, turning around to capture Wyatt's lips in another kiss. His tongue slipped inside as his hands roamed over Wyatt's torso, sliding down to wrap around Wyatt's aching cock as he fumbled with the cap. Aidan rubbed his thumb over the slit, and the sensation combined with Aidan's desire echoing over their bond made Wyatt almost drop the bottle. His hips bucked and he made an incoherent sound that was swallowed by Aidan's mouth and lost in the passion of their kisses.

As Wyatt finally got his fingers to cooperate, Aidan kissed his way along Wyatt's jaw, taking advantage of Wyatt's extra height to nibble lightly at the underside of it before whispering in his ear, "I wanna ride you."

"Yes," Wyatt breathed, and then his hands cooperated fully, swiftly coating his dick and dropping the bottle carelessly. He clutched Aidan's hips and lifted until he was looking up at Aidan instead of down.

Aidan wrapped his arms and legs around Wyatt's shoulders and hips, leaning back to brace his shoulders against the wall as Wyatt guided him downward. He shifted slightly as the blunt end of Wyatt's cock pressed against him, and then he let himself fall just a little, taking Wyatt in with one swift movement that left them both seeing stars. Aidan tensed at the intrusion, letting out a low moan as his head thunked back against the wall, but then Wyatt lifted and lowered him again, changing the angle just a little, and those stars exploded.

They moved quickly, Wyatt lifting and thrusting, and Aidan helping as much as he could, bracing himself against the wall and rocking his hips so Wyatt hit him just right inside with every plunge. It didn't take long before they were on the edge, their bond amplifying the pleasure as it bounced between them, and they came at the same time, crying out each other's names and clinging desperately as their bodies shuddered.

Wyatt slowly sank to the floor, leaning heavily on Aidan and the wall as he tried to control his descent, and they ended up tangled in a pile on the floor, their bodies still joined as they sagged together, breathing heavily. They lay unmoving for a minute, relishing the renewed connection of their bond, and then Aidan shifted, rolling off Wyatt and stretching out next to him, his hand coasting over Wyatt's nipple as he propped his head on his other hand and gazed down with a contented look on his face.

Wyatt grinned up at him, and when Aidan's hand moved lower, he moaned and tugged Aidan down for a kiss. "We should…."

"Yeah." Aidan climbed to his feet, faltering for a moment on shaky legs before pulling Wyatt up with him and kissing him again, only stopping when they were gasping for breath. "Bedroom," he managed in a low growl, swiftly hitting the buttons on the alarm while Wyatt grabbed the lube. They careened down the hallway, bumping into the walls and bookcases, not caring about anything other than touching, teasing, and losing themselves in the sensation as they prepared for round two.

It lasted significantly longer.

Chapter Forty-Two

THE fourth time Wyatt walked out of the closet holding a button-down shirt and a pair of dress pants only a slightly different shade than any of the other three outfits laid out on the bed, Aidan took the clothes from him and immediately returned them to their places on the rack. "Any of these are fine, Wyatt," he admonished gently, taking Wyatt's fluttering hands in his and leading him to the couch in the corner of the bedroom. "Any one of them is appropriate for tomorrow."

"I know." Wyatt sank onto the soft cushions with a sigh. "I just...." He ran his hand through his hair. "It's stupid, isn't it? I mean, they're not going to decide the verdict based on my clothes, right?"

"No, they're not." Aidan couldn't keep all of the laughter from his tone, but he tried to soften his tone as he sat down next to Wyatt, still holding his hands. "You're going to look marvelous in whatever you wear, and the jury is going to love you."

"Are you sure?"

"Of course." Aidan squeezed Wyatt's hands. "But I don't think it's the jury you want to impress."

Wyatt smiled despite his nervousness. "It's not." He blew out a puff of air, deflating as it left his lungs. "I need Elliott to see that I'm not broken. That *we're* not broken."

"He will," Aidan assured him firmly, looking him straight in the eyes and sending his confidence along their Bond. "But it won't be because of how either of us are dressed. It will be because you're *not* broken, because *we* aren't broken. We could show up dressed like we don't have a penny to our names and he would be able to see that. I promise."

"Thanks." Wyatt's smile widened and he tugged Aidan forward, capturing his lips in a soft kiss. Aidan raised his hand to cup Wyatt's jaw, deepening the kiss, and Wyatt reciprocated, slipping his tongue between Aidan's lips and sending all of his love, trust, and gratitude along their Bond, leaving Aidan overwhelmed with the strength of his feelings.

Wyatt's hand was just sliding under Aidan's shirt when there was a knock on the door, and they broke apart with a groan.

"Your brother and sister have the worst timing." Aidan scowled, brushing imaginary lint off his pants as he stood. "Why couldn't they have been late?"

"They *are* late," Wyatt countered with a laugh after glancing at the clock. "They were supposed to be here five minutes ago."

"Then they should have been on time." Aidan pulled Wyatt close again, stretching up to kiss him once more, putting all of his desire, passion, and frustration into the brief touch of their lips. He pulled back to go let Damon and Tabatha in, leaving Wyatt desperately wanting more and left with a raging hard-on.

By the time Wyatt got out to the front room, Aidan had rearmed the alarm and he, Damon, and Tabatha were sitting on the couch and love seat waiting for him. He sat down next to Aidan with a grin, but the smile fell quickly from his face when he noticed his siblings' expressions. The feeling of dread that crept over him when he saw Tabatha's tear-reddened eyes increased when he took in the somber look on Aidan's face and the nervous anxiety his Bondmate was trying to suppress. "What is it?"

Damon held out his phone. "I got a message today."

Wyatt furrowed his brow as he took the slender device from his brother. "Okay...."

"Just—" Damon cut himself off, swallowing hard. "Just read it. Please?"

Slowly, Wyatt slid his thumb over the phone's screen, unlocking it. The message icon was easy to find, large and prominent in the middle of the screen, and with trepidation, Wyatt moved his thumb over to it and pressed down. Immediately, words filled the screen, so many of them crowding into the small space that a scroll bar appeared at the side to let him read the whole message.

He didn't need to. The From-line was enough to send a chill down his spine, and the first sentence made him feel ill. He handed the phone back to Damon without reading the rest of the message. "Did you—?"

"I haven't responded," Damon said firmly as he closed the message and dropped the phone back in his shirt pocket. "I don't want to see her, and I definitely don't want her anywhere near *you*."

"Does she really think that I'll want to see her?" He couldn't even imagine. He was happy he'd reunited with Tabatha and Damon, and the dinner he'd had with Lilly and Quinton a few weeks ago had gone well, but Wyatt wasn't anxious to reunite with anyone else from his old life, particularly not his parents.

Tabatha let out a little laugh. "Probably. She, um. On your birthday, that year, she cried in the car on the way home. Dad didn't. He kept saying we were better off without you and spent all this time trying to convince us of how much better things were going to be. I think maybe Mom convinced herself that he was right 'cause that's the only way she could deal with it."

Wyatt snorted. "So she felt a little guilty at first. Is that supposed to make it all better?"

"No." Damon rubbed his hand over his face. "Even if she felt guilty then, she doesn't now. She got over it as soon as the first check was cashed, it seemed like."

"Yeah." Tabatha shook her head. "I mean, occasionally she'd seem a little, I don't know, depressed, maybe, but she hasn't in years. Even if she was feeling guilty, she didn't do anything about it then, and she started believing the lies about everything being for the best before I moved out."

"So why would she even want to see me?"

"To ease her conscience?" Aidan suggested, and Damon and Tabatha nodded their agreement.

"She's probably convinced that since you're okay *now*, that what they did doesn't matter. Hell," Damon continued with a snort, "she might be congratulating herself. After all, what they did led to you meeting Aidan."

"And that's exactly the kind of thing she would love to take credit for," Tabatha added. "She's gotten bitter lately. I think she feels like she deserves some praise or reward she's not getting and she'll jump on any excuse to get some."

Aidan slipped his arm around Wyatt's shoulders, tugging him close, and Wyatt gave in easily, slumping in Aidan's arms so he leaned heavily against his lover. "Why now?" he asked in a quiet voice, his eyes firmly fixed on the buttons of Aidan's shirt.

"Because they're in town," Damon said flatly. "They're staying at a hotel near the courthouse."

Wyatt's eyes narrowed, and he lifted his head to glare at his brother. "How do you know that? I thought you hadn't responded?"

"It's in the message, Wyatt." Aidan rubbed his hand up and down Wyatt's arm, soothing him. "She put where she was staying so that you would be able to contact her if Damon didn't feel comfortable giving her your contact information."

"Which I didn't," Damon assured him. "Like I said, she's not getting anywhere near you if I have any sort of say in the matter."

"Same here," Tabatha added firmly.

Aidan let the possessive way he was holding Wyatt close and the love and determination he was sending over their Bond do his talking for him. No one had any doubt that he would do everything in his power to keep Wyatt as far from his parents as possible.

"Thanks." Wyatt straightened a little, though he stayed tucked under Aidan's arm and kept their bodies pressed as closely together as he could manage. "Does she say why she wants to see me? I only read the first sentence."

"She claims she wants to apologize." Tabatha rolled her eyes. "Likely she's panicking and wants to try to guilt trip you and remind you that she's your mother. She's terrified that she and Dad are going to be arrested once this trial is over, and she may try to convince you not to press charges against them. Or at least against her. I'm not sure if she cares what happens to him anymore."

"She doesn't?" Damon asked in a surprised tone. He hadn't expected that any more than Wyatt had, and he found himself suddenly feeling a bit out of his depth. "What do you mean?"

"Oh, right. I didn't tell you."

"Tell me what?"

Tabatha rubbed the bridge of her nose, pinching it between her thumb and forefinger as she contemplated the best way to phrase this. "She called me last week, and I answered without looking at the ID on the phone, so I was stuck talking to her. I tried to get off as soon as I could, 'cause I wasn't going to tell *her* anything, but she did tell me that things were getting rough at home. Apparently, the two of them disagree on the way they should handle this trial, and she didn't want to come out here for it. I guess they've been fighting a lot lately, more than normal since their extra money cut out."

"Good." Wyatt surprised even himself with the vehemence in his tone, but he couldn't help but be happy that his parents weren't anymore. They didn't deserve happiness, and though he wouldn't normally wish misery on even his worst enemy, he did wish that his parents would experience it just a little.

"Yeah. Except now she's here, and I'm sure she's doing everything she can to mitigate the consequences for herself, which includes trying to sway you." Tabatha slumped back on the couch and crossed her arms. "Which sucks. Especially since she keeps trying to come through us."

"Better us than calling Wyatt directly," Damon admonished.

"Well, yeah, but that doesn't mean that I *want* to keep getting calls and messages I have to ignore. Hell, the woman filled up my inbox yesterday, and I almost didn't get a message from Garrett because she wouldn't leave me alone. Oh, and she's bugging him, too, now, which is *really* not acceptable."

"Wait. Garrett's your Bondmate, right?" Aidan tilted his head to the side as he looked at Tabatha. "Why is she calling him? He doesn't know how to reach us, does he?" A cold ball of dread grew in his gut as he thought about someone they didn't know, even if that person was Wyatt's brother-in-law, being aware of where they were and how to reach them. They had been threatened too much by people they weren't familiar with who somehow found out where they were to be comfortable with it, even for someone as innocuous as Garrett.

"No," Tabatha confirmed with a shake of her head. "All he knows is that you live in Haverdsford. I guess she's trying to get at me through him. I'm not answering her calls or responding to her messages, so maybe she figured that I would respond to his and he could pass the information along. Not that he would," she added, rolling her eyes, "even if I was going to tell him. He's always disliked her, and he wouldn't choose to help her with this for anything."

Wyatt had to grin at that. "She, uh, doesn't seem to have too many fans."

"Yeah, well, Tabatha and Garrett Bonded while she still lived at home, and our parents tried to convince her that she needed to ditch him and find someone else. He apparently didn't make enough money to suit their tastes or something." Damon snorted. "He does well enough for himself now, but back when they met he was just getting started and trying to pay off debt. That didn't go over well with them."

Aidan shook his head. "They tried to break up her Bond?" He suppressed a shudder as the memory of what had happened when Wyatt was taken from him slipped into the forefront of his mind. "Are they nuts?"

"I think we've long since established that my parents aren't the sanest people out there, Aidan," Wyatt teased, bumping Aidan's shoulder and sending a burst of love along their Bond to knock him out of his sudden melancholy. "Trying to convince Tabatha that she should pick someone else over her Bondmate is downright normal for them, actually. Lots of parents don't like the people their kids Bond with, at least at first."

"Yeah, well, Garrett and ours still hate each other." Tabatha grinned. "But that's fine. Makes it that much easier to avoid seeing our parents. I always end up going over to his folks' place for holidays. They're much more welcoming."

Wyatt smiled at the memory of his time at Aidan's parents' place, warmth growing in his belly as he remembered the way they'd welcomed him and how, despite Aidan's father's initial unease, they'd all accepted him for who he was and had even encouraged him to use his abilities to help them. *That* was what a family was supposed to be like, and Wyatt was glad his sister had found a family that welcomed her as well. It was reassuring to know she wasn't alone.

"Essentially," Damon said, leaning forward so he was resting his elbows on his knees and lacing his fingers together, "she's desperate. And she's going to do anything she can, even if it has less than no chance of working. That's why we were worried. You guys aren't listed in any directory she'd be able to find, are you?"

Aidan's gut twisted. "Our personal lines aren't, but I do a lot of freelance advertisement work, and my business line is. It has to be, or I wouldn't get any jobs. I can't expect people to call me if they don't have easy access to my number. Wyatt never answers that, though."

"Don't," Damon insisted.

Wyatt shook his head. "I don't plan to. I never wanted to, and I especially don't want to now." He and Aidan had playfully argued about his refusal to have anything to do with Aidan's business phone, but this was much more serious than discussions that ended with Wyatt insisting he wasn't a secretary and Aidan offering him some of the "perks" of the position. Those discussions usually ended up with their having sex, one of them bent over Aidan's desk or on the floor of the office. This one wouldn't.

"I don't want you to." Aidan rubbed at the back of Wyatt's neck. "I'll screen those calls as much as I can while they're in town. Most of my regular clients know that I'm tied up right now, but I can't let the work go all together. I've spent too long building my client base to just let it go."

"And you shouldn't," Damon agreed, sitting back and cracking his neck. "Just don't let anyone who calls talk to Wyatt."

Aidan nodded his agreement, but Wyatt didn't feel any better. Just the knowledge that his mother was looking for him had his stomach in knots, and the more they discussed the possible ways she could try to get ahold of him, the more nervous he became. "What if she gets ahold of me? What then?"

"She won't." Aidan turned so he could look Wyatt straight in the eyes. "There's no way she can know where you are, you're off work for the duration of the trial, and she doesn't have your phone number. There's no way she can reach you."

"What if she calls the hospital and they give her the information?"

"I don't think they can, Wyatt. Employee files are confidential."

"Then what about the court records? If she's part of this, she could have a lawyer who has access to the witness information!"

"If they're doing this properly, only your name is listed there, Wyatt." Damon made sure he had his brother's full attention before continuing. "You are the victim here. They don't just make your contact information available to anyone who wants it. That would be counterproductive, and they'd find it hard to get a lot of people to agree to testify."

"Yeah, but—"

Aidan pulled Wyatt close against him. "Listen to me, okay?" He waited for Wyatt to nod against his chest before continuing. "There is no one who knows how to reach you who is going to share that information with anyone, and especially not with your parents. If you're worried, we can call the hospital and call Carina to make sure that everything is locked down, but I know that no matter who she manages to reach, no one is going to pass anything along to her. Okay?"

"Yeah." Wyatt nodded and tried to believe, but part of him couldn't help but worry. He had been burned too badly and too many times just when he thought things were starting to go his way to truly believe that his mother wouldn't find some way to cause problems for him, even if it was just by making him worry needlessly. No matter what it was, he wouldn't give it to her, and he didn't want to be asked.

"Do you want to call?" Aidan asked after a minute, leaning back enough that he could look Wyatt in the eyes again, to be sure he was paying attention. "If we're going to, tonight, we need to now. It'll be too late after dinner."

Wyatt took a deep breath. He wanted to say no, that he trusted people to do their jobs and that he didn't need the additional reassurance of what was probably an unnecessary phone call, but he couldn't make himself, so he nodded. "Yeah. I think I would."

"Okay." There was no reprimand or surprise in Aidan's voice, and that more than anything else made Wyatt feel better about calling.

"I'll call the hospital," he said, pulling his phone from his pocket as he stood. "Can you call Carina?"

Aidan nodded and this time, Wyatt could feel his surprise along their Bond. "Are you sure you don't want me to call both?"

"Yeah, I am." And he was, surprisingly enough. It wasn't a phone call he was looking forward to making, but it would have been worse to let Aidan make it for him. It was Wyatt's job, and his responsibility to make sure they were holding up their end of his employment contract.

"Okay." Aidan smiled, sending his approval and pride to Wyatt, and pulled his phone out of his pocket. "This shouldn't take long," he told Damon and Tabatha, "and then we'll head out to dinner."

Damon and Tabatha nodded as Wyatt stepped into the kitchen, hitting the speed-dial button for his department in the hospital and putting the phone up to his ear. It only rang once before it was answered.

The conversation took longer than he'd expected, but when he was done, Wyatt was satisfied that his mother wouldn't get any information out of his employer, and he was smiling slightly as he stepped back into the front room. Aidan was back on the couch, his phone tucked away, and he stood when Wyatt walked in. "Everything taken care of?"

"Yeah, you?"

"Absolutely." Aidan took Wyatt's hand in his and gently kissed him. "You ready for dinner?"

Wyatt tugged Aidan toward the door. "Definitely. I'm starving."

"Of course you are." Aidan shook his head fondly. "What am I going to do with you?"

"Feed me yummy food?" Wyatt batted his eyelashes and leaned in close. "And afterward," he added in a lower tone, "there are lots of other things you can do to me, if you want."

"Oh, I want."

With a serene grin, Wyatt led the way out of their apartment, heading toward the elevator and dinner with his family. His fears weren't totally at rest, but they'd been soothed for the moment, and now he was going to seize the opportunity and spend one last evening relaxing with his loved ones before his life was once more flipped upside down as everything that had been done to him was dragged out into the open.

He would deal with that tomorrow. Tonight, he was going to have fun.

Chapter Forty-Three

WYATT sat down on the wooden bench with a sigh, slumping forward and resting his head in his hands as he tried to get his breathing and heart rate under control. After the first day, he and Aidan had avoided the trial, but they were both called to testify today, and they'd had to come. Wyatt gave his testimony in the morning, an experience he would forever count among the most painful hours of his entire life, and now, after they'd returned from a late lunch, Aidan was giving his. Wyatt had intended to stay and listen, to support Aidan the way Aidan had supported him the entire time he was up on the stand.

He couldn't, though. Everyone in the courtroom had been watching Aidan and the lawyers, but Elliott Sloan had been watching Wyatt. Every chance he got, Wyatt's tormentor turned around, his eyes seeking Wyatt's as he smirked, and Wyatt hadn't been able to take it. Facing Elliott from the witness stand had been hard enough; he couldn't handle staring the other man down every few minutes.

So here he was, hiding like a coward in the hallway while he waited for Aidan to finish, but it was better than staying in the courtroom. Out here, the seat was just as uncomfortable physically, but there weren't strangers crowded around him, jostling to get a glimpse of the poor kid who had been sold away by greedy and unscrupulous parents, nor was he forced to listen to various versions of what had happened to him recounted for the jury by just about everyone who had been involved. The bits of testimony he had caught outside of his own had been horribly painful to hear, and he had hated every minute of listening to Aidan describe what happened after he had been taken from their apartment.

Best of all, Elliott was in *there*, and there was no chance he'd end up out *here*. He wasn't allowed to leave his chair except when escorted by the officers of the court, which made the hallway much, much safer than inside the courtroom, as far as Wyatt was concerned. Even if the entire population of the courtroom migrated out into the hallway right this minute, it would still be better than facing Elliott's stares.

Slowly, Wyatt managed to calm himself, his breathing steadying and his heart rate returning to something close to normal. He sat up, ran his hands through his hair to tame it again, and was contemplating returning to the courtroom to meet Aidan when he heard the clicking sound of high heels hitting the marble floor.

He couldn't see who it was, but she was approaching quickly, and if Wyatt stood now, he'd be right in her path and faced with at least a few moments of awkward conversation he would rather miss. Instead, he stayed seated, slumping forward with his head in his hands and his fingers twisting in his hair, trying to make his body language look as uninviting as possible so the woman would pass him by. She didn't.

The clicking sounds got louder as the woman neared, but they stopped when she was right in front of him, leaving him looking at a pair of hideous red shoes that were far too risqué for a sober court appearance. The owner was wearing red stockings as well, the color just enough different from that of the shoes that they looked really terrible, even to Wyatt's untrained eye, and that alone was enough to make him reluctant to look up. He could only think of one woman who would feel she had a reason to stop in front of him. She was one of only two people not in the courtroom who could make him wish he'd stayed in his seat to continue the staring contest with Elliott.

His mother.

"Hello, Wyatt," Ursula Mettler said in a soft voice that had veins of steel running through it. "I know that's you, so there's no use pretending you don't know who I'm talking about. Look up and say hello to your mother, my dear."

Wyatt lifted his head and glared. "I'm not your *dear*. I'm not your *anything*."

"You are my son, Wyatt," she said, sitting down on the bench next to him and patting his knee.

He jerked away, hissing at the touch. "Parents don't do that to their children," he insisted, rising to his feet so he could stare down at her. The urge to run was strong, but he held his ground, crossing his arms and spreading his feet just slightly as he met her pleading gaze with his defiant one. "You are the woman who gave birth to me. That's *all*."

"Wyatt," she started, standing and reaching out to him. "Please. Just listen to me."

He dodged the hand, raising his eyebrows in warning when she tried again. "Why should I listen to anything you have to say?"

"I'm your mother, dear. You at least owe me that much."

It was the wrong thing to say. "*I* owe *you*?" Wyatt threw back his head and let out a hysterical laugh that he had to fight to control before he could continue. "*I* owe *you*? What kind of twisted logic led you to that belief? You got everything you could out of me. You took away my life. You *sold* me. And for what? A bigger house? A nicer car?"

"A good night's sleep!" Ursula snapped, her eyes blazing for a moment before she managed to get herself back under control. "We were thinking of Damon and Tabatha, dear. They couldn't be expected to do their best with you running around in their heads all the time, and with you gone, we were able to give them everything they deserved. I was just looking out for my children."

"Two minutes ago, you were trying to convince me that *I* was one of your children. Either I was or I wasn't." Wyatt shook his head, smiling grimly. "We both know you made that decision over twelve years ago. You can't change it now, just because you think it would benefit you."

"Wyatt," she said in a hurt tone, stepping closer again, but stopping when he took a small step back, "what makes you think that I'm here for me? I just wanted to make sure you were all right."

"If you wanted to be sure I was all right, you never would have sold me in the first place."

"I didn't—"

"Yes, you did." His father had signed the papers, but his mother hadn't stopped him, hadn't done anything to help him, even when she was supposedly feeling guilty about what they'd done. "Don't lie to me. After everything you've done, you at least owe *me* that much."

"I wasn't lying, dear." Her voice went back to that sickeningly smooth sound that was clearly trying to win him over and grated horribly on his nerves. "I do want to make sure you're all right. I heard that you found a Bondmate and that you're doing well for yourself now."

"I am," he admitted cautiously, "not that it's any of your concern."

"It is. You're my son."

"No. I'm not."

"Wyatt, please."

"You're too late." Wyatt closed his eyes for a second, and when he opened them, he met his mother's gaze with a resolute stare. He wasn't backing down from this. "Damon and Tabatha told me you felt guilty after I was taken away."

Ursula grabbed onto the straw as if it were a lifeline on a sinking ship. "I did."

"That doesn't matter, though." A wave of sadness washed over Wyatt as he realized she truly didn't understand. "If you really saw me as one of your children and not a burden you had to put up with until you could get rid of me, you never would have let it happen in the first place."

"Wyatt, you don't understand. Your father—"

"You would have found a way to stop it. You would have fought against it."

"I couldn't."

"Yes, you could have." Her denial stung almost as much as the knowledge of what she had done. "You lied to everyone about where I was. You took the money and *enjoyed* it." He took a step forward, using his height to his full advantage as he loomed over her. "If you really felt guilty about what happened, if you were truly *sorry* for what you had done, you would have spent the last twelve years trying to undo it, not living off it."

"I didn't really have a choice!" Ursula protested, crocodile tears springing to her eyes. Everything Wyatt was saying was true, but she had spent so long convincing herself otherwise that she couldn't let herself think about what he was saying. "Your father—"

"What about me, dear?" Lorne Mettler approached from down the hall and stopped next to his Bondmate, raking his gaze up and down Wyatt. "I see you found him," he added in a flat tone, sneering.

"Don't worry, I was just leaving." Wyatt kept his own sneer in check as he turned to go. He had no desire to face his father and rehash the conversation he'd just had with his mother.

Or worse.

Everything he'd been told indicated that his father never felt any remorse at all.

"You're not walking away from me, are you, son?"

Wyatt stiffened and slowly turned to meet Lorne's gaze with a deliberately calm expression. "I'm not your son," he said in a surprisingly even tone. His fingers clenched into fists at his sides, and he itched to wipe the smirk off his father's face, but he kept his expression serene and his tone level. He wasn't going to stoop to Lorne's level.

"Yes, you are." Lorne wrapped an arm around his Bondmate's shoulders and looked Wyatt up and down again. "Like it or not, you are my child, and you will listen to what I have to say, especially after all the trouble you've caused me."

"All the trouble I have caused *you*?" Wyatt raised his eyebrows as he put every bit of the incredulity he was feeling into his voice and expression. "I don't—" He broke off, took a deep breath, and shook his head. He couldn't let himself push this. Doing so would only lead to bad things. "You know what?" he said, smiling faintly. "It's not worth it."

He was turning to walk away when Aidan slipped out of the courtroom, his worry echoing through their Bond, though his face was passive. He approached Wyatt with a smile and laced their fingers together as he stopped by Wyatt's side. He briefly glanced at Ursula and Lorne before focusing his attention on Wyatt, letting the look in his eyes and the concern resonating along their Bond say what his voice couldn't. "Everything okay?"

Wyatt answered with a curt nod that didn't fool Aidan at all. "This is Aidan, my Bondmate. Aidan, this is Ursula and Lorne Mettler." He wouldn't introduce them to Aidan as his parents. That implied some sort of familial connection they didn't have.

Wyatt's parents gaped in astonishment, but Aidan just raised an eyebrow as he focused on what he could feel from Wyatt along their Bond and quirked his lips as he directed his gaze back to the people responsible for this entire situation. "I would say it's nice to meet you, but it's not, so I won't."

Ursula pursed her lips as she surveyed Aidan with a critical eye. "You have a lot of gall being rude to us, especially since we're the whole reason you met our son here."

"That may be," Aidan replied in a cold tone. "But it's not something I'd go bragging about if I were you. I met Wyatt because I found him left for dead behind a dumpster in an alley. I wouldn't change it for the world, but you shouldn't be proud of causing him to end up there."

"I'm not proud of that." Ursula snapped the words defensively as she straightened and crossed her arms. "I was just telling Wyatt how sorry I was for what he went through. I don't see how *you* have any cause to be upset, though. You weren't the one we hurt."

"Hurting Wyatt hurts me." Aidan shook his head. "It's that simple. I don't know how you can't understand that." He looked pointedly between the two of them, focusing on the way Lorne's arm was slung casually around Ursula's shoulder. There was obviously love between them, and it baffled him that they couldn't understand how he felt about Wyatt being hurt.

"I understand how hurting someone you love hurts you," Lorne said softly. "I don't understand how you can love a Dreamer. You'll regret it someday, after years of not being able to sleep and never having a night to yourself. Then you'll understand why we couldn't let him stay with us."

"No, I won't." Aidan squeezed Wyatt's hand in reassurance. "Having him in my dreams is the best thing that's ever happened to me. I hated having him gone, not having him there."

"You won't always feel that way." Lorne narrowed his eyes as he tried to stare Aidan down. Aidan met his gaze calmly, drawing on the strength of Wyatt standing next to him and sending love over their Bond as Wyatt's father continued to rant. "Someday," he said, his free arm waving wildly, "you'll understand why it was best for all of us that he left. We had to protect ourselves and our other children. When you have other people to protect, then you'll know, and you'll be stuck with him."

"I can't think of anything I could want more." Aidan dropped Wyatt's hand so he could wrap an arm around his waist. "The two of you are idiots for doing what you did, but you'll never see it, so I'm not going to waste my time explaining it to you. You clearly don't understand what you gave up, and you never will."

Ursula looked straight into Aidan's eyes, trying not to shake and let her tone betray her true feelings. "We didn't give up anything."

"You gave up a relationship with your son. With all your children, probably. Everyone who knows what you did hates you, and you're never again going to have the life that you gave it all up to get."

"We'll get it back." Ursula stepped forward. "There's nothing you can do to stop us."

"We already have." Wyatt held his head high as he looked at the people who had been his parents. "We spoke to the authorities in Ambridia last week, via video, at our lawyer's request. They're watching the results of this trial closely, and once Elliott Sloan is convicted, you can expect them to be contacting you."

"You can't do that!" Lorne stepped forward angrily, his hands balled into fists and held ready as his eyes flickered between Wyatt and Aidan. "You're our son; they can't make you testify."

"I'm not going to. I won't need to. They have my statement, and Aidan's, and the only debate is going to be whether you should be tried out there, or here where the rest of the trials are taking place." Wyatt grinned wryly as he leaned against Aidan. "Our lawyer tells us that it's a bit of a hot topic right now. You're going to pay for what you did, and even if you somehow managed to convince me that you don't deserve it, it's too late. It's out of my hands."

"You little...." Lorne stepped forward and swung his fist, aiming for Wyatt's face. Wyatt dodged easily, leaning back to let it fly by as Lorne cursed.

Aidan stepped forward and grabbed Lorne's arm, stopping him before the officer stationed on the other side of the lobby moved. "Walk away," he said in a firm tone that brooked no argument. "If you leave right now and don't look back, we'll forget this ever happened. But if you *ever* try to contact us again, or try to convince anyone that you don't deserve everything that's coming to you, we *will* remember this, and we *will* make sure you pay for it."

"You can't."

"Watch me." Aidan glanced over toward the guard. "I can get him over here with just one word, and I will, if you don't leave. So go ahead, call my bluff, if that's what you think this is, but I promise you, I'm *not* bluffing."

Lorne glared hard at Aidan, but Ursula stepped up and put a hand on his shoulder. "Come on, dear. It's not worth it."

"You're right." Lorne stepped back, shaking his arms when Wyatt and Aidan let him go, and brushed the wrinkles from his suit jacket. "They're not worth any of it." He took his Bondmate's arm and led her away. "I hope the two of you get everything you deserve." He spit the words like a curse over his shoulder.

"He really doesn't understand who deserves what in this situation, does he?" Wyatt said, feeling a little sorry for them.

"Doesn't look like it," Aidan agreed, slipping his arm back around Wyatt's waist. "Are you okay? Really?"

"Yeah. I am." Wyatt realized. He started to smile as he slung his arm over Aidan's, encircling his waist as well. "I'm actually kind of glad that they cornered me."

Aidan looked at him with a raised eyebrow and a dubious expression. "Oh? You care to explain?"

Wyatt laughed with relief, the sound ringing out like a bell in the empty hallway, and tugged Aidan a little closer as they walked away from the courtroom. "We okay to blow this joint?"

"Yeah, but I still want an explanation. That's not what I was expecting you to say. At all."

"I know. It wasn't what I was expecting to say either." Wyatt led the way out of the building, only releasing Aidan when he had to so they could get through security and out into the sunshine. In the park across from the ornate building, he sat on one of the benches and tugged Aidan down next to him, twisting sideways a little as they settled so he could look directly at Aidan.

"So. Explanation?" Aidan asked after a minute of silence. "Or are we waiting for something else?"

"No. Just enjoying the scenery."

"You're looking at me."

"Exactly." Wyatt leaned in, cupping Aidan's cheek and gently brushing his lips across Aidan's before pulling back with a grin. "It's great scenery."

"Yeah, well, the scenery would like an explanation." Aidan crossed his arms over his chest and attempted to scowl, but he probably didn't look nearly as upset or intimidating as he was trying for, because he couldn't keep his lips from twitching into a betraying smile. "Please?" he added after a moment, trying for pleading and cute rather than intimidating.

Wyatt laughed. "Yeah, yeah. So long as I can keep enjoying the sights while I talk."

"*Yes.* Just tell me already!" Aidan pulled Wyatt in for a swift kiss and then leaned back on the bench, arranging himself so that Wyatt had the best possible view. "Why are you *glad* they cornered you?"

"Because now it's over." Wyatt shrugged. "I know when Damon and Tabatha mentioned that they wanted to see me, I panicked. And honestly, I panicked a little when my mother first came up to me too. But the things she said, that they *both* said, made me realize it wasn't anything I had done, or I could have done differently, or anything like that. They're just crazy and prejudiced and there's nothing I can do to change it. Maybe they do think that they were doing what was best for the family, but I know that's not true, and so do Damon and Tabatha, so I don't have to worry about it anymore, you know?"

"I guess that makes sense." Aidan took Wyatt's hand and squeezed. "So that's it? You just realized your parents are psycho, and you're better off without worrying about them?"

"Well, that, and I realized they can't hurt me anymore. I'm bigger than both of them," he said with a laugh. "But more than that, I *know* that the things they were telling me aren't true. They can't do anything to me, so why should I be afraid of them?"

"That's... remarkably healthy," Aidan observed. "And kinda sexy. I *like* confident Wyatt."

"You like me no matter what mood I'm in."

"True," Aidan admitted easily as he stood and tugged Wyatt to his feet as well. "I want to do something about it right now, though."

"Well, why didn't you just say so?" Wyatt grinned as he let Aidan lead him toward the car and home. "We could have left sooner."

WYATT watched expectantly as Aidan finished the phone call, thanking Carina several times and agreeing to something before he finally hit the end button and set the phone on the table. "Well?" Wyatt asked, urging Aidan to sit next to him. "What did Carina have to say?"

"Verdict came in today. The judge sentenced right away."

"And?" Wyatt had known that was a possibility for several days now. Unlike Elliott Sloan's trial, the case against Lumoinnovations hadn't required his presence in the courtroom and he hadn't gone, but that didn't mean he hadn't followed the trial. Carina kept them updated almost daily, and it was clear for most of the week that the trial was approaching its conclusion. "What did they decide?"

"Fines mostly, and sanctions." Aidan shrugged. "It's a corporation, so there's not a lot they can do other than that. Their financial records and business practices are going to be audited quite heavily for the next several years, and the people in charge of the project besides Elliott have been named and will have charges brought against them as well."

"So that's it, then? It's over?" Wyatt didn't quite believe it. It didn't *feel* over, and he wondered if it ever would.

"Mostly." Aidan kissed Wyatt's temple softly. "There will be other trials, or at least pleas entered, for the other people who were involved, but honestly, most of them were just doing their jobs, and with the threats Elliott made, it's not likely that many of them will be punished at all, especially since they testified at Elliott's trial."

Wyatt nodded. The big surprise at Elliott's trial had been when his underlings from Lumoinnovations had taken the stand, one by one testifying about what he had made them do to Wyatt and what the consequences would have been if they'd refused. Wyatt hadn't been present for most of it, but he'd been told the employees were candid about the deals they had been offered in exchange for their support, and that most of them expressed regret they hadn't had the ability or the courage to do something sooner. It was far too little, far too late, but knowing what he knew about Elliott, Wyatt couldn't hold their cowardice against them. He still remembered being told about the "position" they'd had difficulty filling and the insinuations Elliott had made about what happened to the people who hadn't lived up to his expectations. "Wow."

"Yeah."

It was a lot to process. Wyatt remembered the last day of Elliott's trial and the way he'd wanted to cling to Aidan for support. But he had stood alone so he could prove to Elliott and his parents that he was strong enough. He'd waited then for the elation that never came, and that night, as they had reassured each other that it really was over, Aidan had suggested that maybe it would come when Elliott was sentenced.

It hadn't, not even when Elliott was sentenced to spend the remainder of his days in a government slave camp, doing manual labor to improve the city during the day and kept from manipulating the Dreamscape by the camp's Dreamers at night. He would never have another day or night of freedom, and still it wasn't enough to satisfy Wyatt.

He had hoped that the verdict against Lumoinnovations would bring him more satisfaction, and the conclusion of his parent's trials in Ambridia even more, but the Lumoinnovations trial was now over, and even with the knowledge that the company had been found in the wrong, he didn't feel any differently.

"It feels anticlimactic," he finally said, sliding down on the couch and letting his head fall against the back. "I keep waiting for some big thing to happen that's going to make me feel like we got through this, and it doesn't. I'm starting to think it never will."

"It's not something that's going to magically be all better, Wyatt." Aidan scooted down so his head was right next to Wyatt's. "All these trials, they might bring a little bit of closure, but they're not going to suddenly make you feel like everyone got what they deserved. I don't think anyone can. Not in this case."

"I know. I just wish that I could feel safe here again, you know?" Wyatt sighed as he looked over toward the door. "I know that everyone involved is being dealt with and that I'm safe, but I don't *feel* that way sometimes, and I hate it."

"We could move." Aidan sat up and pulled Wyatt up with him, grinning at Wyatt's surprised look. He felt the same, honestly, but now that the words had left his mouth, he found that he meant them. "I'm serious. We talked about it before and didn't really decide anything, but it might be a good idea.

Even if we don't move out of the city, even getting a new place that doesn't have those memories associated with it might be a good idea."

"You'd do that?" Wyatt cocked his head to the side as he looked at Aidan, feeling along their Bond for any sense of doubt, but Aidan was completely sincere, and Wyatt had to fight to contain his own shock. "You'd just up and move because I can't get over what happened?"

Aidan leaned in close, making sure he was looking straight into Wyatt's eyes. "First of all—yes. Absolutely. I'd do a lot more than just move for you, Wyatt. You should know that by now."

"I do." Wyatt blushed and ducked his head, trying not to get overwhelmed by the love he felt echoing along their Bond. He *knew* Aidan felt that way, and he felt the same way about Aidan, but it was still shocking at times and occasionally left him wondering what he'd done to deserve someone who loved him that much. "It just still amazes me, is all."

"Yeah, well." Aidan blushed, looking down. His face was still flushed when he looked back up, meeting Wyatt's eyes determinedly as he continued with his list like nothing had been said. "Second, I work from home. You're the one who will have to find a new job if we move out of the city. Your life will be uprooted more than mine will. And third, I'm not exactly thrilled with the memories, either. I don't think I'm ever going to forget the way they just barged in here and took you. I'm the one who couldn't stop them." He dropped his head again, this time in shame. The knowledge that he had failed to keep Wyatt safe burned all these months later.

"Hey." Wyatt lifted Aidan's chin. "We had this conversation, remember? If you'd done any more, things would have been a lot worse." He leaned in and kissed Aidan softly, savoring the feeling of Aidan's lips against his. "Stop feeling guilty."

"I don't. I just…." Aidan sighed as he trailed off. It wasn't guilt, exactly, that he felt, but the emotions associated with the memory weren't pleasant, and he could definitely do without the reminder of what had happened and the nervousness he felt every time someone knocked on the door. "I don't like the memories."

"So maybe we should move, then." Wyatt smiled as he leaned in to kiss Aidan again. "We could start fresh, somewhere out in the country maybe, though still close enough to Haverdsford that we can visit easily. It could be good."

"Do you really want to?" Aidan grasped Wyatt's shoulders, holding him back enough that he could clearly see the expression on Wyatt's face.

"Yeah," Wyatt said in an amazed tone, his smile widening. "I think I do. Do you?"

Aidan barely managed to nod before Wyatt was on top of him, pushing him down to the couch and kissing him passionately. His tongue slipped into Aidan's mouth as his hands slid under Aidan's clothes and his fingers danced over Aidan's skin. He ground their hips together, showing Aidan just how much he approved of the idea.

"We'll, uh, have to start thinking about where so you can, ah, look for a job," Aidan said between kisses, somehow keeping his mind on the topic at hand despite the distraction.

"Later," Wyatt growled.

Epilogue

WET lips circled Wyatt's cock, enveloping it in moist warmth, and a talented tongue swirled around it, then lapped at the end and licked along the length. Wyatt moaned without opening his eyes, wriggling and writhing as he begged for more, his hands fisted in the sheets and his whole body humming with pleasure. He came without ever opening his eyes, crying out as Aidan swallowed and relaxing as Aidan licked him clean.

He opened his eyes with a lazy smile and looked down at Aidan, who peered up at him from between his legs, the covers over his shoulders and his cheeks flushed with pleasure. Wyatt hummed and reached down toward Aidan. "Hey."

Aidan chuckled, crawling up Wyatt's body to capture his lips in a deep kiss. His tongue slid into Wyatt's mouth, stroking and teasing as he kissed Wyatt awake. "Happy Birthday," he said when he pulled back.

Wyatt beamed. "Thanks." He stretched under Aidan, nuzzling the pillow as he pulled Aidan close. "What time is it?"

"Early, still. You can go back to sleep if you want."

Wyatt snickered mischievously. "Will you wake me up like that again?"

"Maybe." Aidan kissed Wyatt again, pulling back much more reluctantly this time. "If you're good."

"What am I going to do while I'm asleep that could possibly be *bad*?"

Aidan simply looked at him with a raised eyebrow. "You get us into more trouble when we're asleep than we get into when we're awake!"

"Yeah, okay." Wyatt conceded the point easily. "But if you're not going to be sleeping with me, what am I going to do?"

"I'm pretty sure I don't want to know, Wyatt."

"You would *love* to know." Wyatt laughed. "But I'm not going to tell you." He swatted lightly at Aidan's shoulder. "Now go fix me breakfast."

"What makes you think I'm fixing breakfast?"

"You always fix breakfast on my birthday."

"I'm not sure twice counts as always, Wyatt," Aidan protested as he climbed from the bed, kissing Wyatt's shoulder as he pulled away. "Maybe I decided not to this year."

"Twice counts as always when it's as long as we've been together. Now go make it thrice." He rolled over, burying his face in the pillow. "I wanna sleep more before our guests arrive."

Aidan rolled his eyes and snickered fondly as he pulled on some pants and padded out to the kitchen. When he got there, he dumped some food in the dogs' bowls and whistled for them, petting the two big animals when they came running in from their room.

When they'd moved in, the plan had been to use that room as a second guest bedroom, but they'd never gotten around to putting a bed in it. Then Wyatt had found Belle by the side of the road and they'd rescued Kashi a few weeks later. Now it was firmly established as the dogs' territory: their beds, blankets, and toys spread out over the floor and the couch and chair covered with golden fur.

It was an odd arrangement, but it worked, and it meant that their bed and their nicer furniture usually stayed dog-free, so Aidan wasn't going to object. Not that he ever would, even if Belle and Kashi shed and drooled on every nice thing they owned. The dogs made Wyatt too happy for Aidan to do anything but love them.

When they had finished eating, he let the dogs out and spent a moment looking out over their backyard as he watched the dogs play. The house was perfect for them, even though it had seemed a little big at the time they'd bought it. Aidan wouldn't trade any of it for anything. Two years ago, he never would have thought they'd end up here: in a house about a forty-five minute drive from Haverdsford, Wyatt working at the clinic in the nearest town, and the graphic novel Aidan had been illustrating intermittently for years before he met Wyatt now on the verge of being released.

It was almost unfathomable, especially after what they'd gone through not too long after Wyatt's twenty-eighth birthday. Things had been rough then, especially after all the verdicts came in and they both realized that no matter what happened to Elliot, Lumoinnovations, and Wyatt's parents, it would never be enough to make up for what had happened.

The sentence delivered against Wyatt's parents—permanent slavery, the same fate they'd tried to deliver their son to, only this time given legally—just emphasized the point. They were serious about moving after the verdict against Lumoinnovations came down, but it was the one against Wyatt's parents that prompted them to stop looking for a new place in the city and focus on finding something out in the country. They'd needed a completely fresh start, and they'd gotten it.

After encouragement from Carina and the rest of their friends, Wyatt pursued a civil suit against his parents as well, and the money Ursula and Lorne were paid for Wyatt's services was reclaimed—their house and other assets sold to cover it all—and given to Wyatt. He insisted he wanted nothing to do with it and instead donated it to charity. He made enough working at the clinic as their Dreamer, and Aidan still made plenty as a freelance graphic designer and illustrator. With the graphic novel Aidan had illustrated about to hit shelves, they weren't hurting for money, especially since their huge house ended up costing less than the luxury apartment in the heart of Haverdsford. Even with the dogs and the occasional trips into the city to visit their friends and out to Montwick to visit Aidan's family, they were doing just fine.

When the dogs started barking crazily at a squirrel as it scampered along the trees, Aidan called them inside, sending them to their room while he fixed breakfast. They wouldn't stay there for long—they were convinced that everything cooked in the house was really for them—but it gave him a few minutes' peace while he started the chocolate chip pancakes.

By the time the pancakes were done, the dogs were seated by his side, tongues lolling as they looked at him with wide eyes, begging him for food they couldn't have. "This isn't for you, guys. I'm sorry." To assuage his conscience, he pulled out the bag of treats and gave them each one before he loaded the breakfast tray with all the pancakes. He had a Bondmate to reawaken.

THE last guest didn't leave until after midnight, and Wyatt was more than a little tipsy when they left. "Night," he called out as he shut the door behind the last one. He leaned against it as it clicked and grinned at Aidan.

Aidan pounced. "So," he said, looping his hands over Wyatt's head. "Good day?"

"The best." Wyatt pulled Aidan close, resting their foreheads together. "Thanks."

Aidan kissed him briefly before pulling back. "So, Ratri gave me something before he left. I thought you might want to see it."

"Oh?" Wyatt arched his eyebrows. His plans for the evening hadn't included anything that Ratri might have left behind, but if Aidan was bringing it up now, it must be important. "What is it?"

"Come on." Aidan tugged Wyatt into the kitchen, picked up a slip of paper, and held it out to Wyatt. "He printed this out before they came over today."

Wyatt took it hesitantly, frowning down at it. It was a news article, dated that morning, and his eyes widened as he read it. *Reyes Frontier Declares Bankruptcy*, the headline read, the bold letters jumping off the page. Astonished, Wyatt looked up at Aidan. "Really?"

"Keep reading," Aidan urged, leaning his chin on Wyatt's shoulder so he could read along.

Wyatt did, skimming at first, but then taking in every word as he got caught up in the article. It detailed how Reyes Frontier, the parent company of Lumoinnovations, Fabrisystems, and several other subsidiaries, had been under increased financial watch since a scandal two years earlier involving mistreatment of a Dreamer and that the increased monitoring had uncovered other scandals as well. The company had floundered for a time and hoped to salvage operations but hadn't managed to recover financially. The company was currently reorganizing in order to save as much of the corporation as possible, but the departments implicated in the scandal had already been eliminated and would not be part of the corporate restructure.

When he finished reading, Wyatt slowly lowered the paper to the table. "So it's over. Completely."

"Yeah." Aidan grinned as he circled to face Wyatt, arms still around Wyatt's waist. "The company that did that to you won't even exist in a few months, and no one who was heavily involved in it will ever be free again. It's completely over."

The feeling of satisfaction that had been missing after the verdicts from each trial two years earlier still didn't come, and Wyatt wasn't suddenly filled with feelings of safety and light and warmth, but he *did* feel satisfied, and he managed a firm nod as he slowly pulled his hand back from the printout and turned to Aidan. "Good." He leaned in, kissed Aidan soundly, and when he pulled back, they were both smiling. "Now, what else do we have planned for the evening?"

"Oh, I'm sure I can think of a few things."

"Only a few?" Wyatt waggled his eyebrows comically. "I can think of *lots*, and I'd like to try them all." He furrowed his eyebrows and frowned. "Though, possibly not all tonight. It's late, and I know you need a bit of recovery time."

"Only as much as you do."

"In your dreams, maybe."

Aidan laughed as he took a bottle of red wine from underneath the counter and poured them both a glass. He handed Wyatt his and clinked them together as he slipped his arm back around Wyatt's waist. "To a great day and many more to come. Happy birthday."

"Thanks," Wyatt whispered, taking a sip of his wine and then setting his glass down. He gently pulled Aidan's from his hand as well, set it on the countertop, and then leaned in, cupping his hands around Aidan's chin and kissing him. He savored the way the spicy flavor of Aidan mixed with the bitter tannins of the wine. This was what he wanted many more days of, and as long as he could have it, no matter what else happened, life would be good.

NESSA L. WARIN lives in southwestern Ohio with a cat who graciously allows her to pay all the bills and demands pampering on a regular basis. She enjoys wine tastings and travel and can easily get lost in science fiction or fantasy stories. She's a true geek, enjoys costuming, and can be found dressed up at at least one Renaissance festival and fantasy convention each year. When she's not having fun, Nessa works in Corporate America coordinating the production and mailing of marketing materials and wishing she had more time to write.

Visit Nessa's blog at http://nessa-l-warin.livejournal.com and follow her on Twitter @nessalwarin. She can also be reached at nessa.l.warin@gmail.com.

Also from NESSA L. WARIN

STAMP of FATE

NESSA L. WARIN

http://www.dreamspinnerpress.com

Also from NESSA L. WARIN

Sauntering VAGUELY DOWNWARD

NESSA L. WARIN

http://www.dreamspinnerpress.com

www.ingramcontent.com/pod-product-compliance
Lightning Source LLC
Chambersburg PA
CBHW050033030726
47506CB00001B/256